Stephen Mc...

SPACE BOY

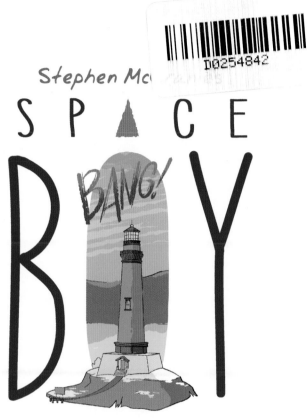

VOLUME 14

Written and illustrated by
STEPHEN McCRANIE

DARK HORSE BOOKS

President and Publisher **Mike Richardson**
Editors **Brett Israel** and **Freddye Miller**
Assistant Editors **Sanjay Dharawat** and **Rose Weitz**
Designer **Anita Magaña**
Digital Art Technician **Allyson Haller**

STEPHEN McCRANIE'S SPACE BOY VOLUME 14

This book collects *Space Boy* episodes 211–223 and 225–226, previously published online at WebToons.com.

Library of Congress Cataloging-in-Publication Data
Names: McCranie, Stephen, 1987- author, illustrator.
Title: Space Boy / written and illustrated by Stephen McCranie.
Other titles: At head of title: Stephen McCranie's
Description: First edition. | Milwaukie, OR : Dark Horse Books, 2018- | "This book collects Space Boy episodes 1-16 previously published online at WebToons.com." | Summary: Amy lives on a colony in deep space, but when her father loses his job the family moves back to Earth, where she has to adapt to heavier gravity, a new school, and a strange boy with no flavor.
Identifiers: LCCN 2017053602 | ISBN 9781506706481 (v. 1)
Subjects: LCSH: Graphic novels. | CYAC: Graphic novels. | Science fiction. | Moving, Household--Fiction. | Self-perception--Fiction. | Friendship--Fiction.
Classification: LCC PZ7.7.M42 Sp 2018 | DDC 741.5/973--dc23
LC record available at https://lccn.loc.gov/2017053602

Published by Dark Horse Books
A division of Dark Horse Comics LLC, 10956 SE Main Street, Milwaukie, OR 97222
StephenMcCranie.com | DarkHorse.com

To find a comics shop in your area, visit comicshoplocator.com

MIX
Paper from responsible sources
FSC www.fsc.org FSC® C016973

First edition: November 2022
ISBN 978-1-50672-877-3
10 9 8 7 6 5 4 3 2 1
Printed in China

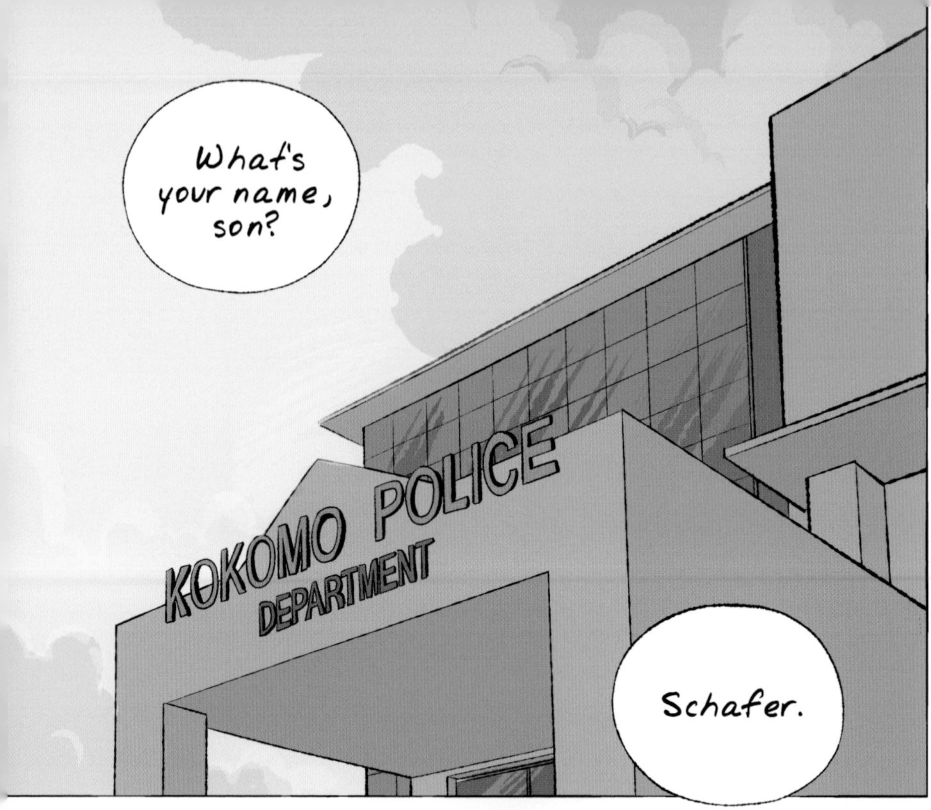
What's your name, son?
KOKOMO POLICE DEPARTMENT
Schafer.

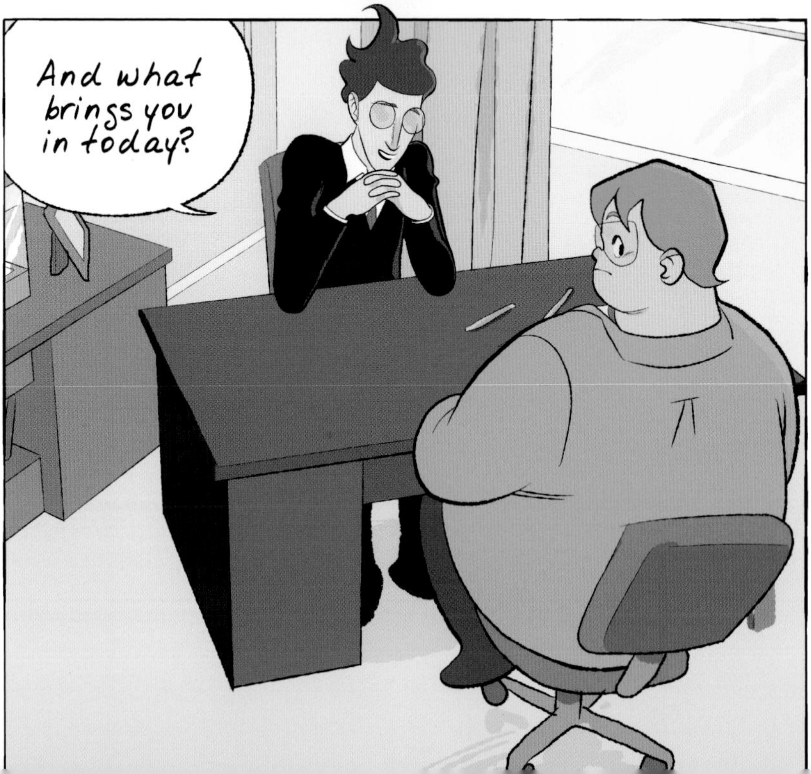
And what brings you in today?

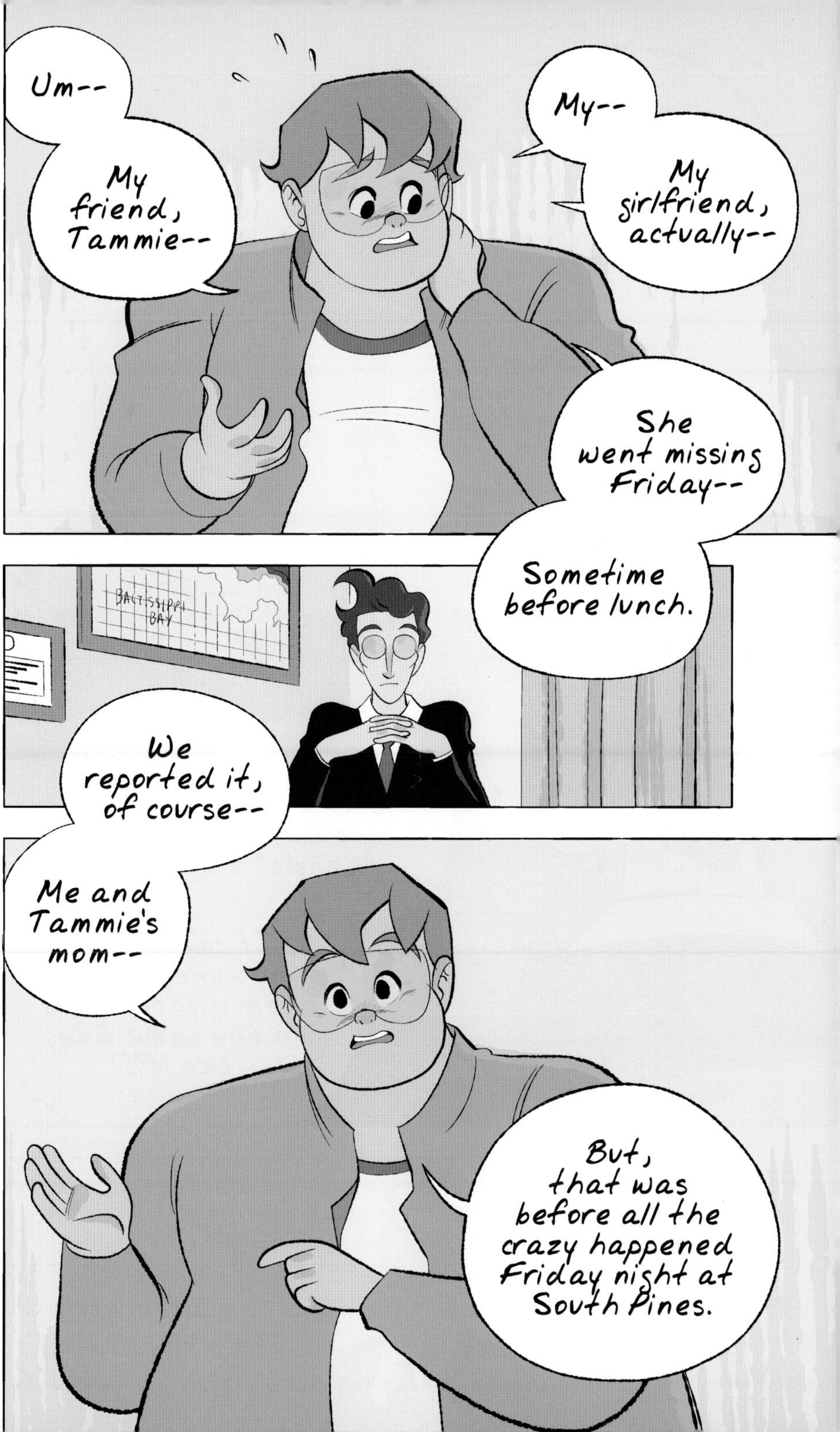
Um--
My friend, Tammie--
My--
My girlfriend, actually--
She went missing Friday--
Sometime before lunch.
We reported it, of course--
Me and Tammie's mom--
But, that was before all the crazy happened Friday night at South Pines.

When I saw the news yesterday about the masked men invading campus, I thought:
"What if Tammie's case is related somehow?"
I mean, she and Amy are close friends!
It can't be a coincidence both of them disappeared on the same day, can it?!

Hmm.
Interesting.

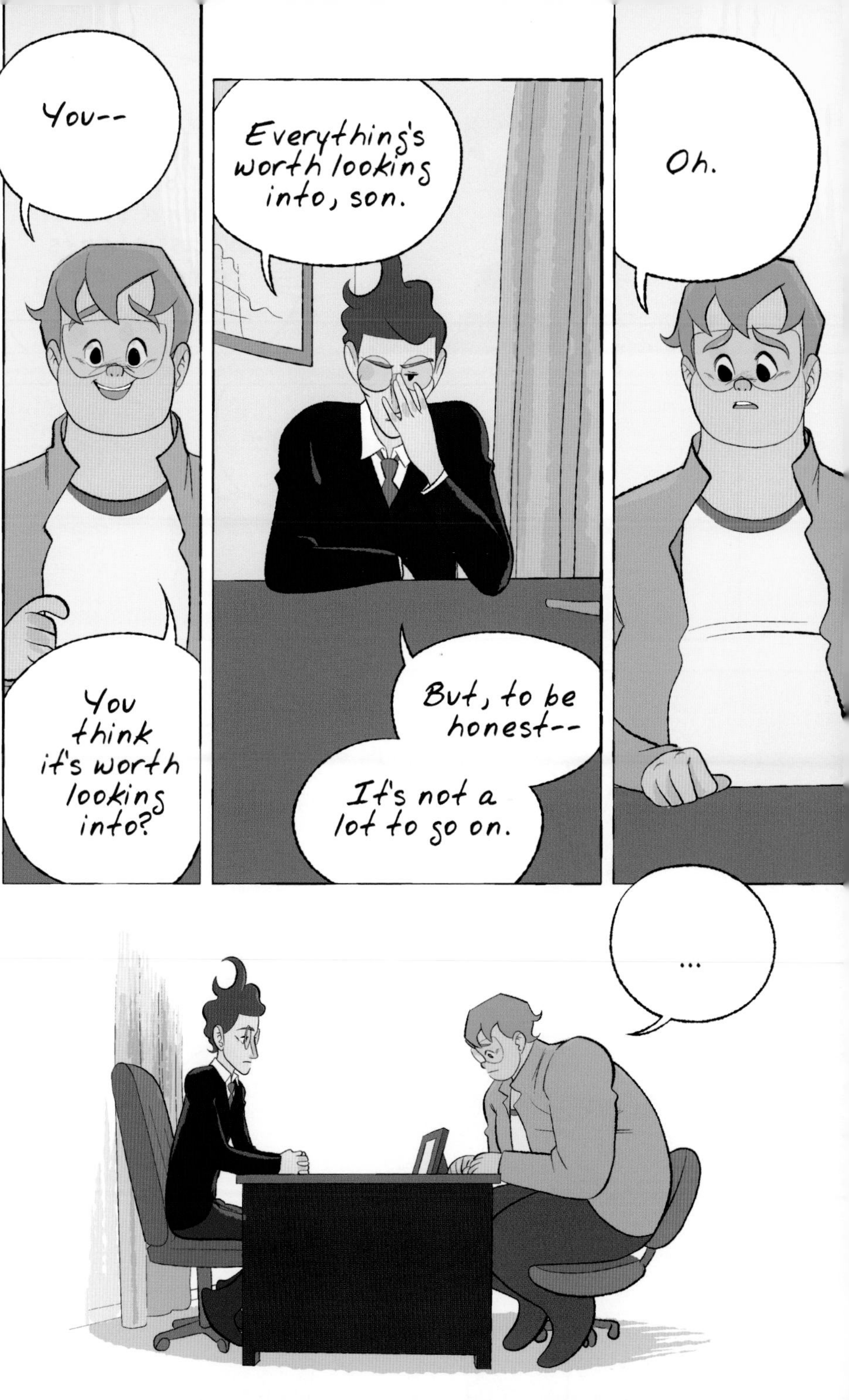
You--
You think it's worth looking into?
Everything's worth looking into, son.
But, to be honest--
It's not a lot to go on.
Oh.
...

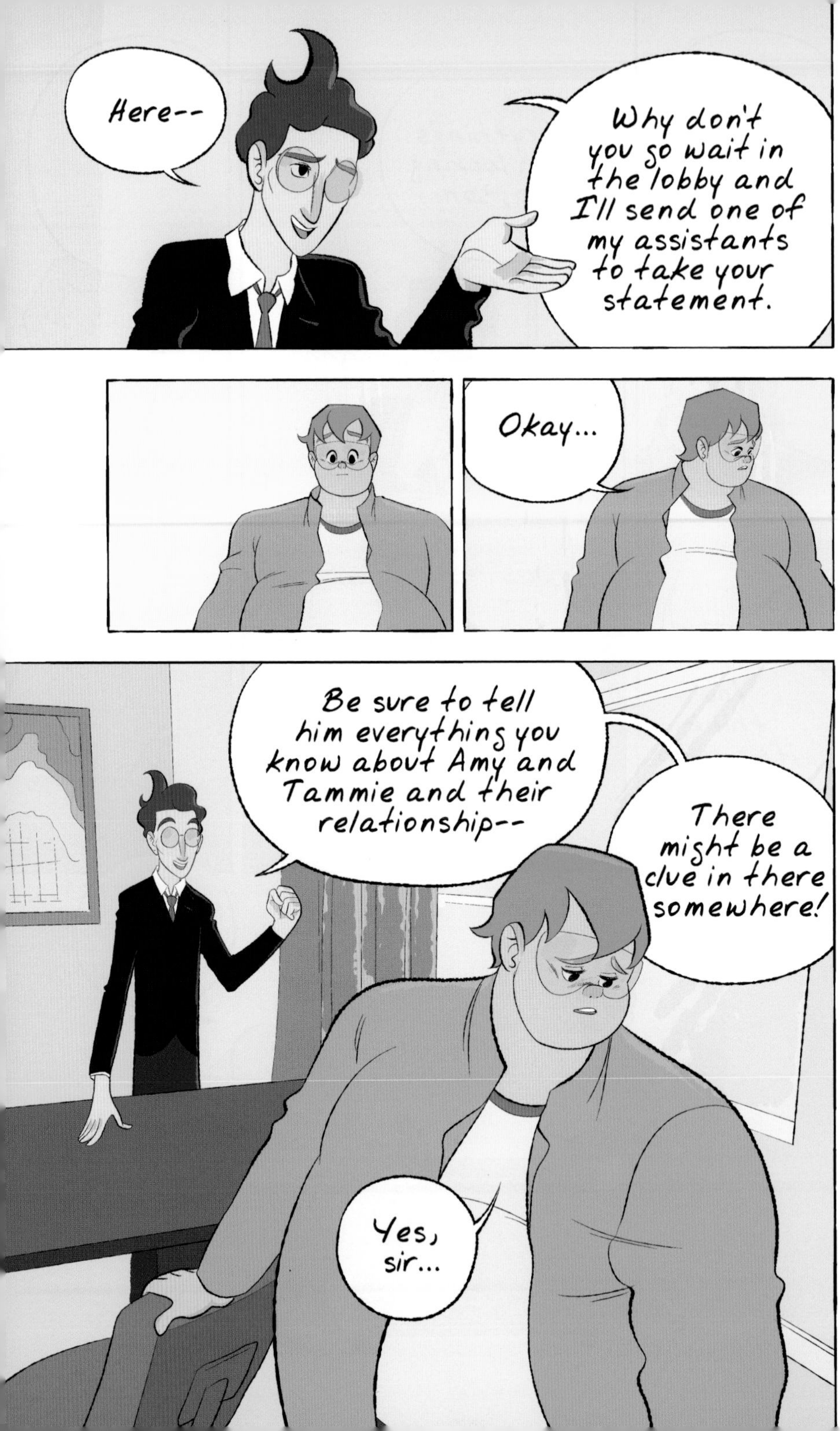
Here--
Why don't you go wait in the lobby and I'll send one of my assistants to take your statement.
Okay...
Be sure to tell him everything you know about Amy and Tammie and their relationship--
There might be a clue in there somewhere!
Yes, sir...

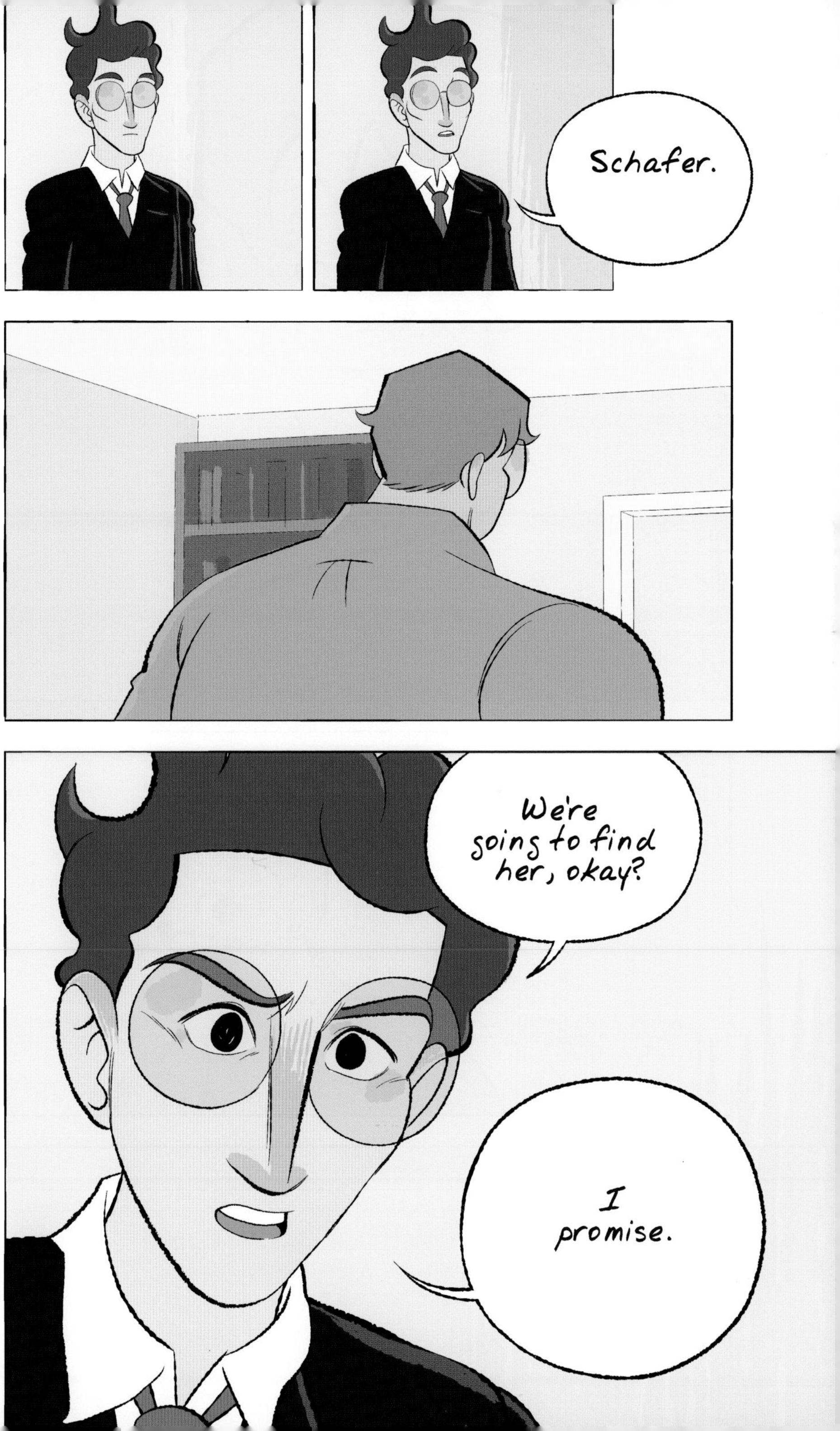
Schafer.
We're going to find her, okay?
I promise.

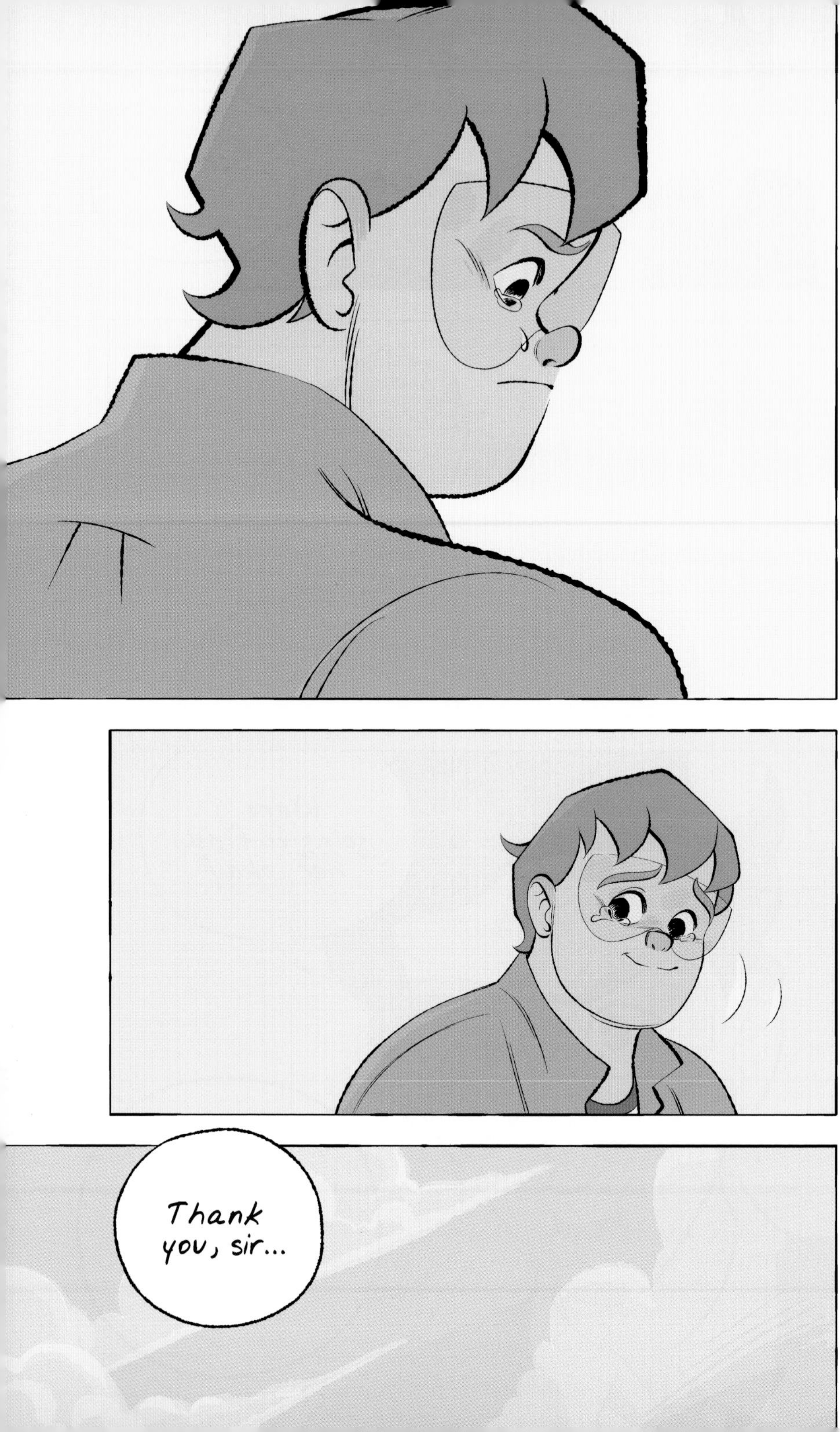
Thank you, sir...

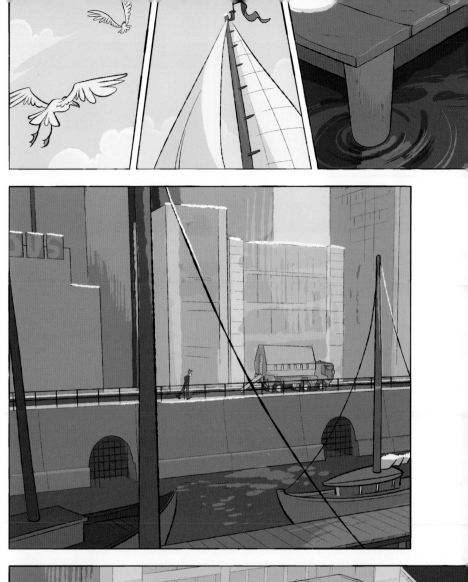

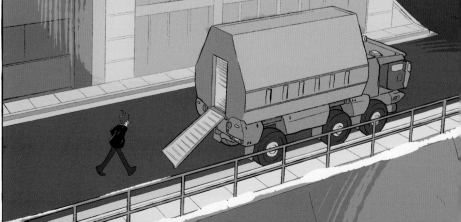

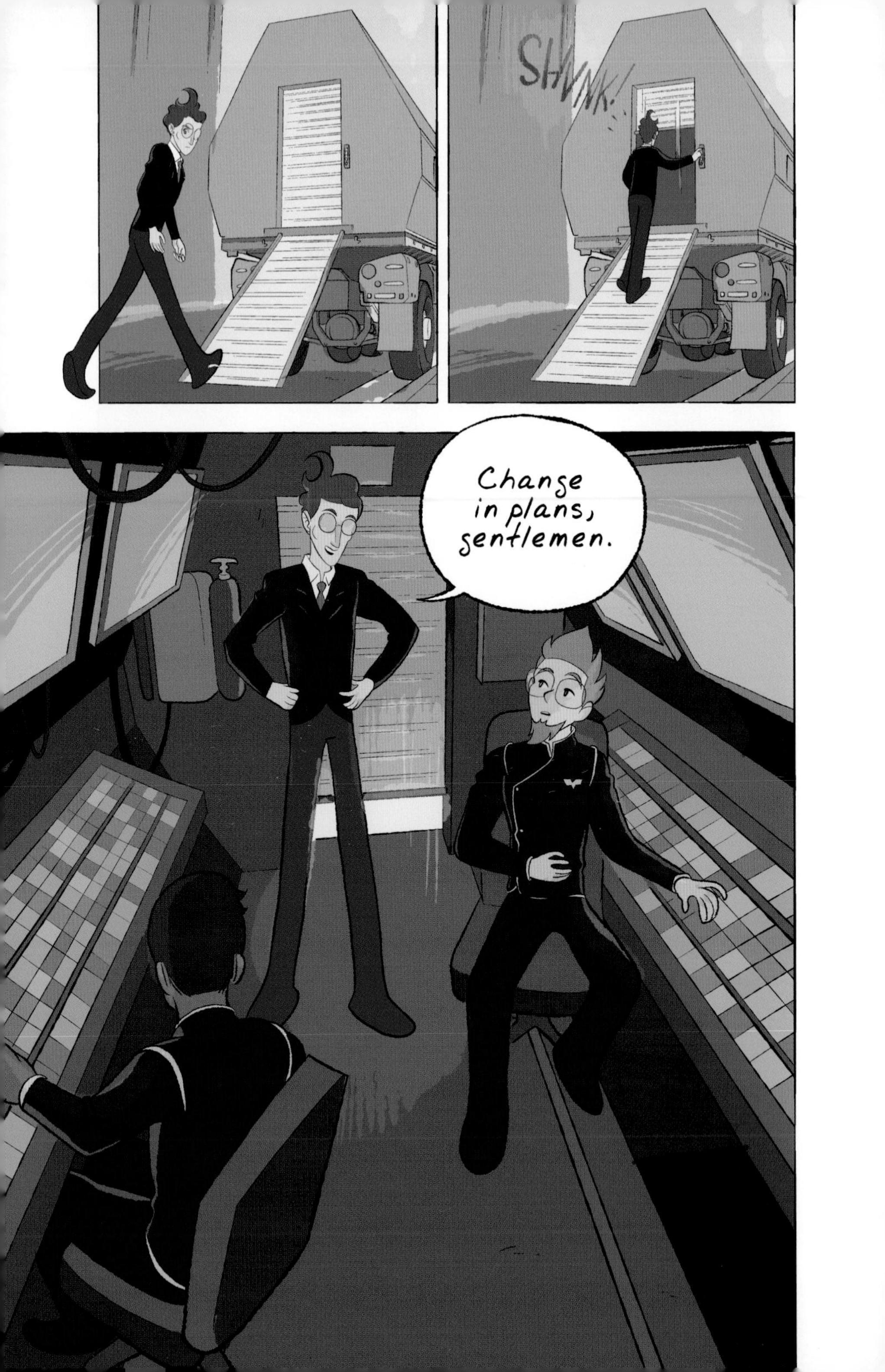
SHNNK!
Change in plans, gentlemen.

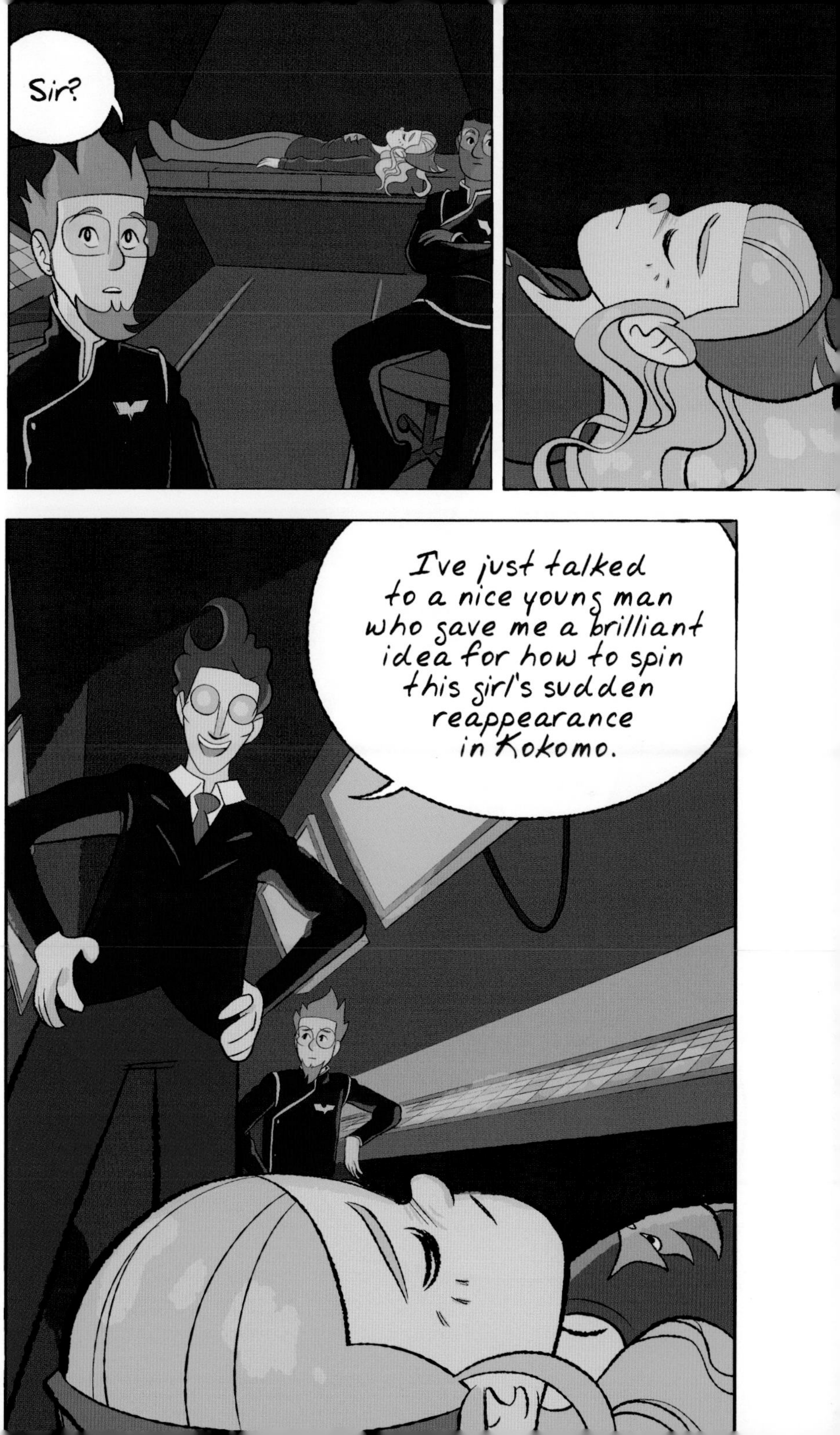
Sir?
I've just talked to a nice young man who gave me a brilliant idea for how to spin this girl's sudden reappearance in Kokomo.

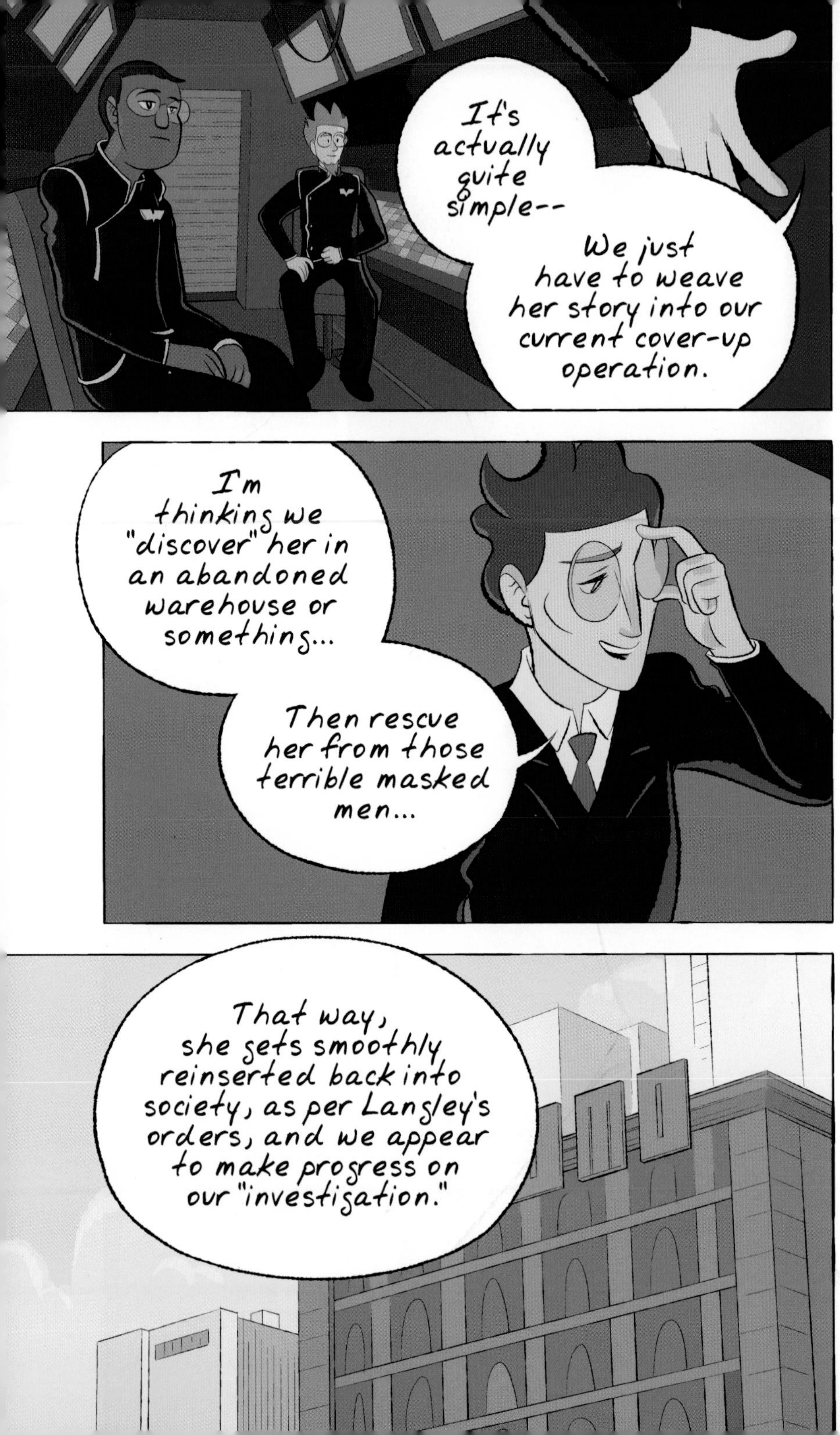
It's actually quite simple--
We just have to weave her story into our current cover-up operation.
I'm thinking we "discover" her in an abandoned warehouse or something...
Then rescue her from those terrible masked men...
That way, she gets smoothly reinserted back into society, as per Langley's orders, and we appear to make progress on our "investigation."

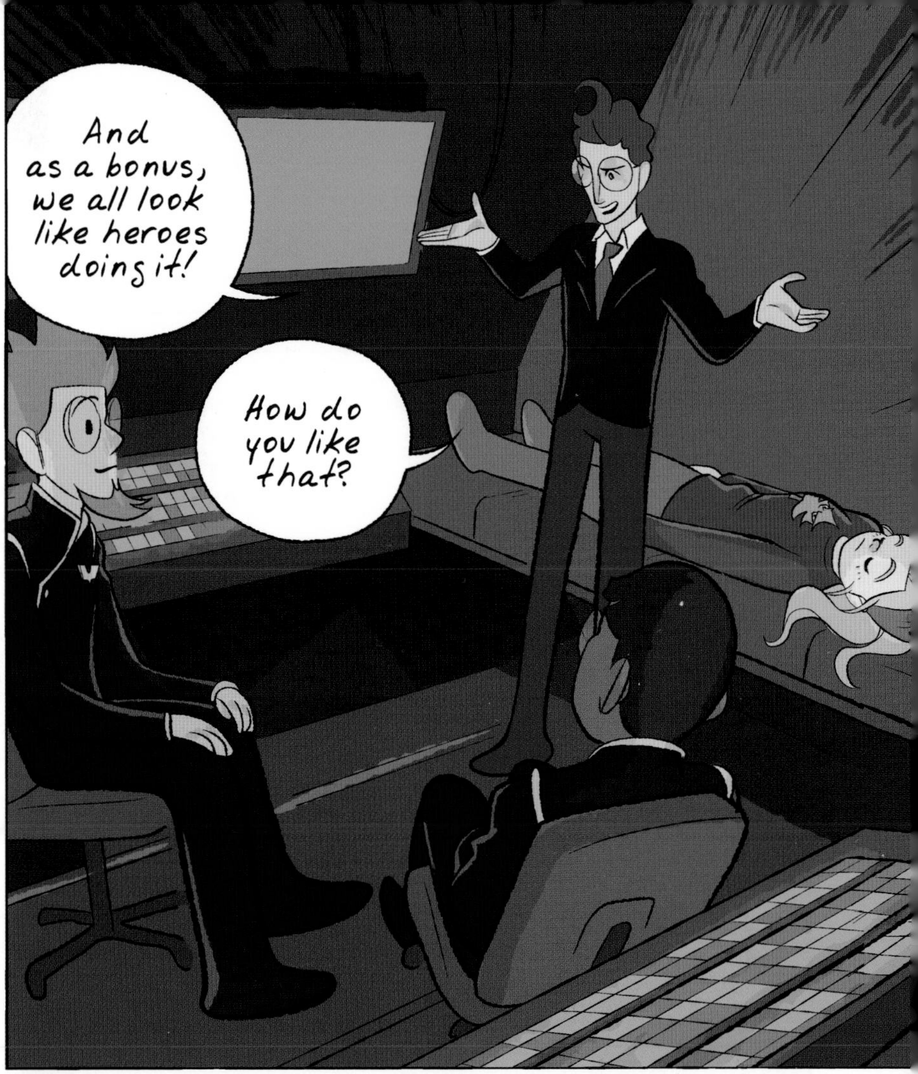
And as a bonus, we all look like heroes doing it!
How do you like that?

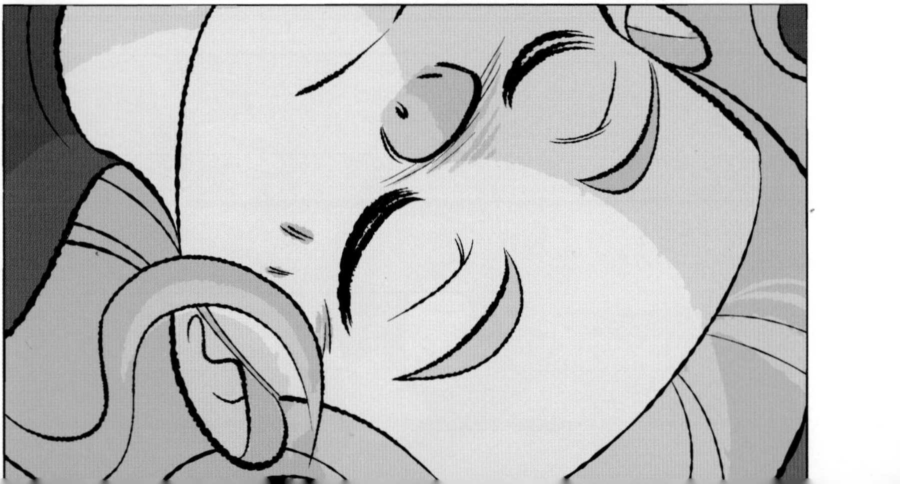

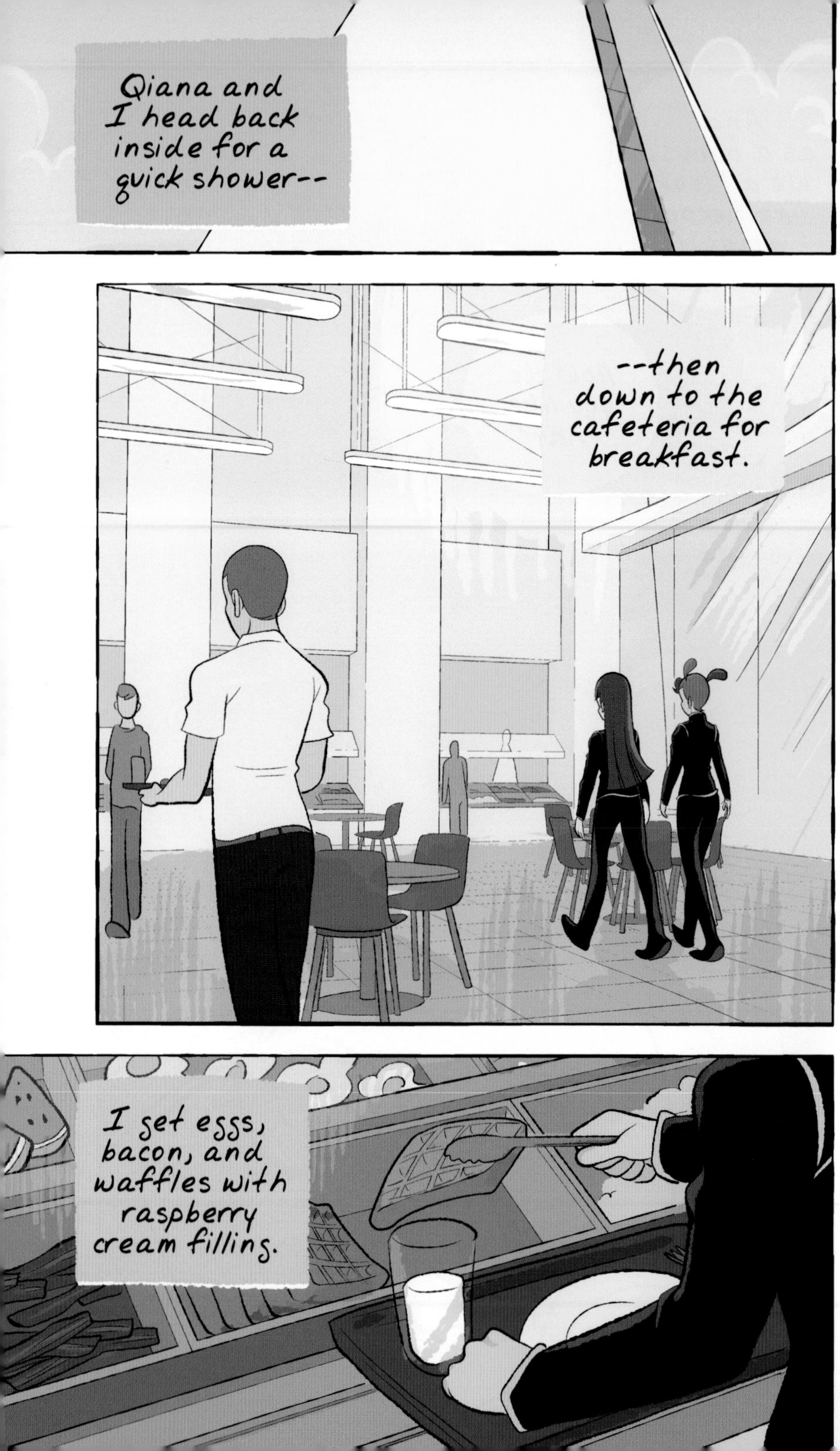
Qiana and I head back inside for a quick shower--
--then down to the cafeteria for breakfast.
I get eggs, bacon, and waffles with raspberry cream fillings.

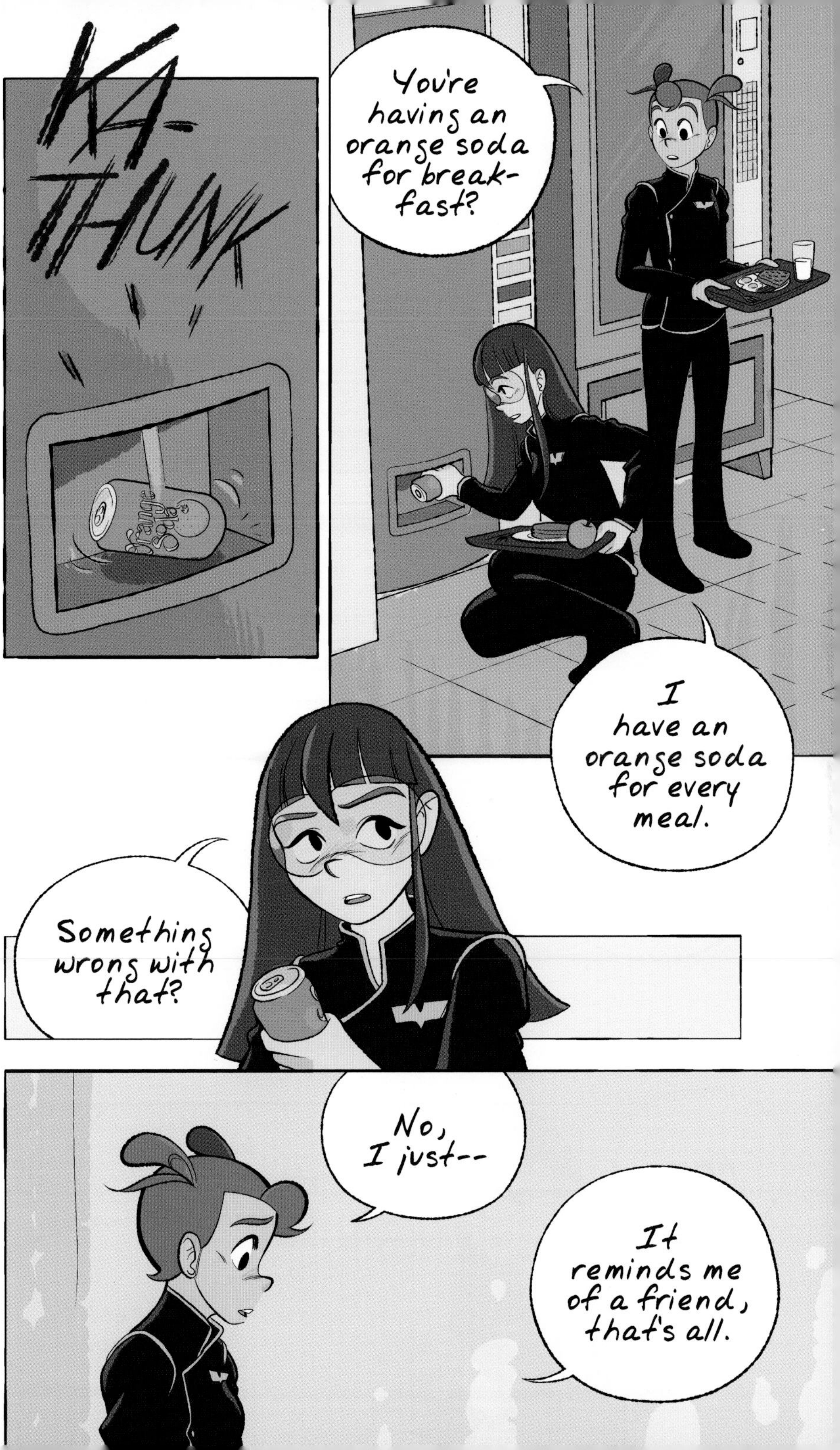
KA-THUNK
Orange Soda
You're having an orange soda for break-fast?
I have an orange soda for every meal.
Something wrong with that?
No, I just--
It reminds me of a friend, that's all.

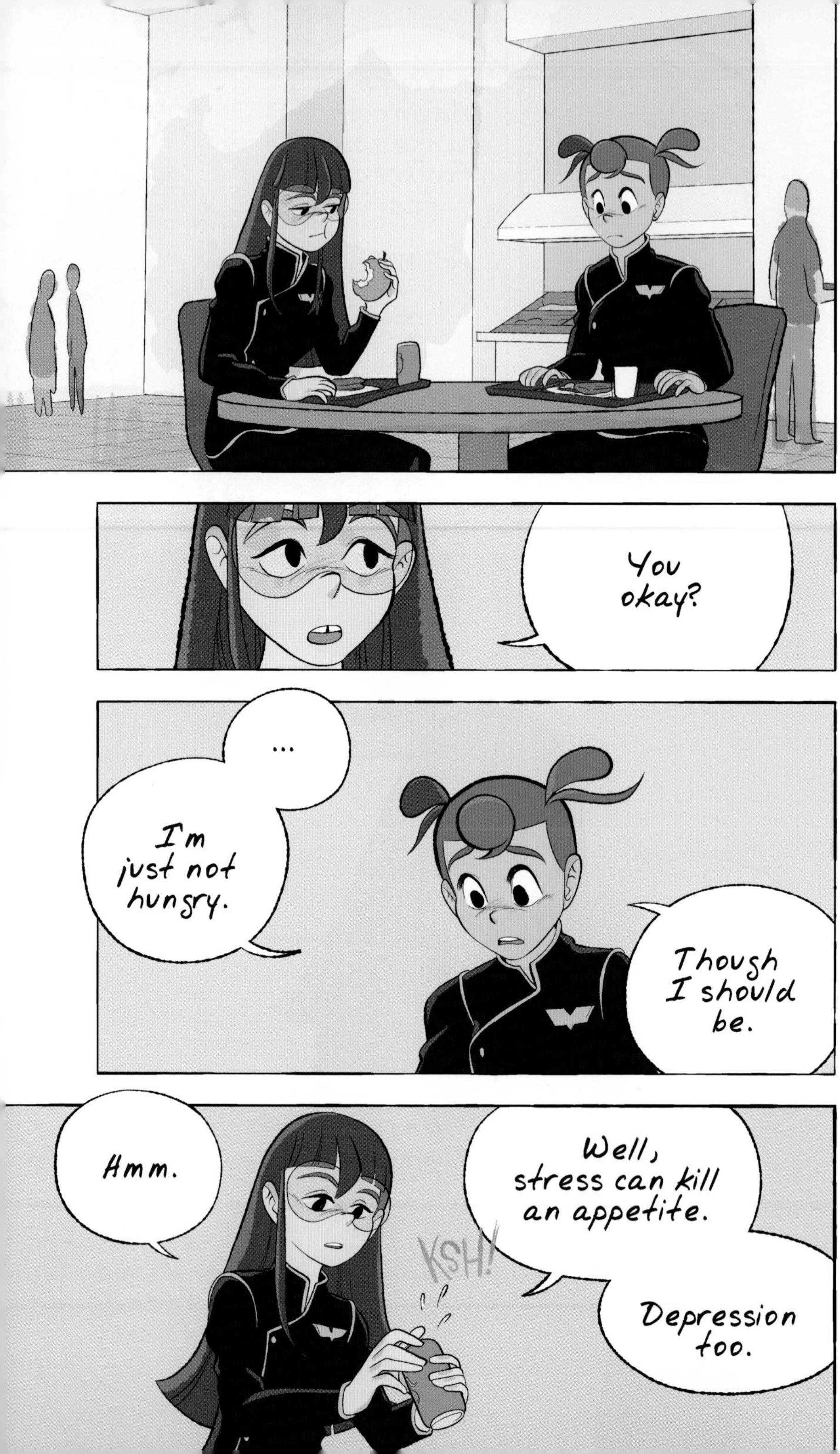
You okay?
...
I'm just not hungry.
Though I should be.
Hmm.
Well, stress can kill an appetite.
KSH!
Depression too.

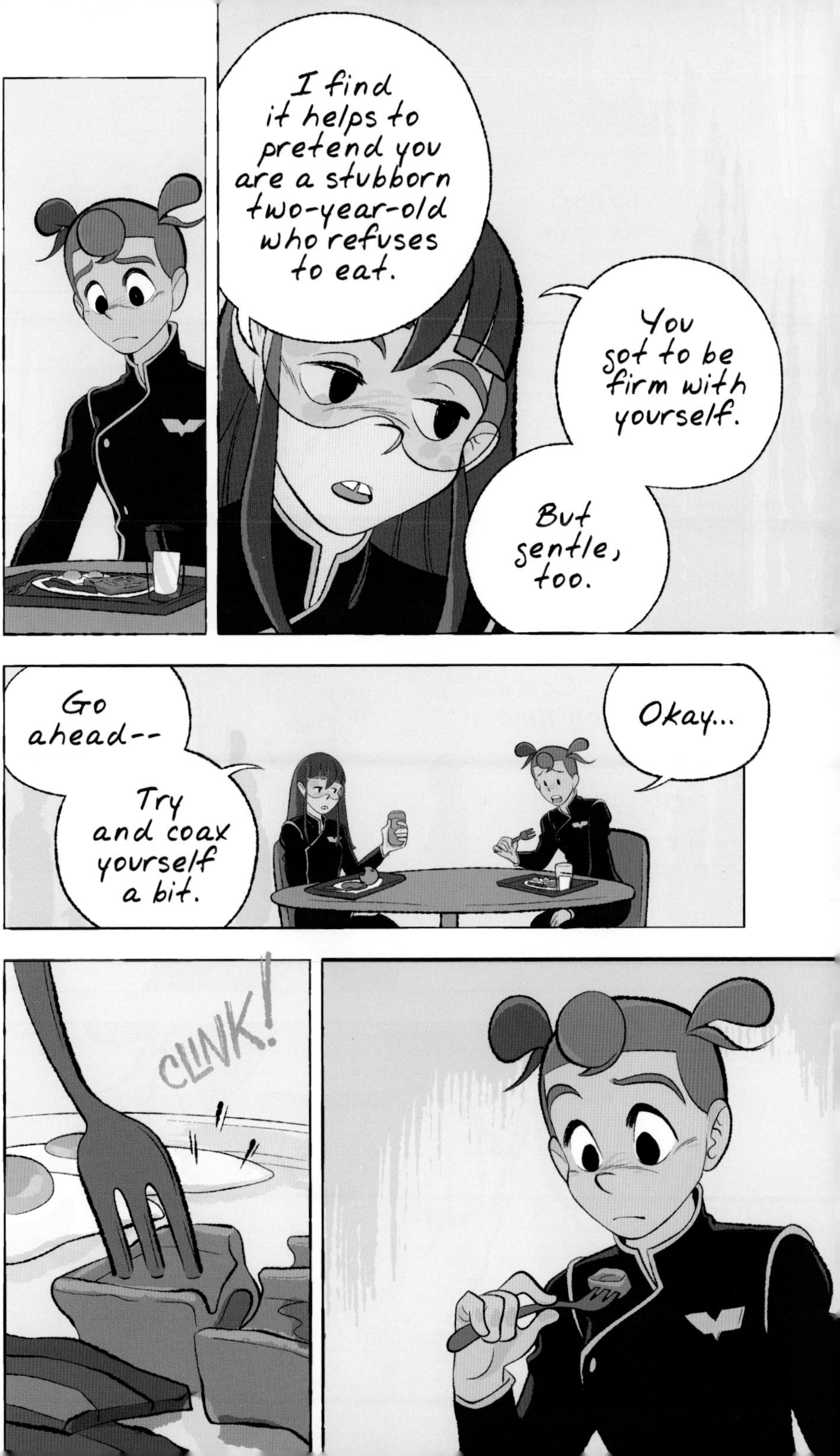
I find it helps to pretend you are a stubborn two-year-old who refuses to eat.
You got to be firm with yourself.
But gentle, too.
Go ahead--
Try and coax yourself a bit.
Okay...
CLINK!

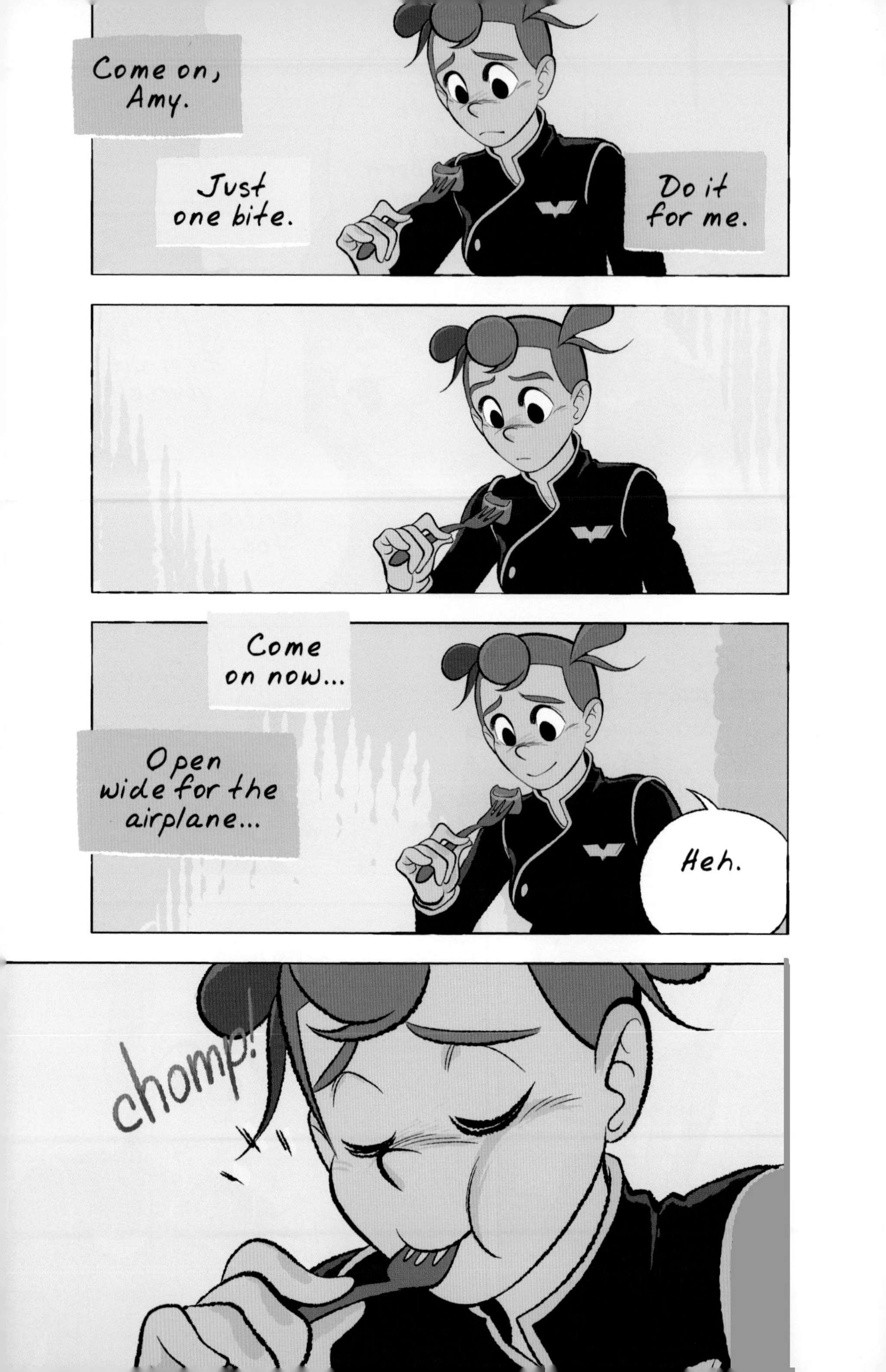
Come on, Amy.
Just one bite.
Do it for me.
Come on now...
Open wide for the airplane...
Heh.
chomp!

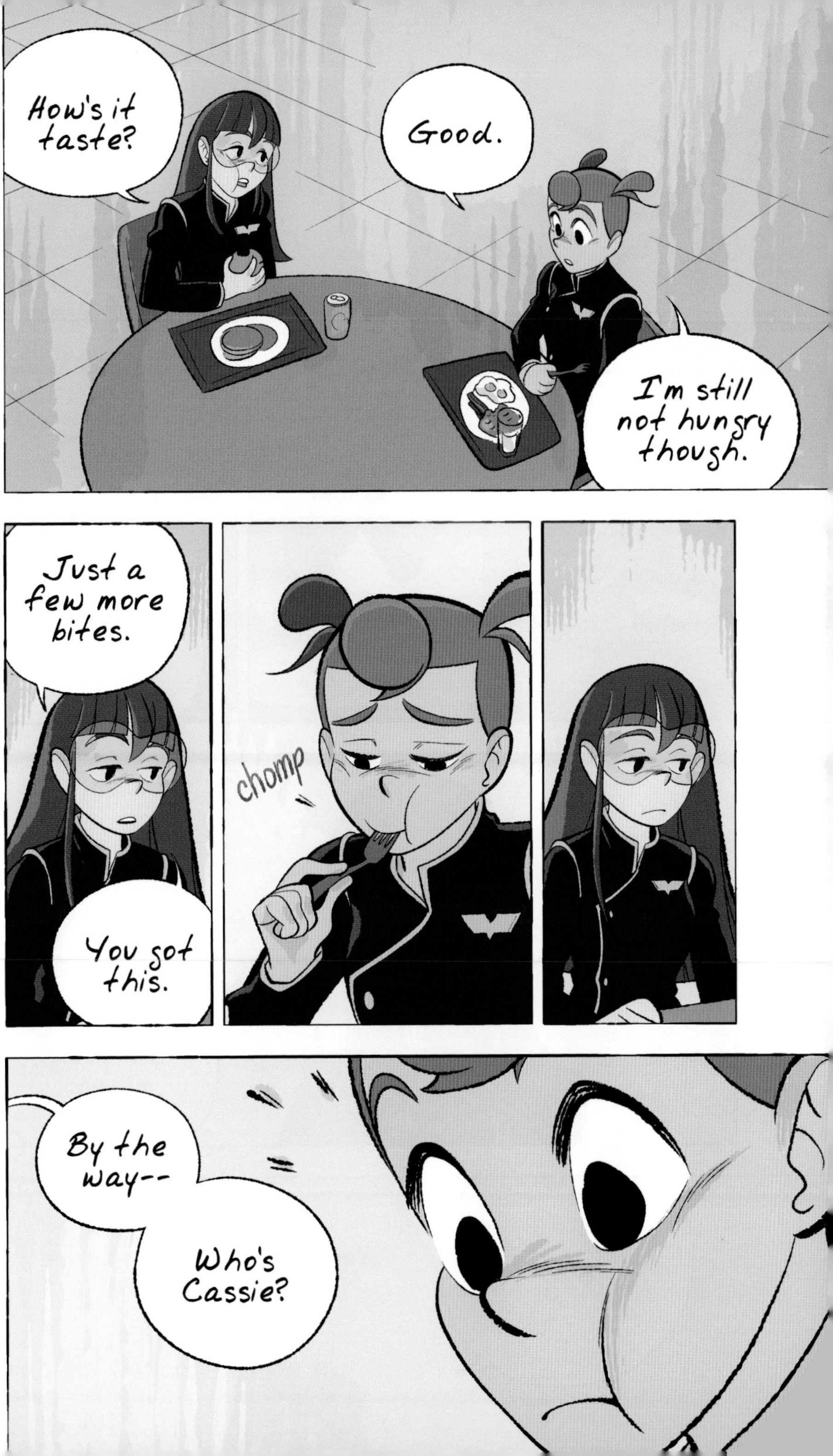
How's it taste?
Good.
I'm still not hungry though.
Just a few more bites.
You got this.
chomp
By the way--
Who's Cassie?

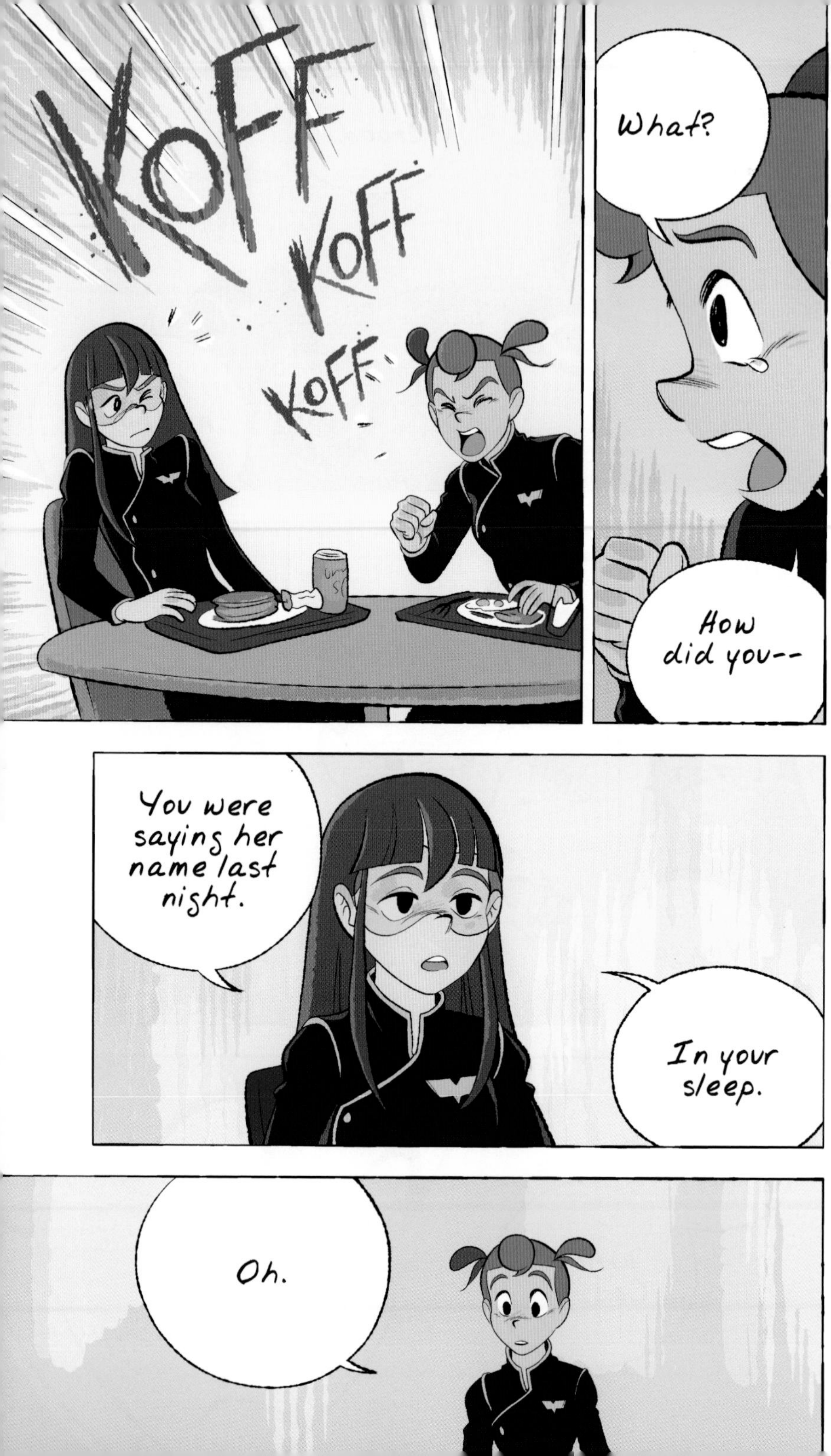
KOFF
KOFF
KOFF
What?
How did you--
You were saying her name last night.
In your sleep.
Oh.

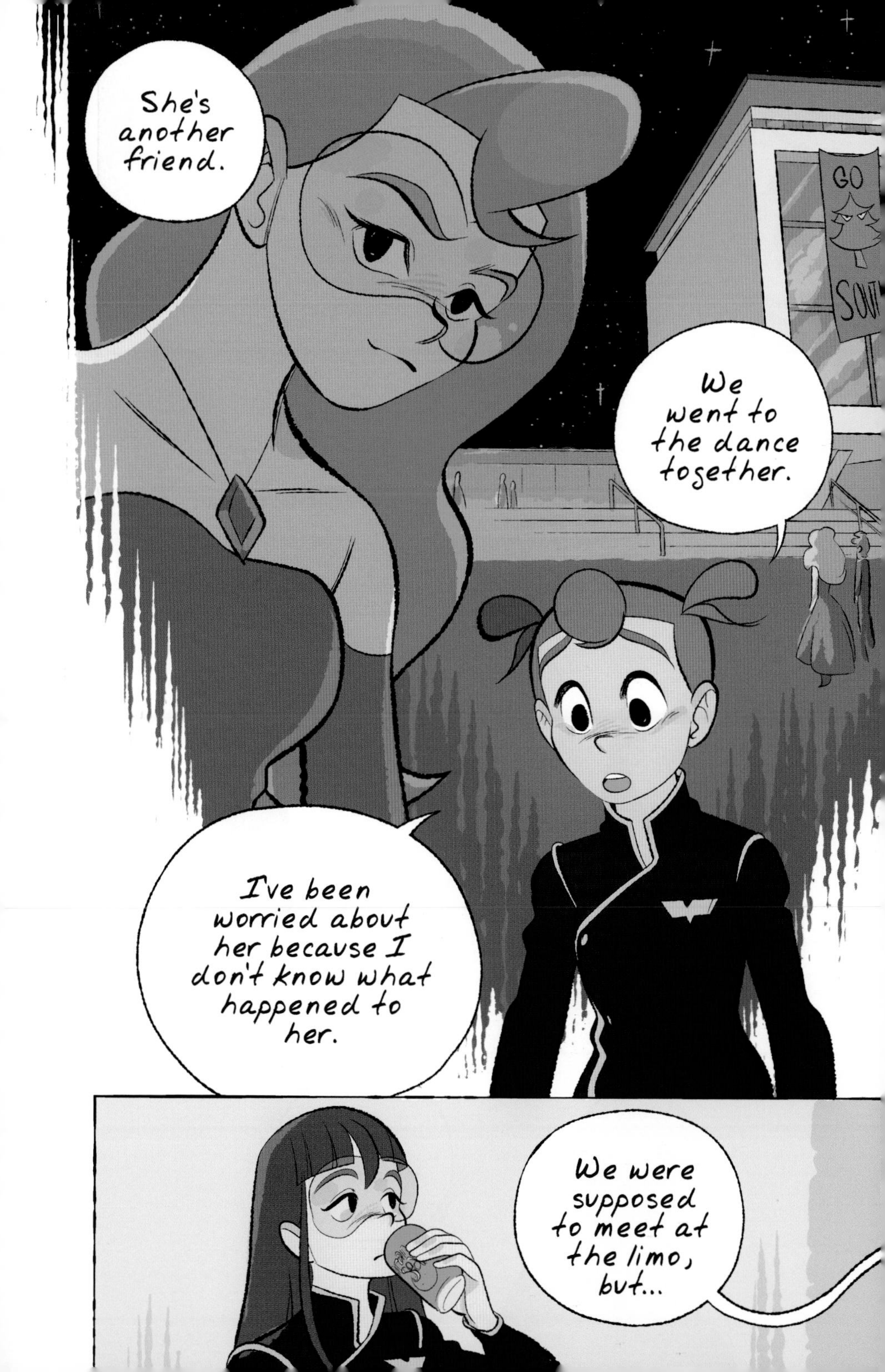
She's another friend.
We went to the dance together.
I've been worried about her because I don't know what happened to her.
We were supposed to meet at the limo, but...

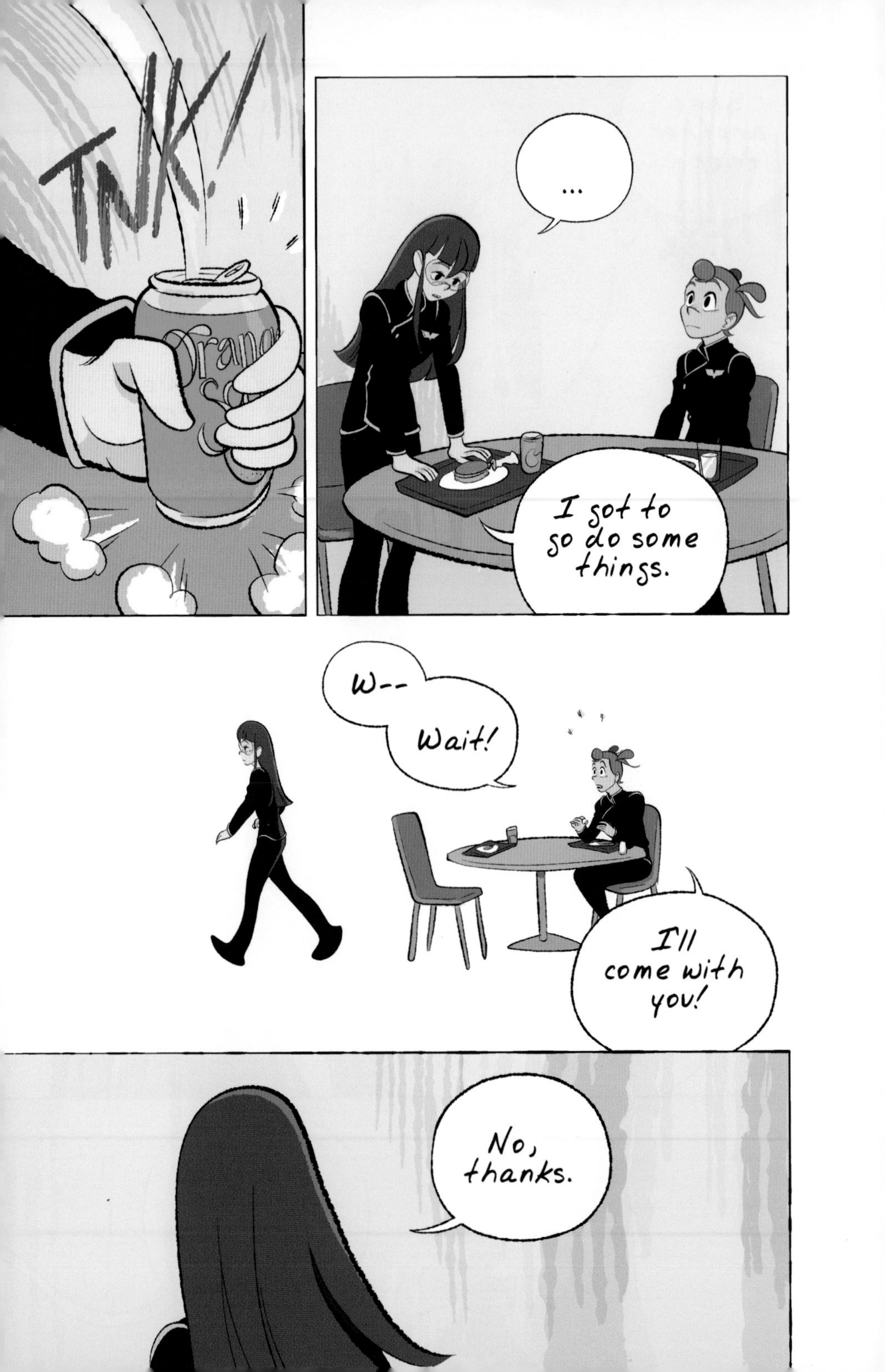
TNK!
Orange Soda
...
I got to go do some things.
W--
Wait!
I'll come with you!
No, thanks.

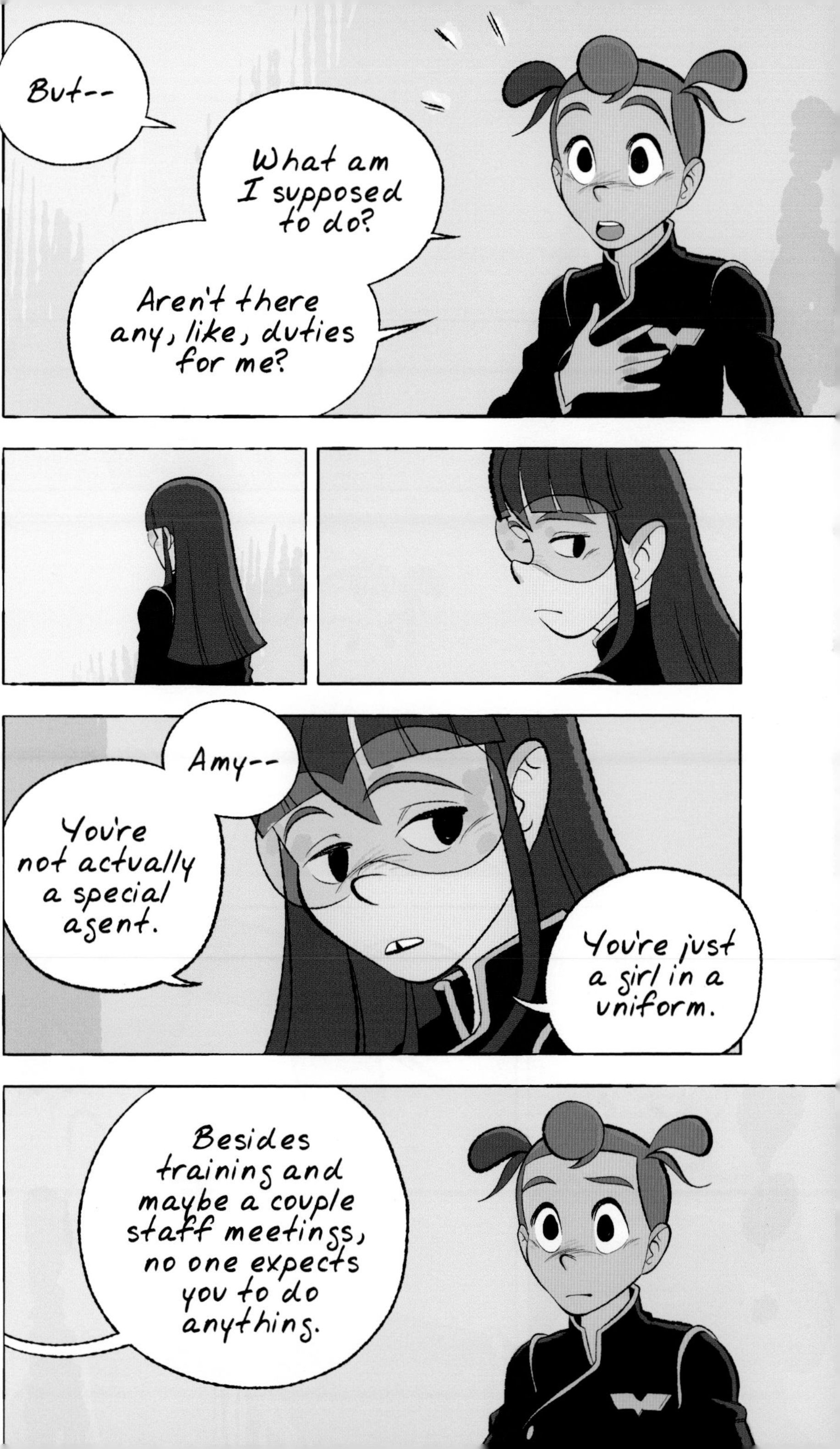
But--
What am I supposed to do?
Aren't there any, like, duties for me?
Amy--
You're not actually a special agent.
You're just a girl in a uniform.
Besides training and maybe a couple staff meetings, no one expects you to do anything.

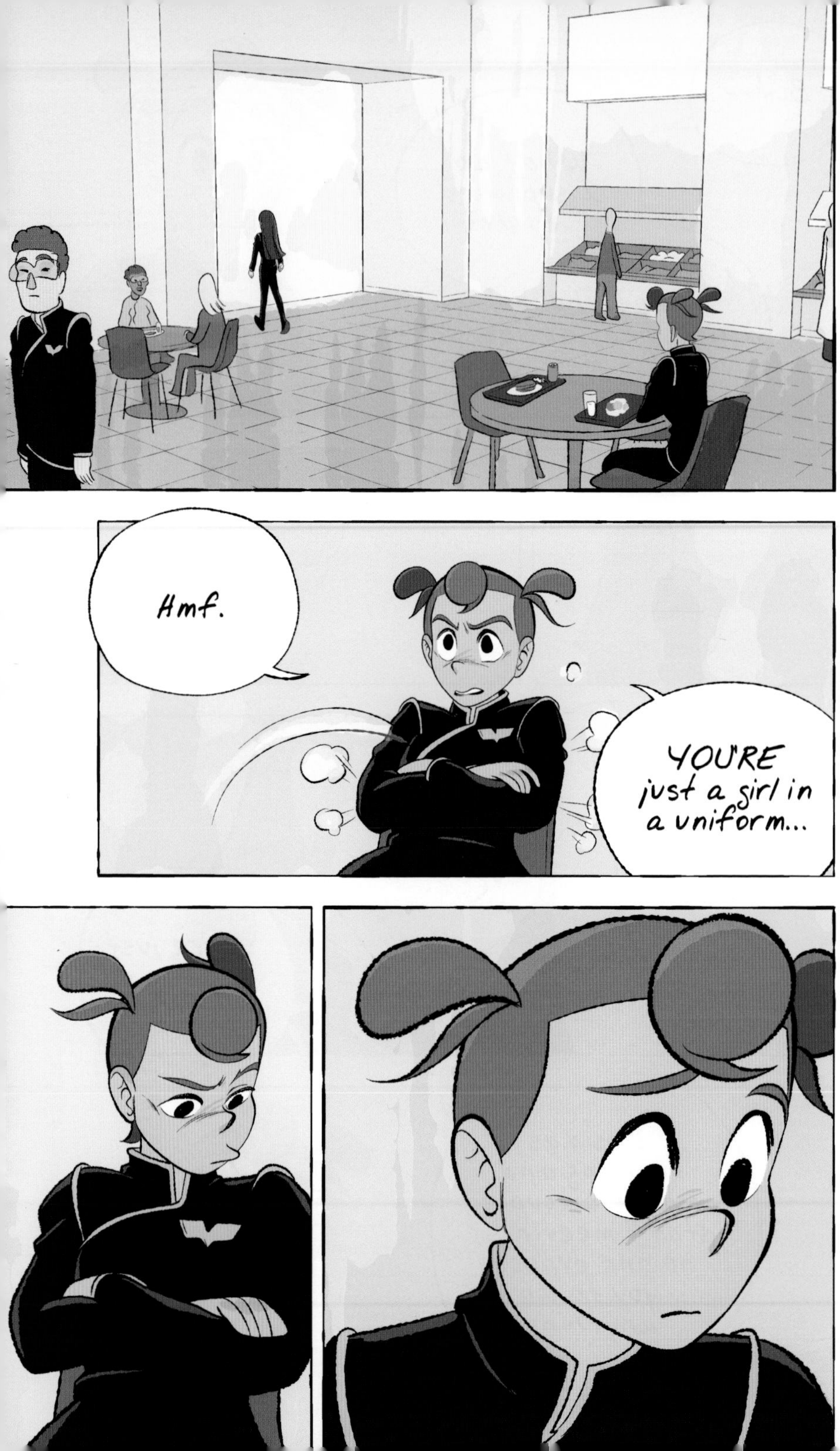
Hmf.
YOU'RE just a girl in a uniform...

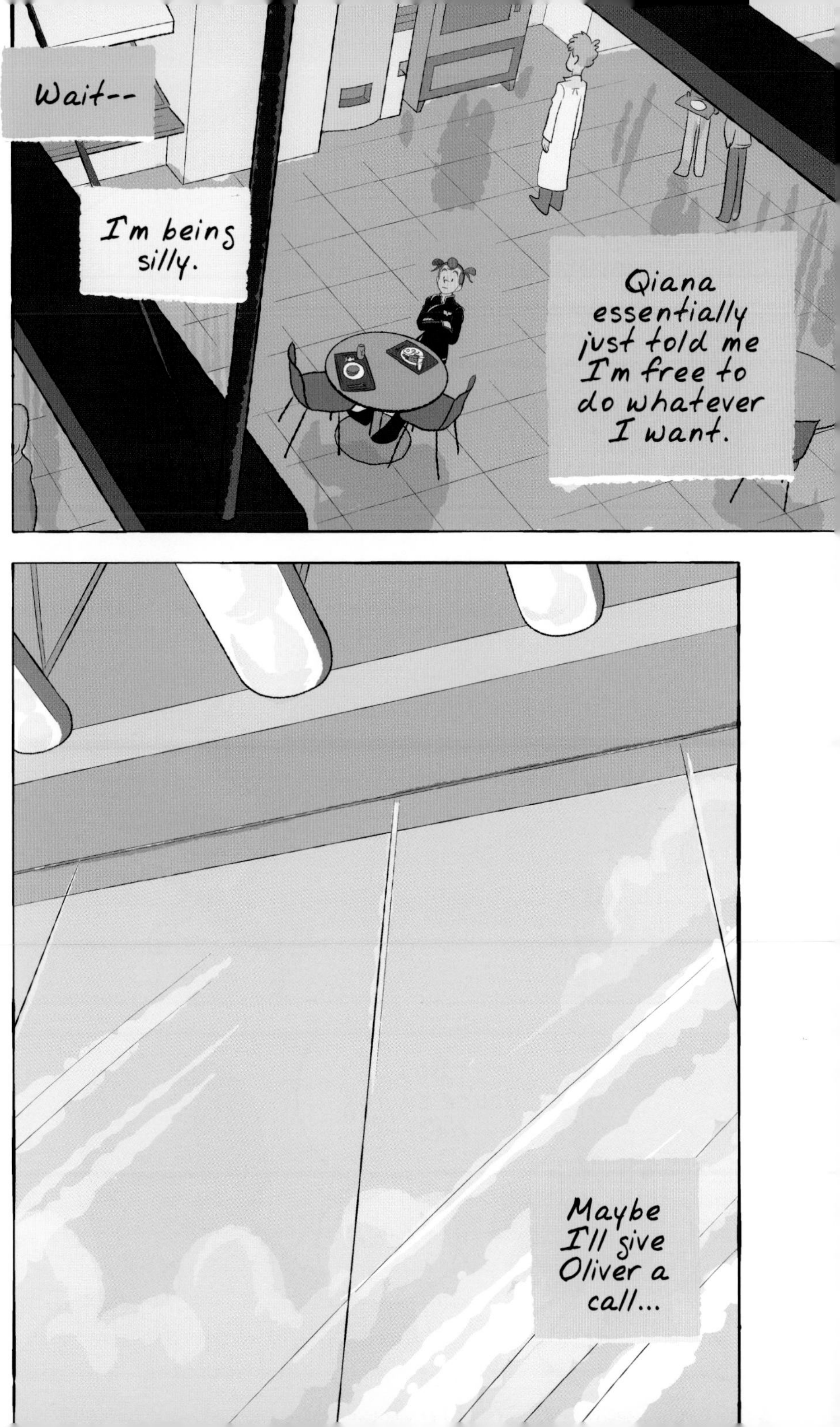
Wait--
I'm being silly.
Qiana essentially just told me I'm free to do whatever I want.
Maybe I'll give Oliver a call...

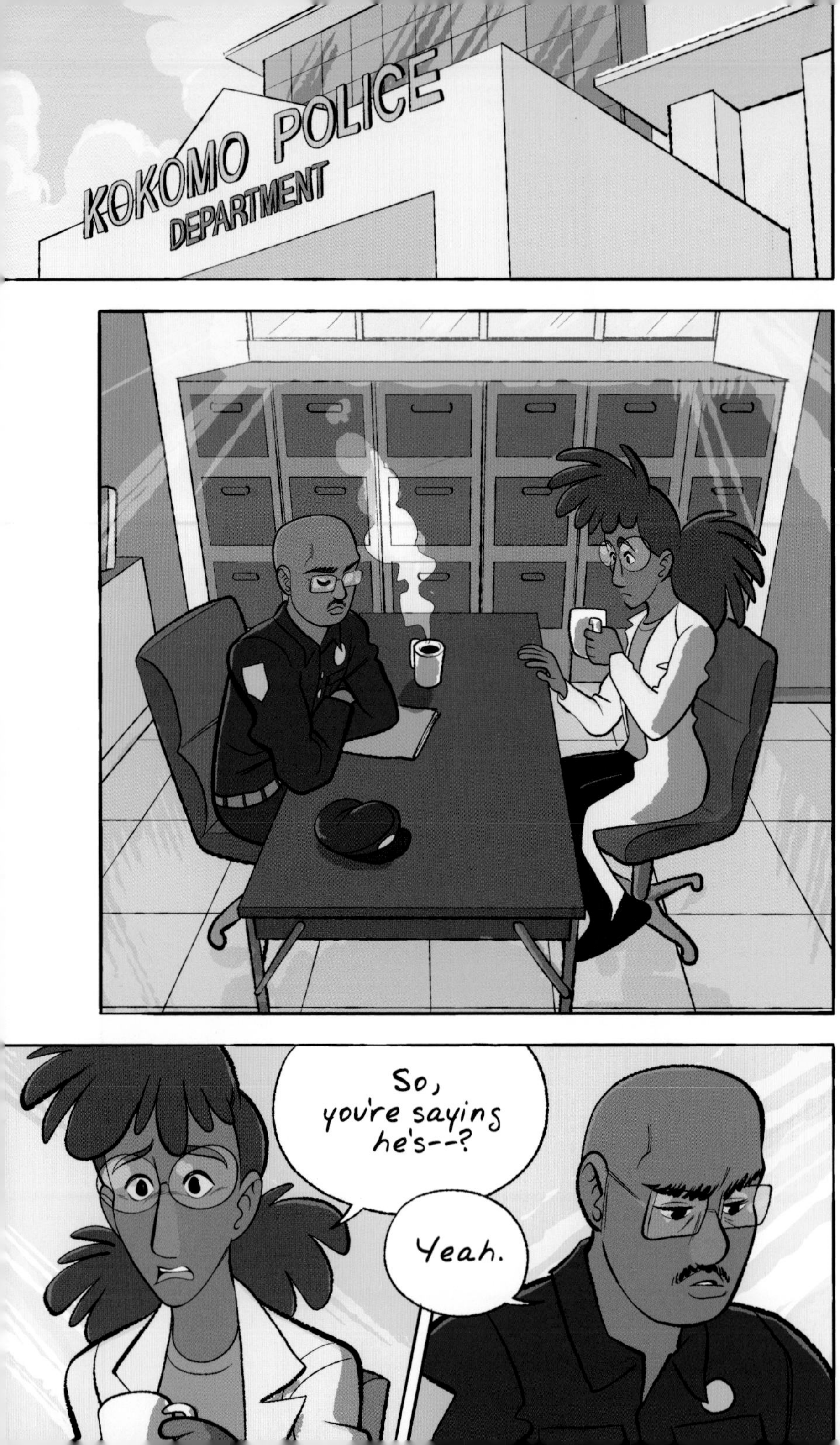
KOKOMO POLICE
DEPARTMENT
So, you're sayins he's--?
Yeah.

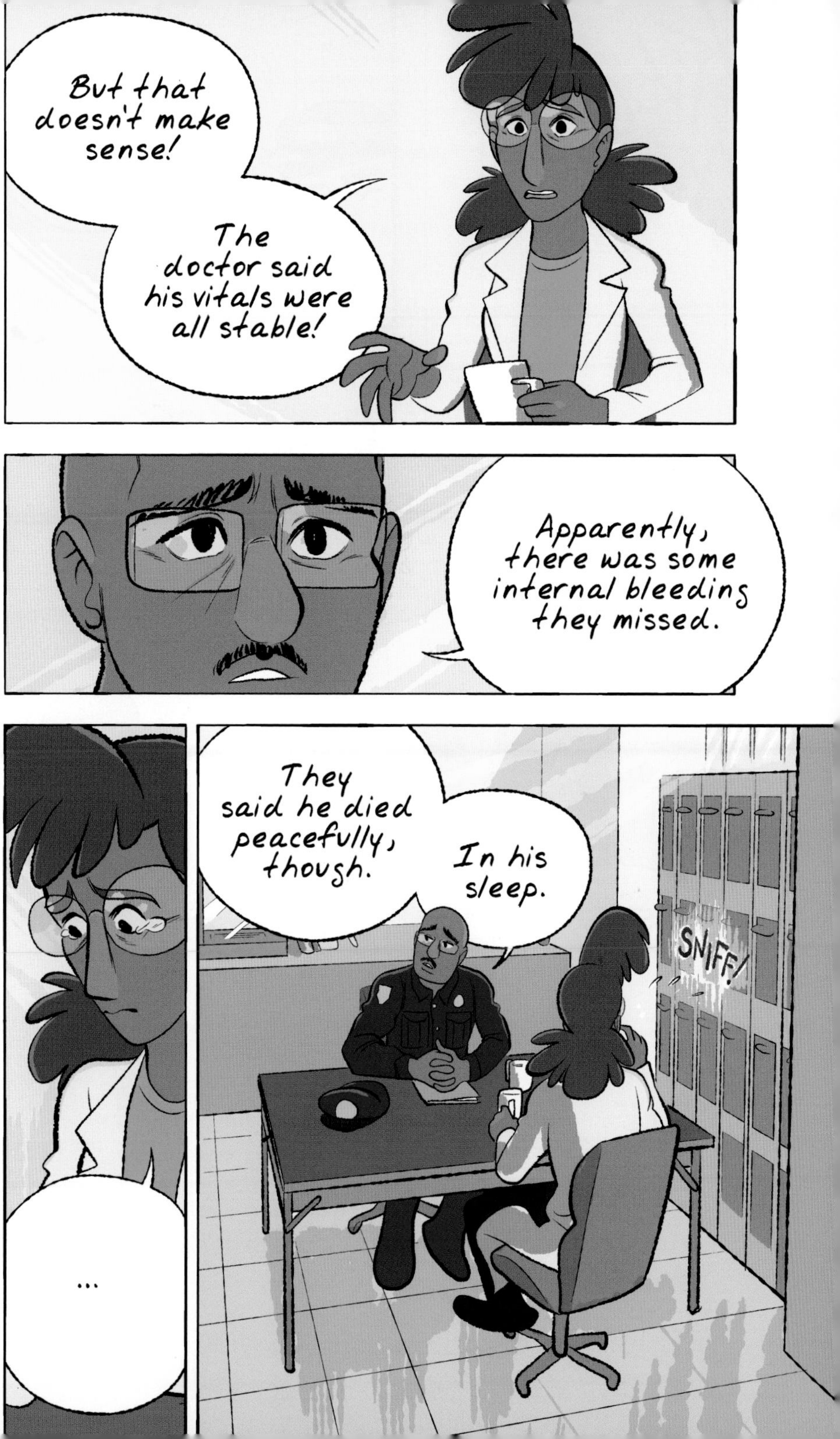

But that doesn't make sense!
The doctor said his vitals were all stable!
Apparently, there was some internal bleeding they missed.
They said he died peacefully, though.
In his sleep.
SNIFF!
...

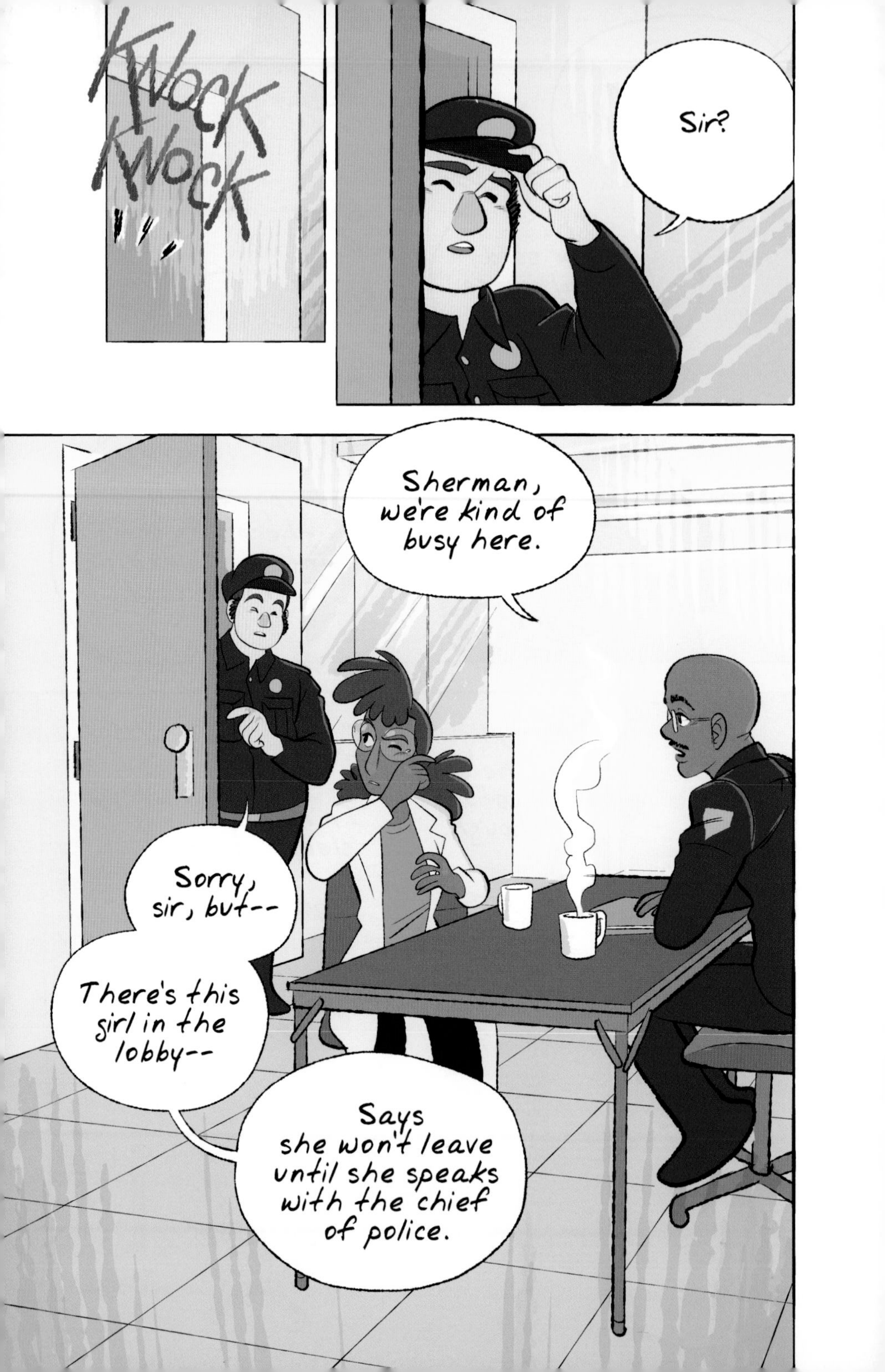
KNOCK KNOCK
Sir?
Sherman, we're kind of busy here.
Sorry, sir, but--
There's this girl in the lobby--
Says she won't leave until she speaks with the chief of police.

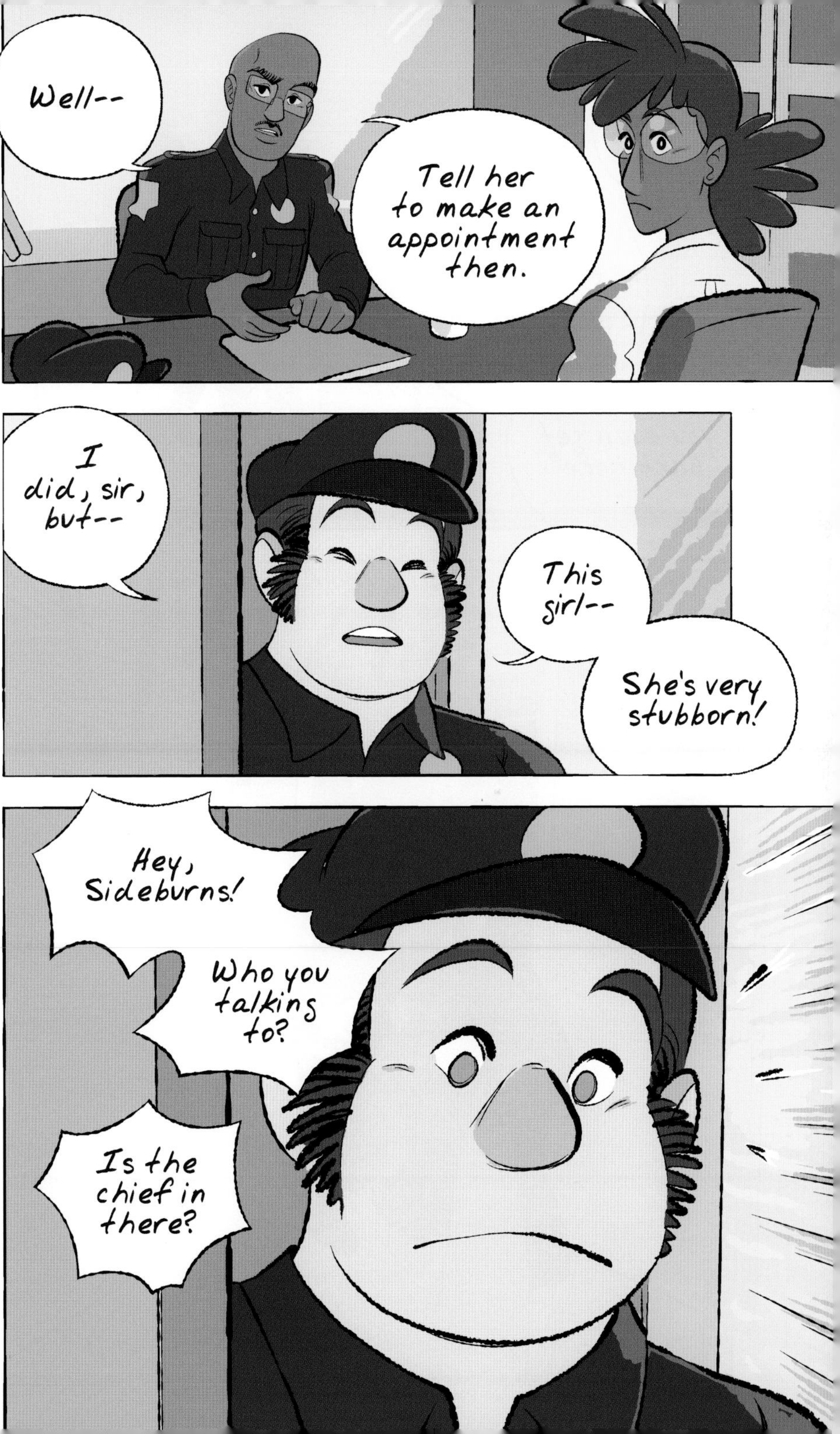
Well--
Tell her to make an appointment then.
I did, sir, but--
This girl--
She's very stubborn!
Hey, Sideburns!
Who you talking to?
Is the chief in there?

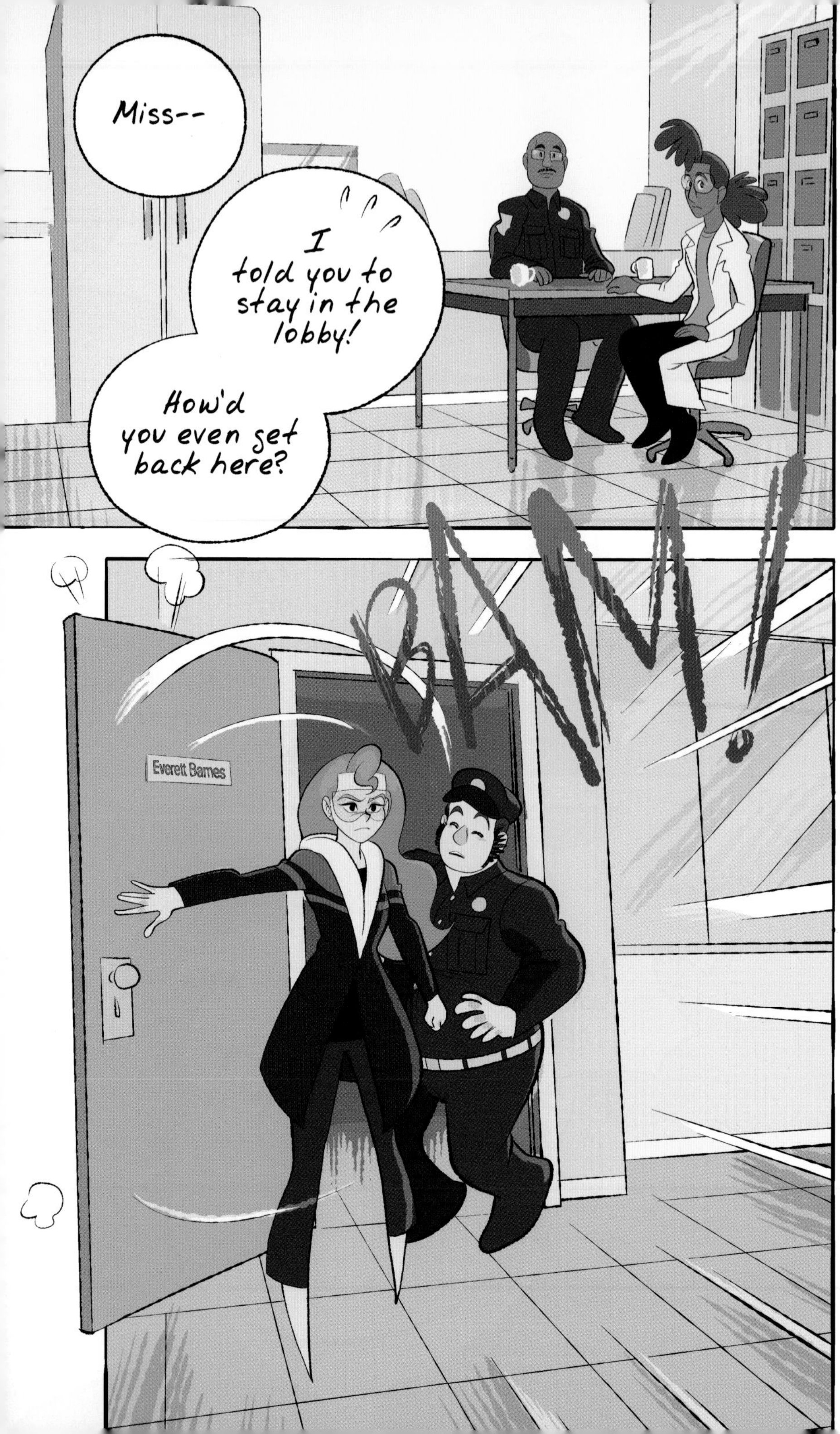
Miss--
I told you to stay in the lobby!
How'd you even get back here?
BAM!
Everett Barnes

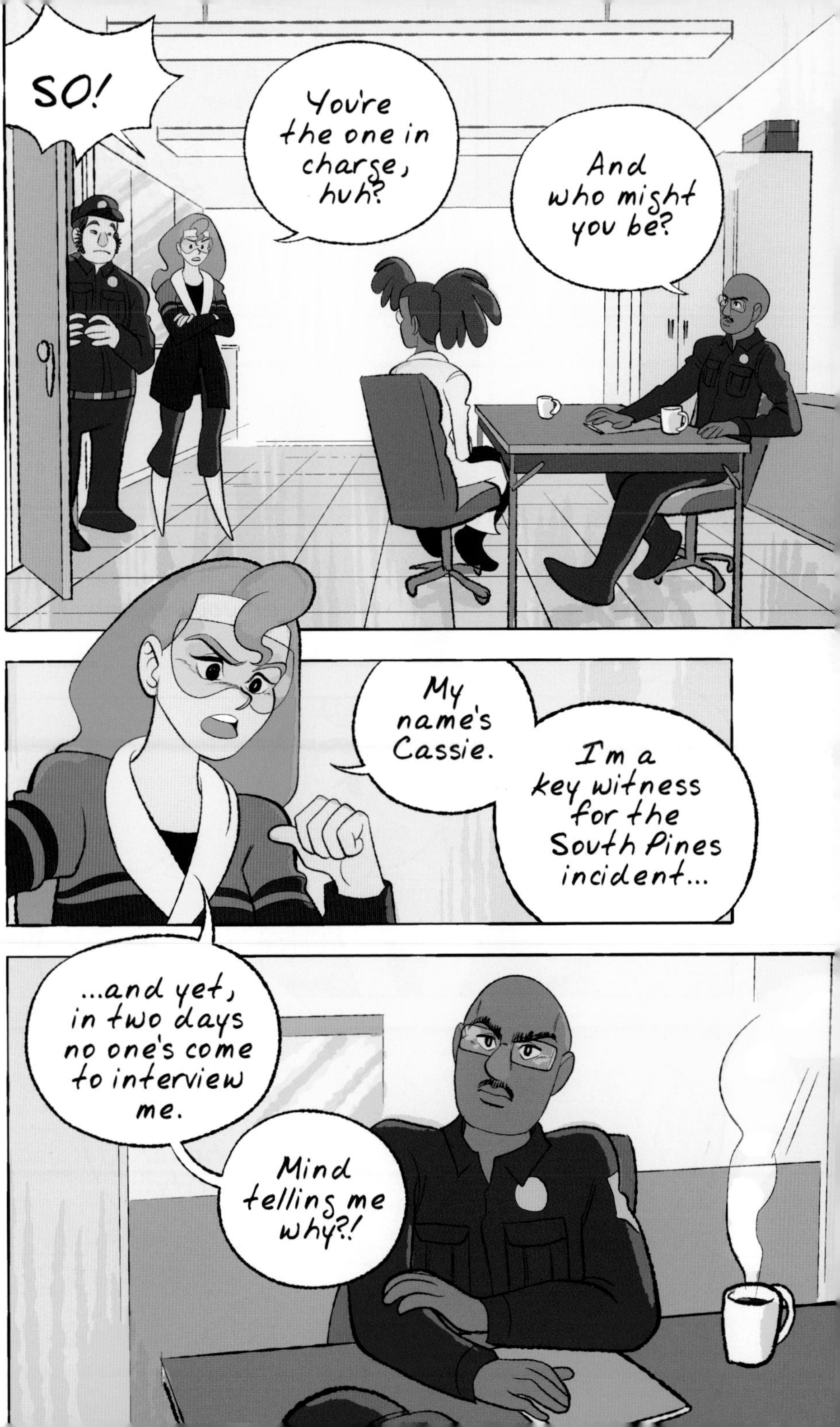
SO!
You're the one in charge, huh?
And who might you be?
My name's Cassie.
I'm a key witness for the South Pines incident...
...and yet, in two days no one's come to interview me.
Mind telling me why?!

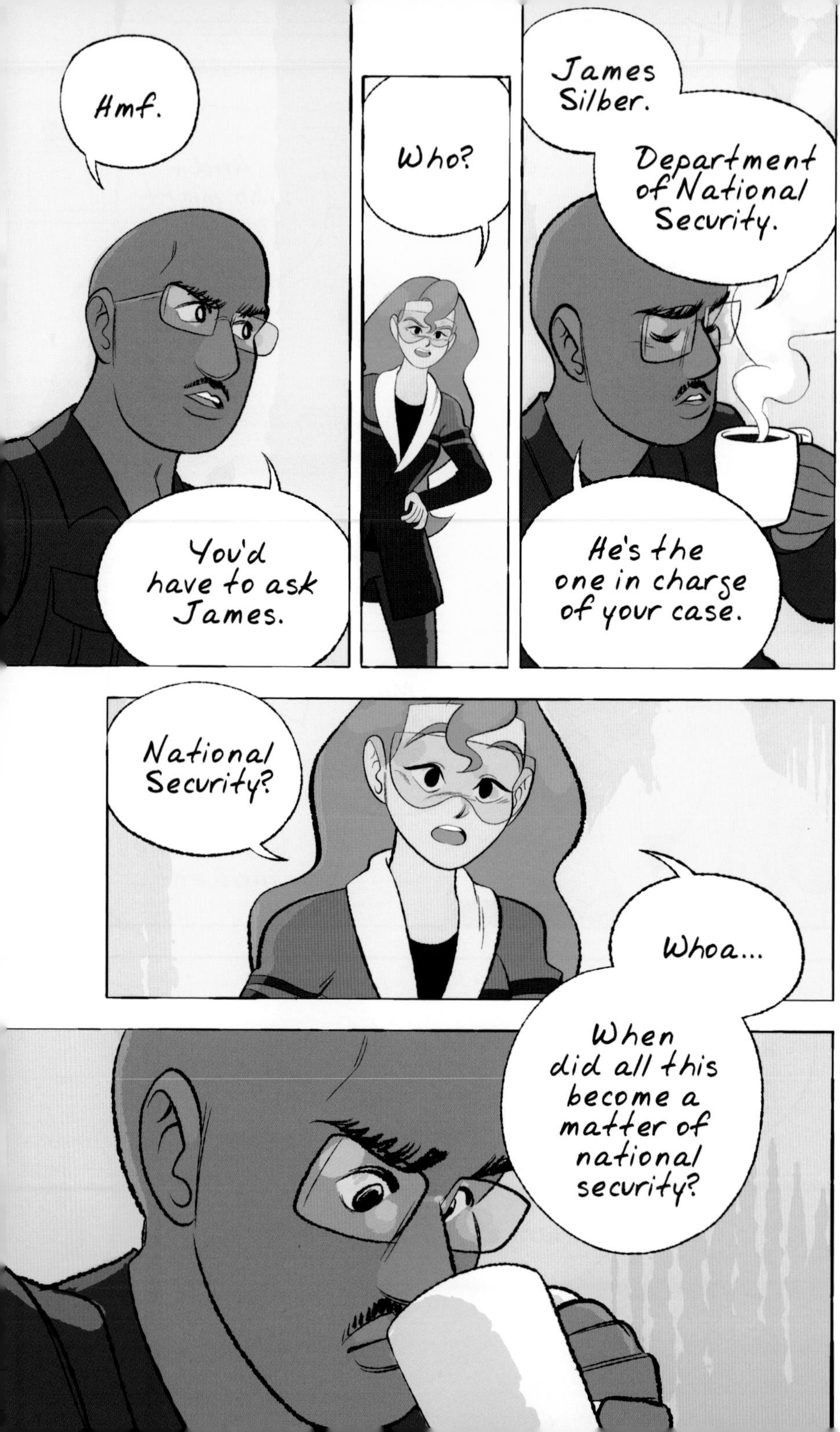
Hmf.
You'd have to ask James.
Who?
James Silber.
Department of National Security.
He's the one in charge of your case.
National Security?
Whoa...
When did all this become a matter of national security?

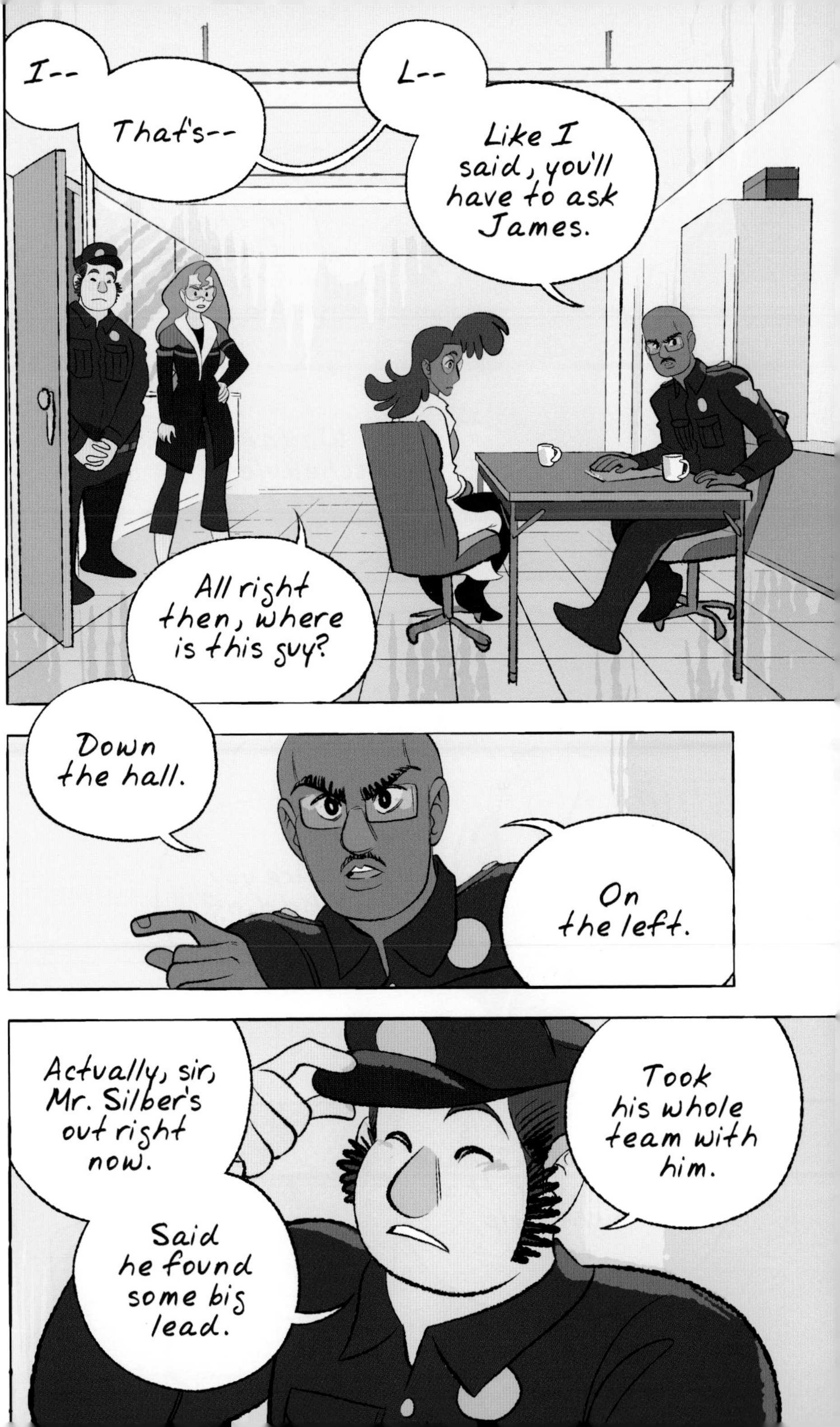
I--
That's--
L--
Like I said, you'll have to ask James.
All right then, where is this guy?
Down the hall.
On the left.
Actually, sir, Mr. Silber's out right now.
Said he found some big lead.
Took his whole team with him.

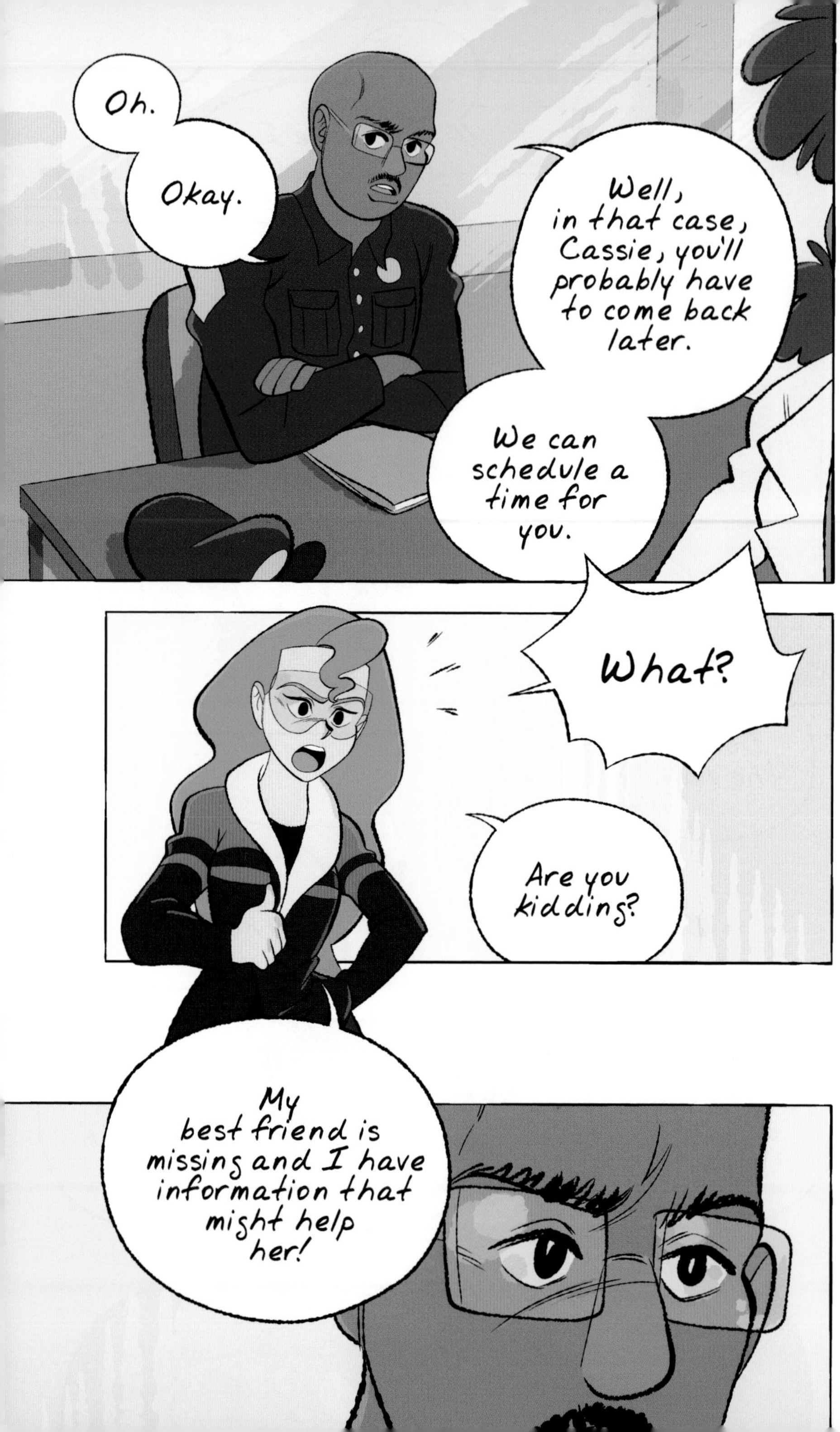
Oh.
Okay.
Well, in that case, Cassie, you'll probably have to come back later.
We can schedule a time for you.
What?
Are you kidding?
My best friend is missing and I have information that might help her!

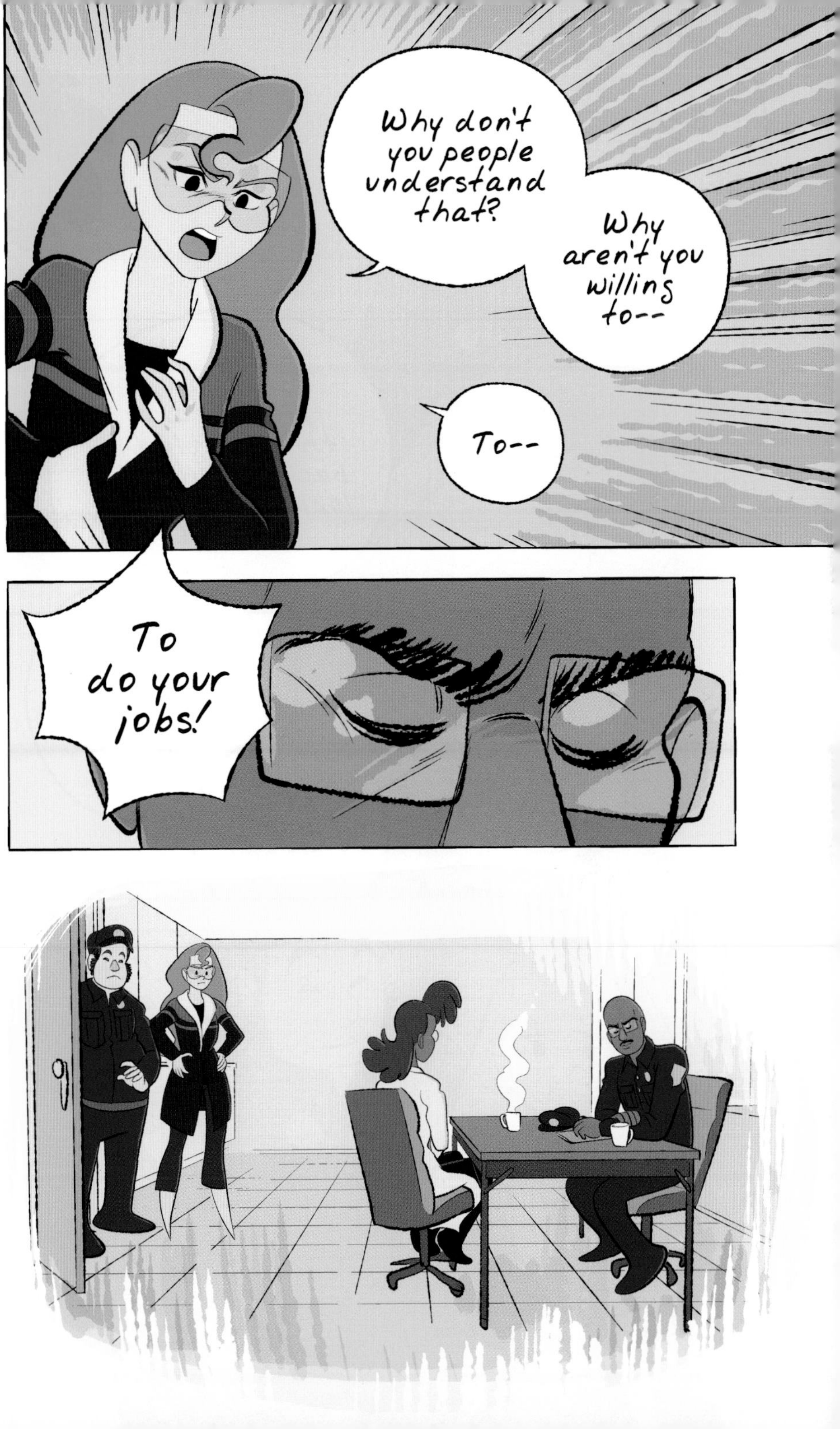
Why don't you people understand that?
Why aren't you willing to--
To--
To do your jobs!

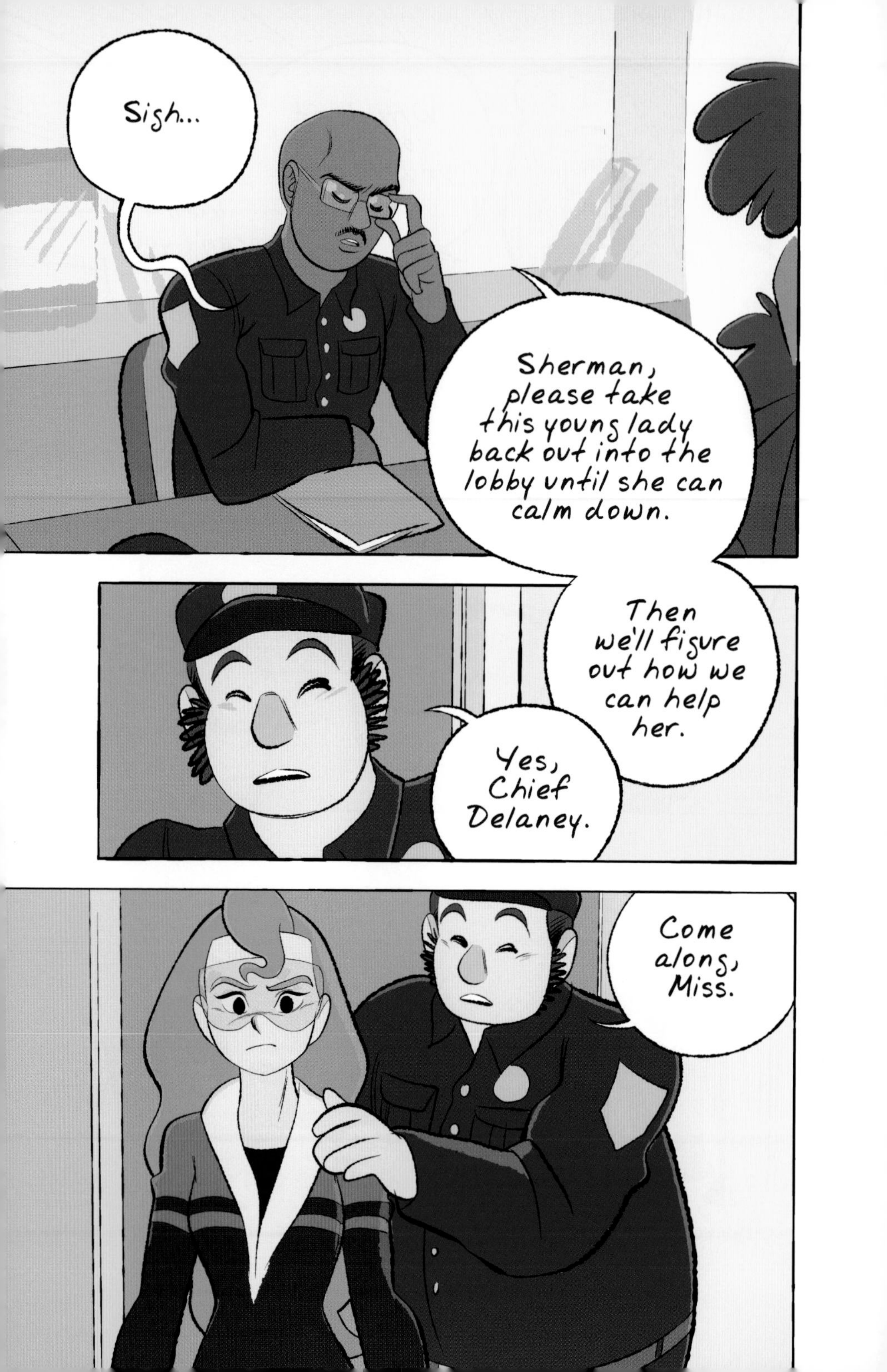

Sigh...
Sherman, please take this young lady back out into the lobby until she can calm down.
Then we'll figure out how we can help her.
Yes, Chief Delaney.
Come along, Miss.

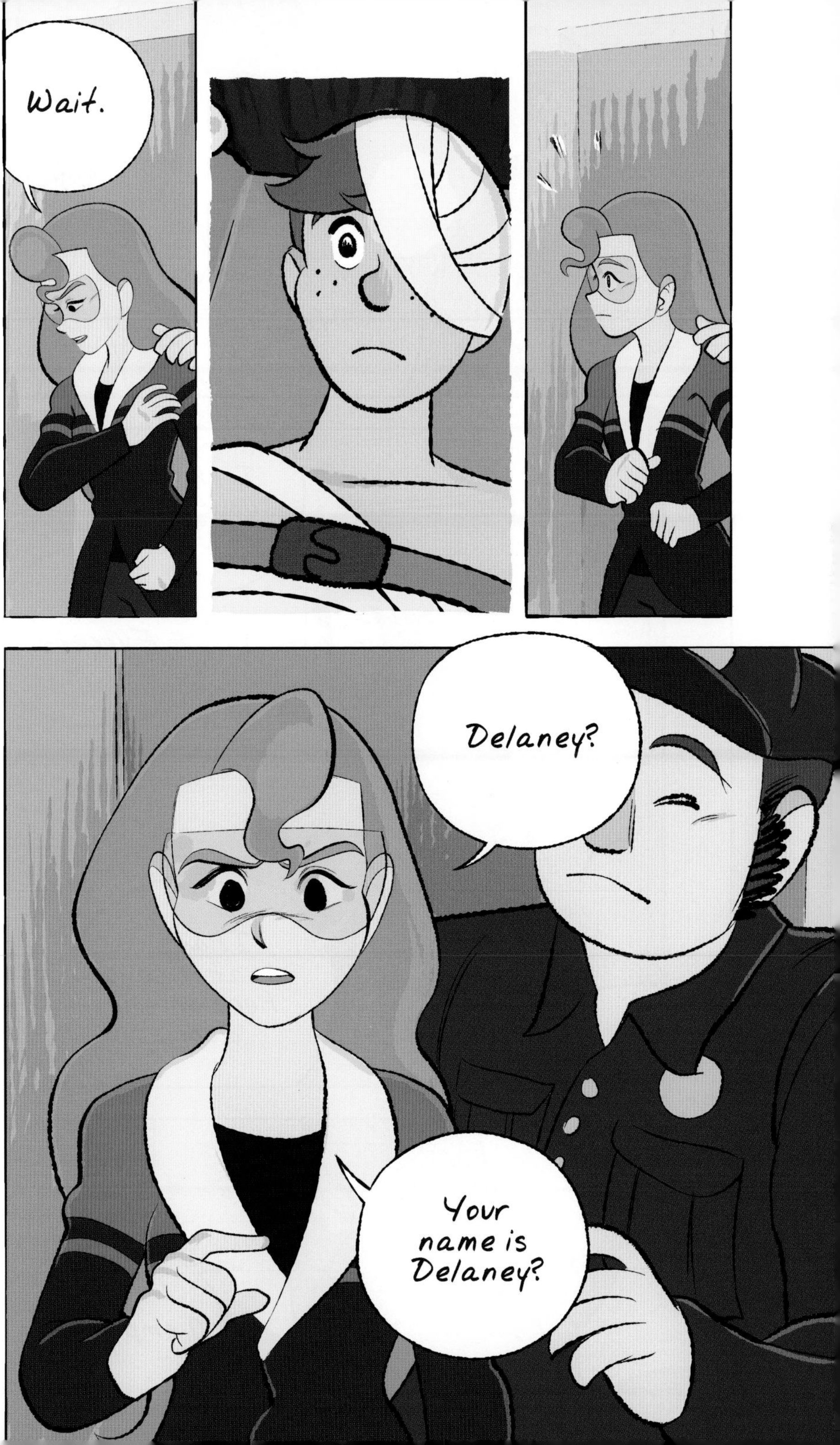
Wait.
Delaney?
Your name is Delaney?

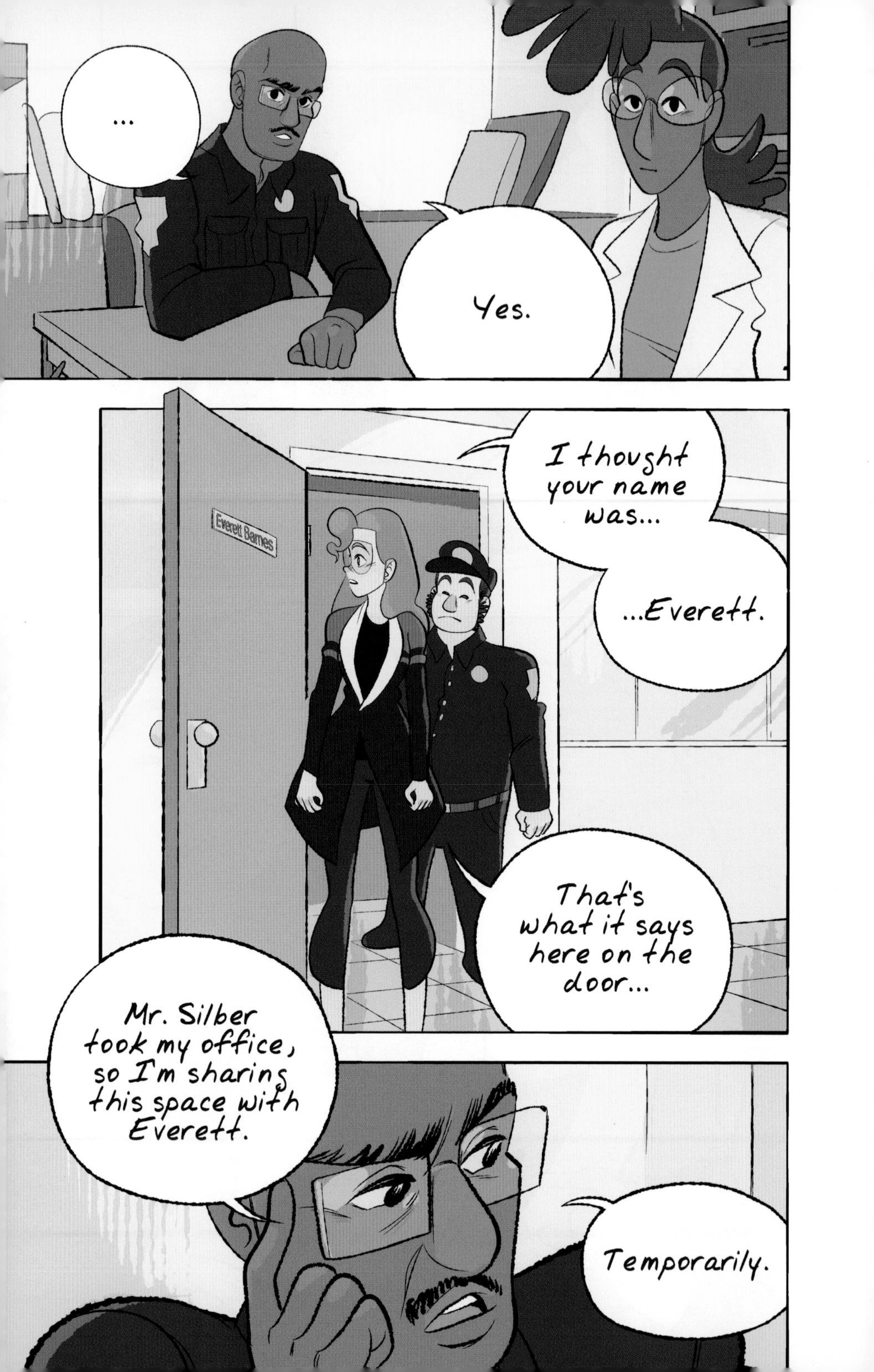
...
Yes.
Everett Barnes
I thought your name was...
...Everett.
That's what it says here on the door...
Mr. Silber took my office, so I'm sharing this space with Everett.
Temporarily.

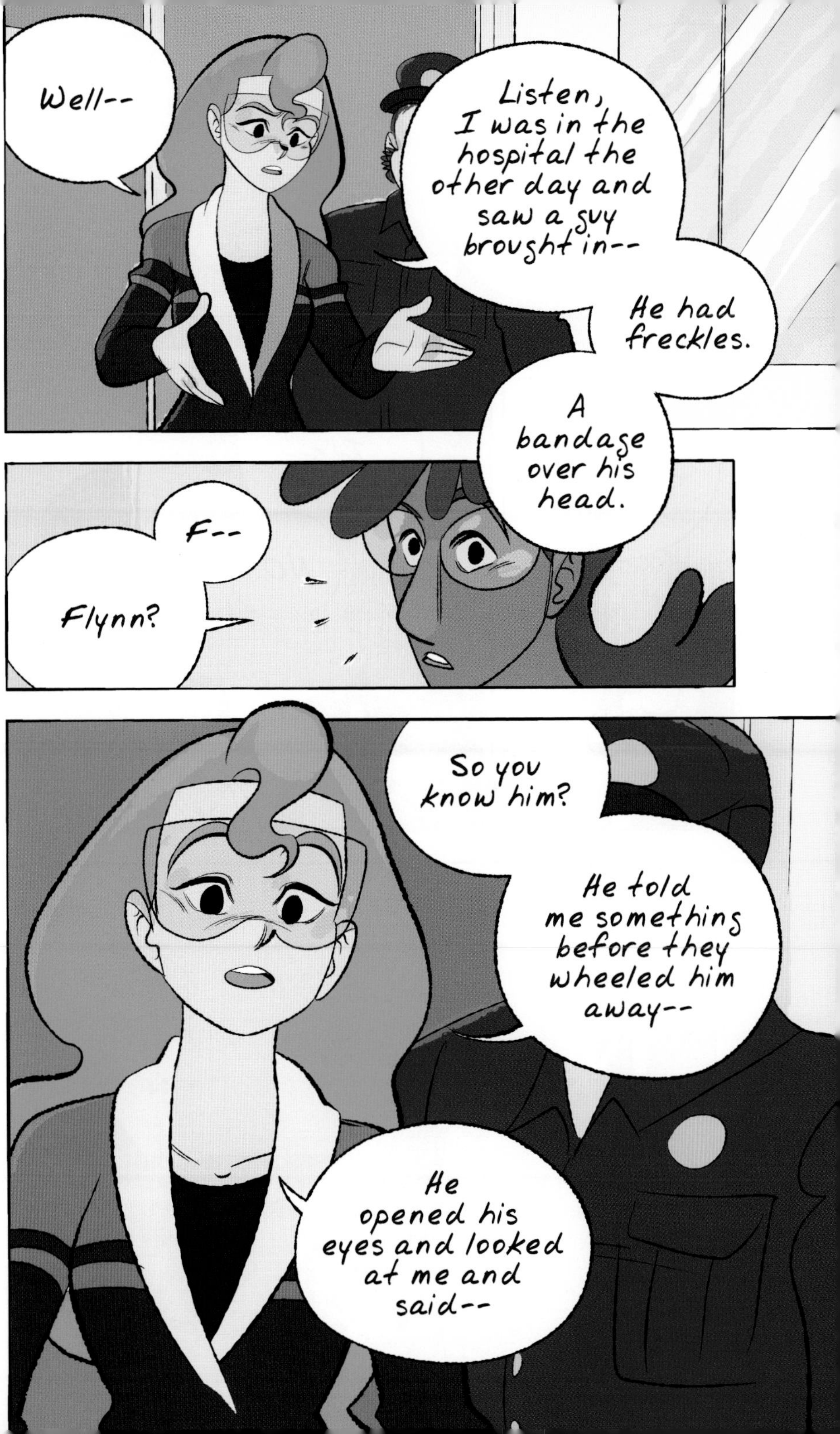
Well--
Listen, I was in the hospital the other day and saw a guy brought in--
He had freckles.
A bandage over his head.
F--
Flynn?
So you know him?
He told me something before they wheeled him away--
He opened his eyes and looked at me and said--

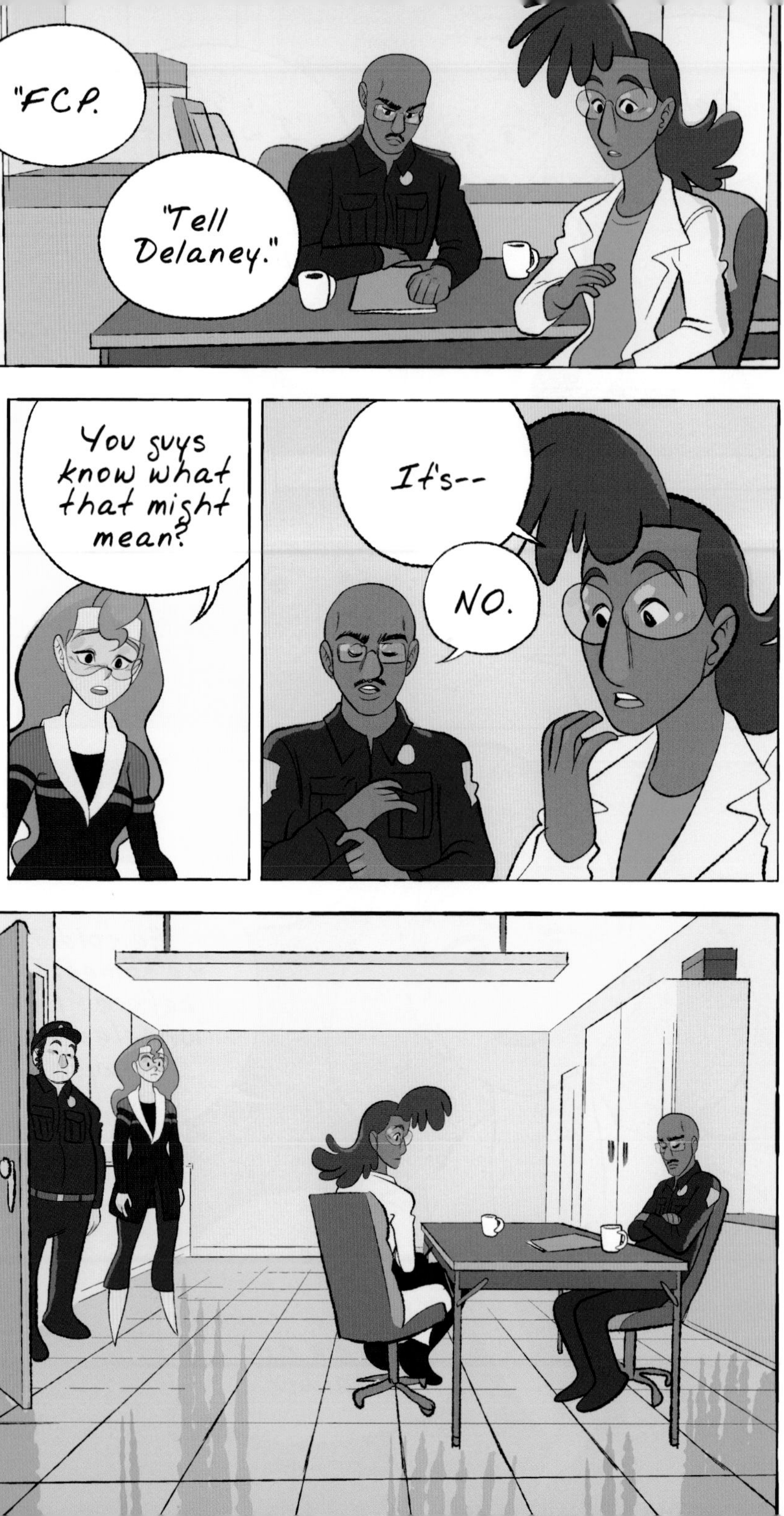
"FCP.
"Tell Delaney."
You guys know what that might mean?
It's--
NO.

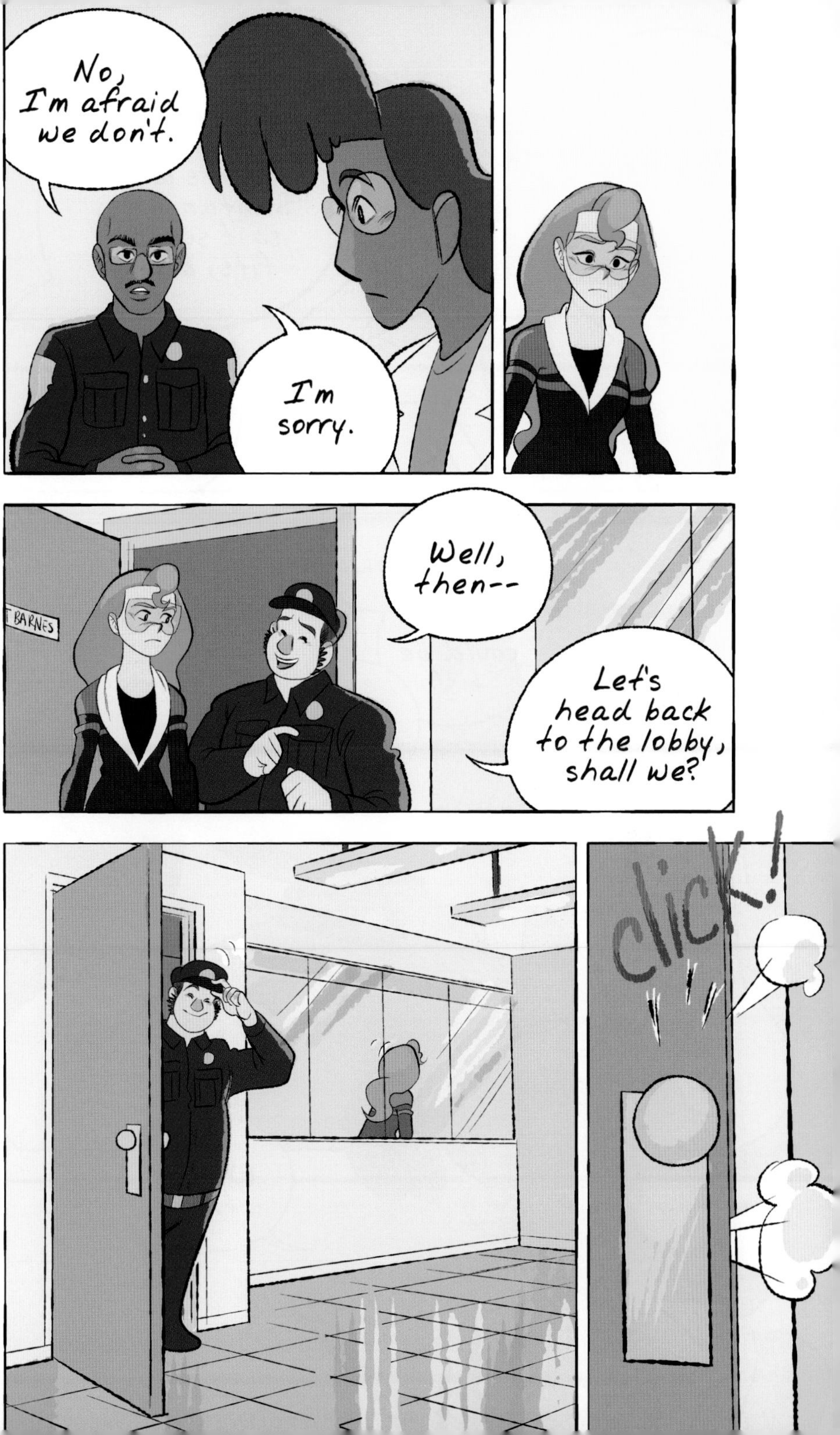

No, I'm afraid we don't.
I'm sorry.
BARNES
Well, then--
Let's head back to the lobby, shall we?
click!

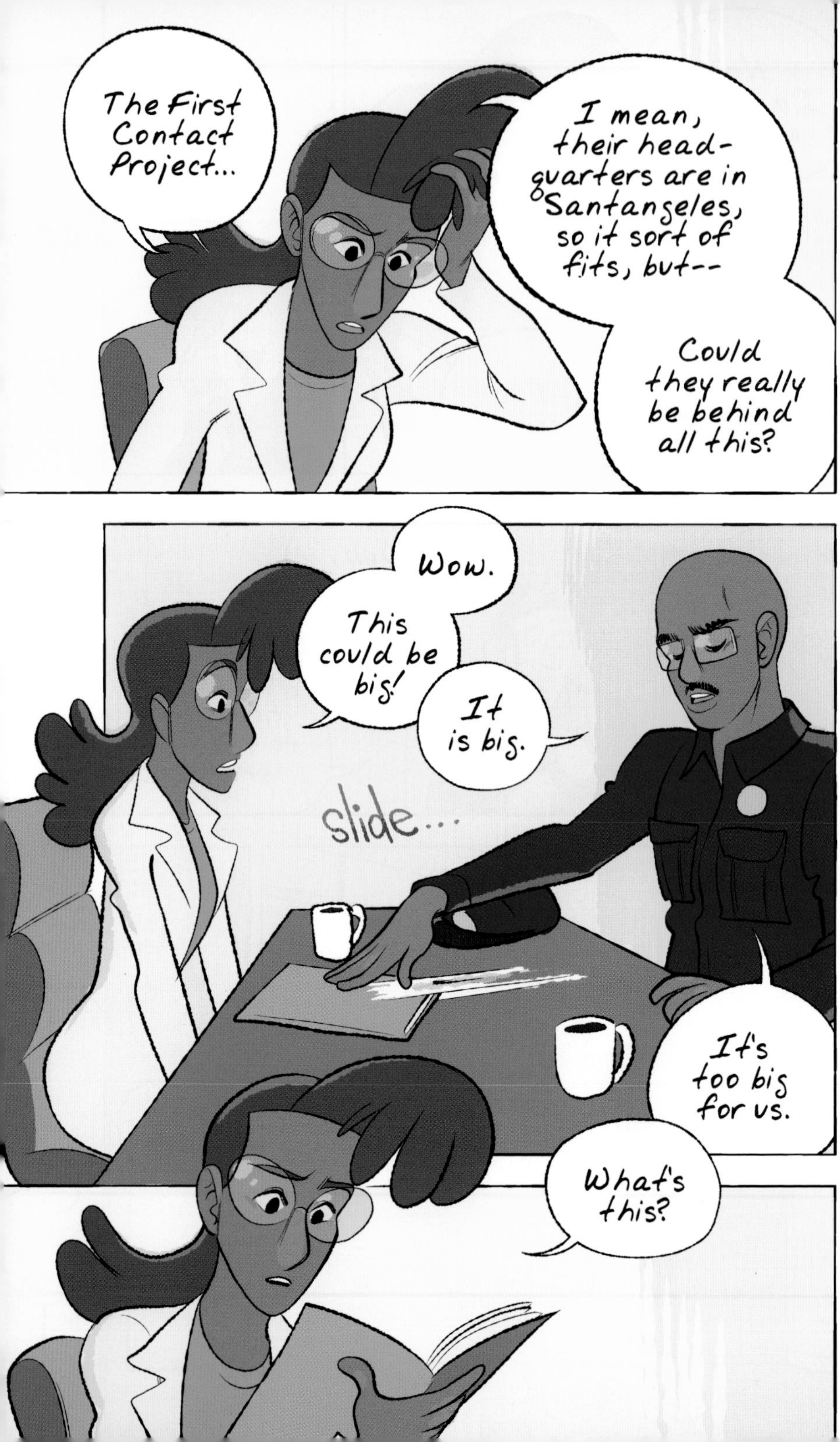
The First Contact Project...
I mean, their head-quarters are in Santangeles, so it sort of fits, but--
Could they really be behind all this?
Wow.
This could be big!
It is big.
slide...
It's too big for us.
What's this?

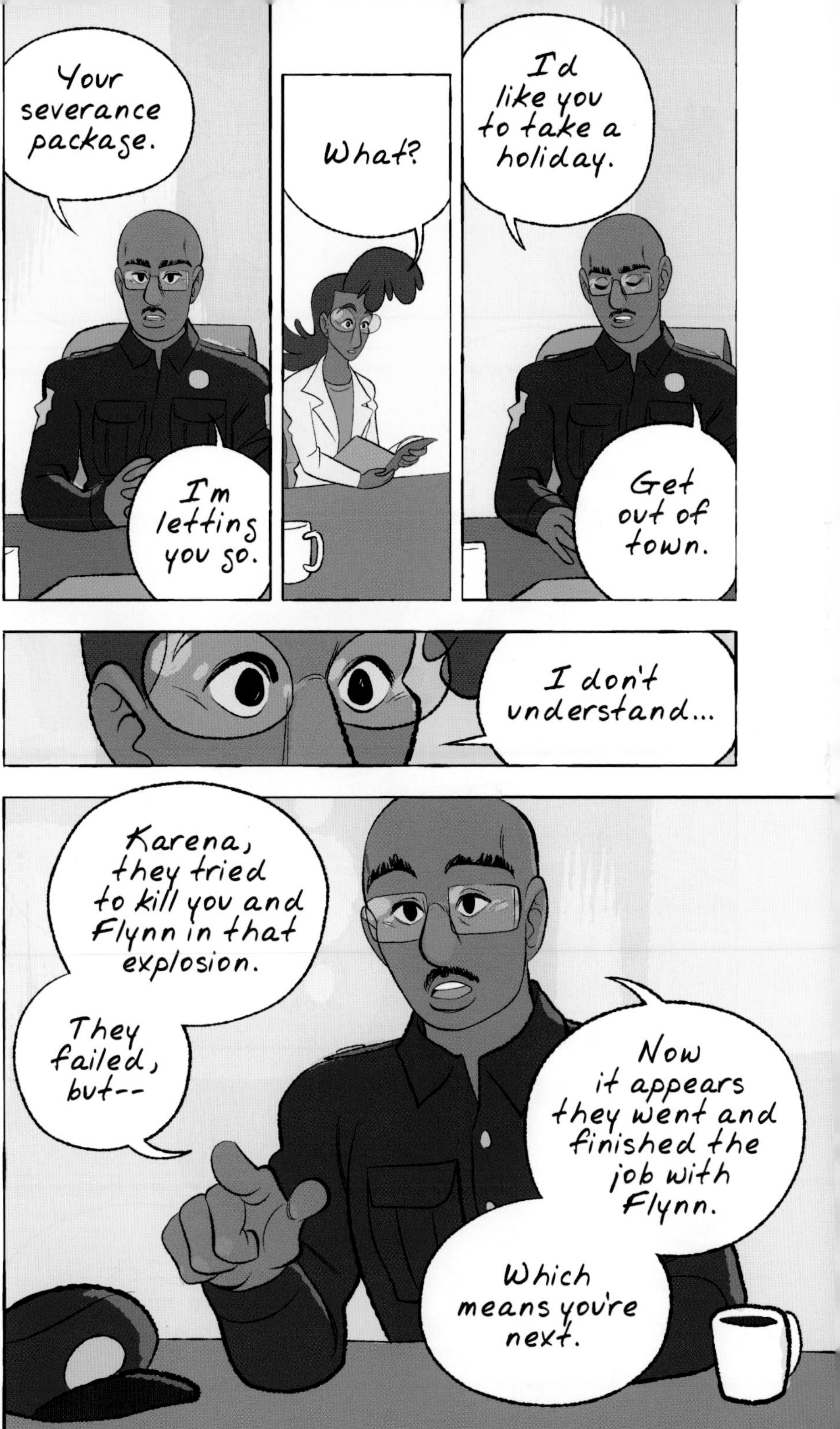
Your severance package.
I'm letting you go.
What?
I'd like you to take a holiday.
Get out of town.
I don't understand...
Karena, they tried to kill you and Flynn in that explosion.
They failed, but--
Now it appears they went and finished the job with Flynn.
Which means you're next.

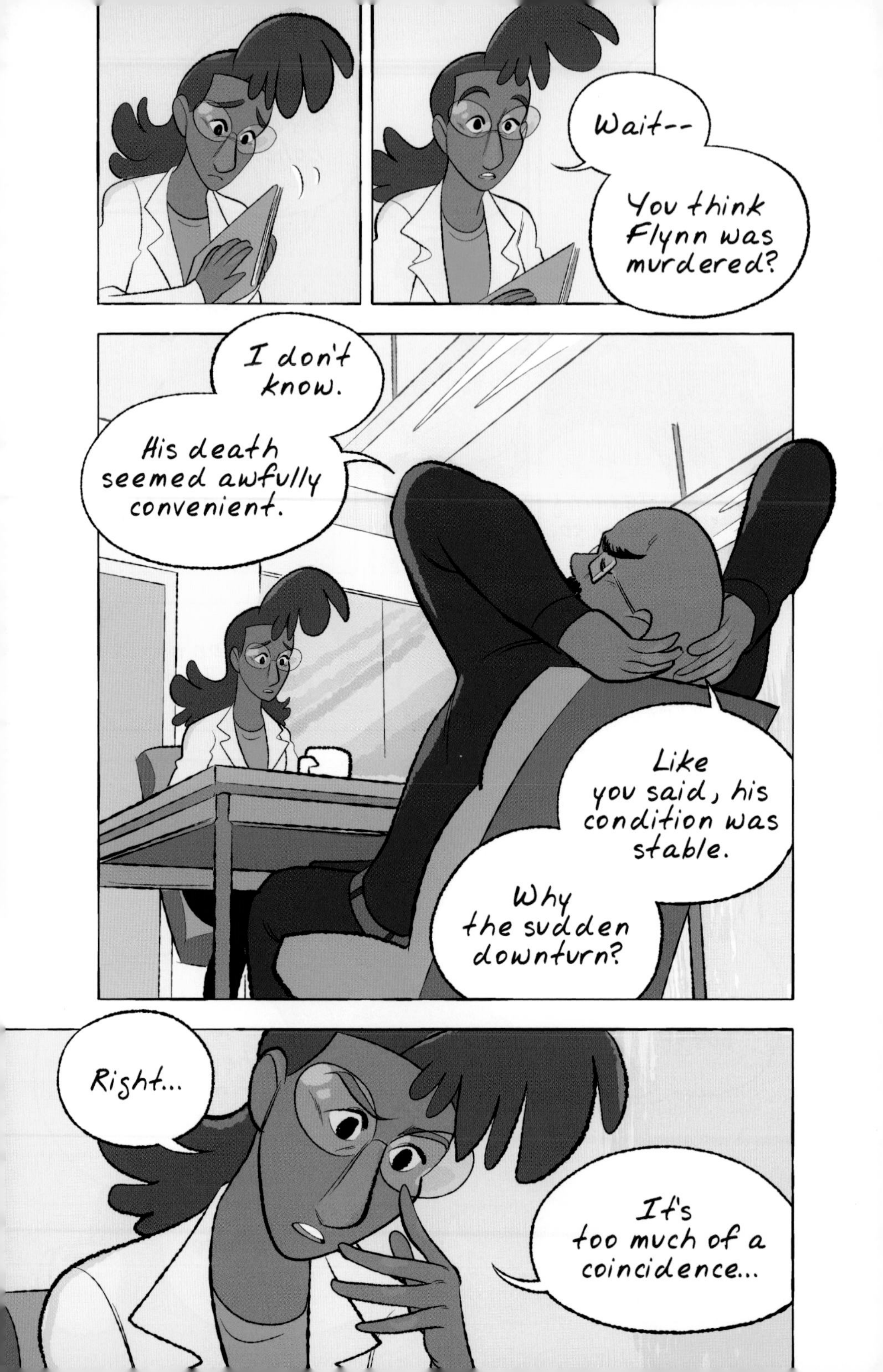
Wait--
You think Flynn was murdered?
I don't know.
His death seemed awfully convenient.
Like you said, his condition was stable.
Why the sudden downturn?
Right...
It's too much of a coincidence...

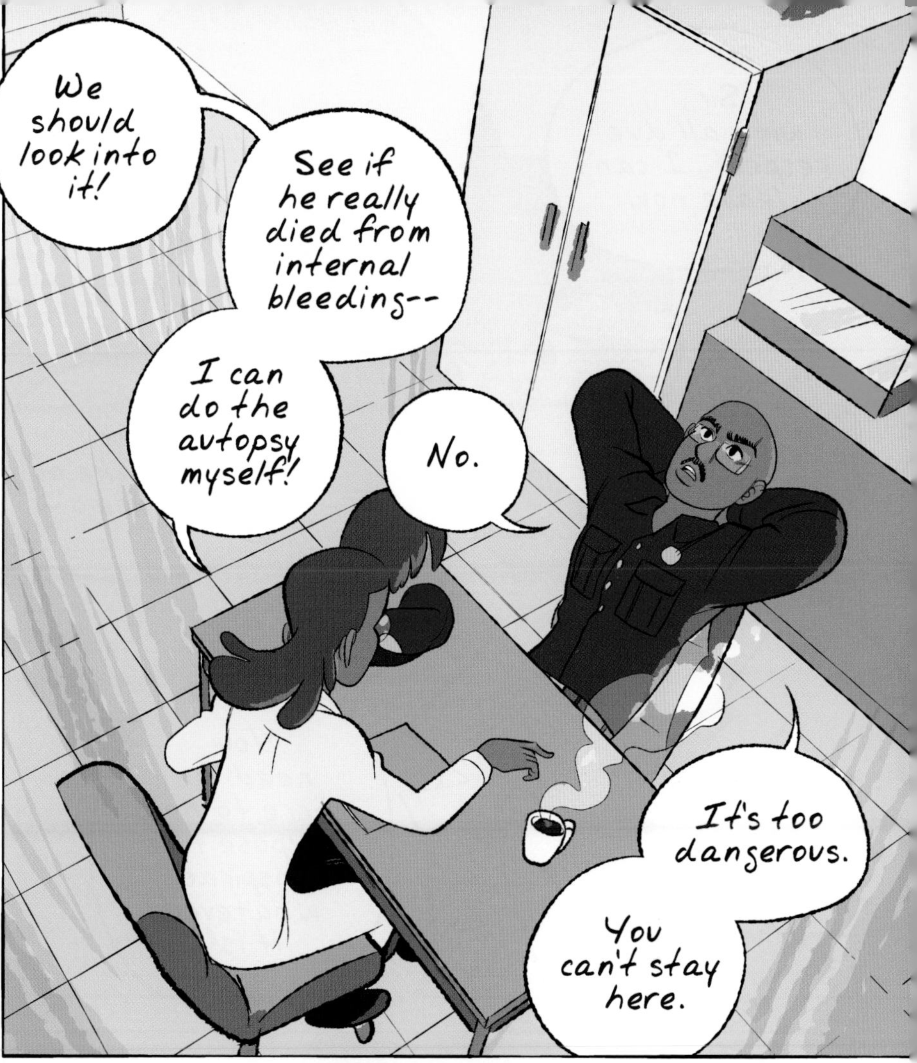
We should look into it!
See if he really died from internal bleeding--
I can do the autopsy myself!
No.
It's too dangerous.
You can't stay here.

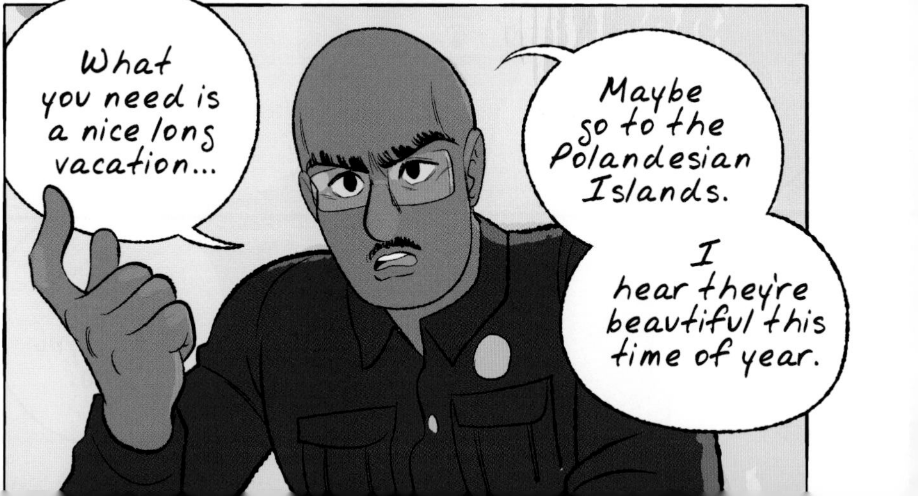
What you need is a nice long vacation...
Maybe go to the Polandesian Islands.
I hear they're beautiful this time of year.

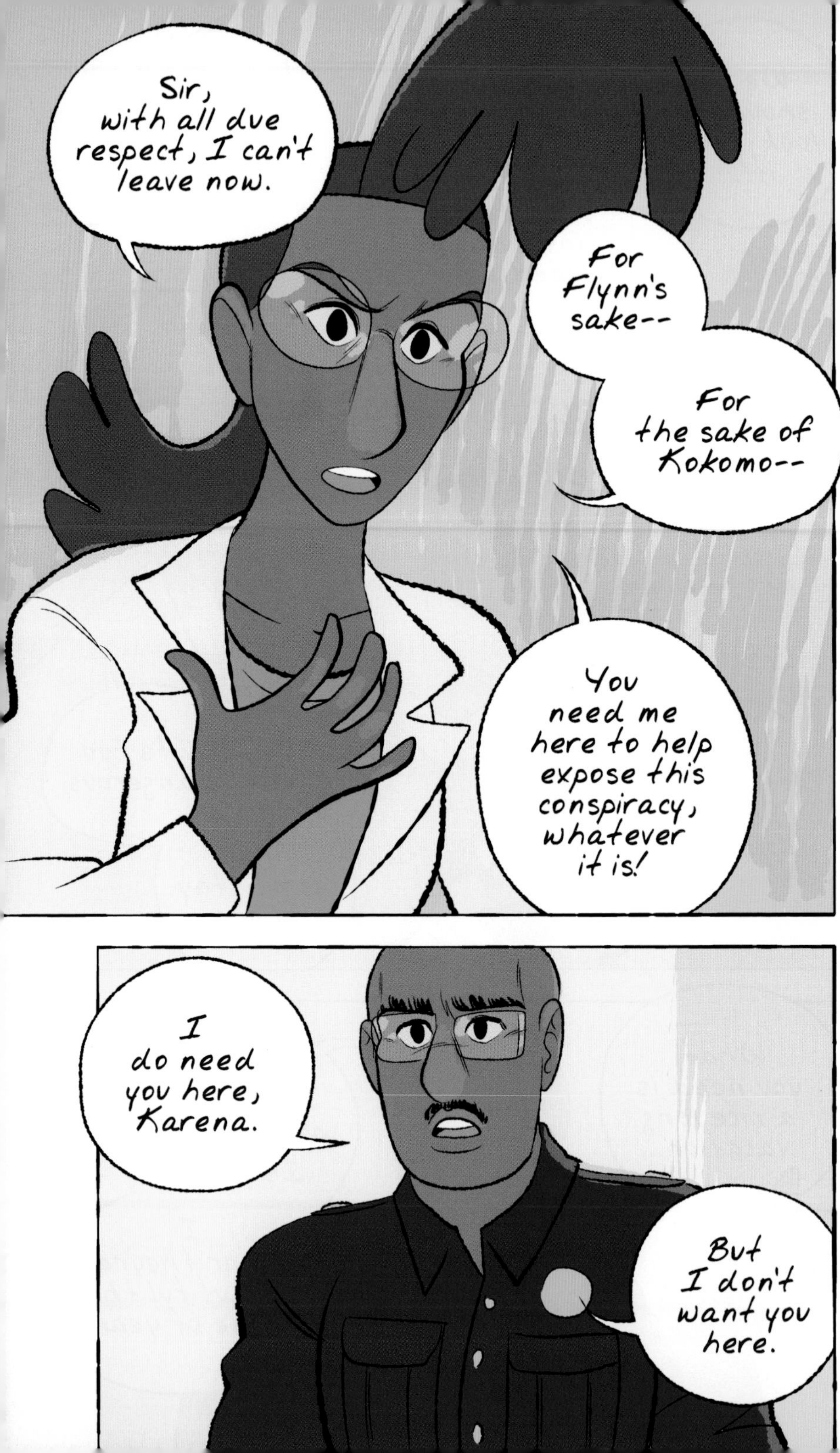
Sir, with all due respect, I can't leave now.
For Flynn's sake--
For the sake of Kokomo--
You need me here to help expose this conspiracy, whatever it is!
I do need you here, Karena.
But I don't want you here.

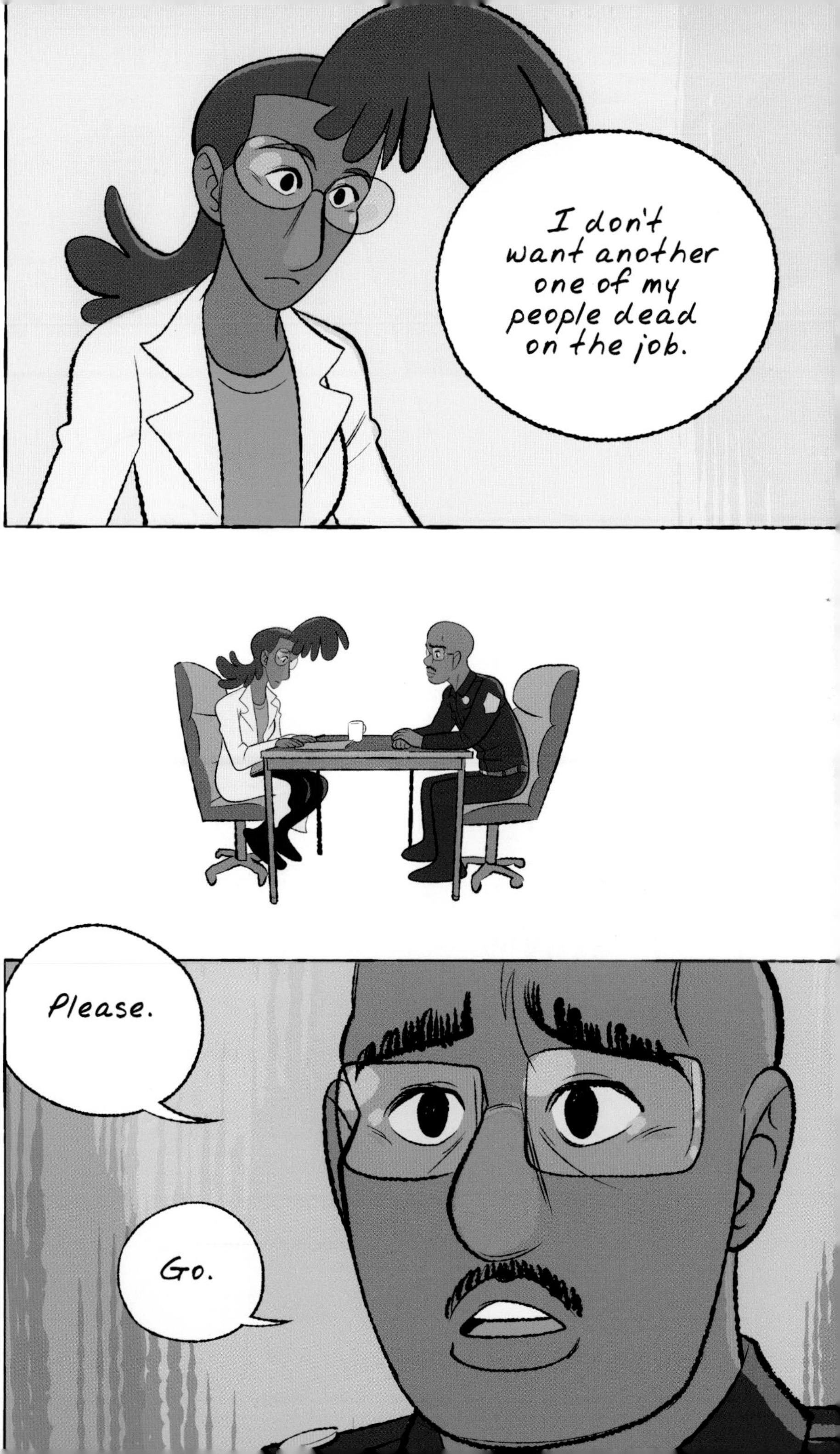
I don't want another one of my people dead on the job.
Please.
Go.

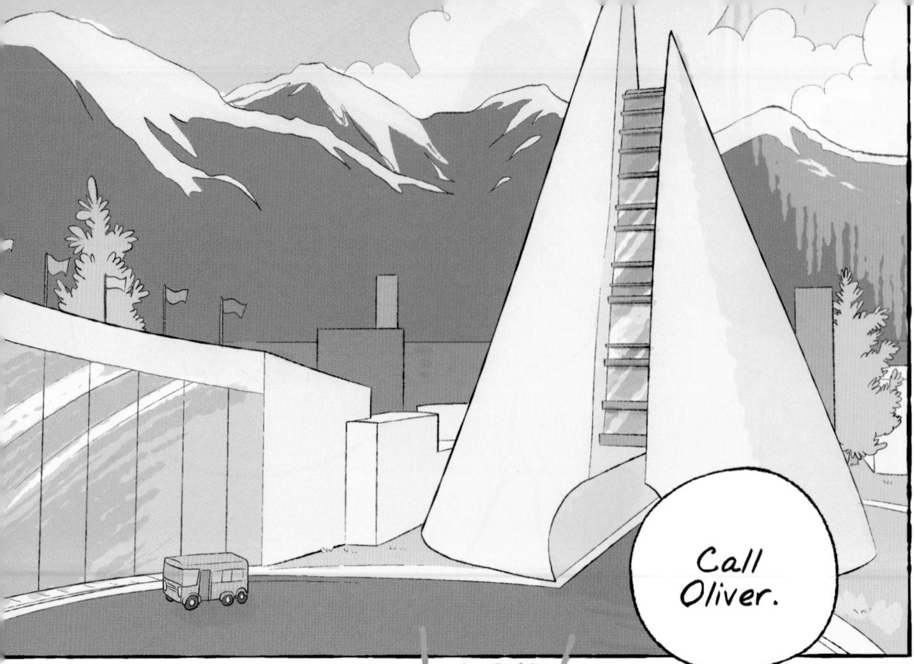
Call Oliver.

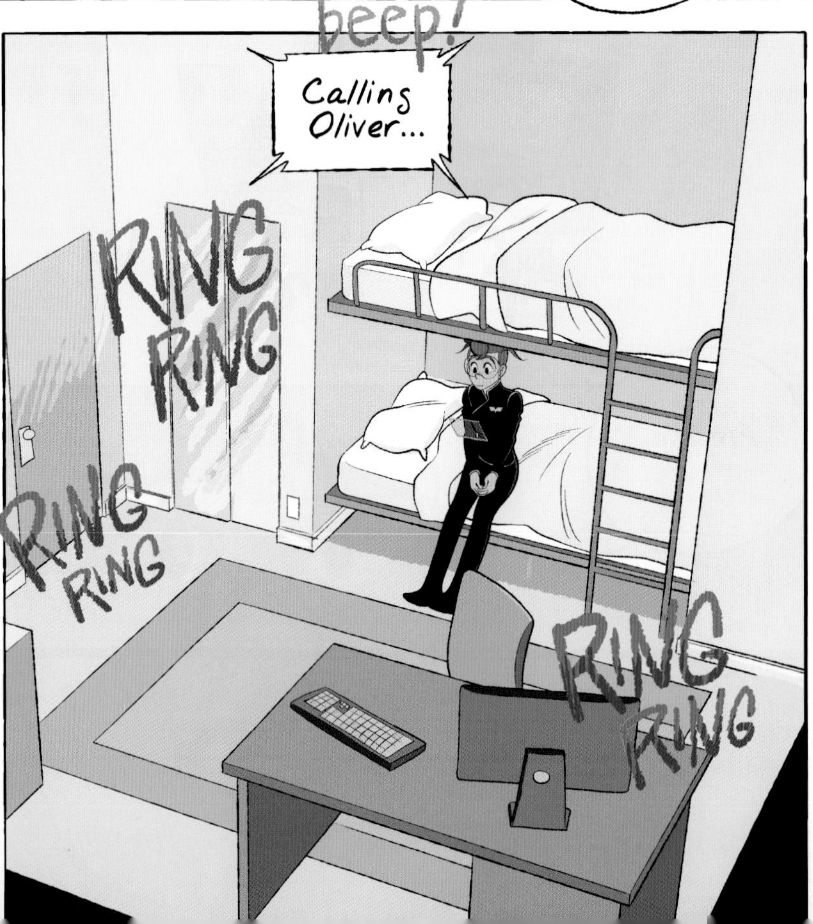
beep!
Callins Oliver...
RING RING
RING RING
RING RING

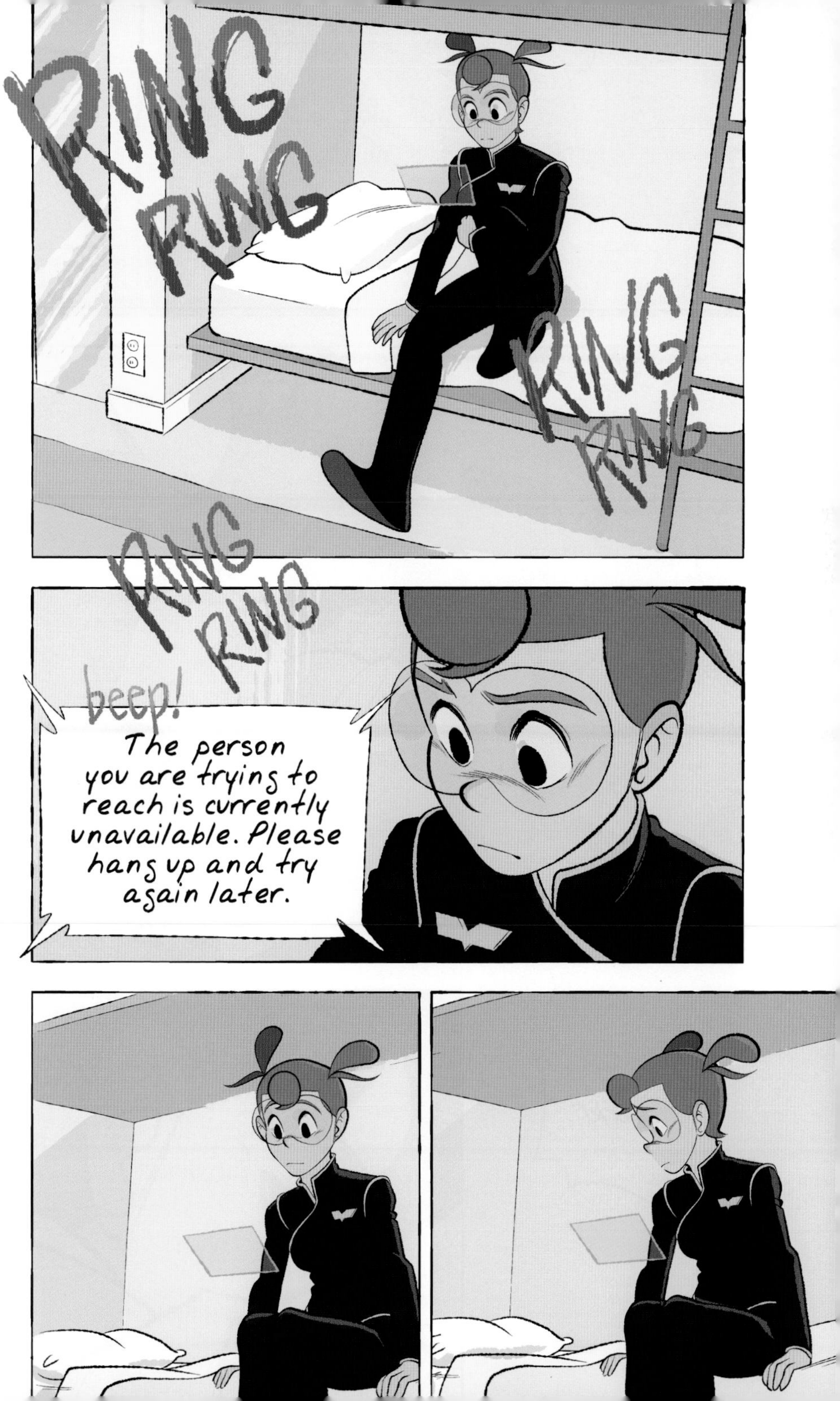
RING RING
RING RING
RING RING
beep!
The person you are trying to reach is currently unavailable. Please hang up and try again later.

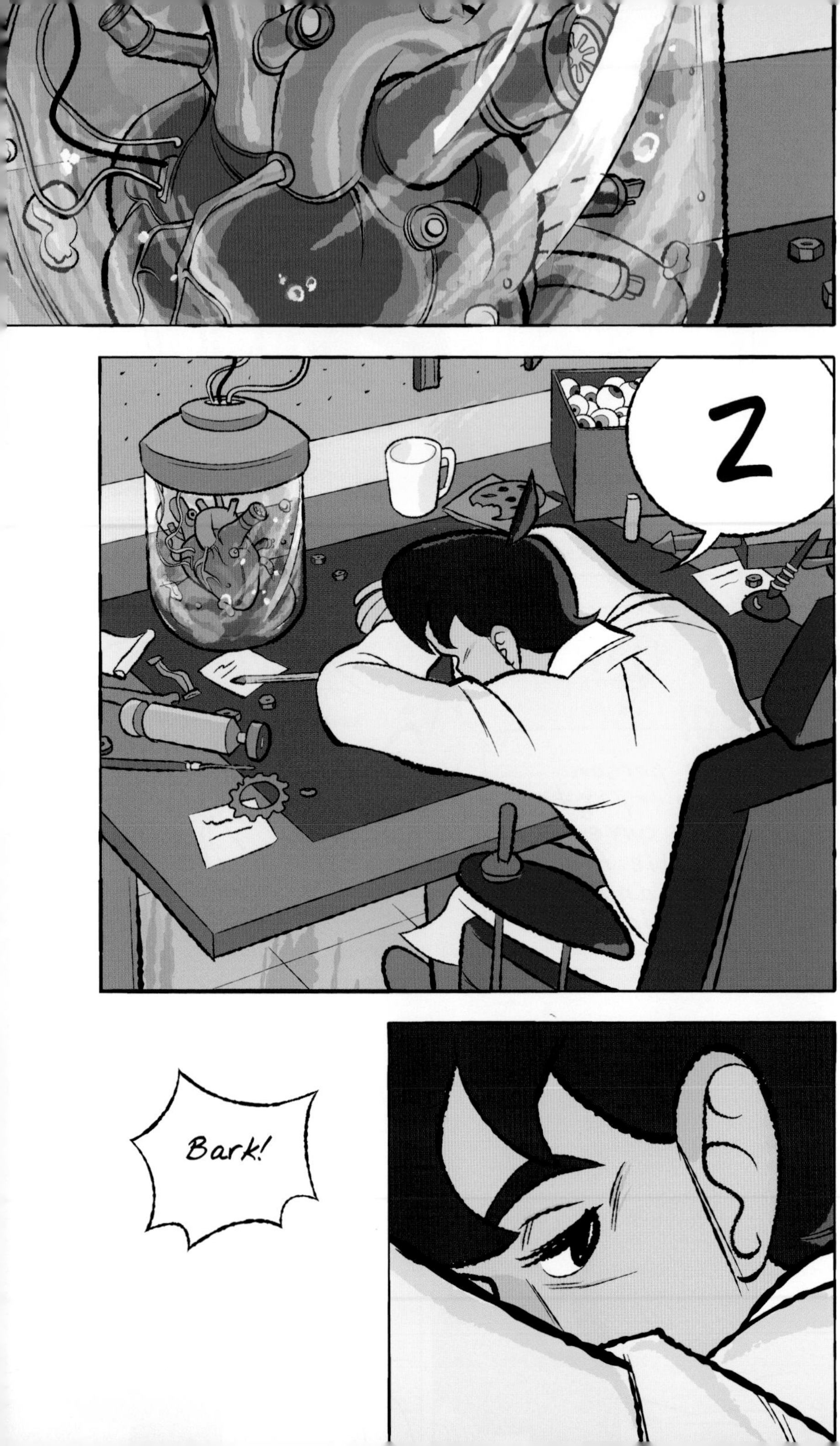
Z
Bark!

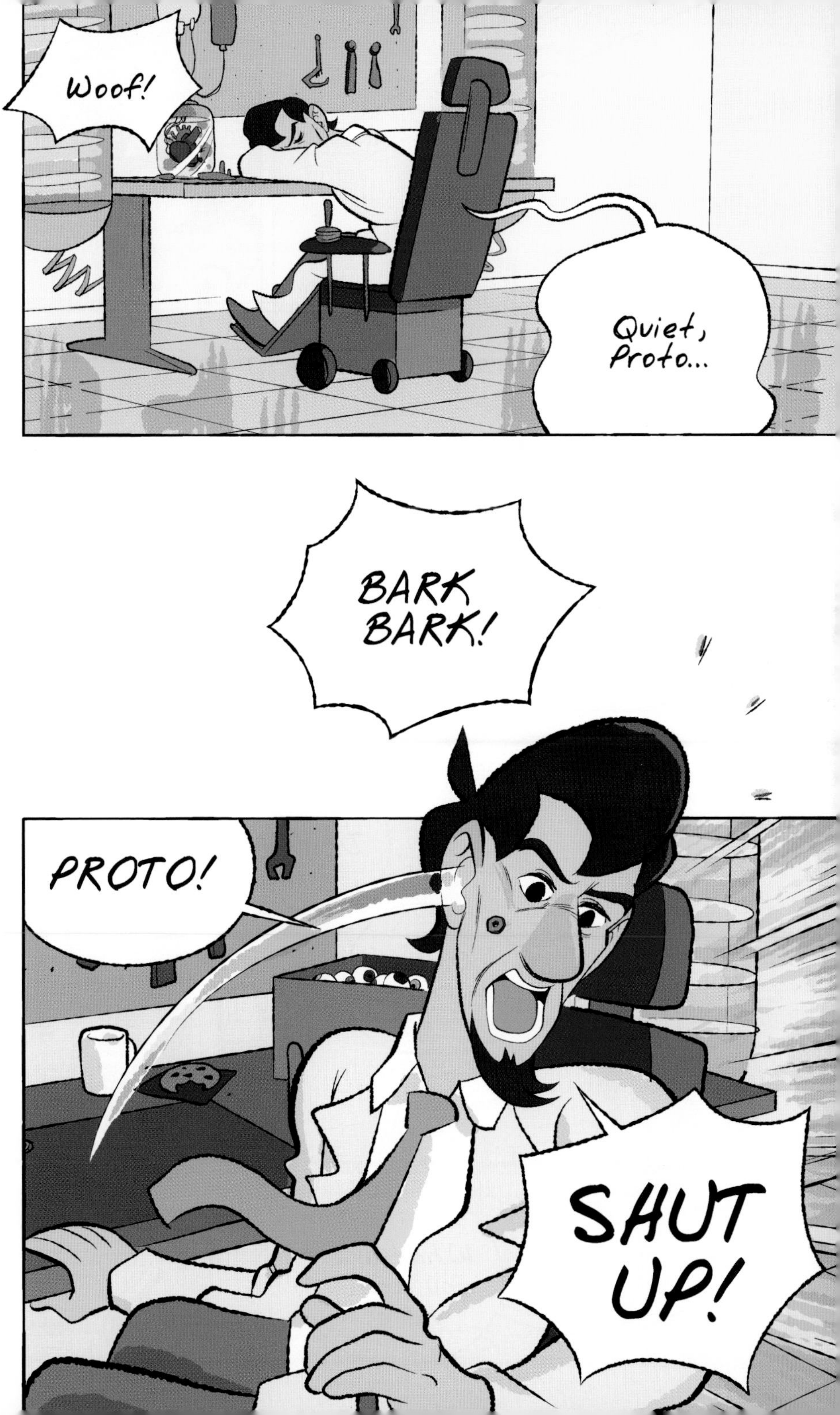
Woof!
Quiet, Proto...
BARK BARK!
PROTO!
SHUT UP!

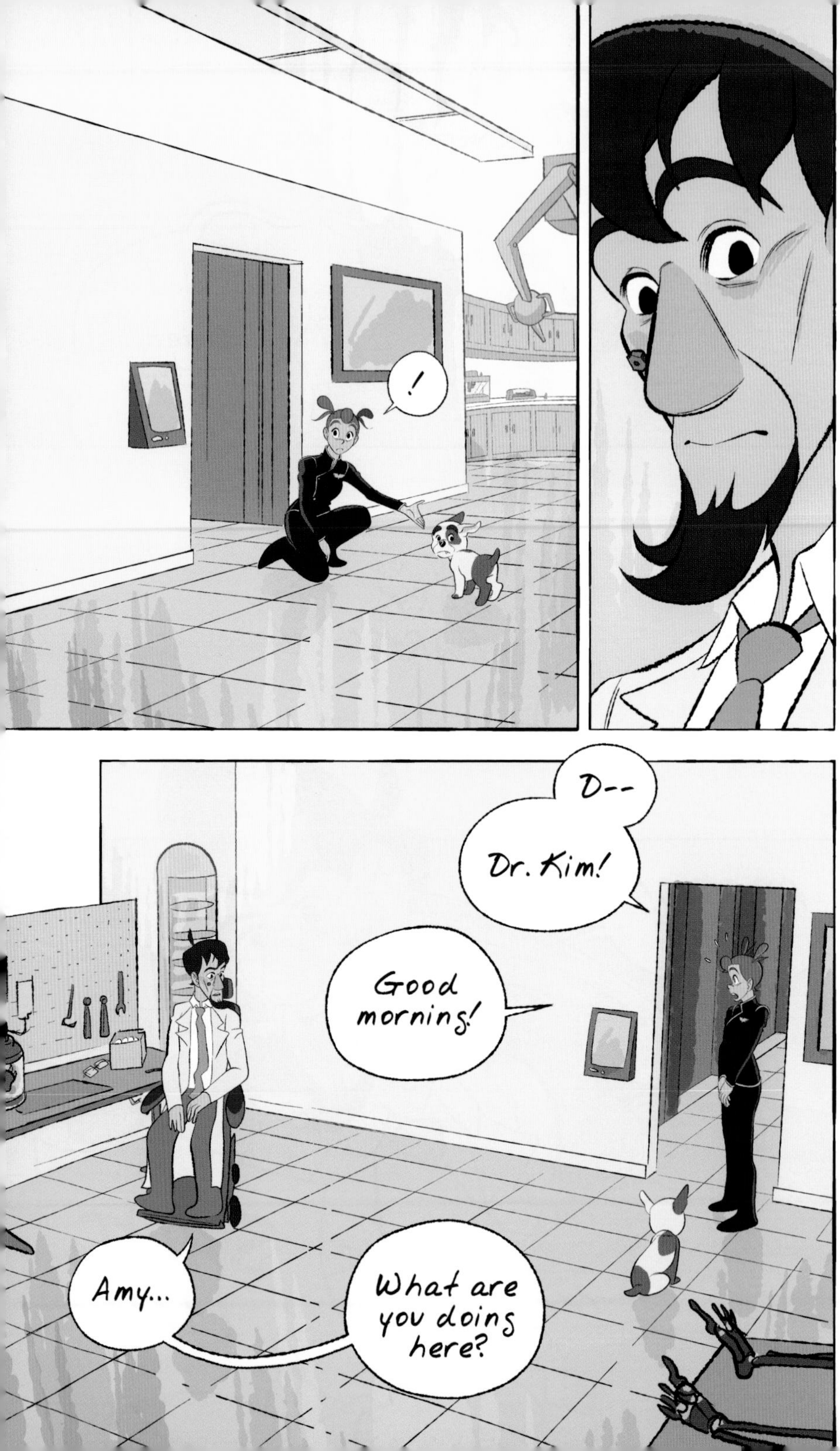
!
D--
Dr. Kim!
Good morning!
Amy...
What are you doing here?

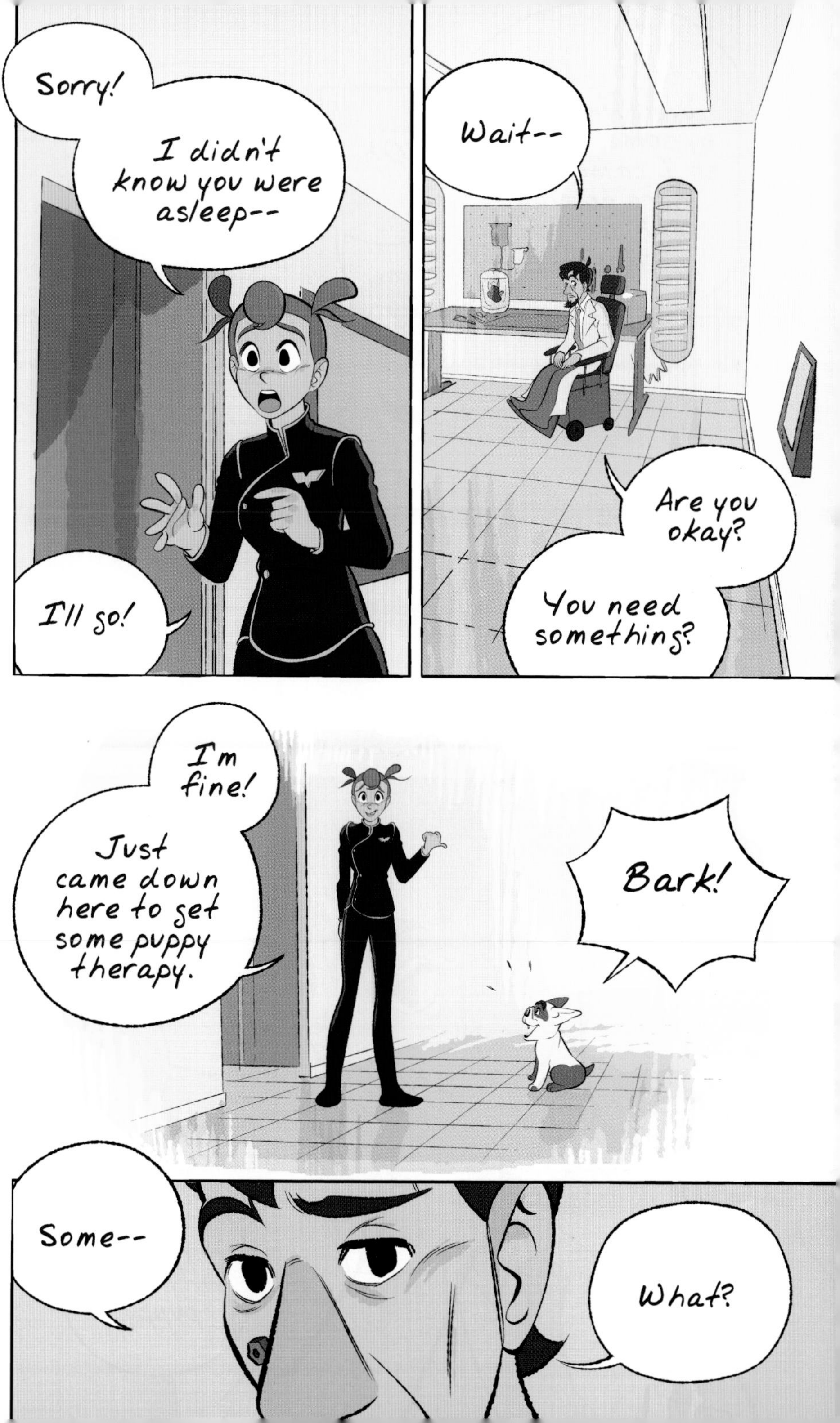
Sorry!
I didn't know you were asleep--
I'll go!
Wait--
Are you okay?
You need something?
I'm fine!
Just came down here to get some puppy therapy.
Bark!
Some--
What?

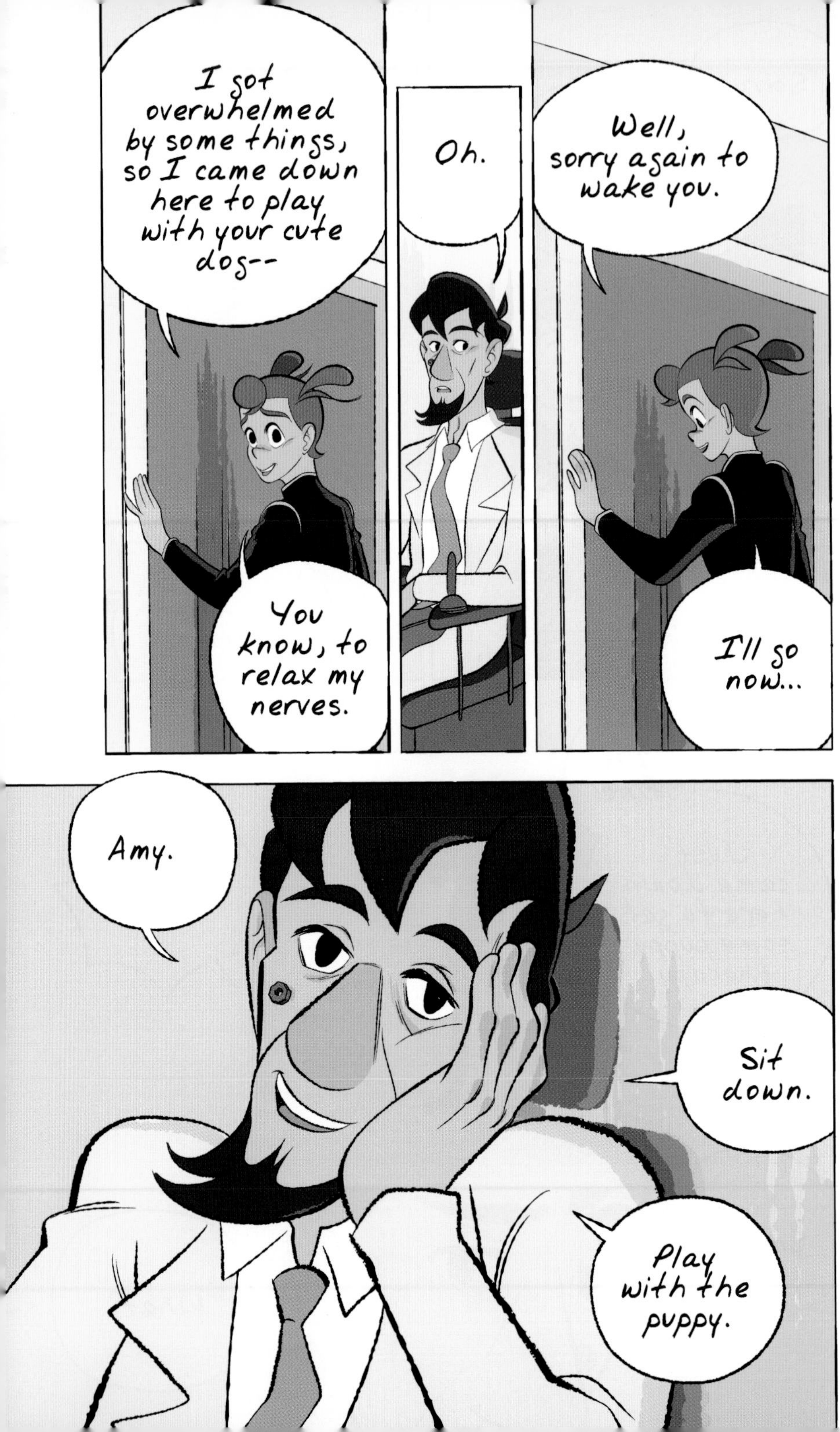
I got overwhelmed by some things, so I came down here to play with your cute dog--
You know, to relax my nerves.
Oh.
Well, sorry again to wake you.
I'll go now...
Amy.
Sit down.
Play with the puppy.

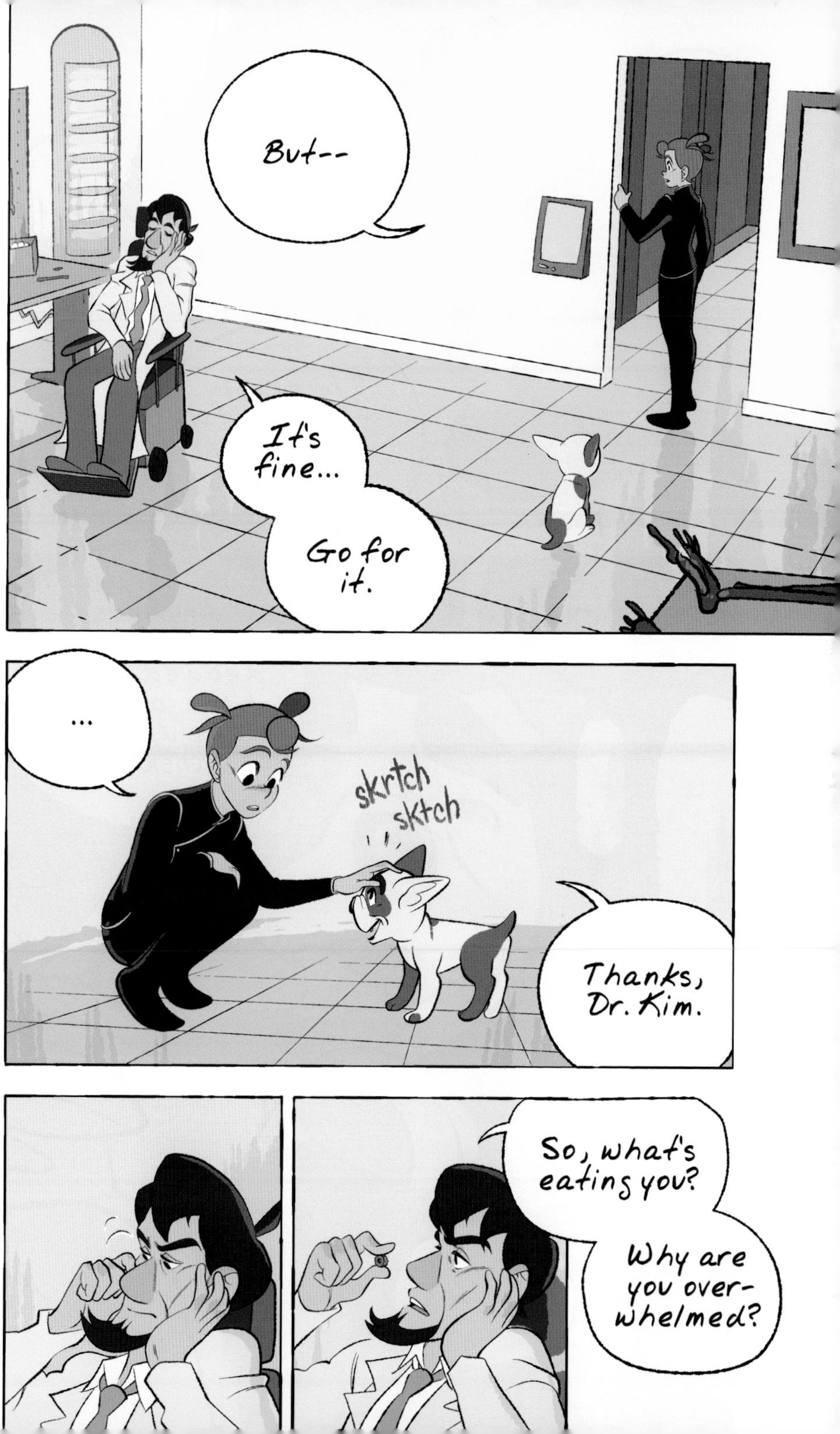
But--
It's fine...
Go for it.
...
skrtch
sktch
Thanks, Dr. Kim.
So, what's eating you?
Why are you over-whelmed?

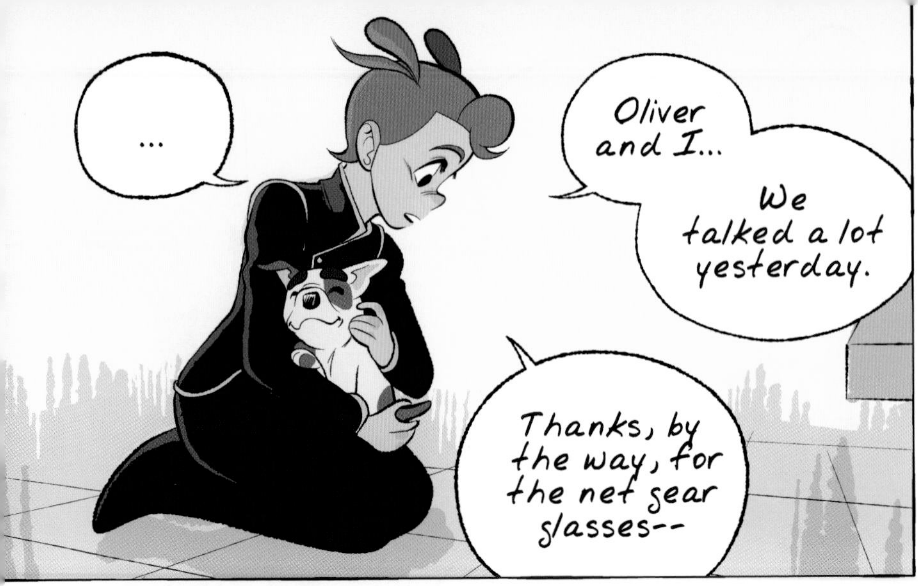
...
Oliver and I...
We talked a lot yesterday.
Thanks, by the way, for the net gear glasses--

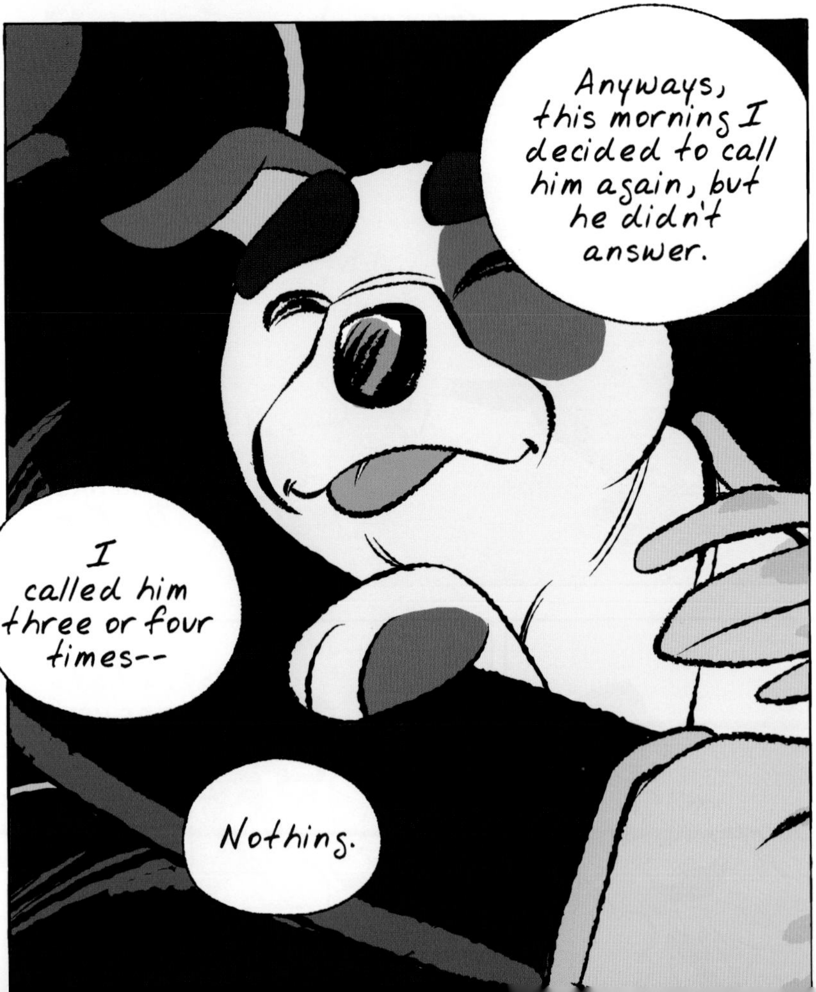
Anyways, this morning I decided to call him again, but he didn't answer.
I called him three or four times--
Nothing.

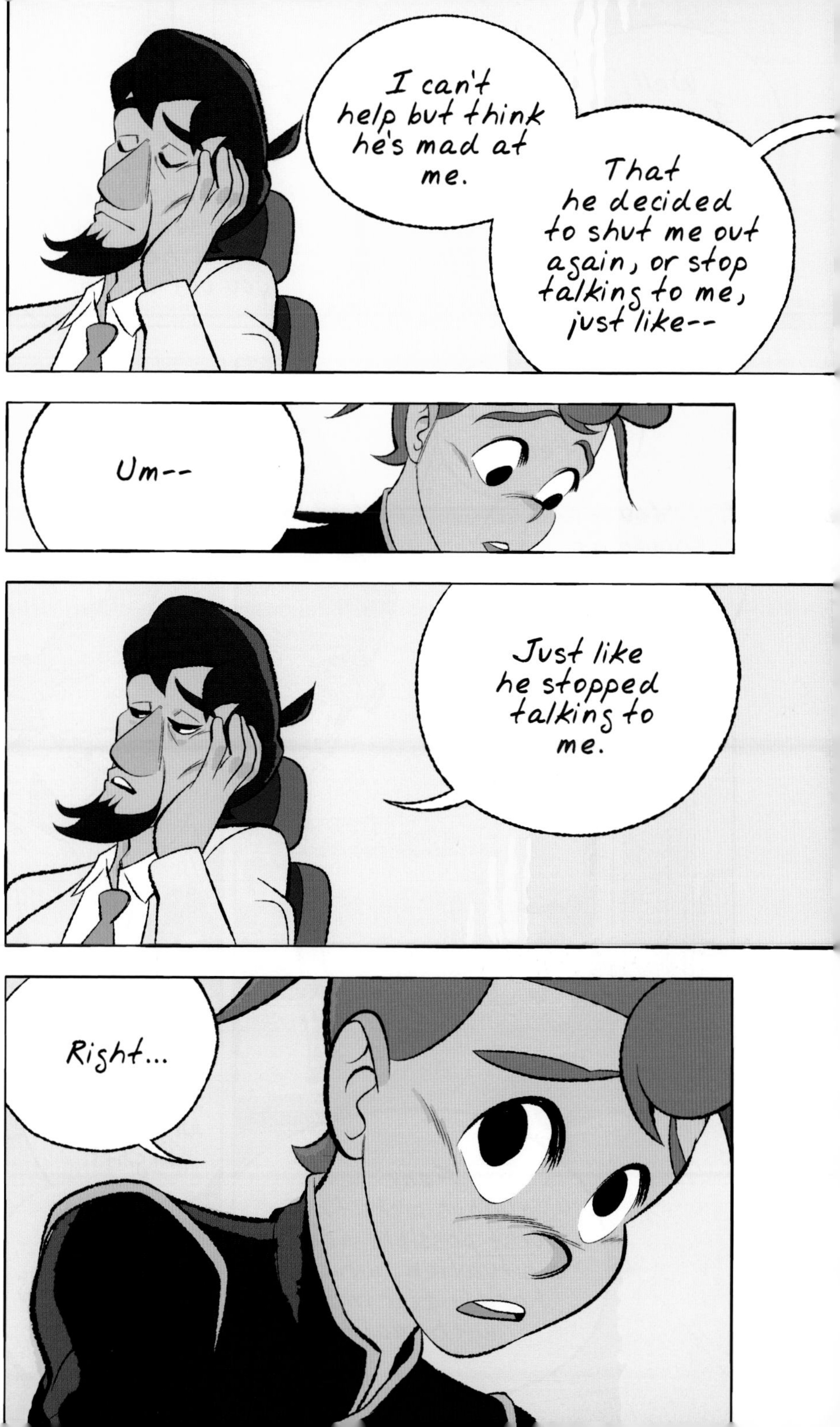
I can't help but think he's mad at me.
That he decided to shut me out again, or stop talking to me, just like--
Um--
Just like he stopped talking to me.
Right...

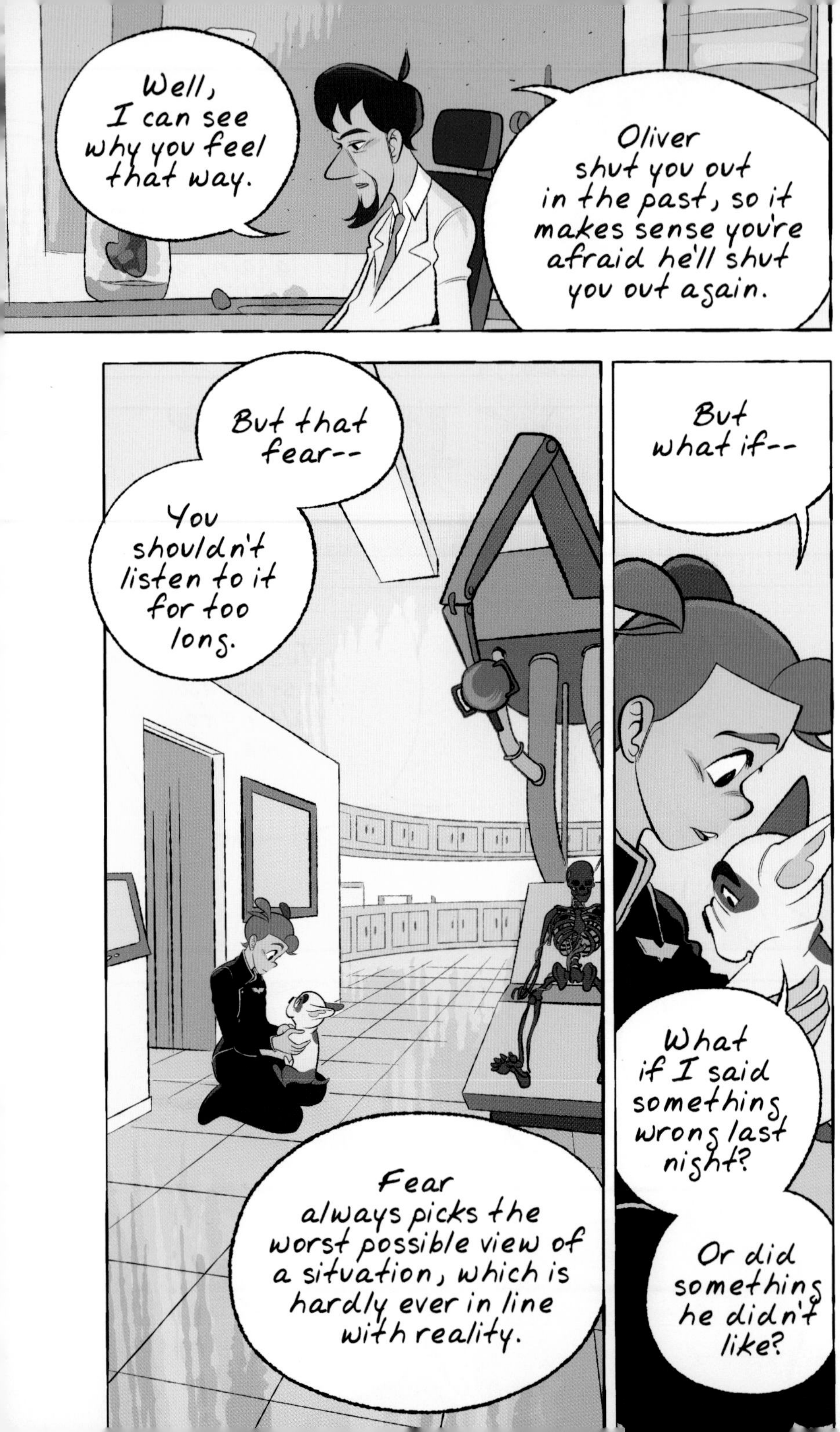
Well, I can see why you feel that way.
Oliver shut you out in the past, so it makes sense you're afraid he'll shut you out again.
But that fear--
You shouldn't listen to it for too long.
But what if--
What if I said something wrong last night?
Fear always picks the worst possible view of a situation, which is hardly ever in line with reality.
Or did something he didn't like?

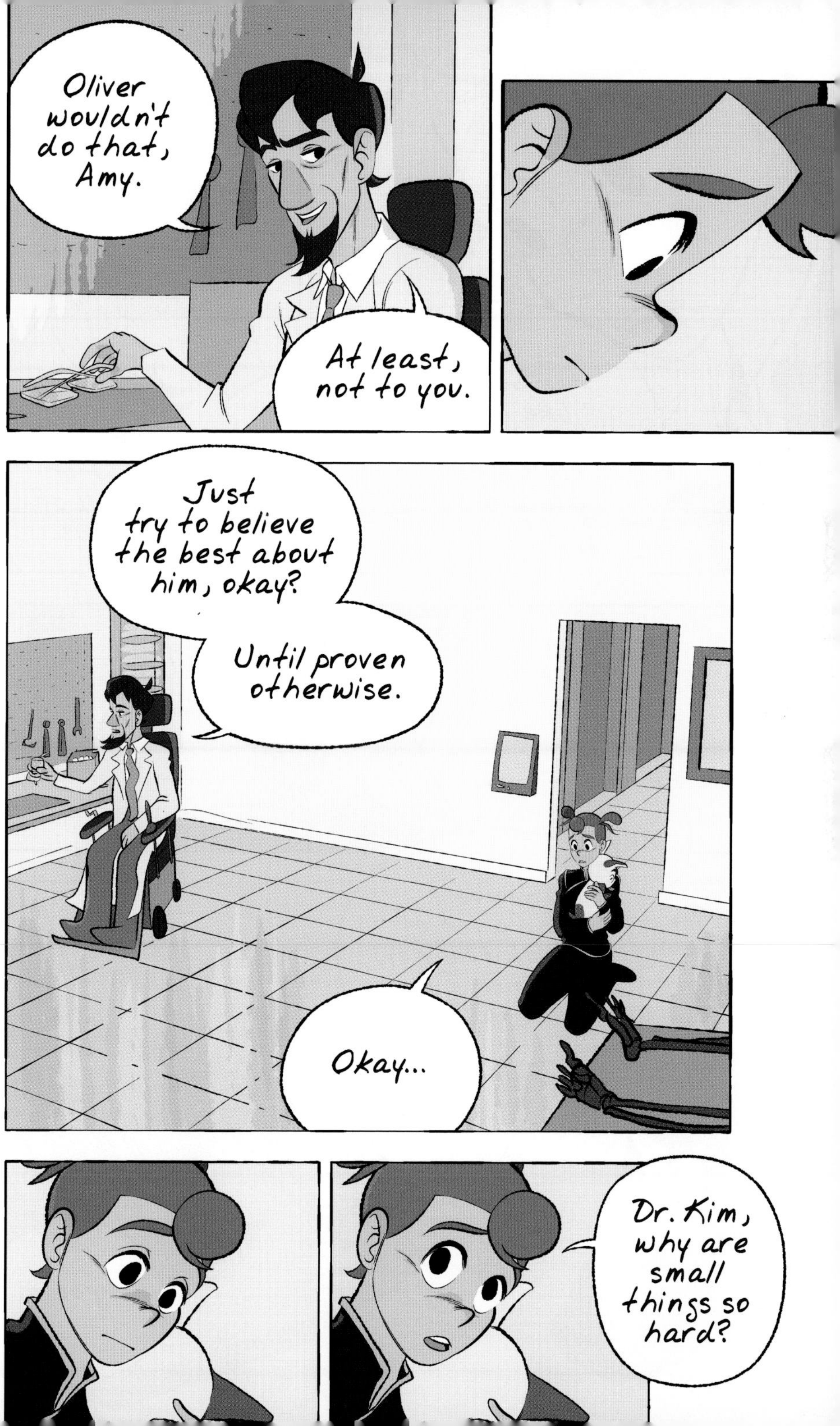
Oliver wouldn't do that, Amy.
At least, not to you.
Just try to believe the best about him, okay?
Until proven otherwise.
Okay...
Dr. Kim, why are small things so hard?

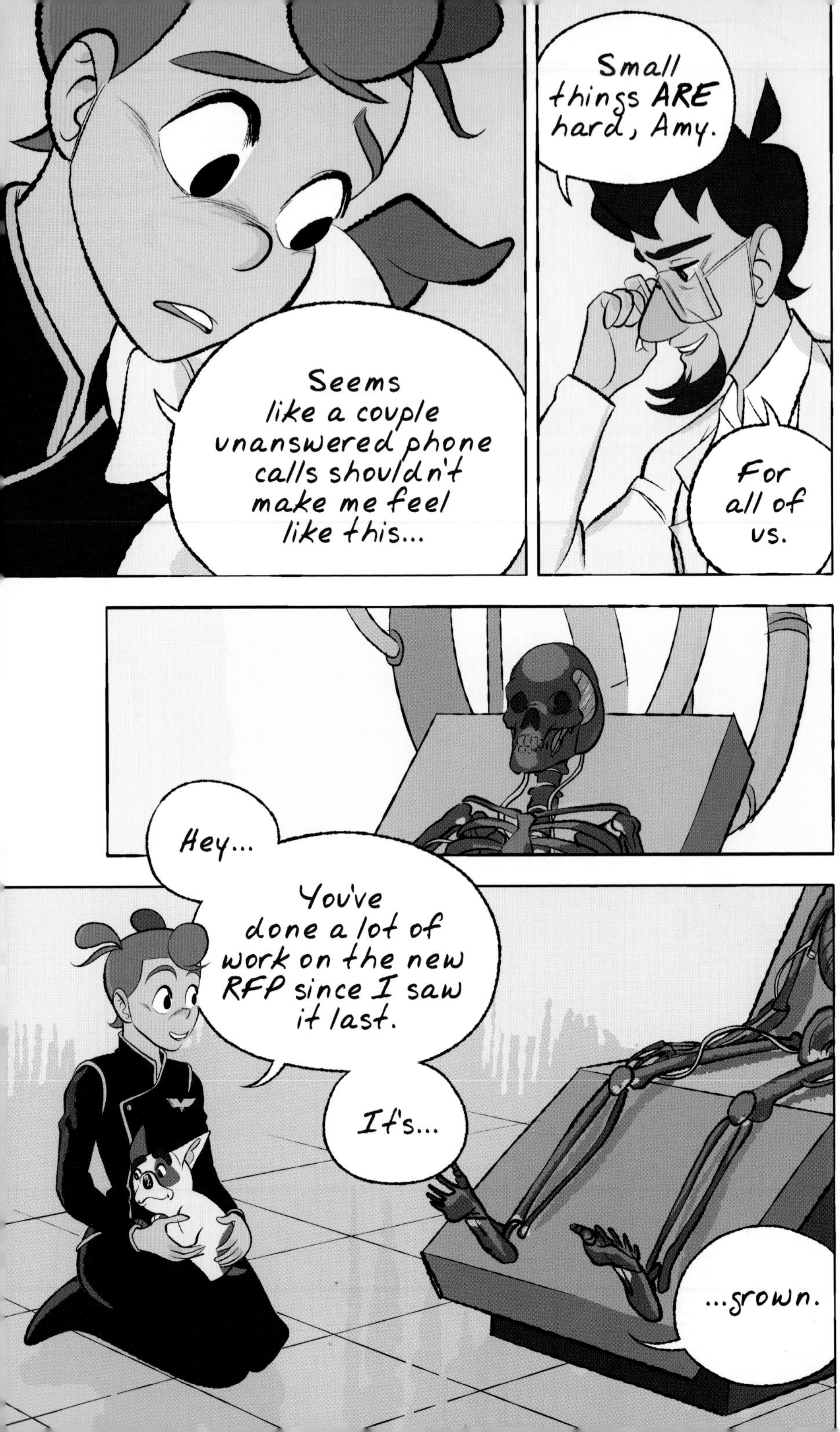
Seems like a couple unanswered phone calls shouldn't make me feel like this...
Small things ARE hard, Amy.
For all of us.
Hey...
You've done a lot of work on the new RFP since I saw it last.
It's...
...grown.

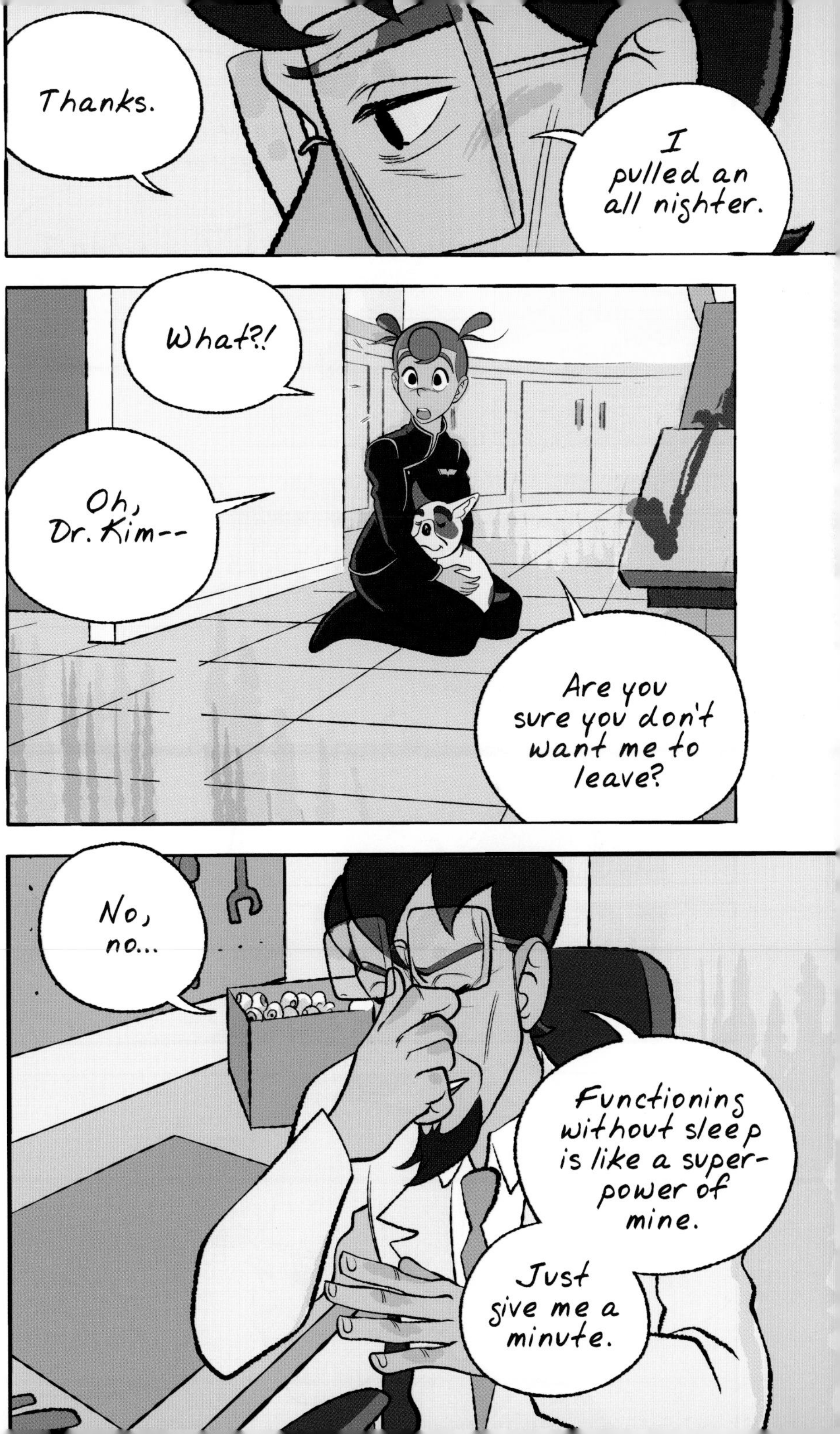
Thanks.
I pulled an all nighter.
What?!
Oh, Dr. Kim--
Are you sure you don't want me to leave?
No, no...
Functioning without sleep is like a super-power of mine.
Just give me a minute.

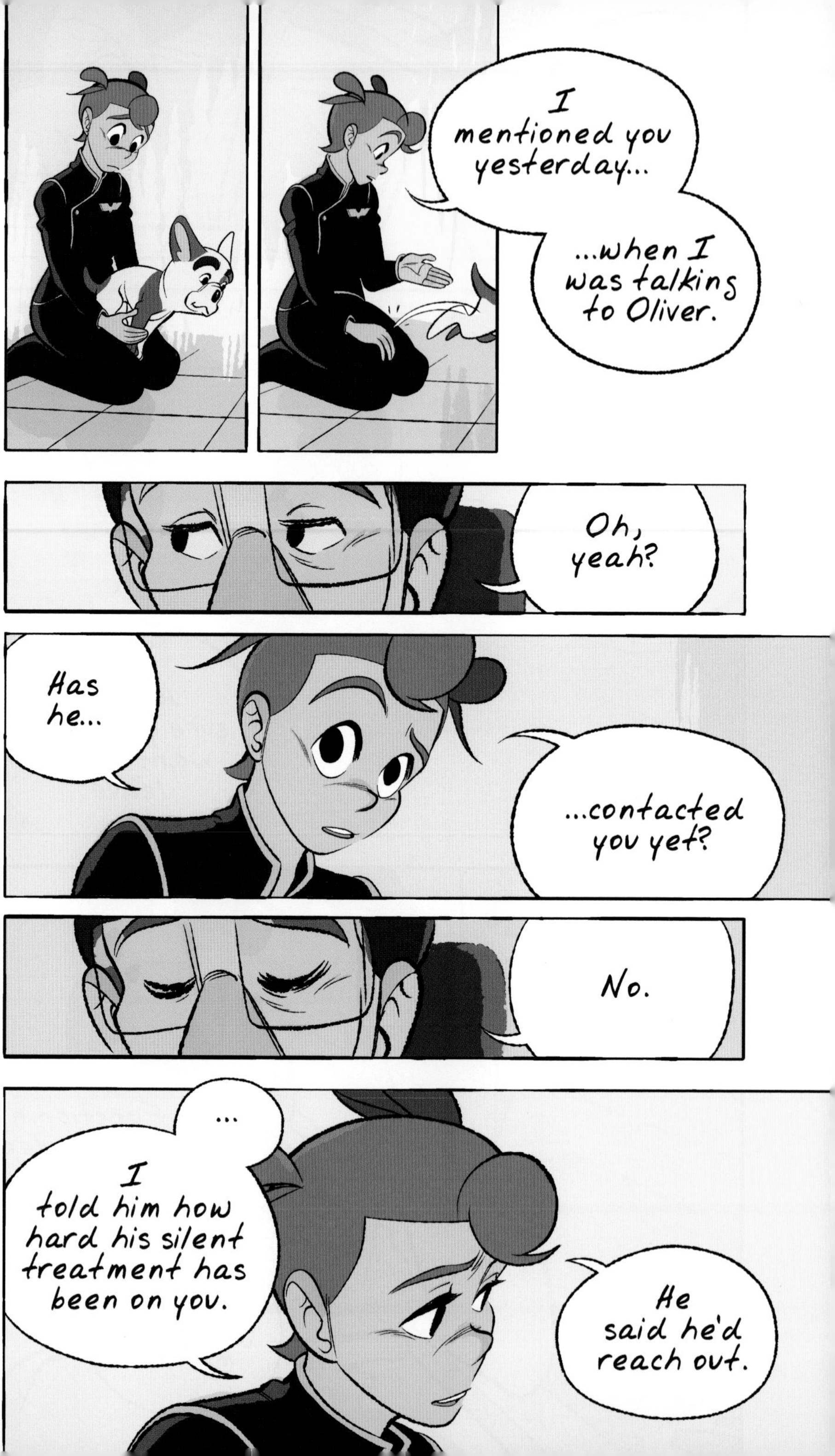
I mentioned you yesterday...
...when I was talking to Oliver.
Oh, yeah?
Has he...
...contacted you yet?
No.
...
I told him how hard his silent treatment has been on you.
He said he'd reach out.

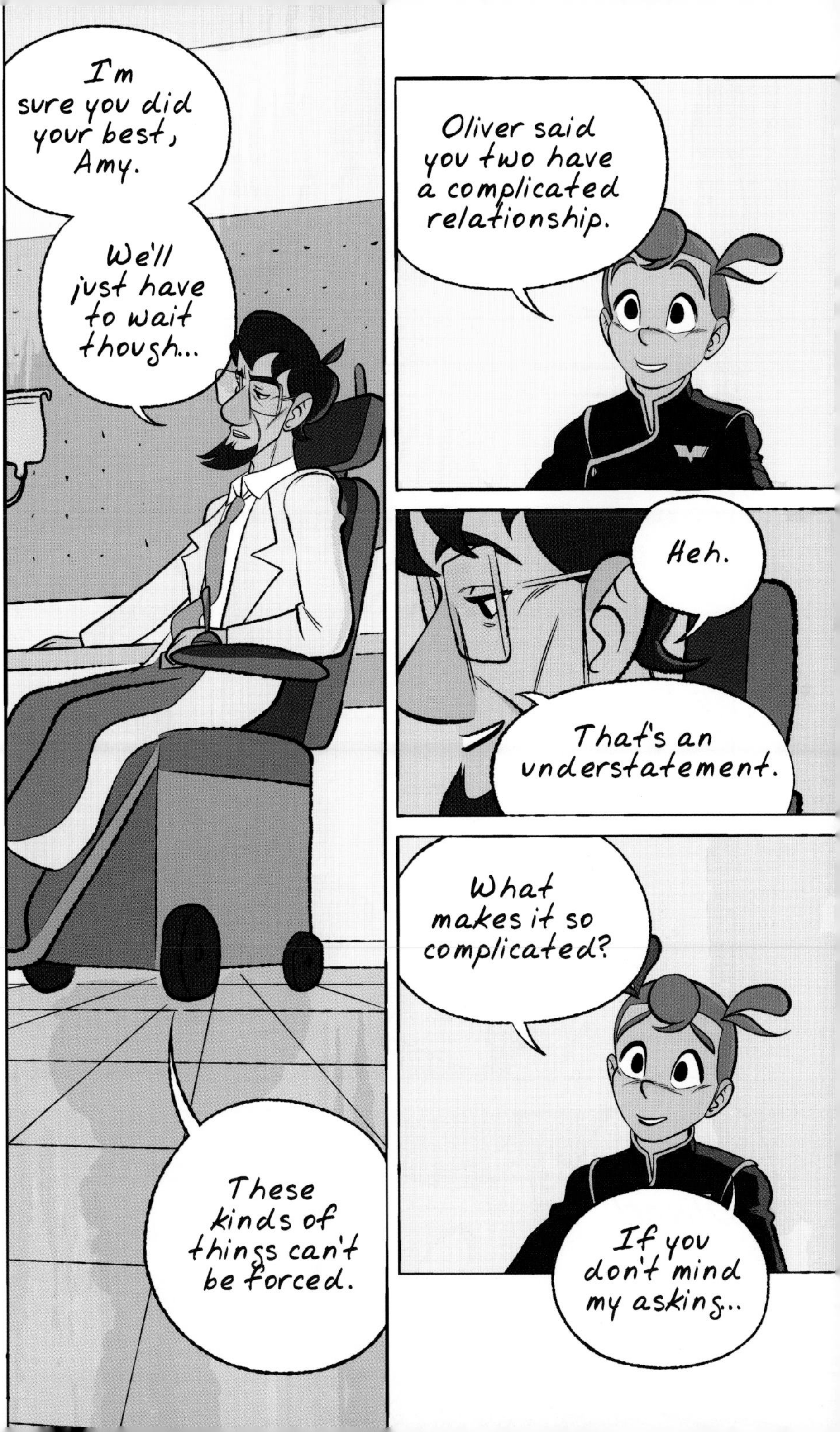
I'm sure you did your best, Amy.
We'll just have to wait though...
These kinds of things can't be forced.
Oliver said you two have a complicated relationship.
Heh.
That's an understatement.
What makes it so complicated?
If you don't mind my asking...

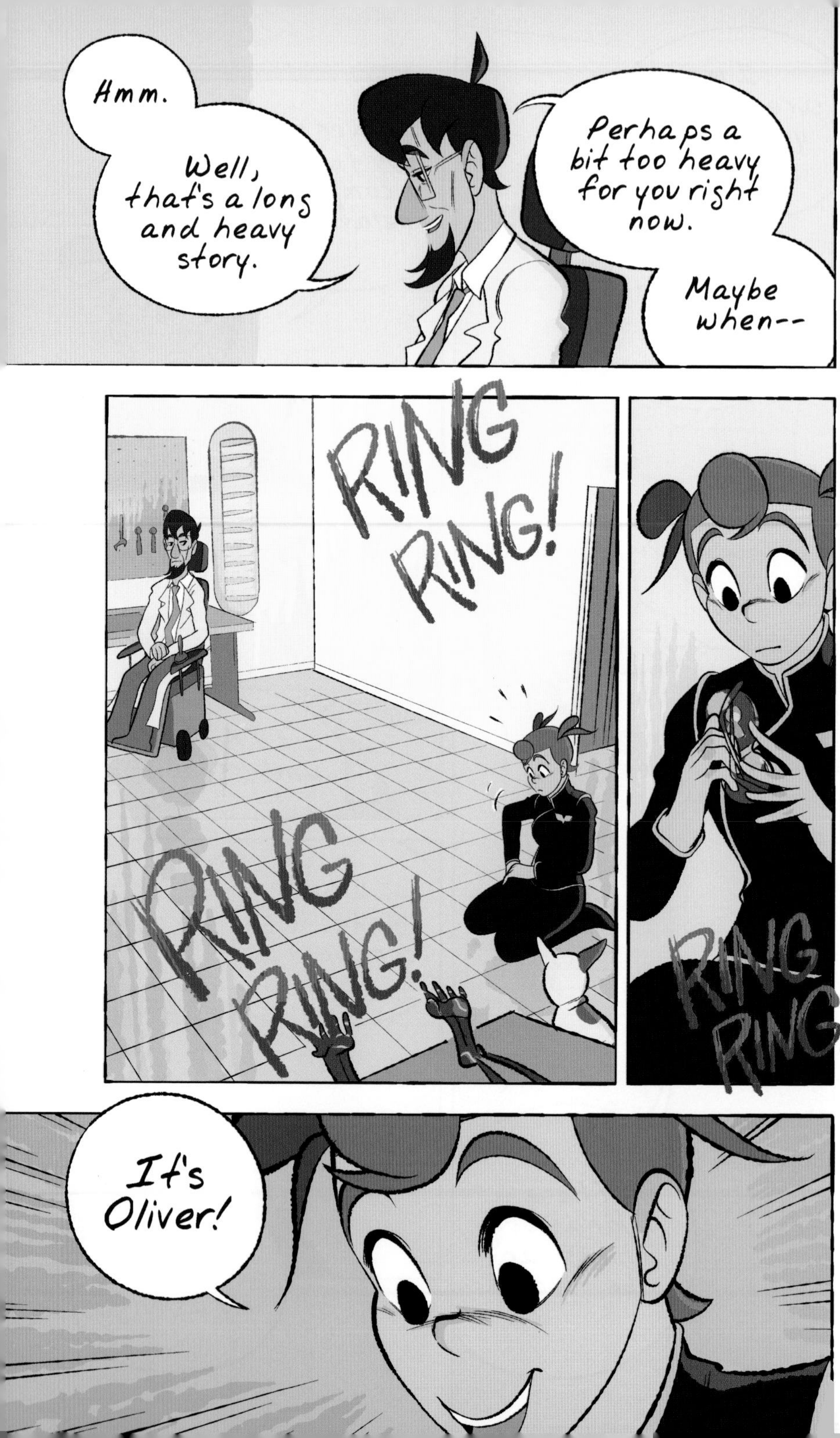
Hmm.
Well, that's a long and heavy story.
Perhaps a bit too heavy for you right now.
Maybe when--
RING RING!
RING RING!
RING RING!
It's Oliver!

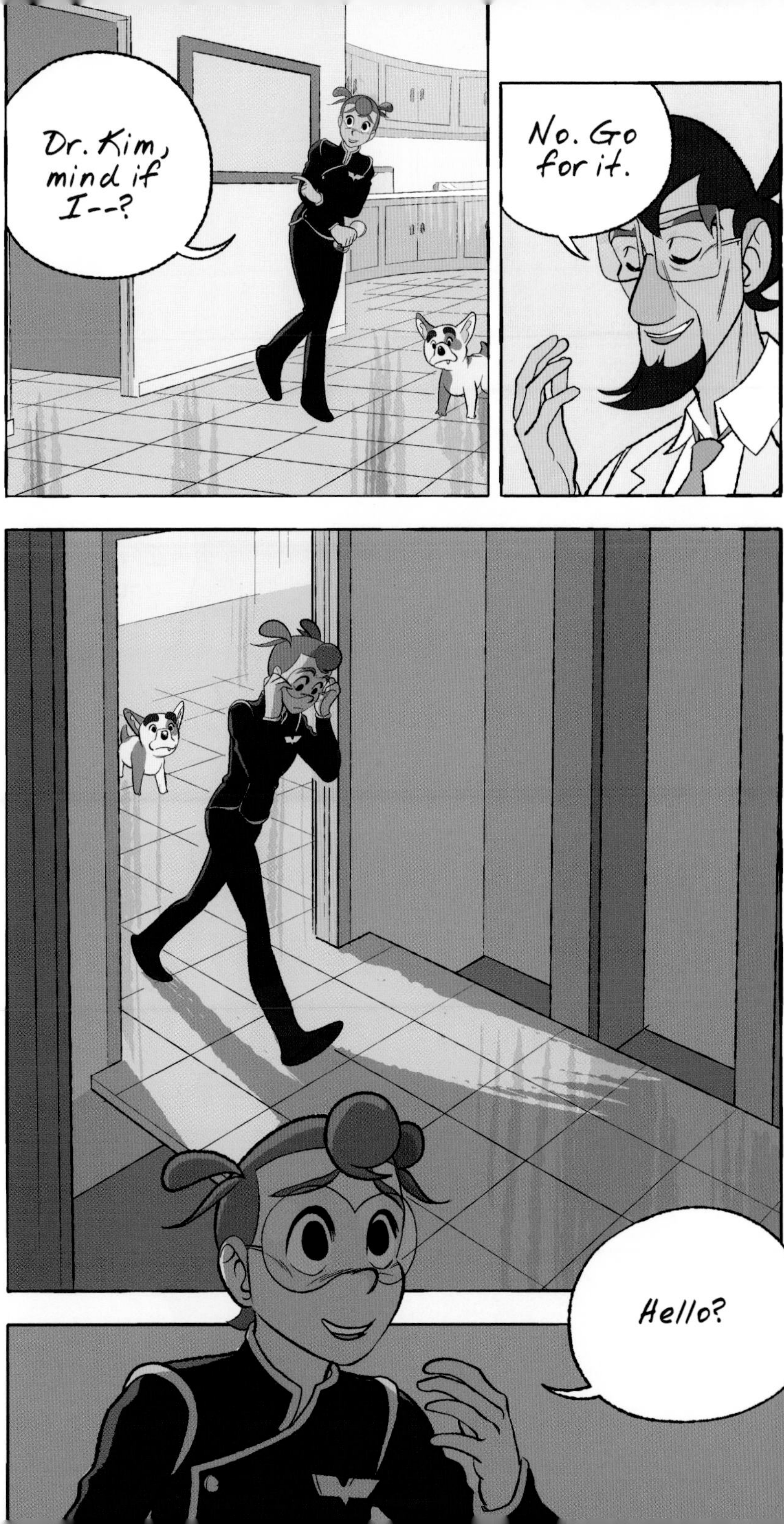

Dr. Kim, mind if I--?
No. Go for it.
Hello?

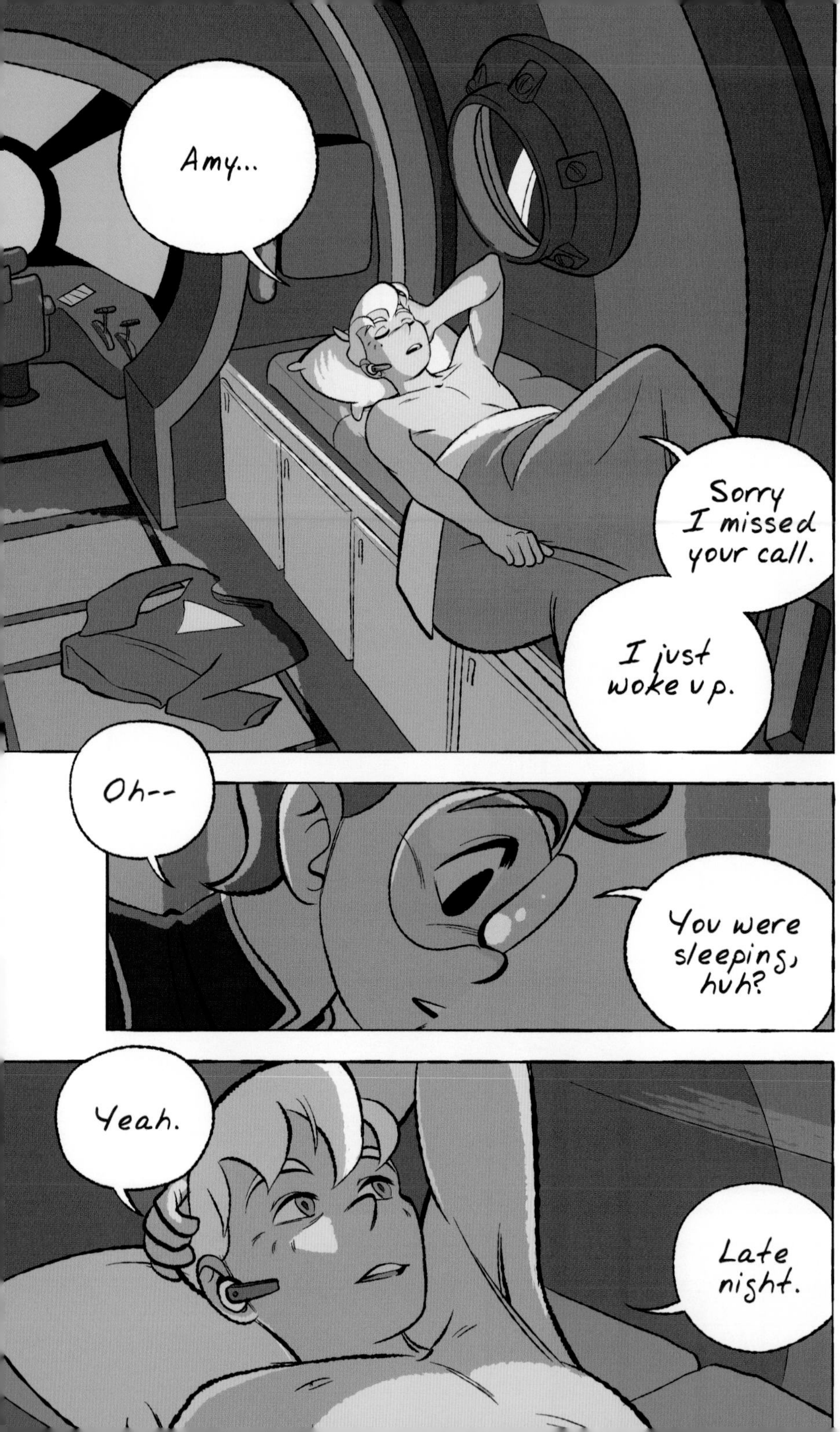
Amy...
Sorry I missed your call.
I just woke up.
Oh--
You were sleeping, huh?
Yeah.
Late night.

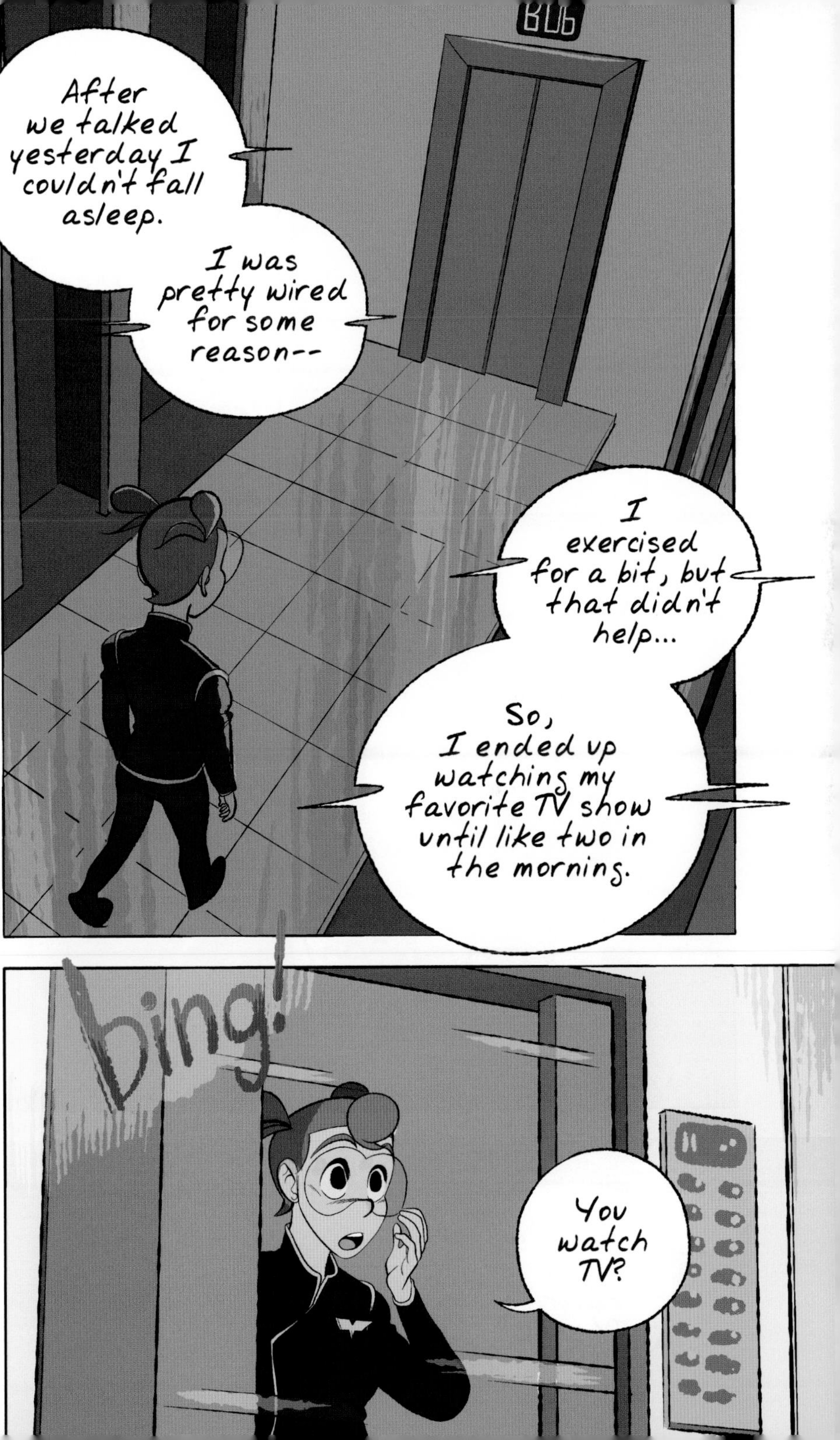
B06
After we talked yesterday I couldn't fall asleep.
I was pretty wired for some reason--
I exercised for a bit, but that didn't help...
So, I ended up watching my favorite TV show until like two in the mornings.
bing!
You watch TV?

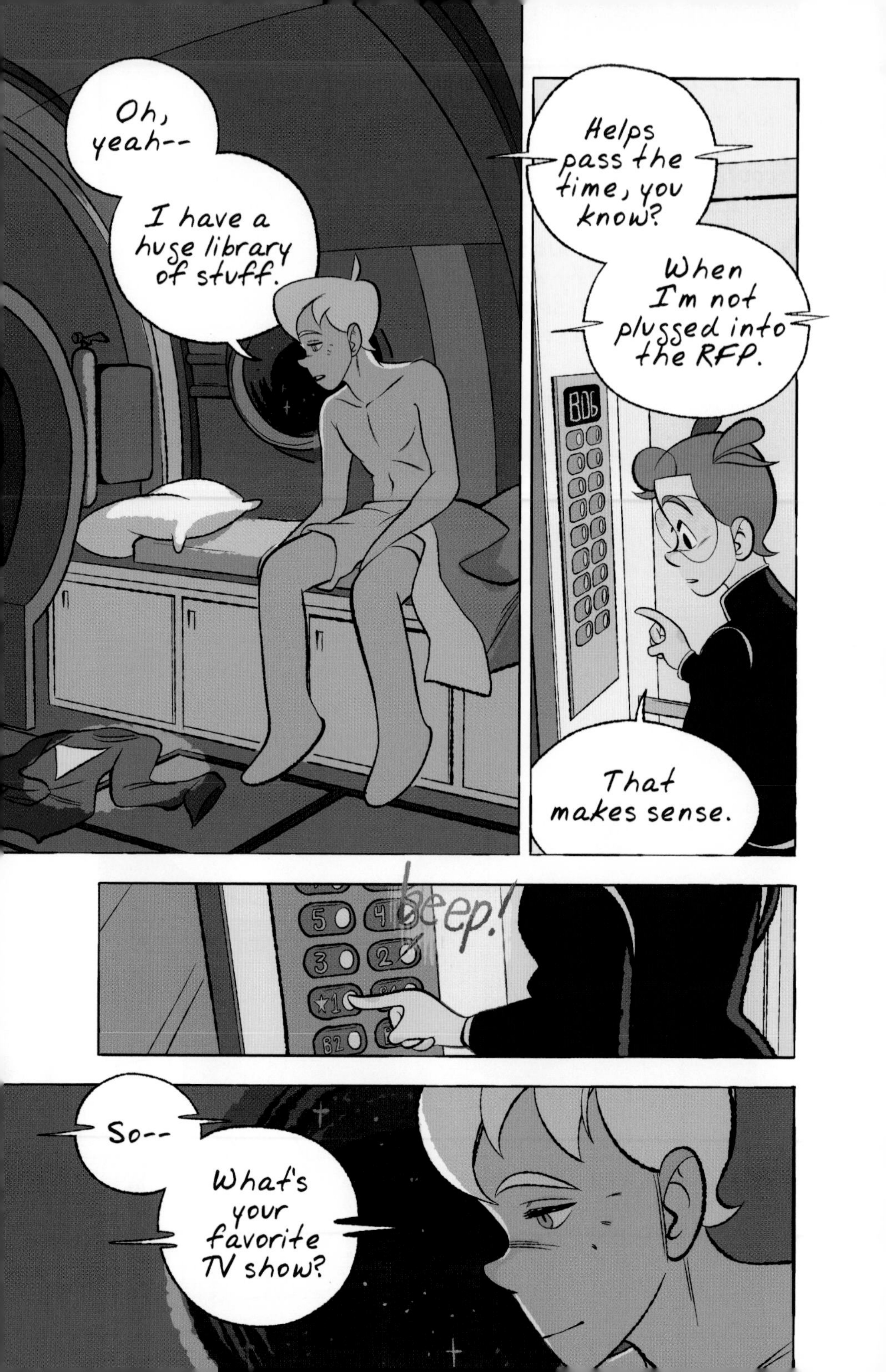

Oh, yeah--
I have a huge library of stuff.
Helps pass the time, you know?
When I'm not plussed into the RFP.
BD6
That makes sense.
beep!
So--
What's your favorite TV show?

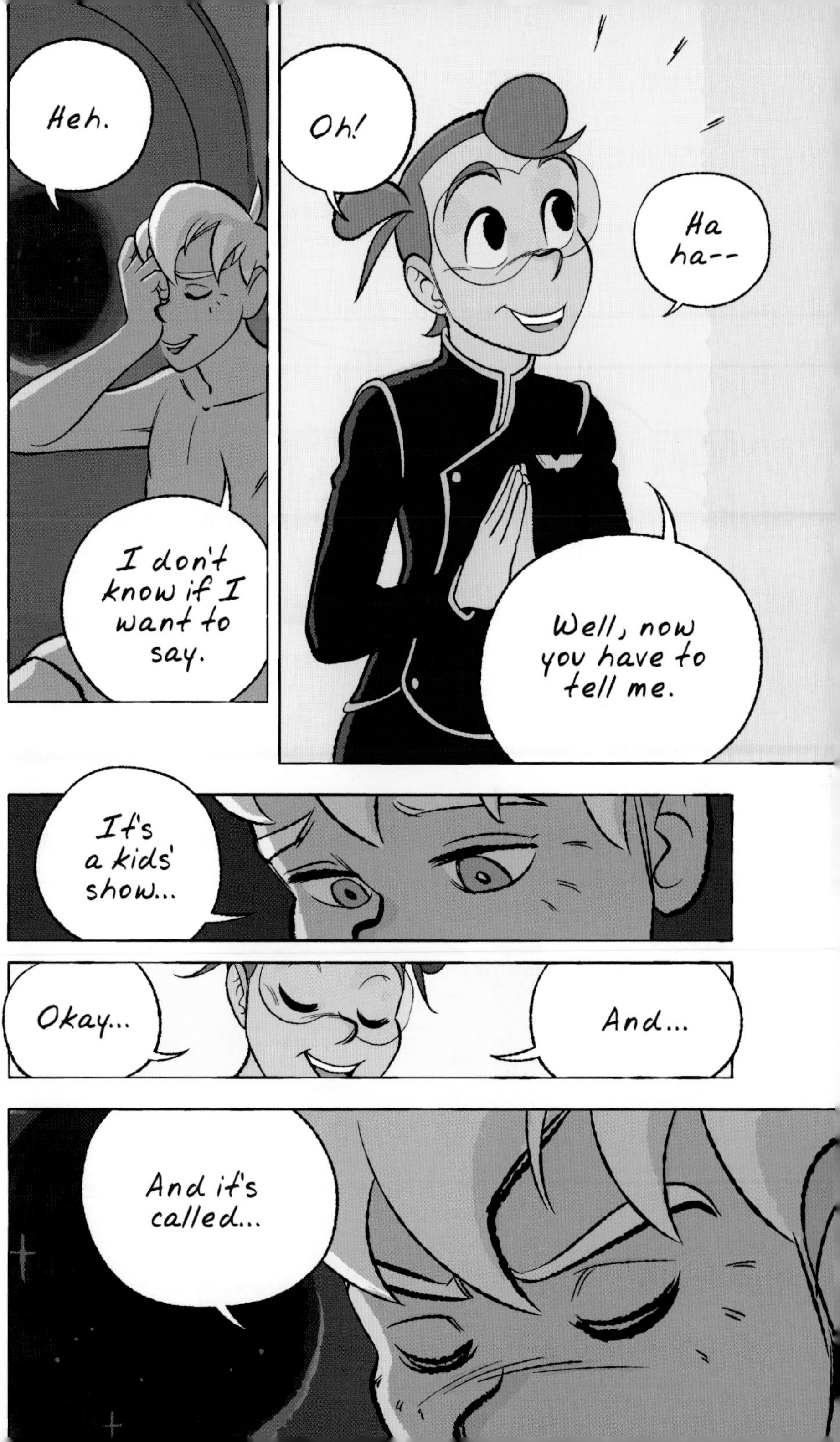
Heh.
Oh!
Ha ha--
I don't know if I want to say.
Well, now you have to tell me.
It's a kids' show...
Okay...
And...
And it's called...

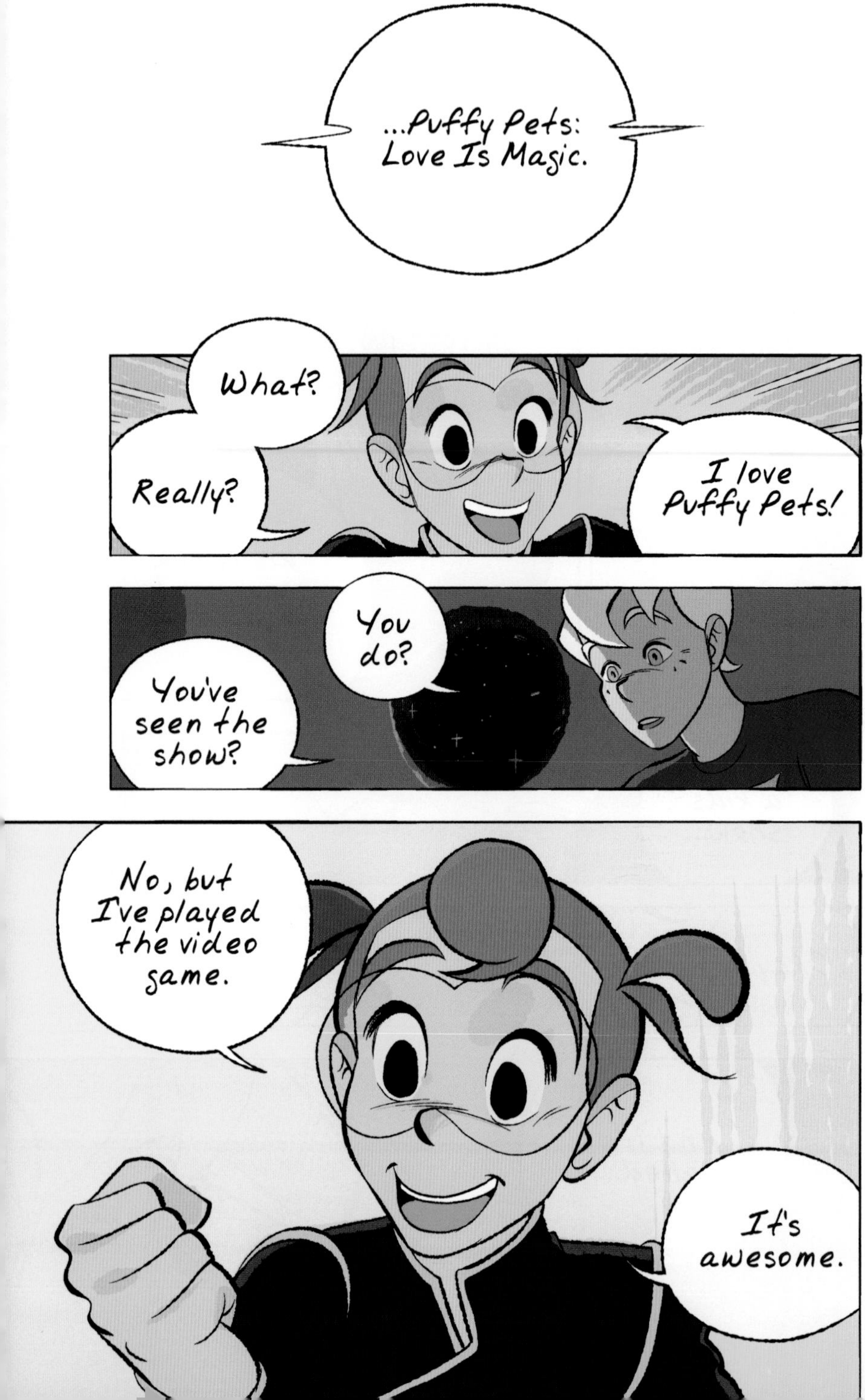
...Puffy Pets:
Love Is Magic.
What?
Really?
I love Puffy Pets!
You do?
You've seen the show?
No, but I've played the video game.
It's awesome.

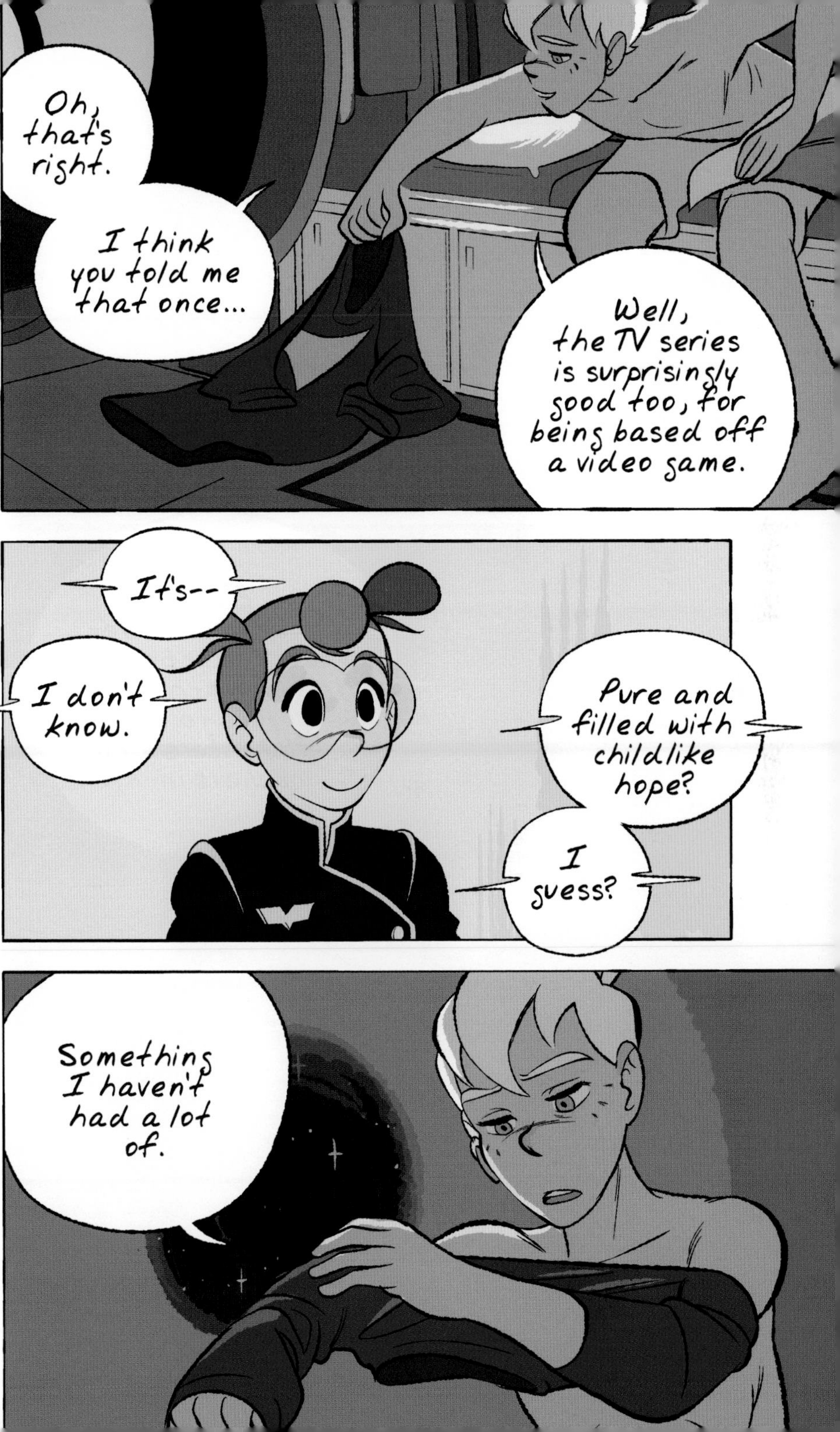
Oh, that's right.
I think you told me that once...
Well, the TV series is surprisingly good too, for being based off a video game.
It's--
I don't know.
Pure and filled with childlike hope?
I guess?
Something I haven't had a lot of.

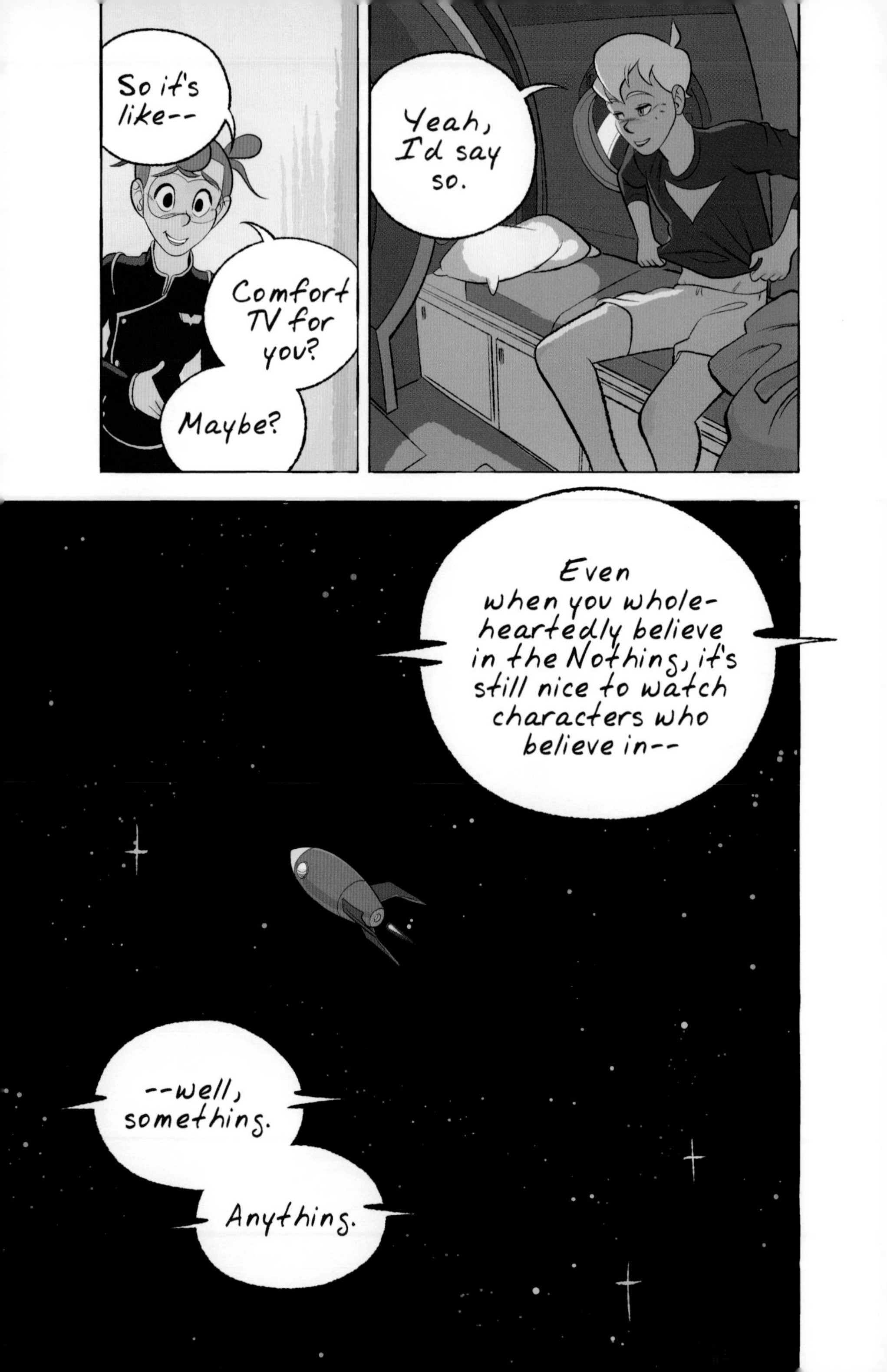
So it's like--
Yeah, I'd say so.
Comfort TV for you?
Maybe?
Even when you whole-heartedly believe in the Nothing, it's still nice to watch characters who believe in--
--well, something.
Anything.

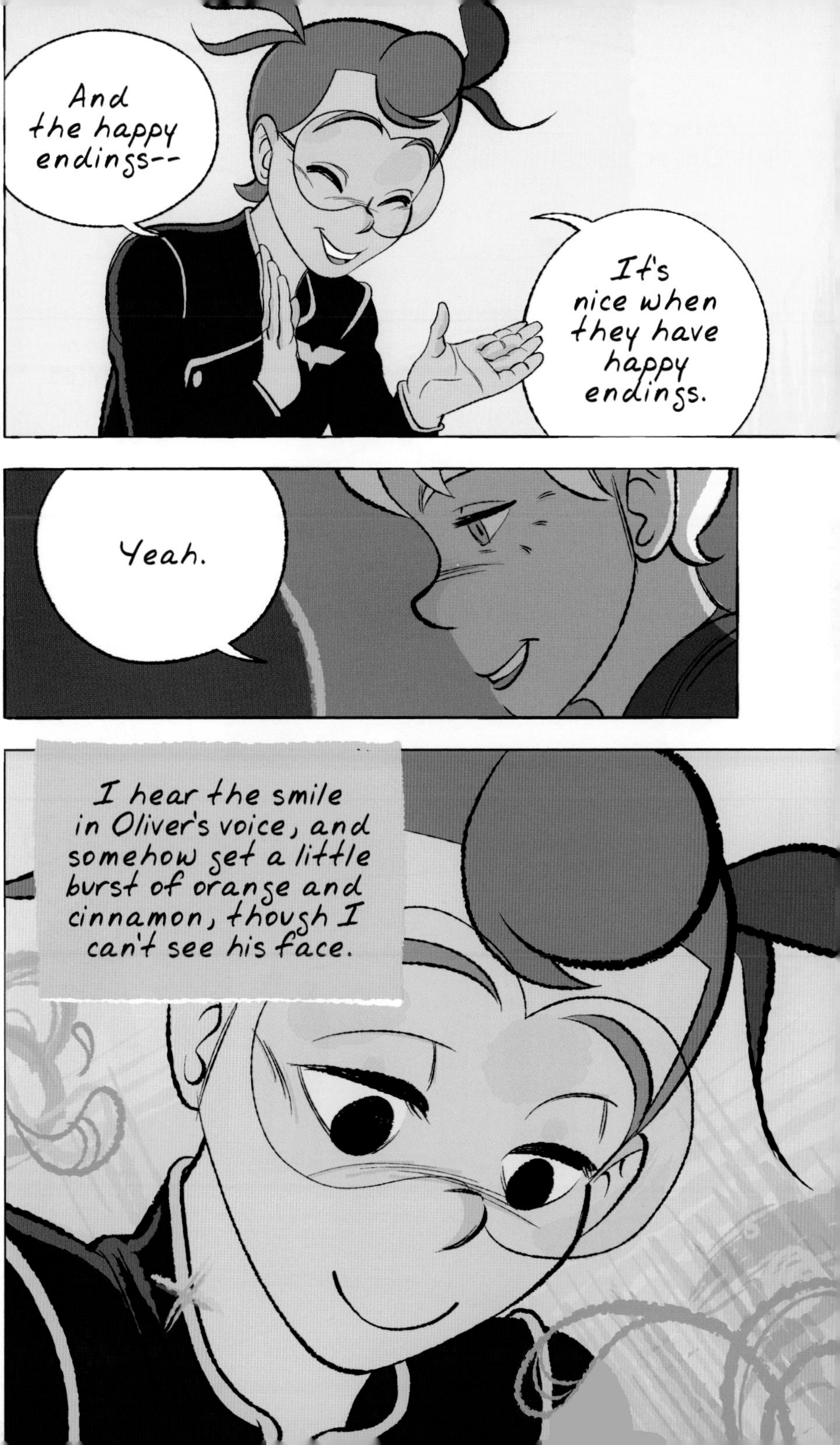
And the happy endings--
It's nice when they have happy endings.
Yeah.
I hear the smile in Oliver's voice, and somehow get a little burst of orange and cinnamon, though I can't see his face.

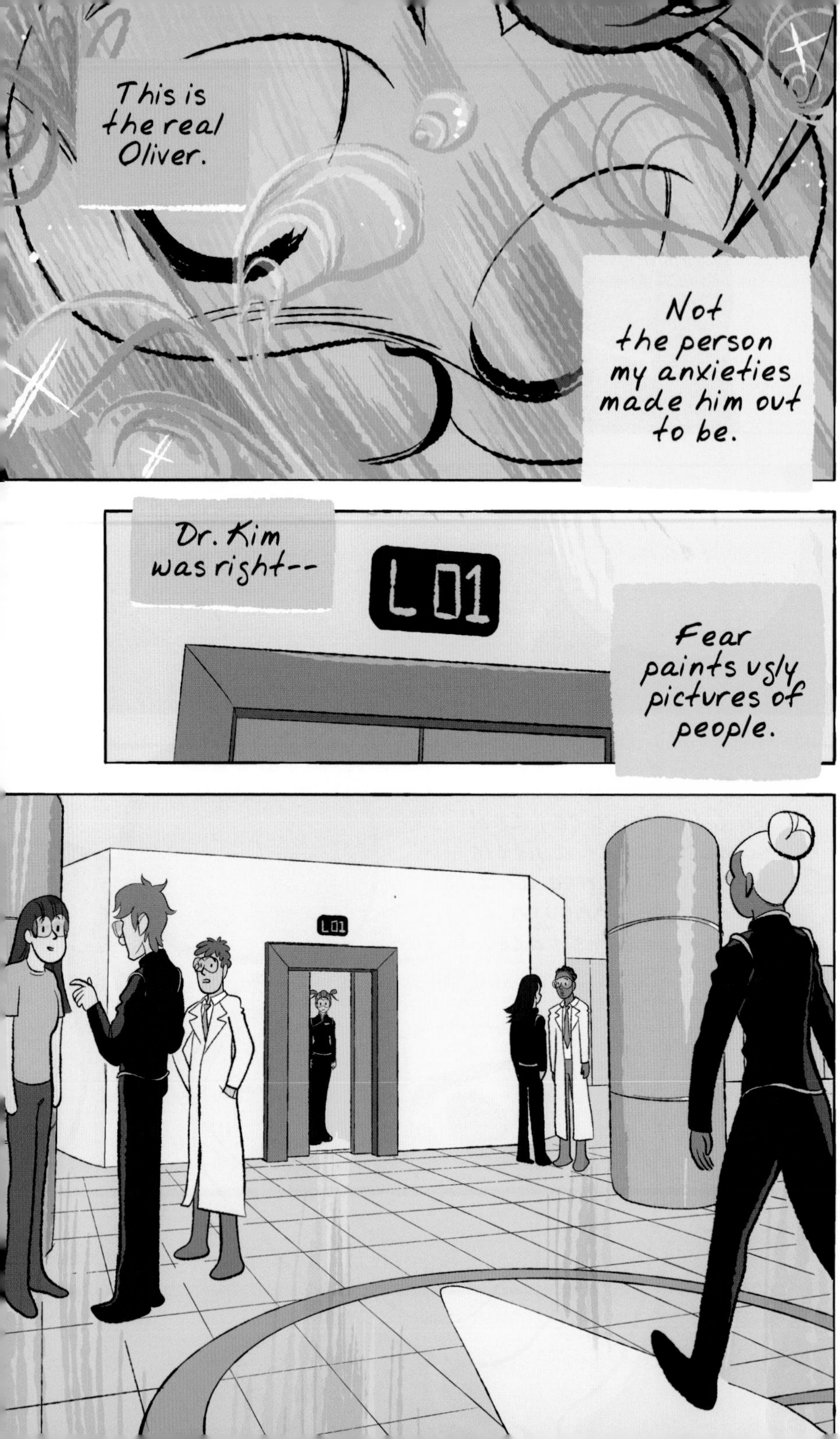
This is the real Oliver.
Not the person my anxieties made him out to be.
Dr. Kim was right--
L01
Fear paints ugly pictures of people.
L01

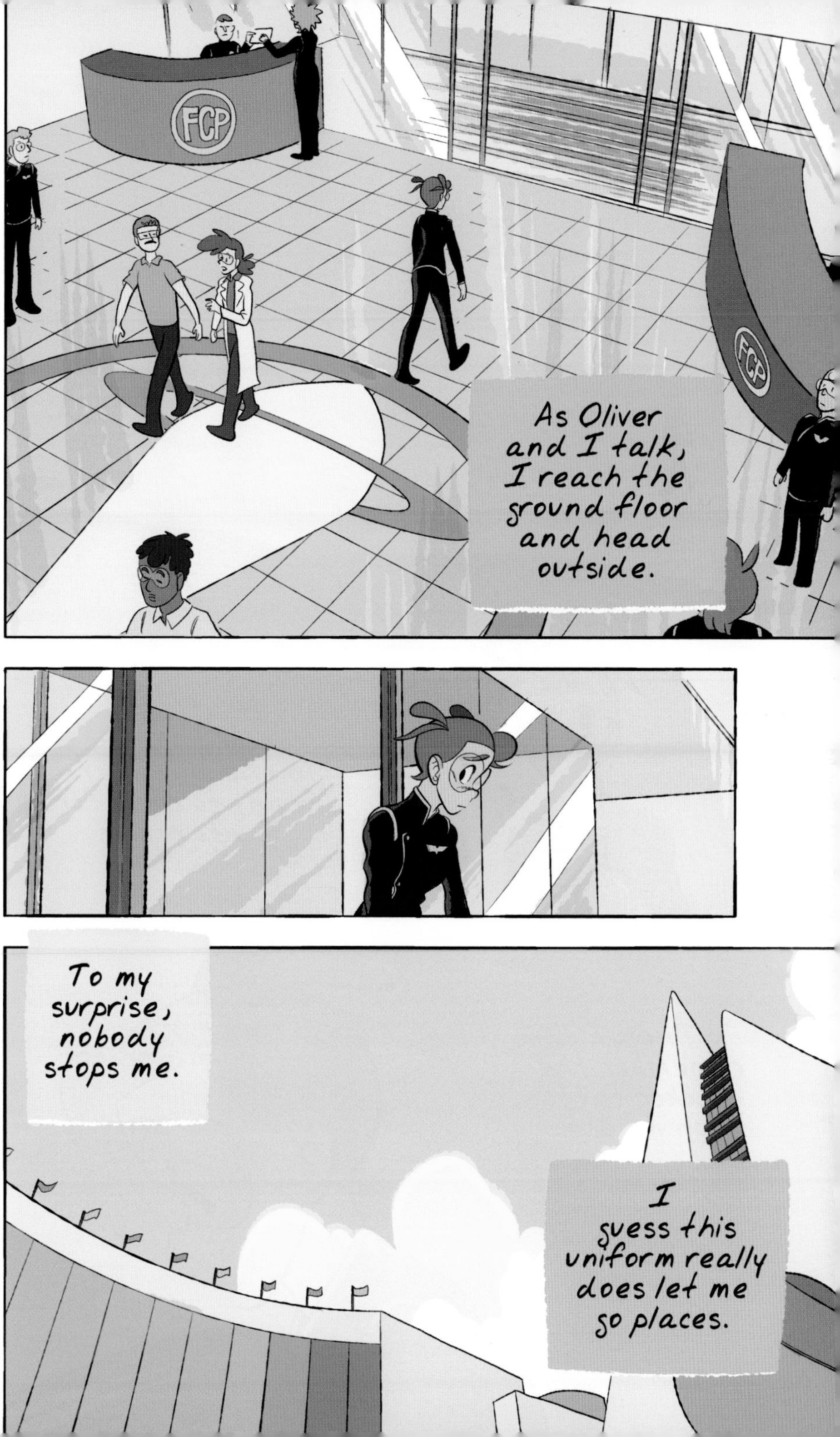
As Oliver and I talk, I reach the ground floor and head outside.
To my surprise, nobody stops me.
I guess this uniform really does let me go places.

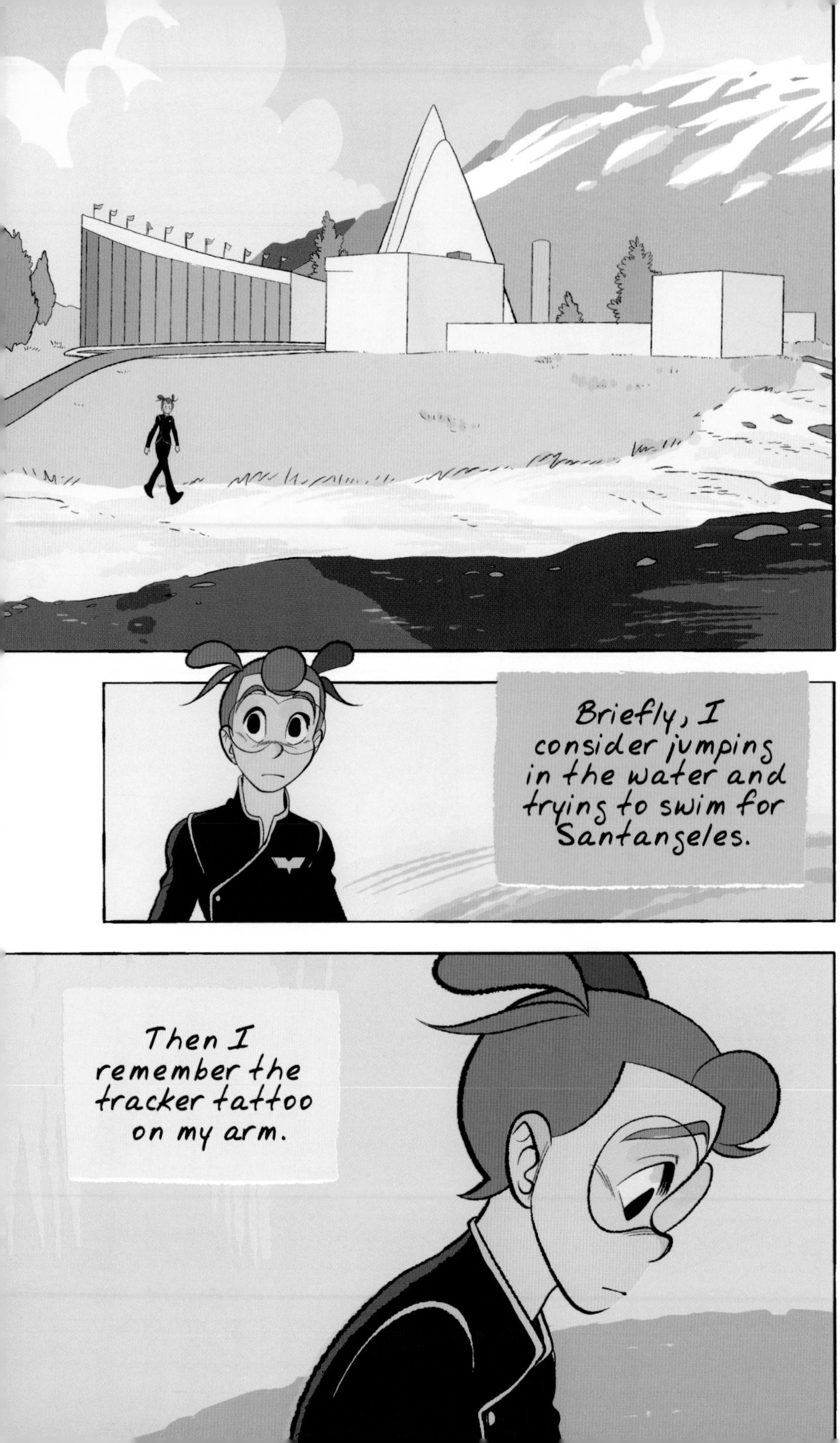
Briefly, I consider jumping in the water and trying to swim for Santangeles.
Then I remember the tracker tattoo on my arm.

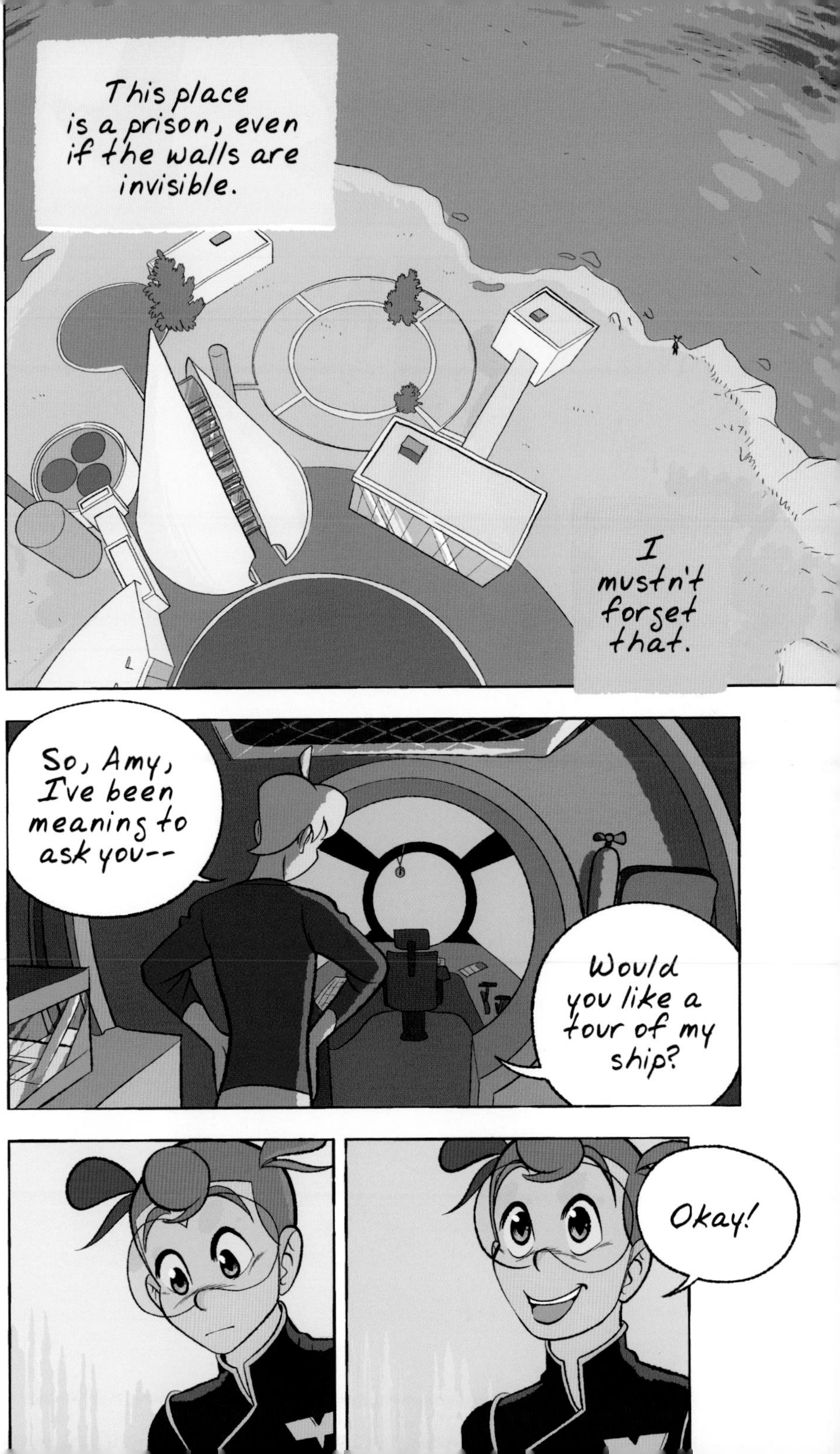
This place is a prison, even if the walls are invisible.
I mustn't forget that.
So, Amy, I've been meaning to ask you--
Would you like a tour of my ship?
Okay!

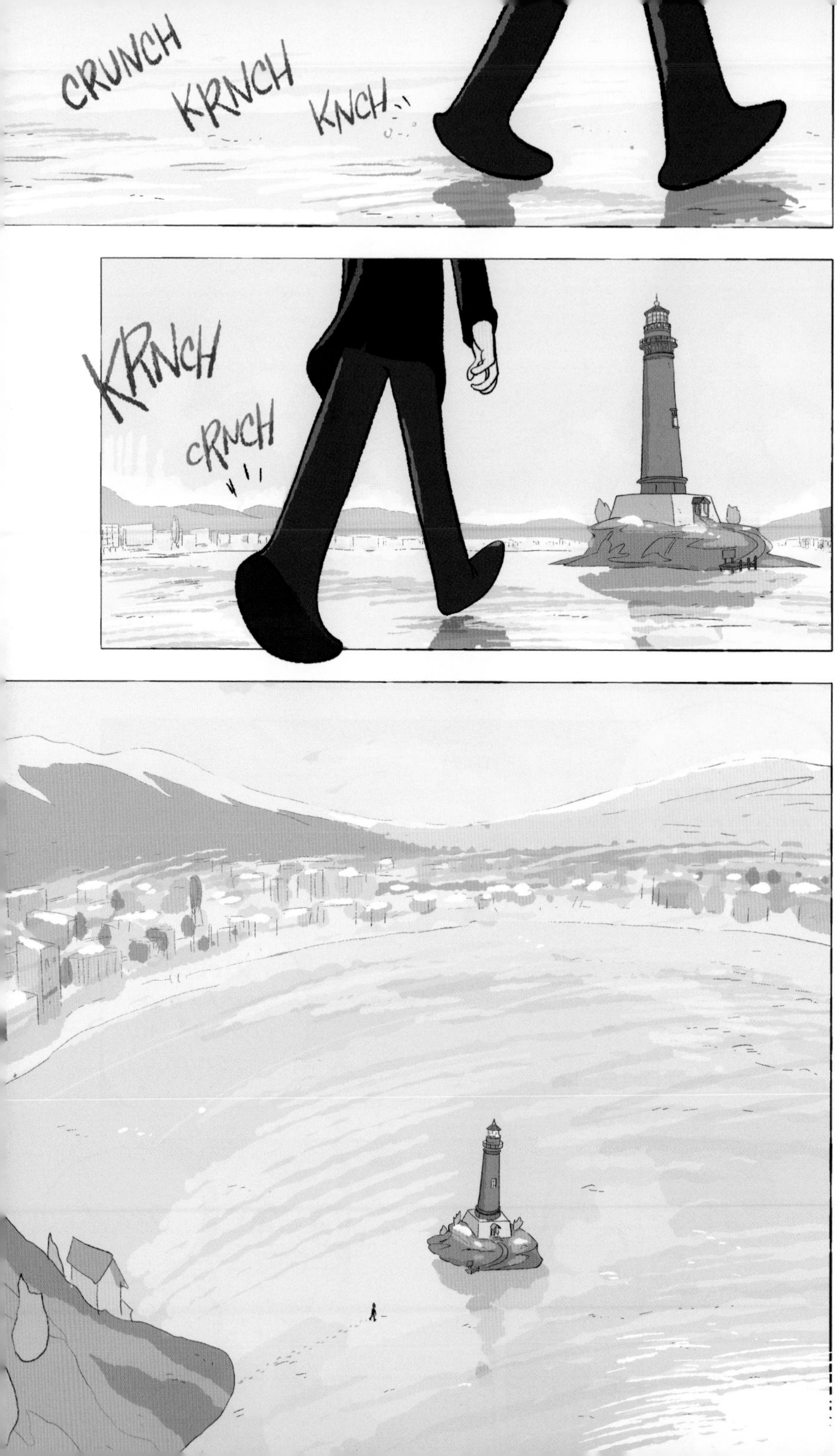
CRUNCH
KRNCH
KNCH
KRNCH
cRNCH

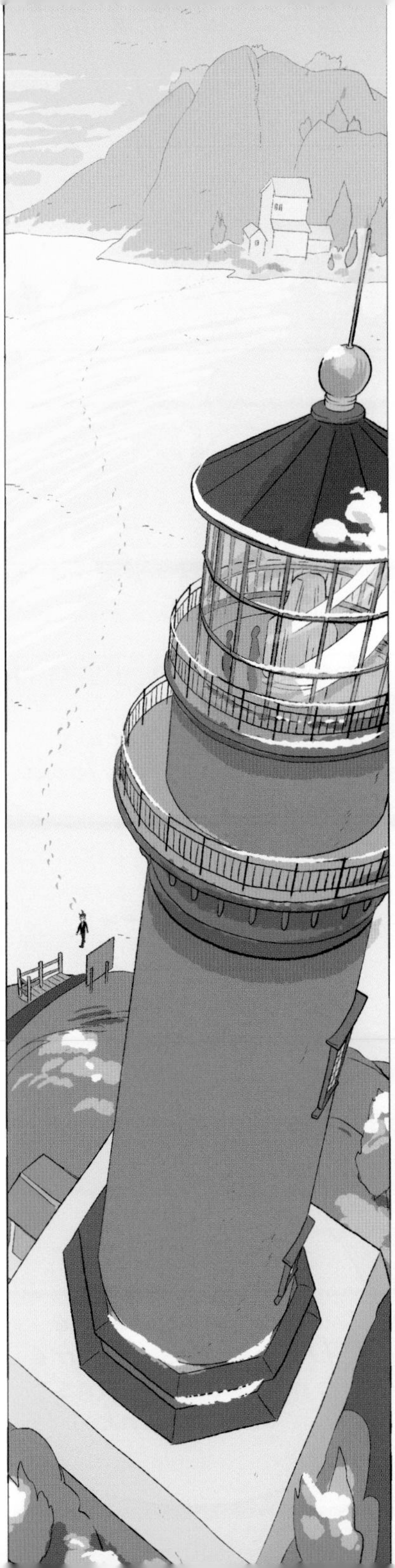

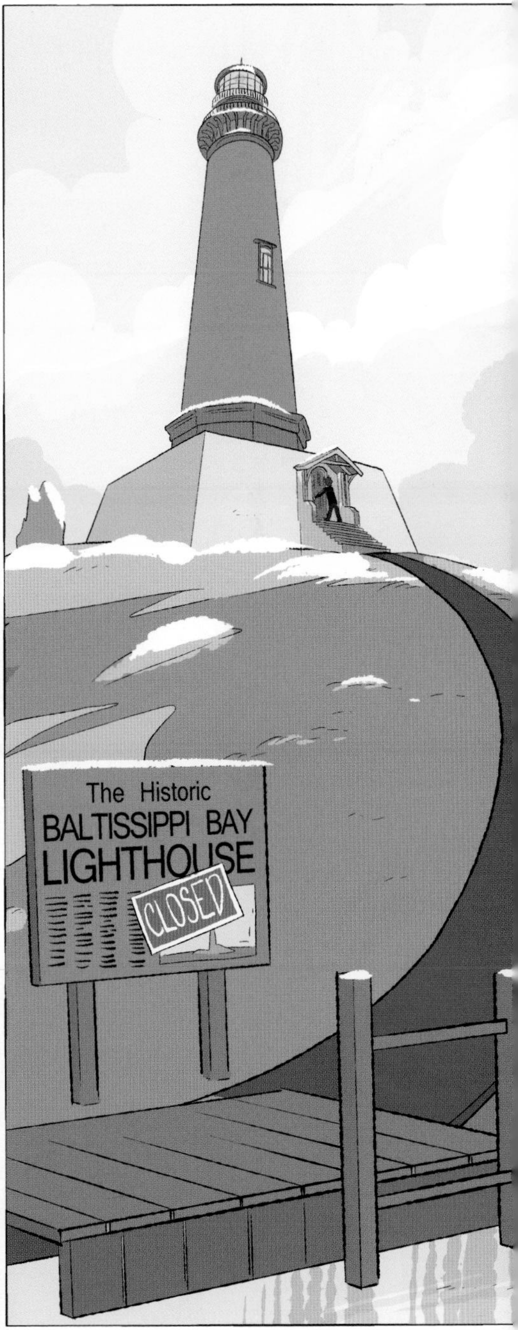
The Historic
BALTISSIPPI BAY
LIGHTHOUSE
CLOSED

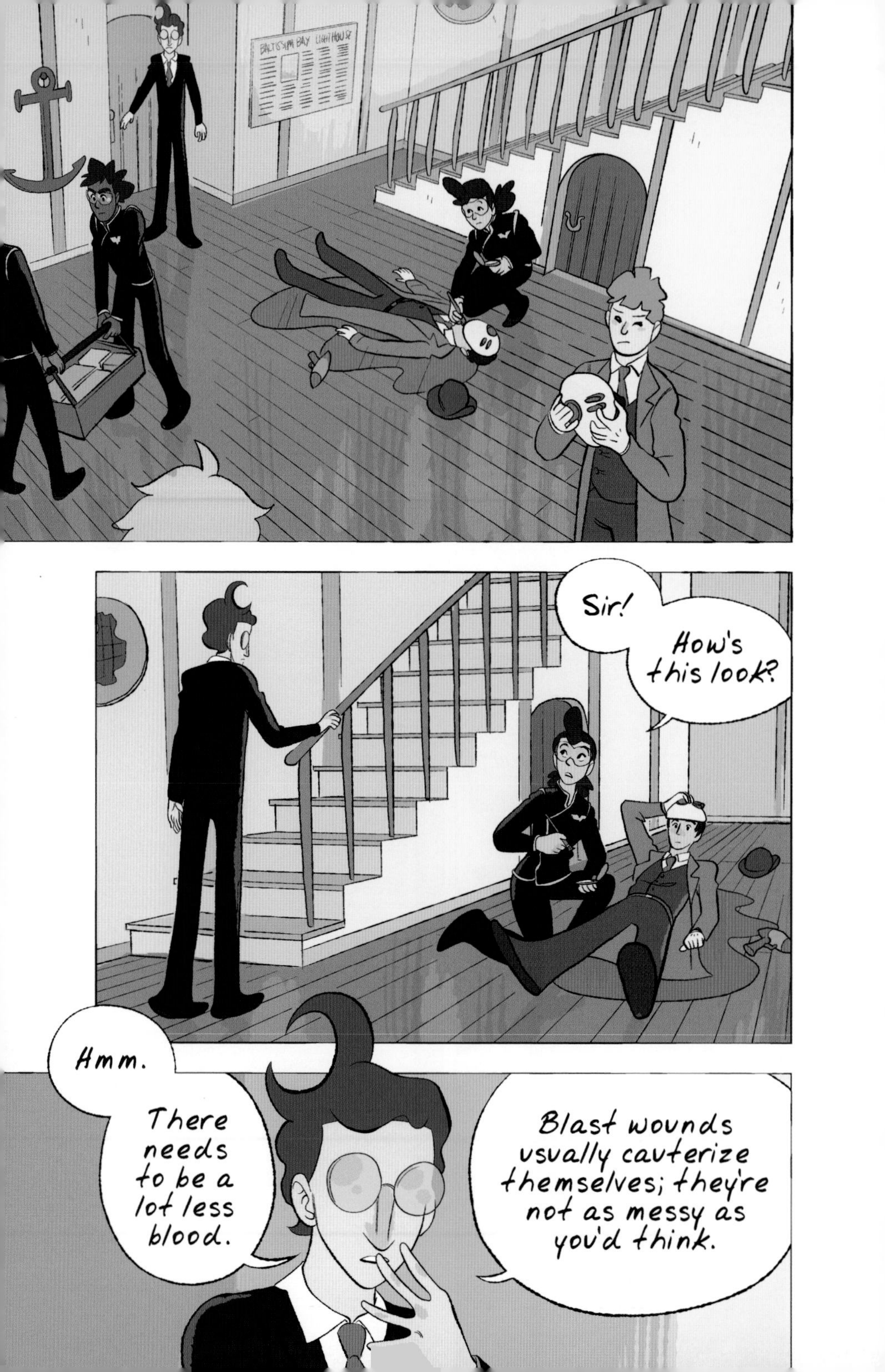
BALTISSIMA BAY LIGHTHOUSE
Sir!
How's this look?
Hmm.
There needs to be a lot less blood.
Blast wounds usually cauterize themselves; they're not as messy as you'd think.

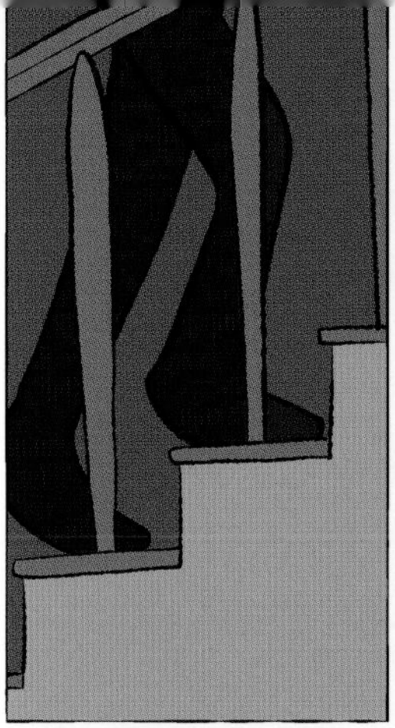
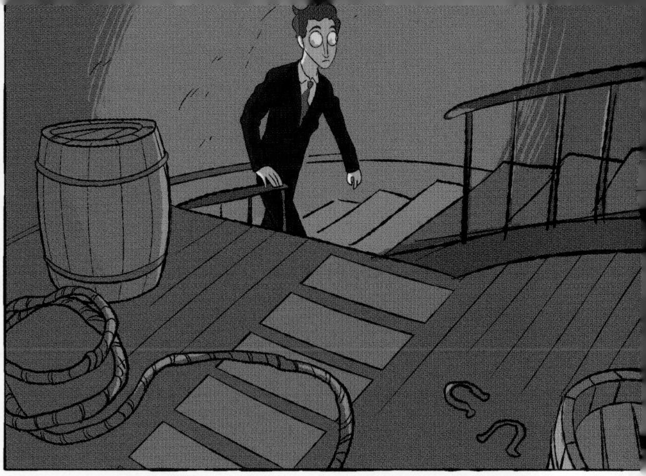
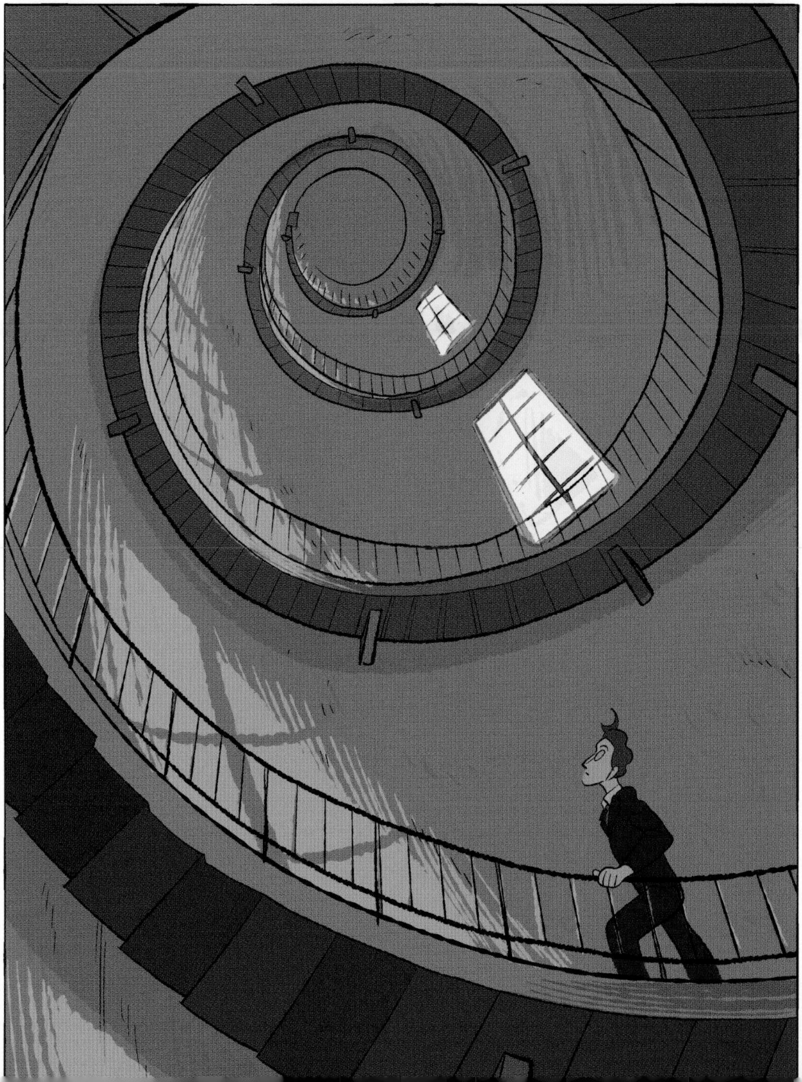

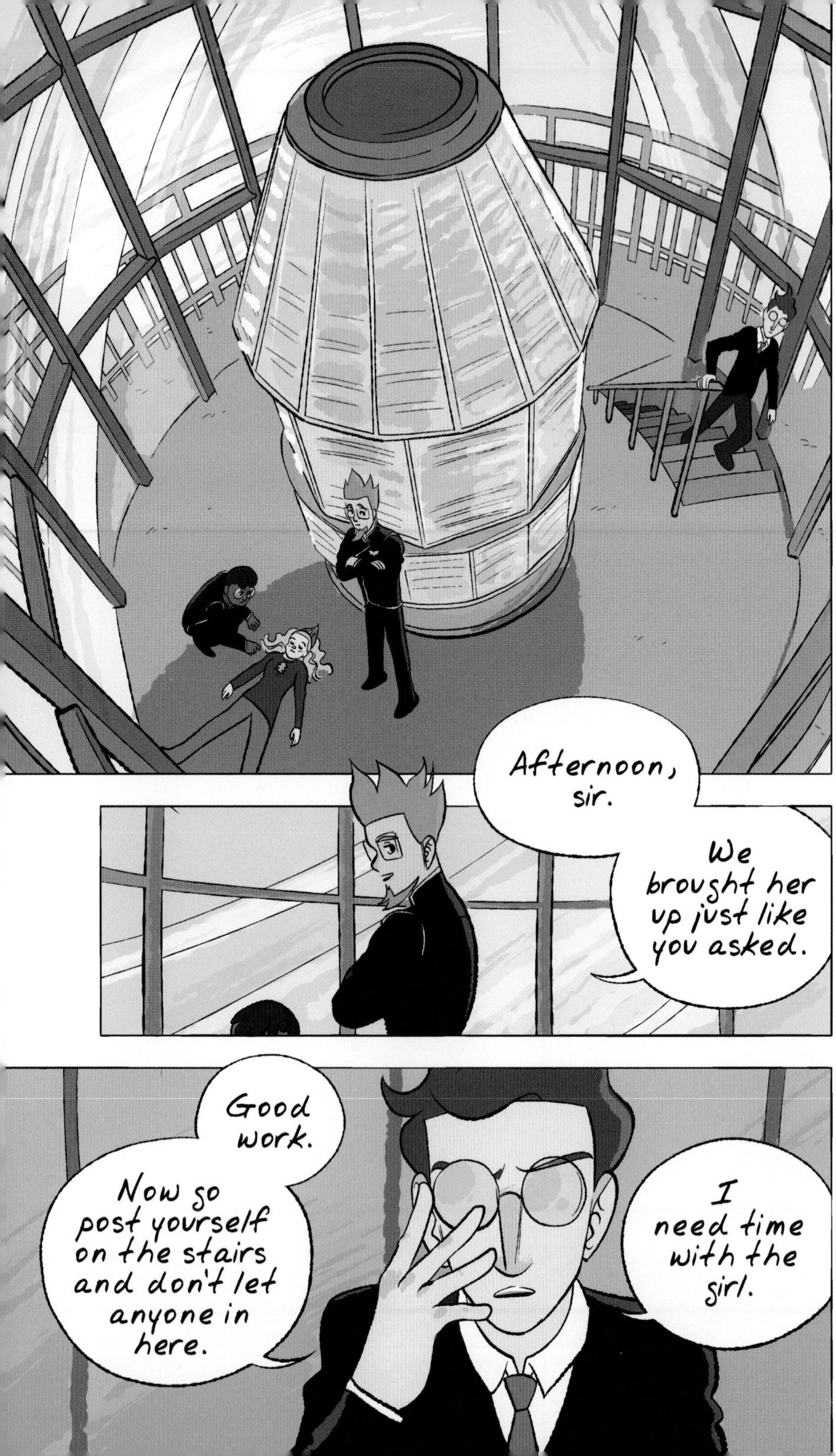
Afternoon, sir.
We brought her up just like you asked.
Good work.
Now go post yourself on the stairs and don't let anyone in here.
I need time with the girl.

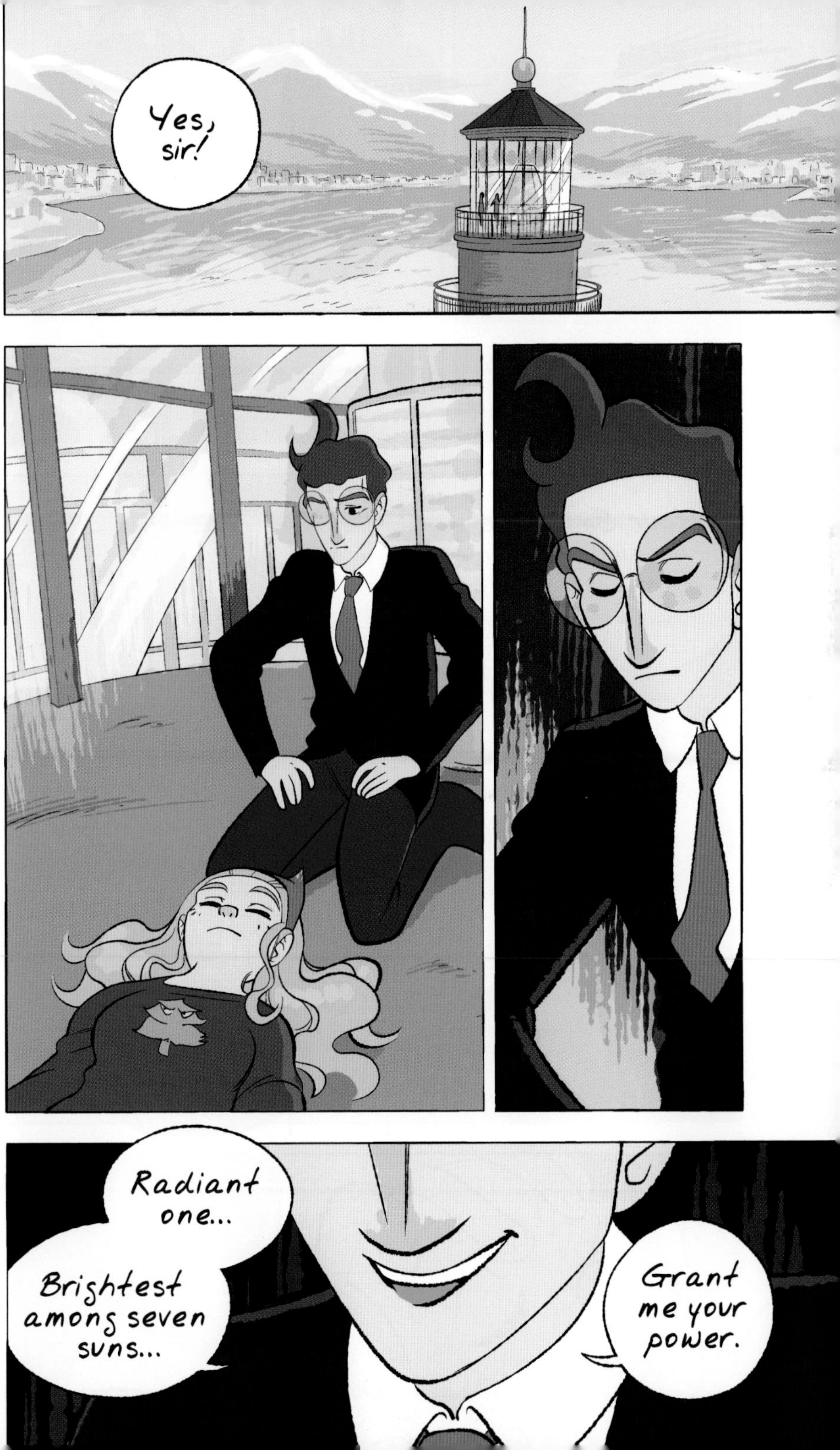
Yes, sir!
Radiant one...
Brightest among seven suns...
Grant me your power.

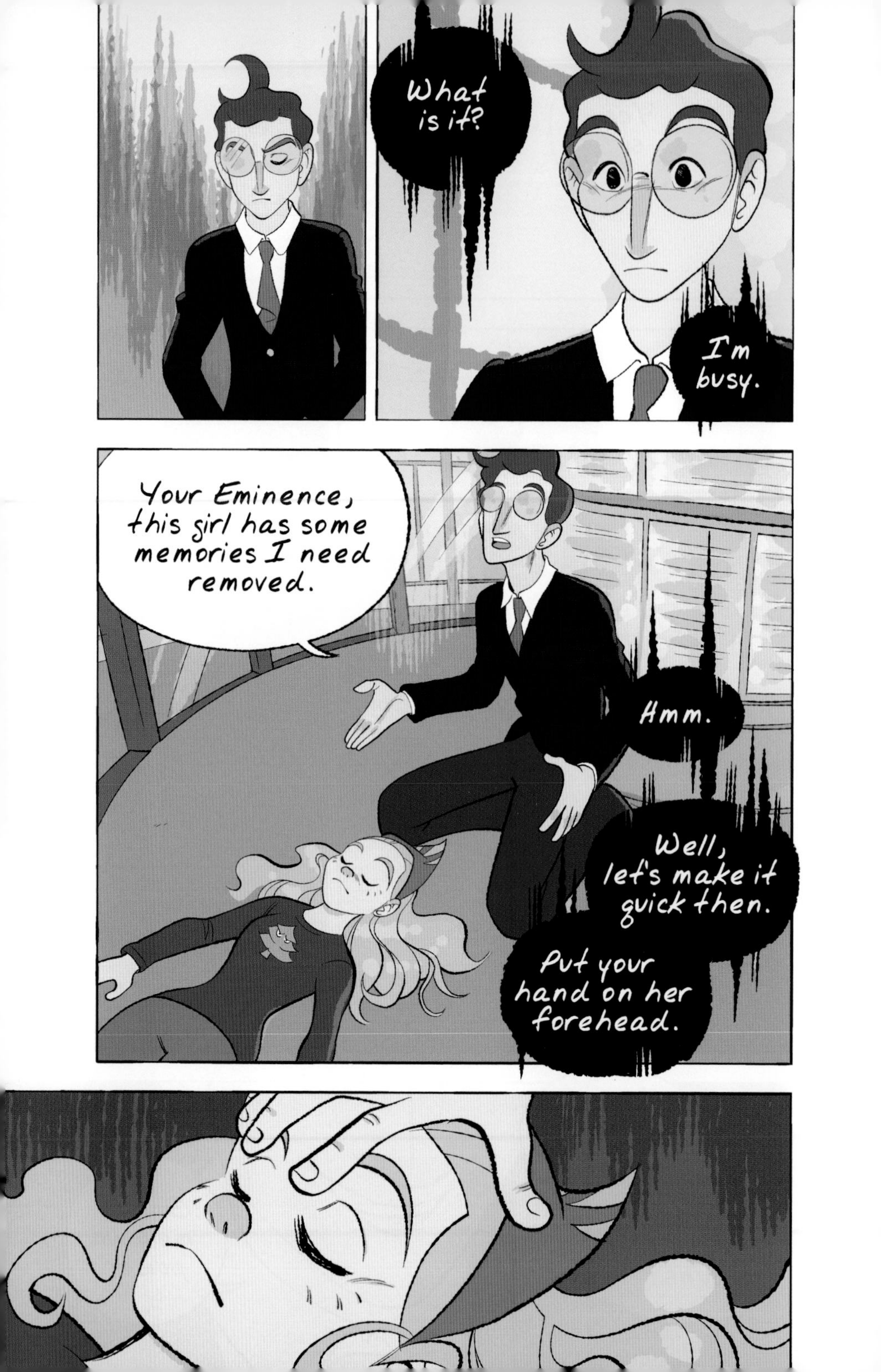
What is it?
I'm busy.
Your Eminence, this girl has some memories I need removed.
Hmm.
Well, let's make it quick then.
Put your hand on her forehead.

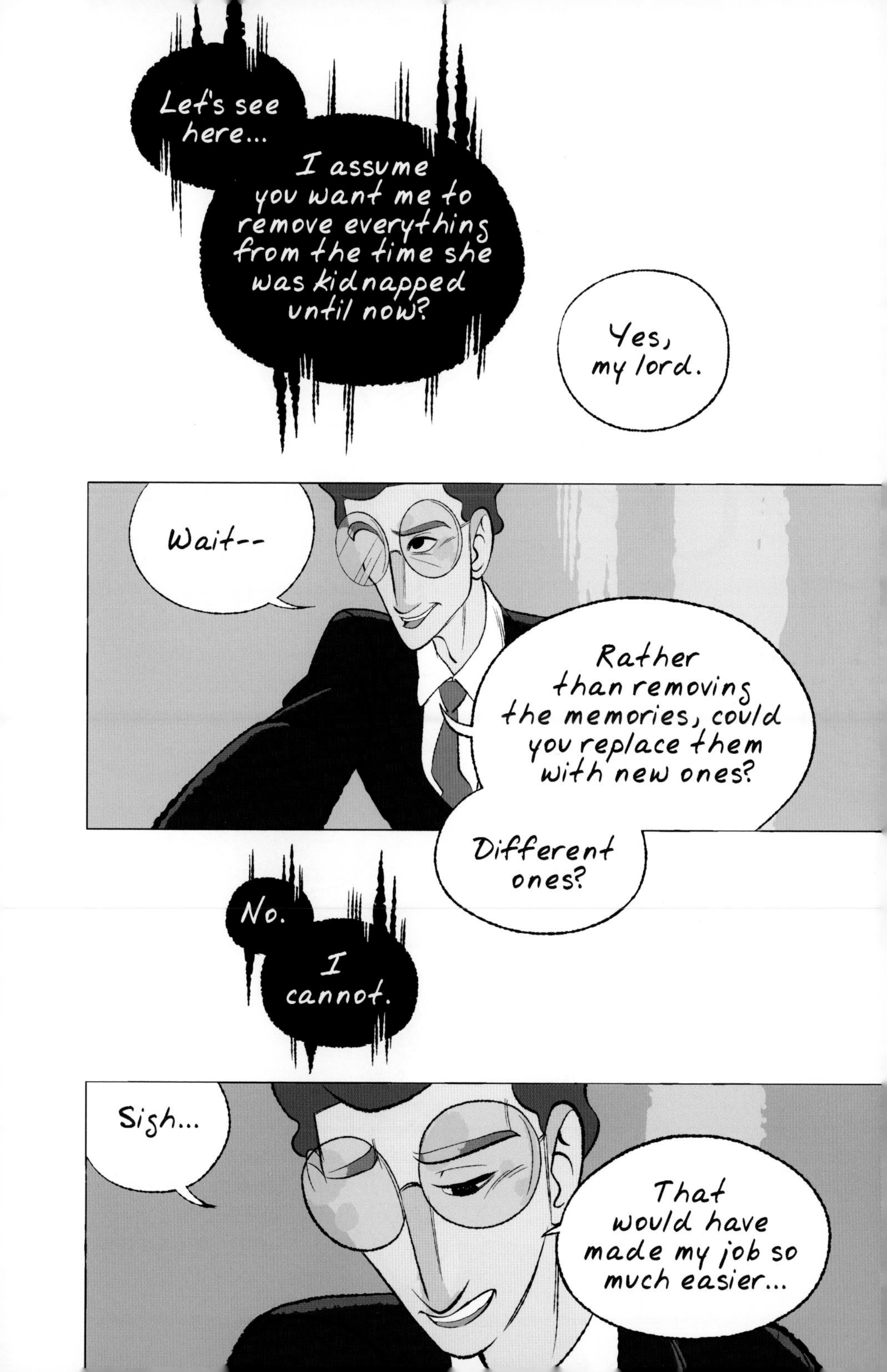
Let's see here...
I assume you want me to remove everything from the time she was kidnapped until now?
Yes, my lord.
Wait--
Rather than removing the memories, could you replace them with new ones?
Different ones?
No.
I cannot.
Sigh...
That would have made my job so much easier...

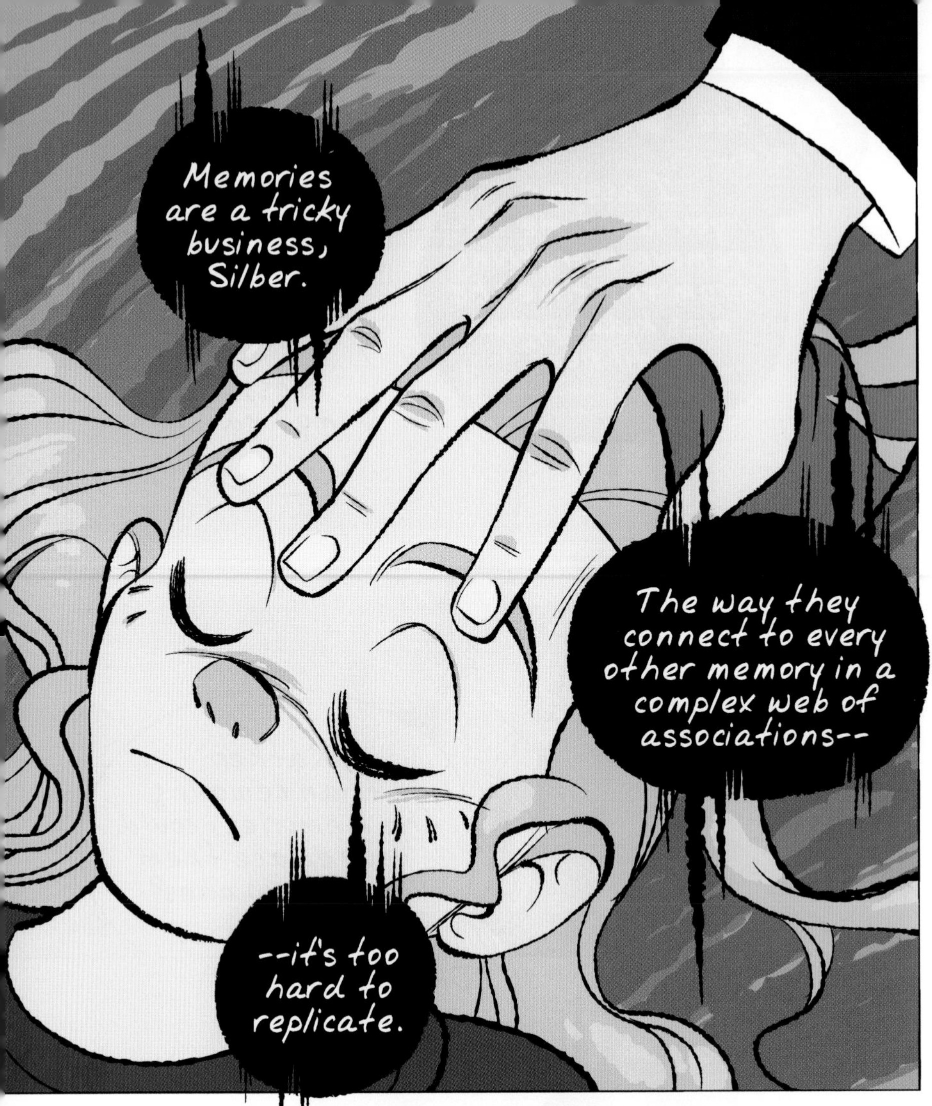
Memories are a tricky business, Silber.
The way they connect to every other memory in a complex web of associations--
--it's too hard to replicate.

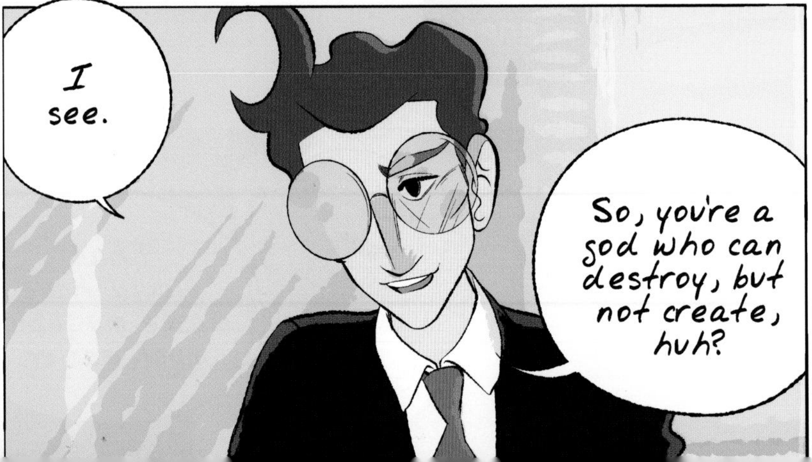
I see.
So, you're a god who can destroy, but not create, huh?

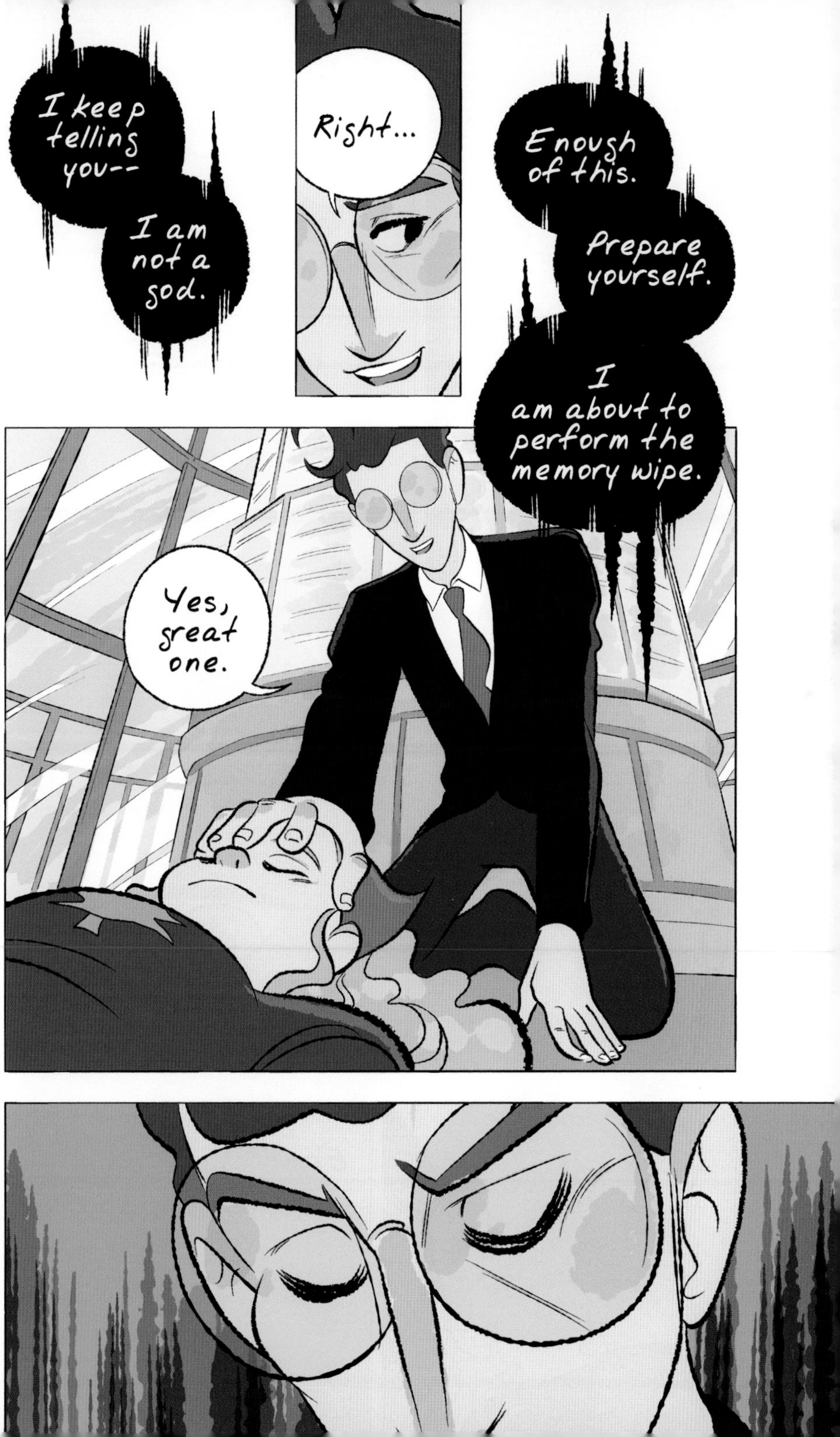
I keep telling you--
I am not a god.
Right...
Enough of this.
Prepare yourself.
I am about to perform the memory wipe.
Yes, great one.

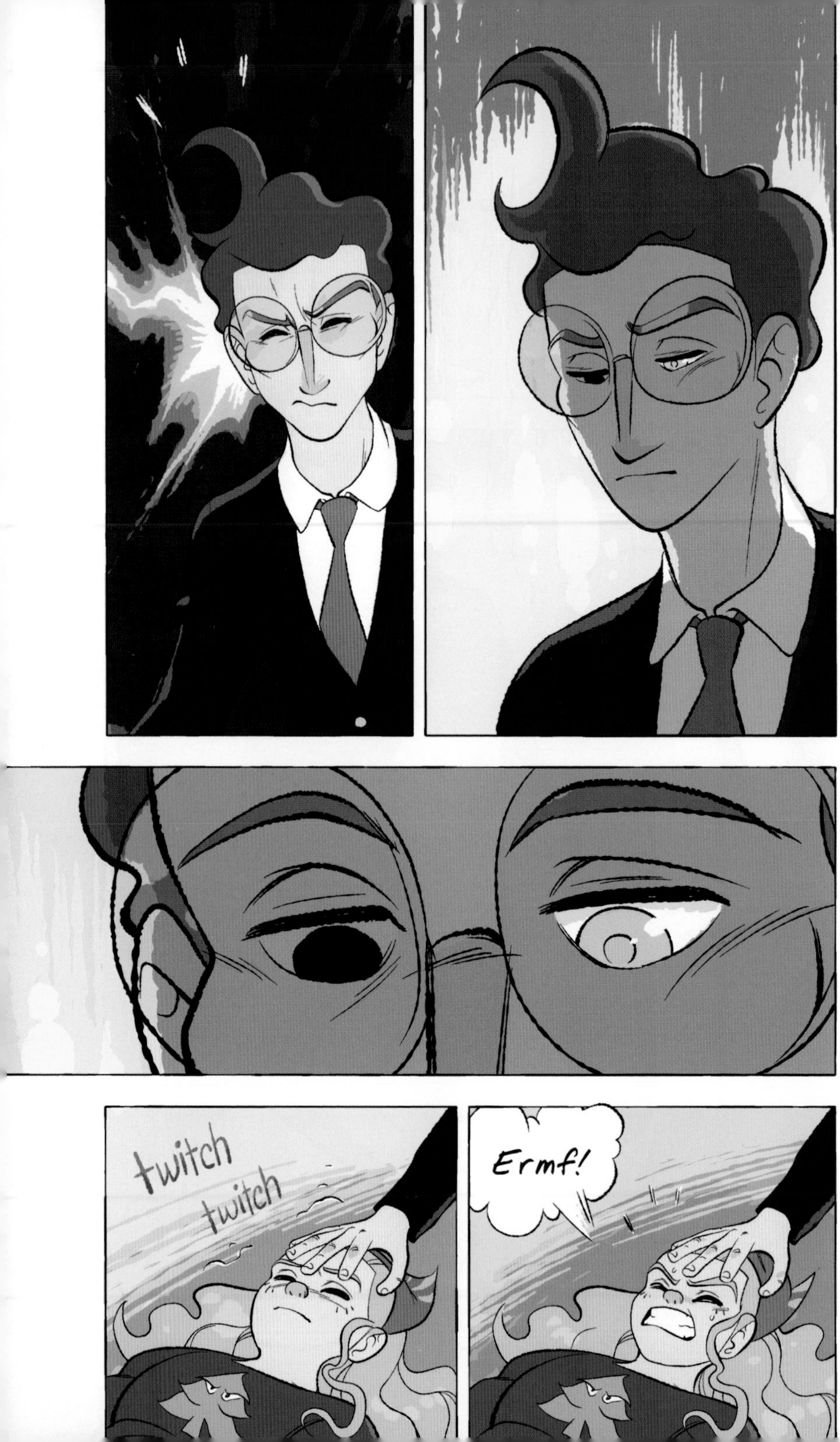
twitch
twitch
Ermf!

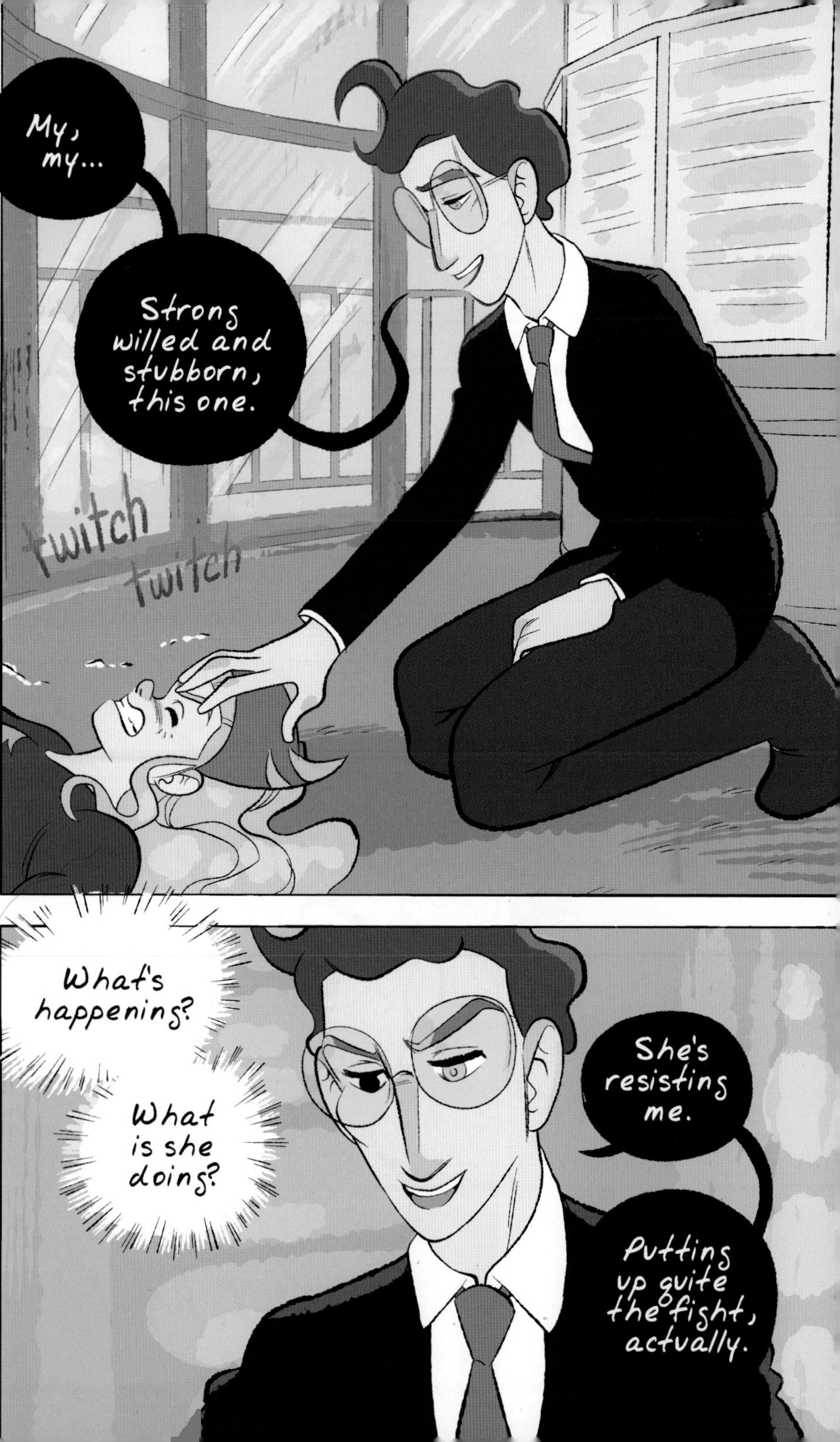
My, my...
Strong willed and stubborn, this one.
twitch
twitch
What's happening?
What is she doing?
She's resisting me.
Putting up quite the fight, actually.

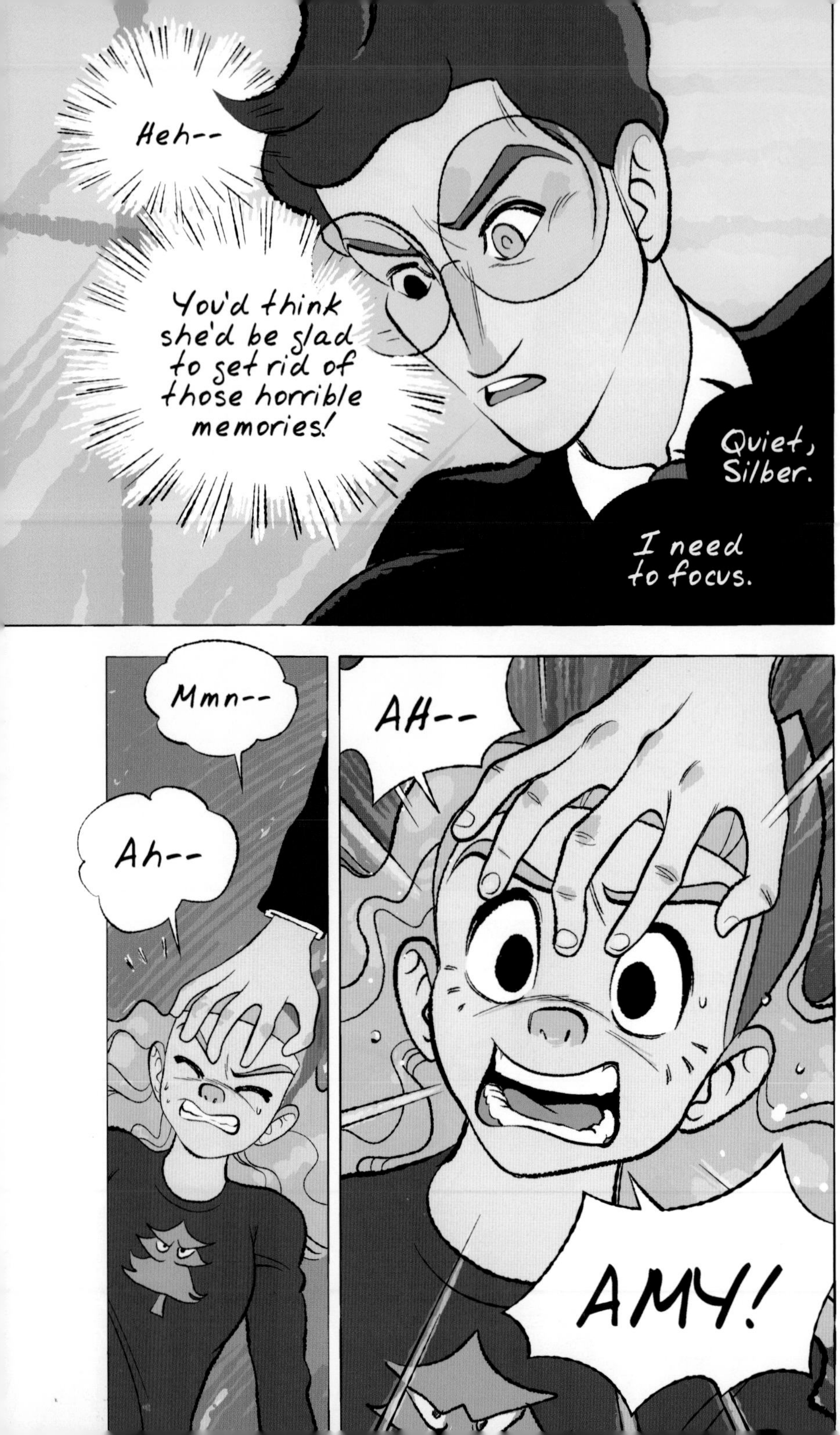
Heh--
You'd think she'd be glad to get rid of those horrible memories!
Quiet, Silber.
I need to focus.
Mmn--
Ah--
AH--
AMY!

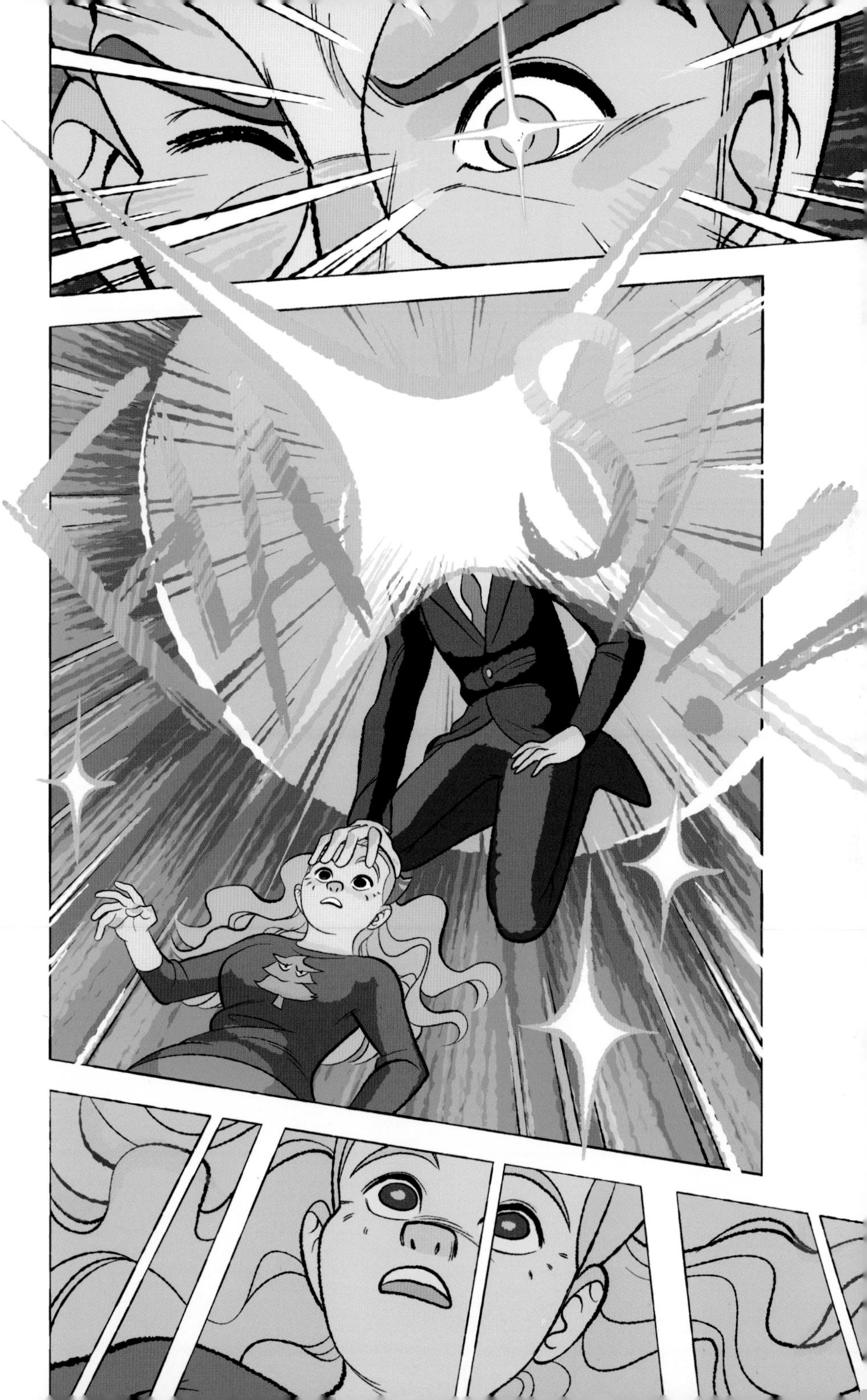

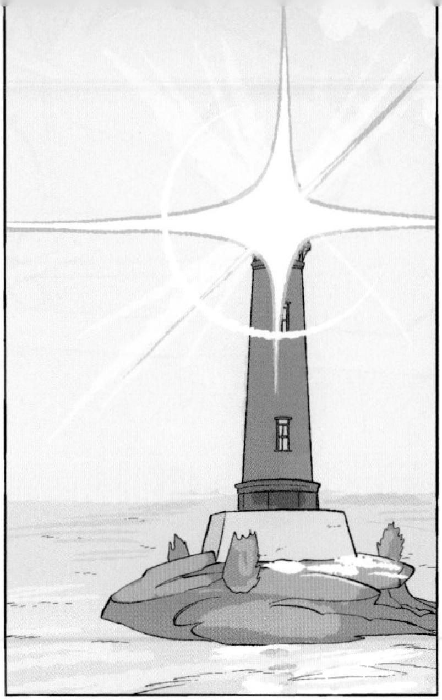
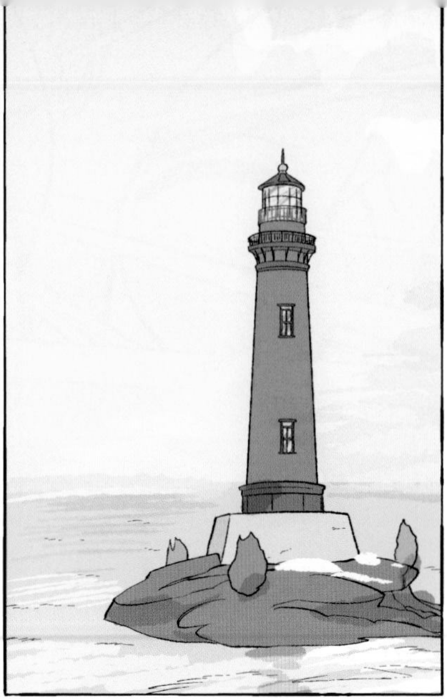
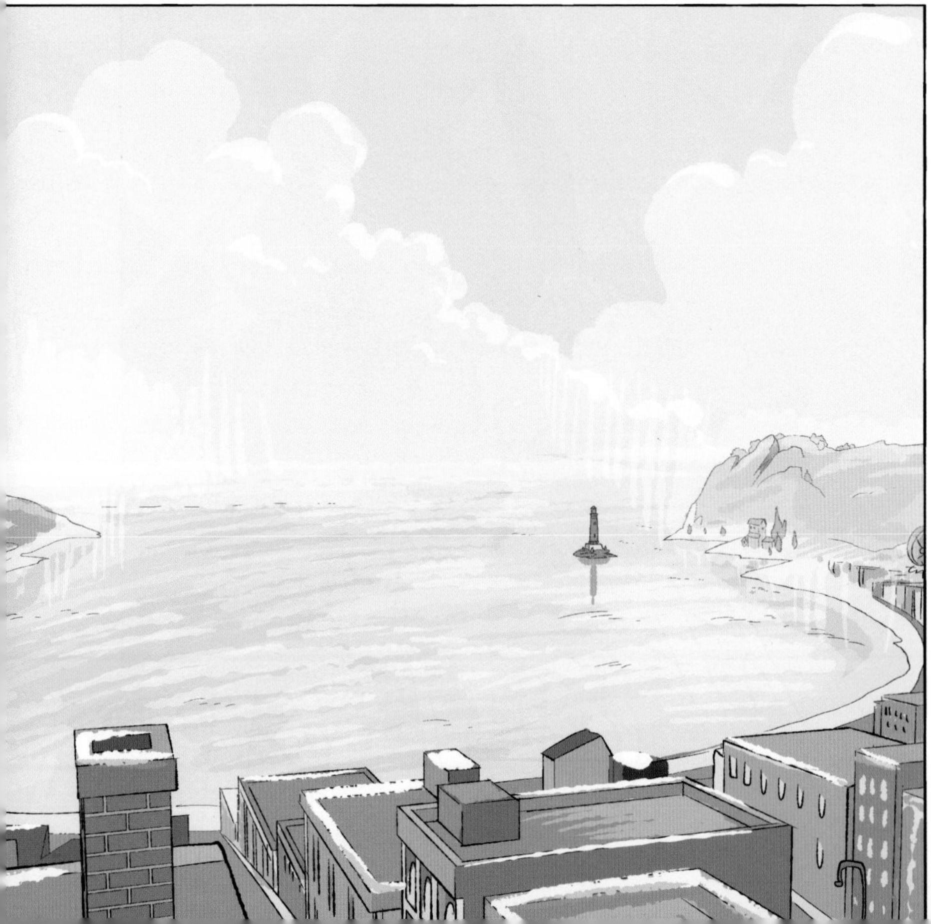

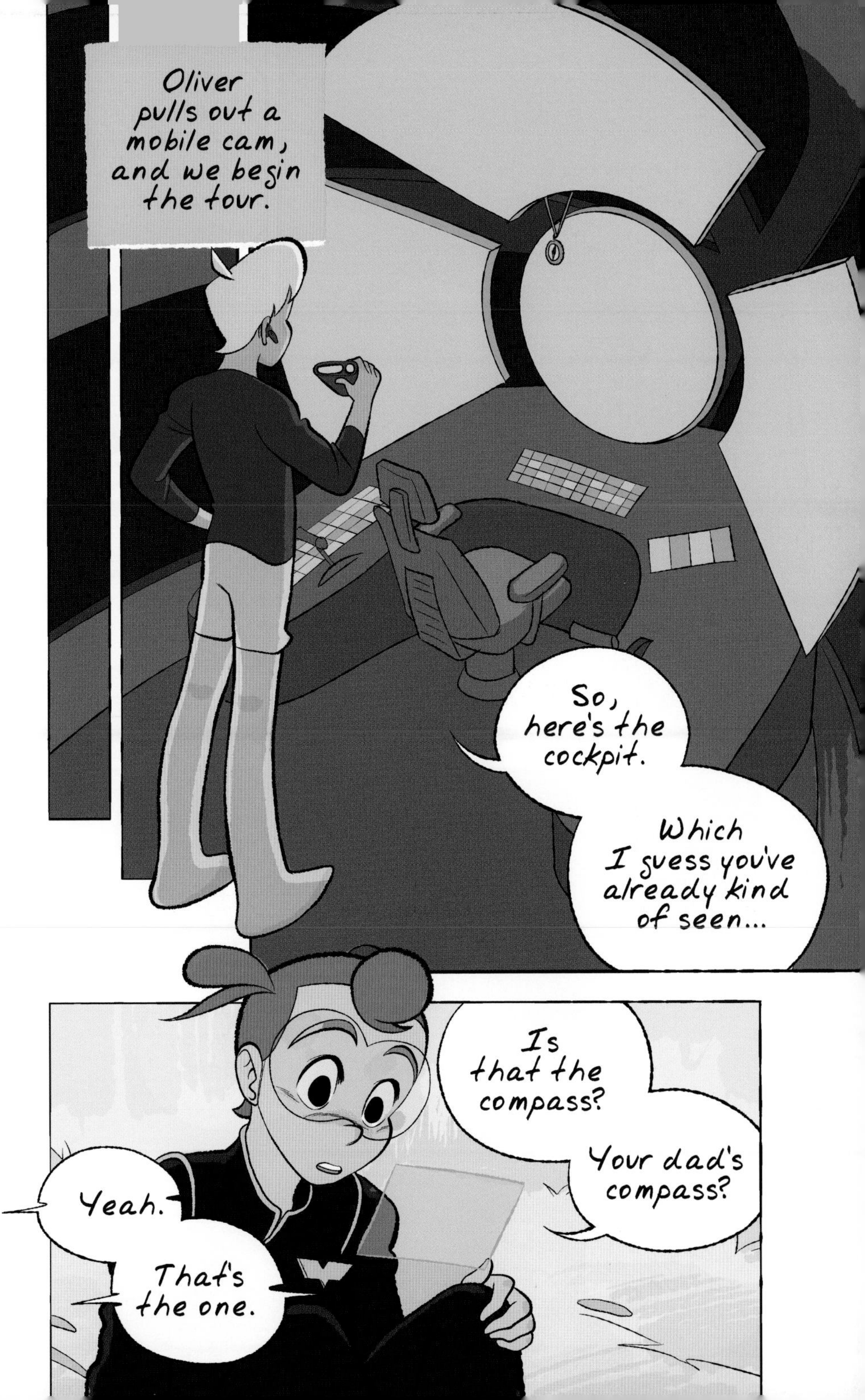
Oliver pulls out a mobile cam, and we begin the tour.
So, here's the cockpit.
Which I guess you've already kind of seen...
Is that the compass?
Your dad's compass?
Yeah.
That's the one.

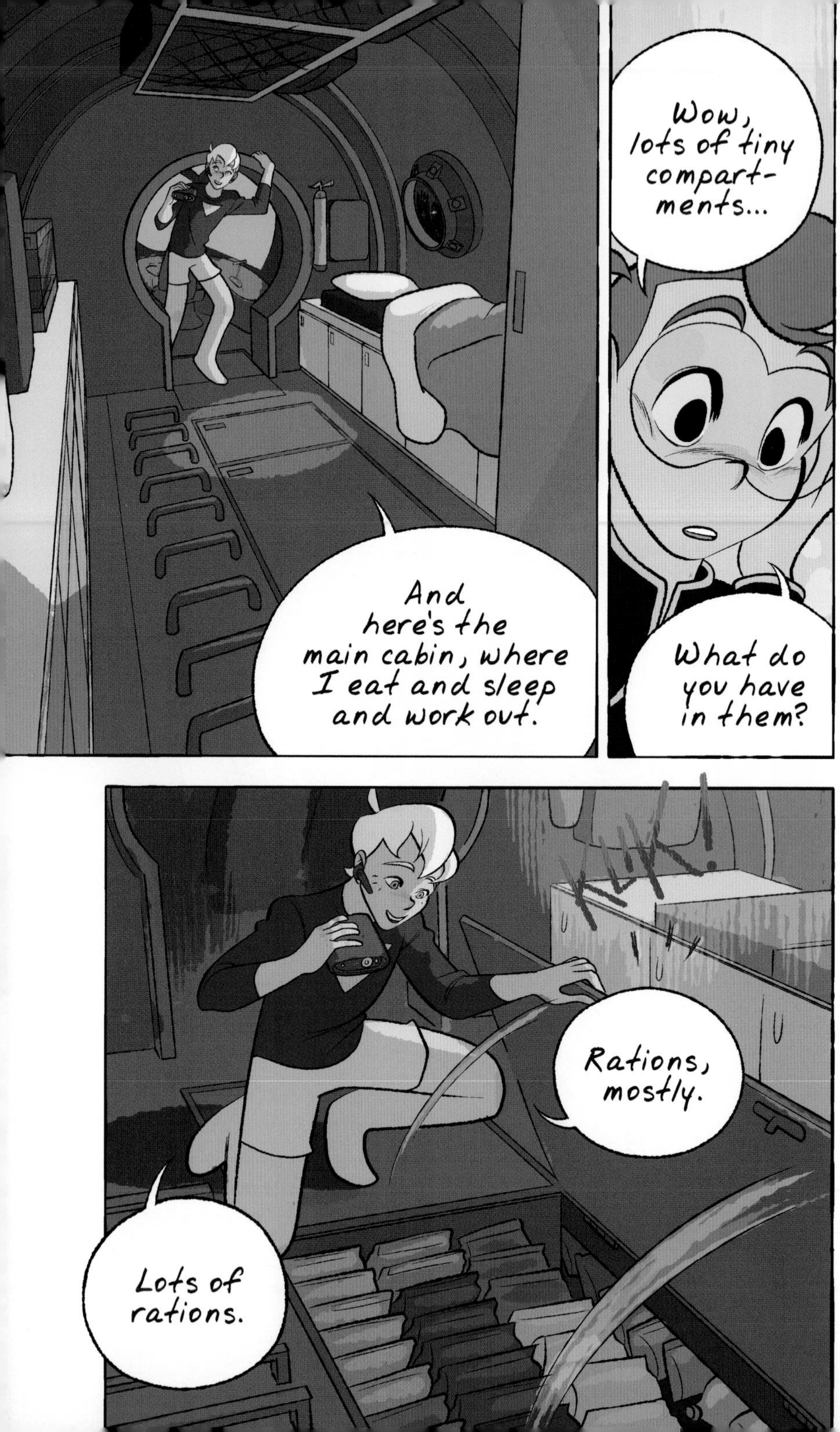
And here's the main cabin, where I eat and sleep and work out.
Wow, lots of tiny compart-ments...
What do you have in them?
Rations, mostly.
Lots of rations.

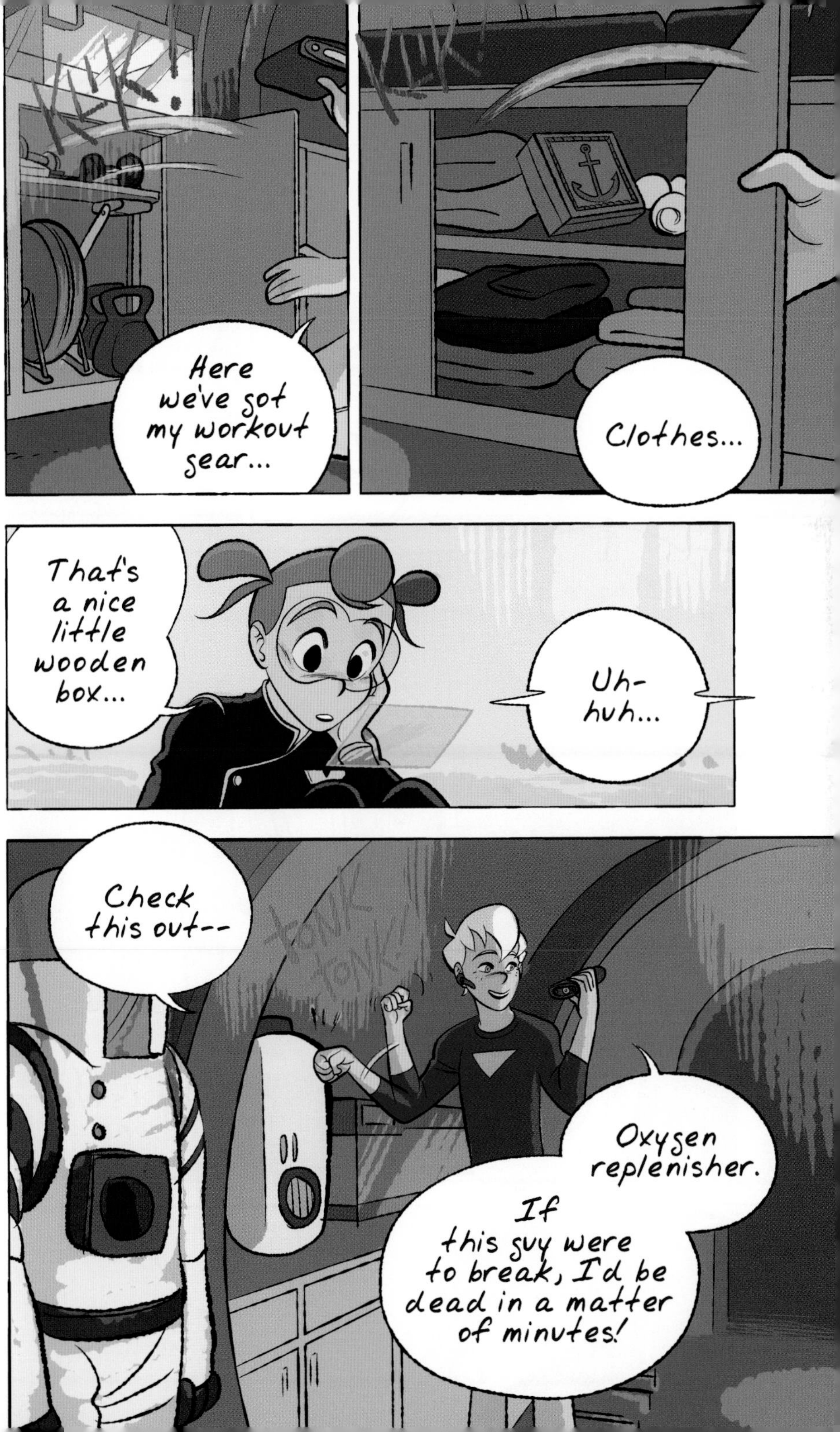
KLIK!
Here we've got my workout gear...
KLIK!
Clothes...
That's a nice little wooden box...
Uh-huh...
Check this out--
TONK TONK!
Oxygen replenisher.
If this guy were to break, I'd be dead in a matter of minutes!

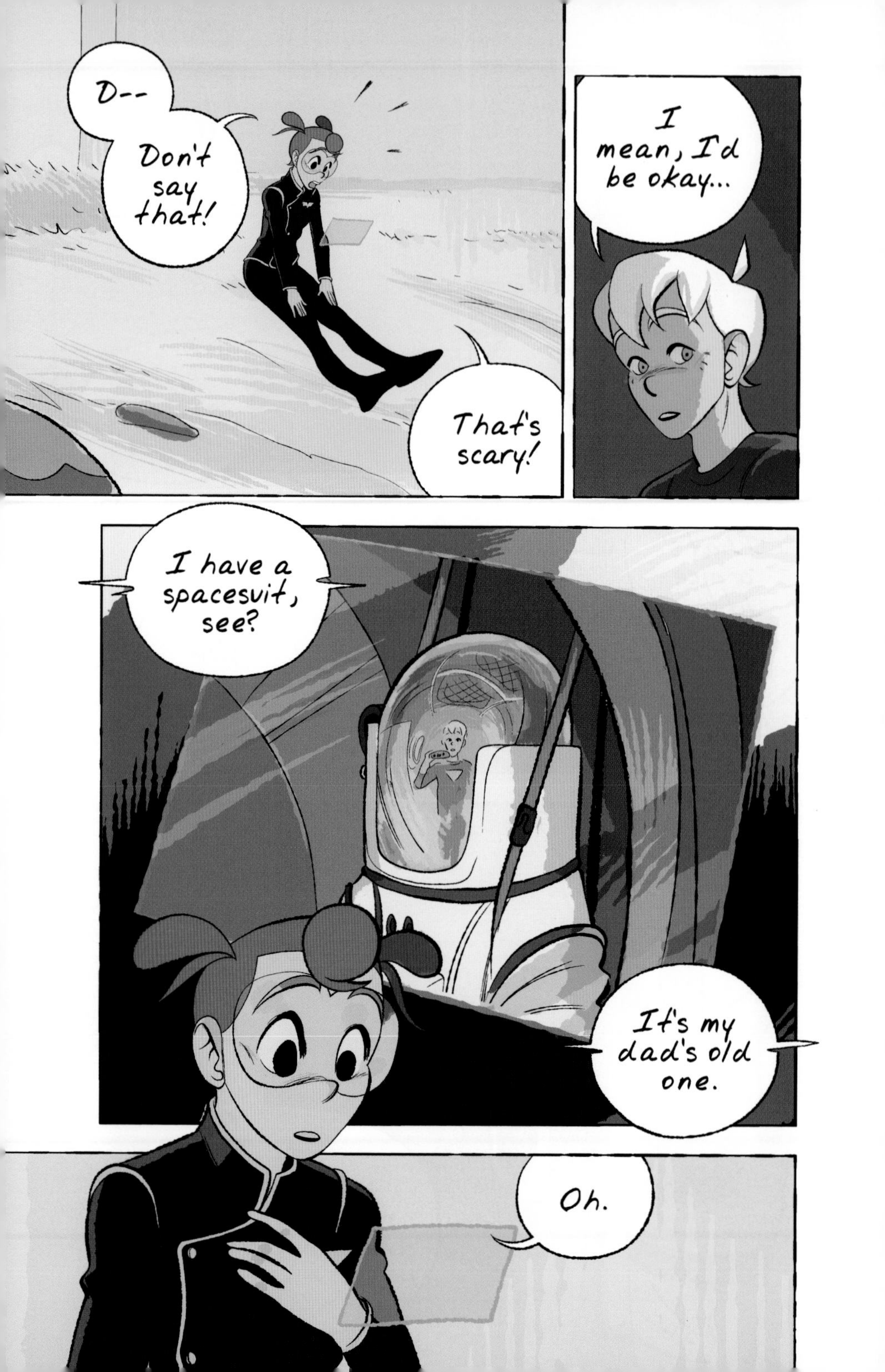
D--
Don't say that!
That's scary!
I mean, I'd be okay...
I have a spacesuit, see?
It's my dad's old one.
Oh.

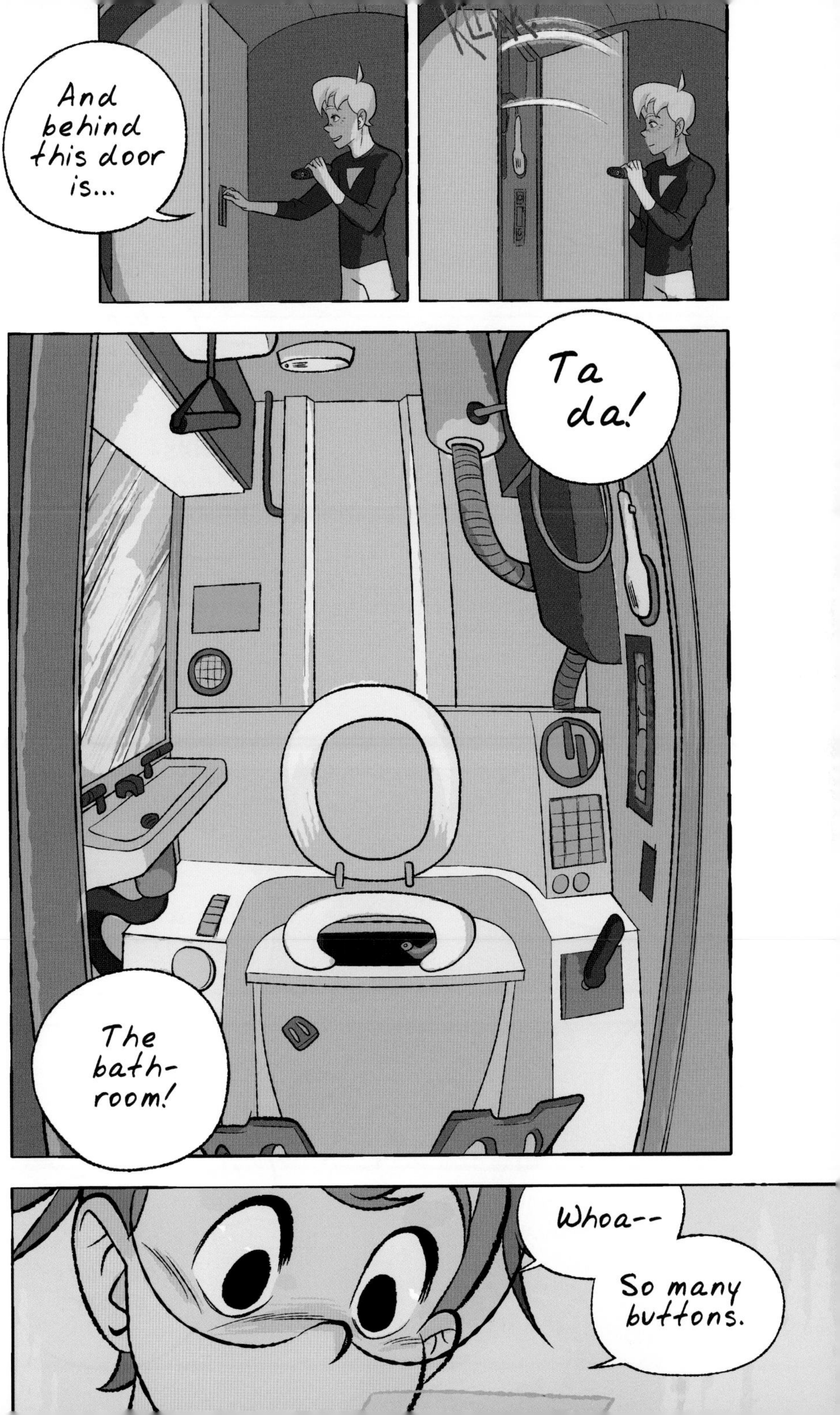
And behind this door is...
Ta da!
The bath-room!
Whoa--
So many buttons.

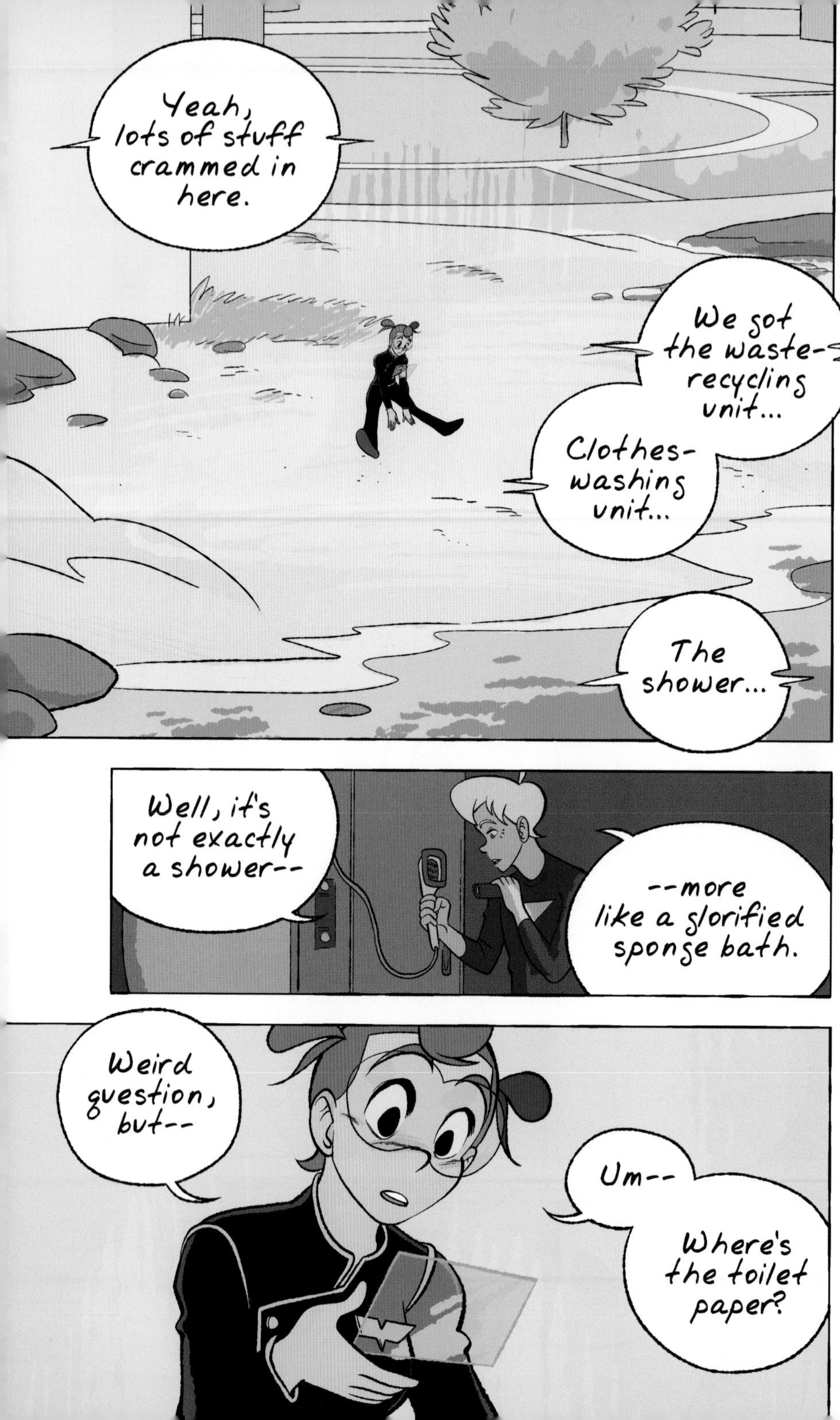
Yeah, lots of stuff crammed in here.
We got the waste-recyclins unit...
Clothes-washing unit...
The shower...
Well, it's not exactly a shower--
--more like a glorified sponge bath.
Weird question, but--
Um--
Where's the toilet paper?

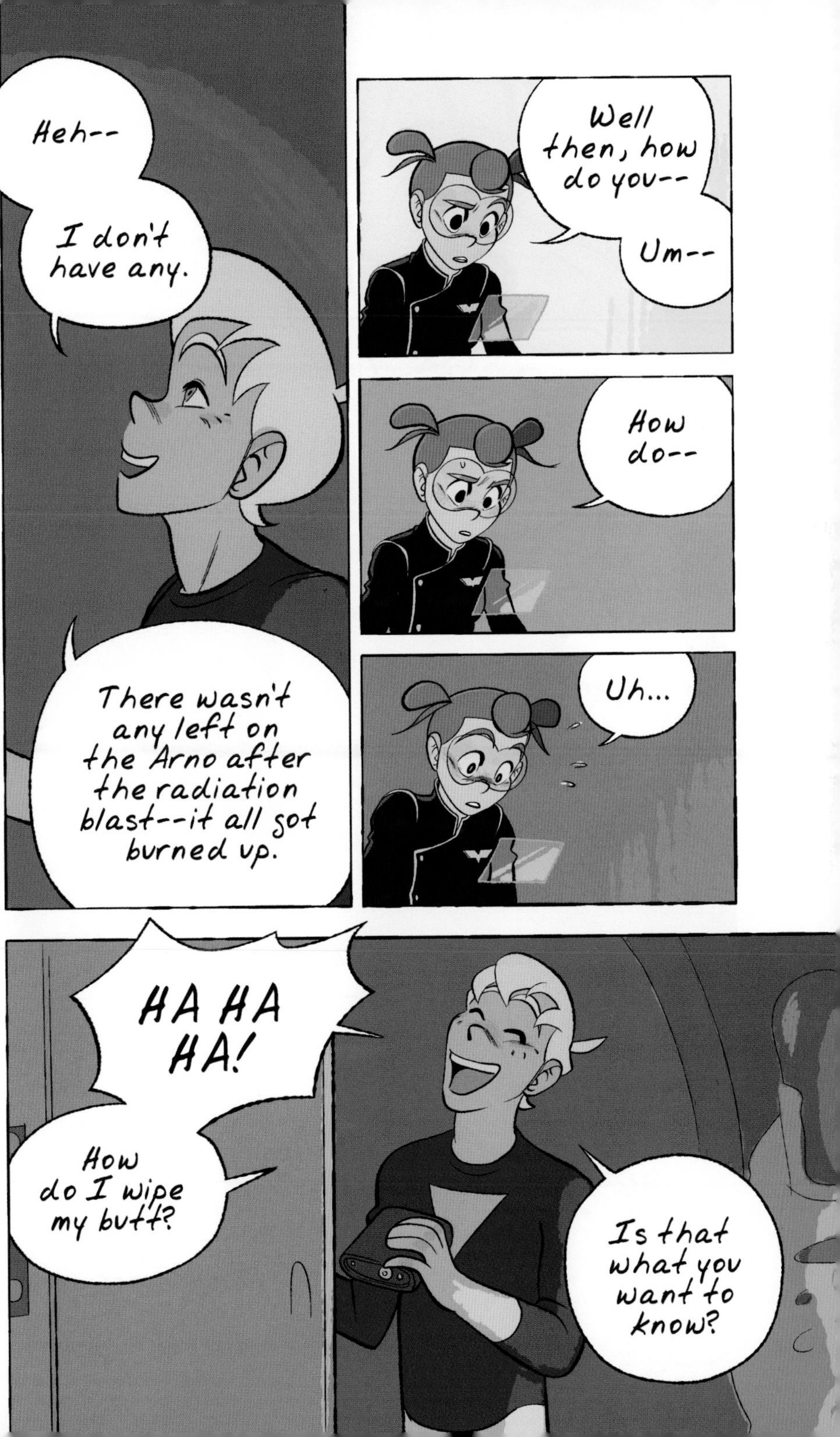
Heh--
I don't have any.
Well then, how do you--
Um--
How do--
Uh...
There wasn't any left on the Arno after the radiation blast--it all got burned up.
HA HA HA!
How do I wipe my butt?
Is that what you want to know?

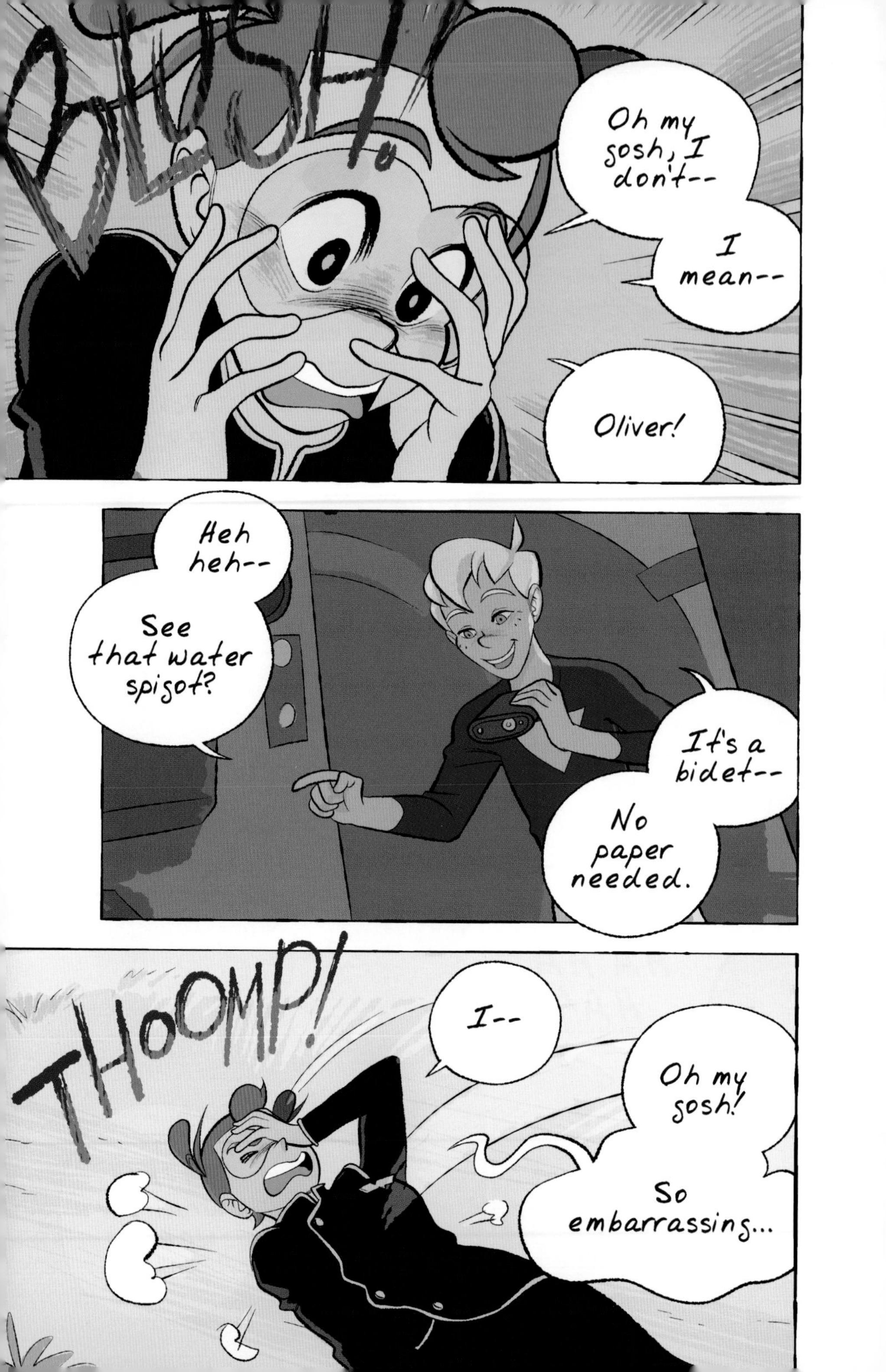
BLUSH!
Oh my sosh, I don't--
I mean--
Oliver!
Heh heh--
See that water spigot?
It's a bidet--
No paper needed.
THOOMP!
I--
Oh my sosh!
So embarrassing...

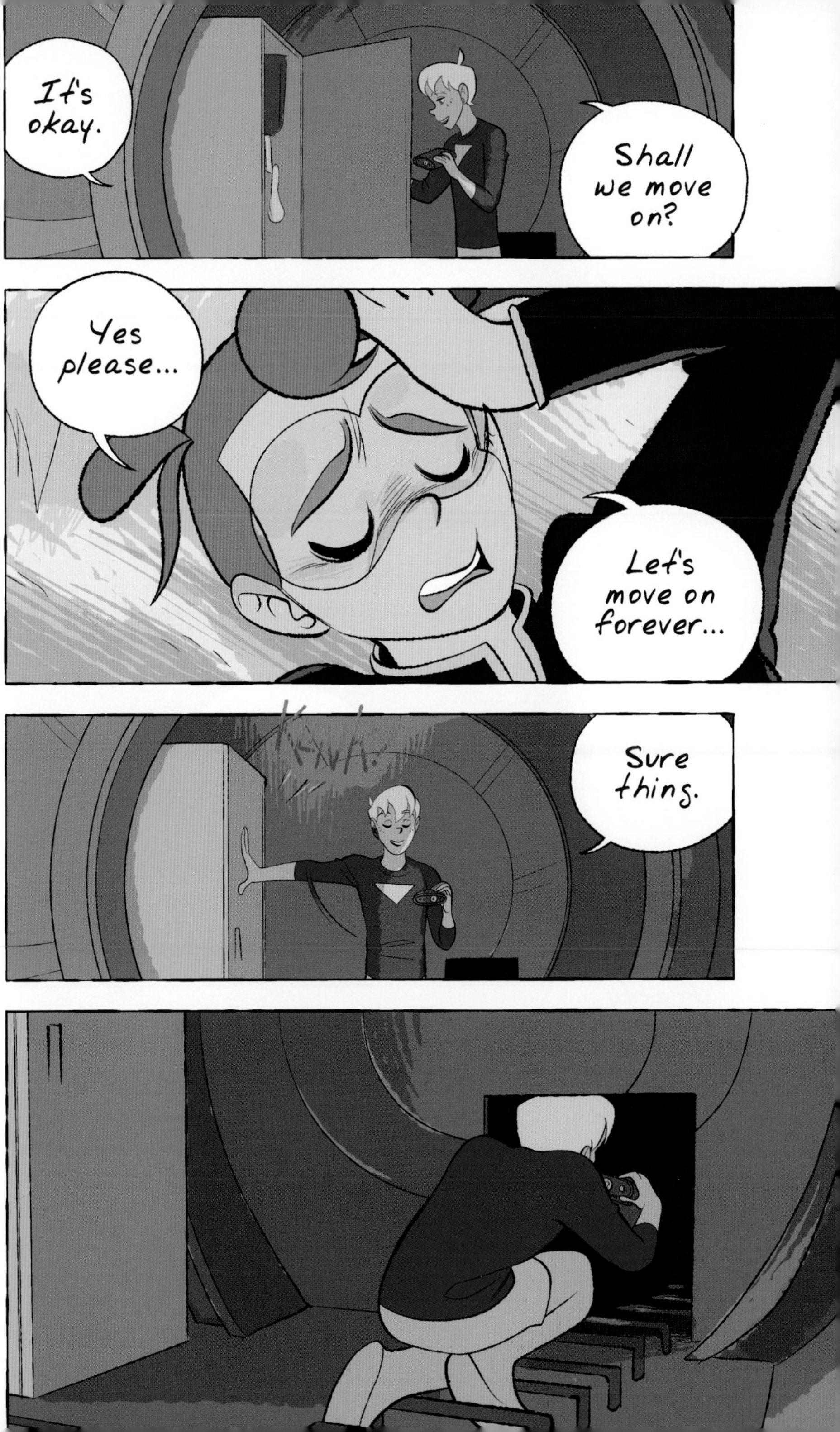
It's okay.
Shall we move on?
Yes please...
Let's move on forever...
Sure thing.

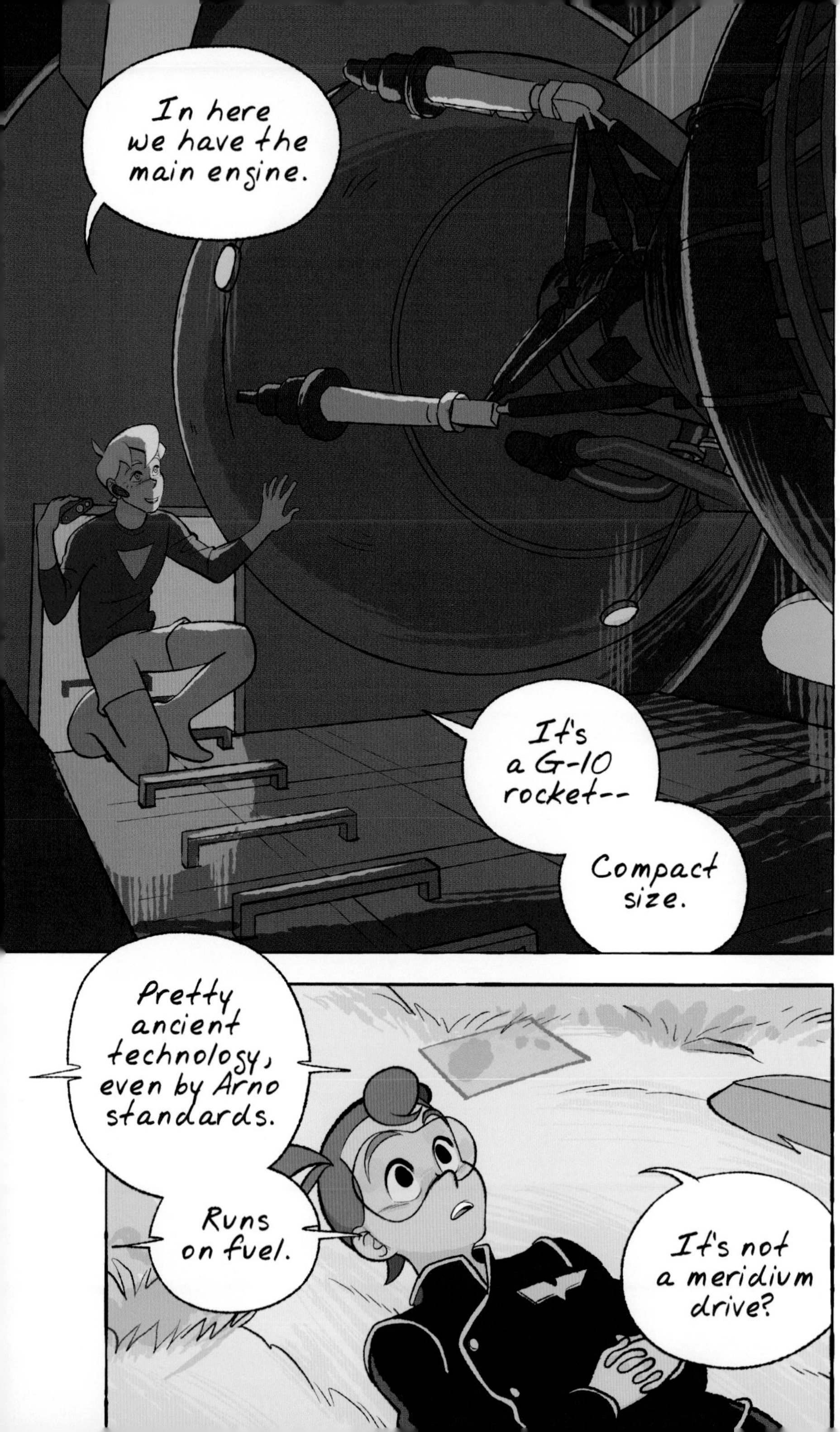
In here we have the main engine.
It's a G-10 rocket--
Compact size.
Pretty ancient technology, even by Arno standards.
Runs on fuel.
It's not a meridium drive?

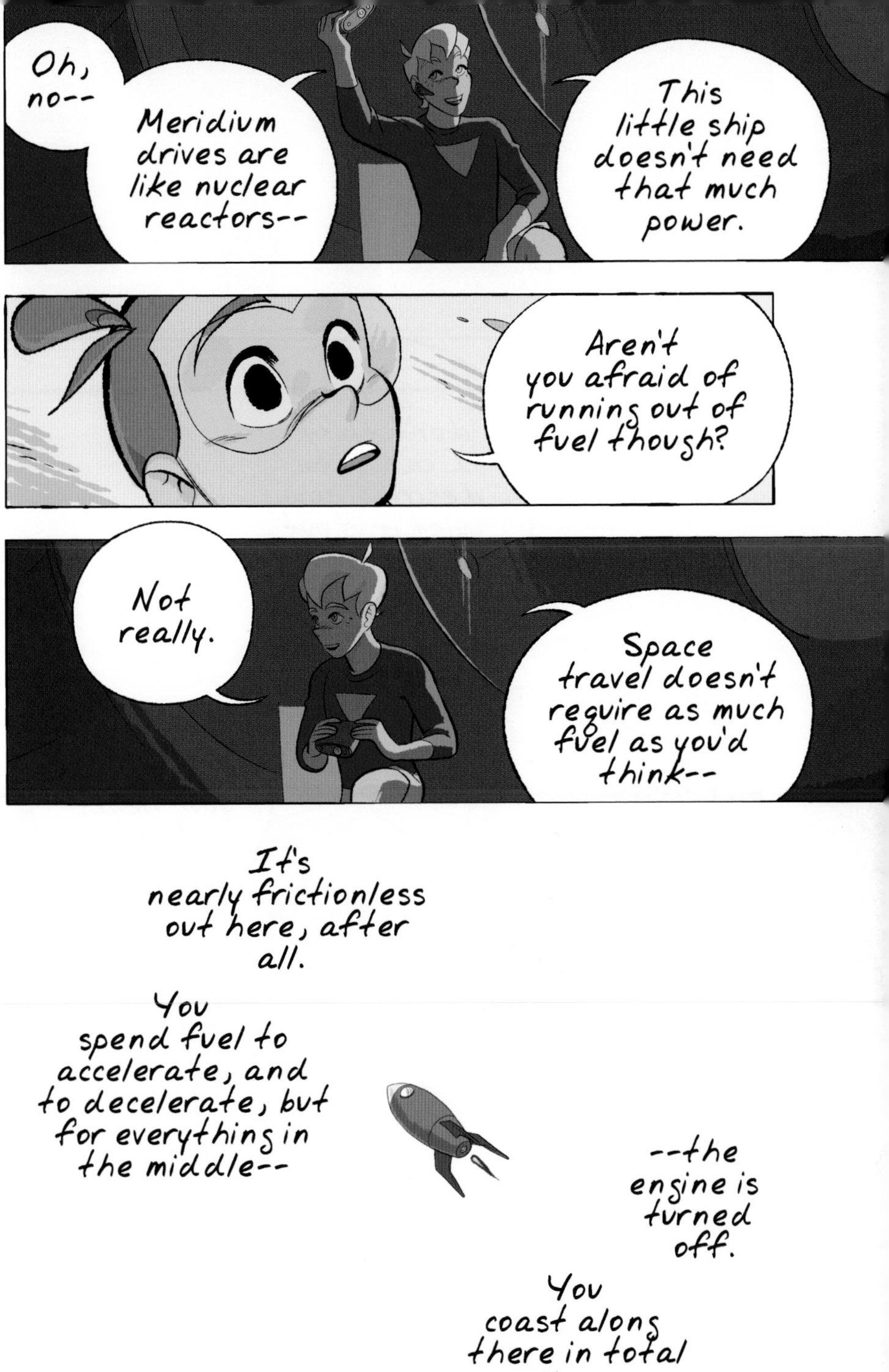
Oh, no--
Meridium drives are like nuclear reactors--
This little ship doesn't need that much power.
Aren't you afraid of running out of fuel though?
Not really.
Space travel doesn't require as much fuel as you'd think--
It's nearly frictionless out here, after all.
You spend fuel to accelerate, and to decelerate, but for everything in the middle--
--the engine is turned off.
You coast along there in total silence.

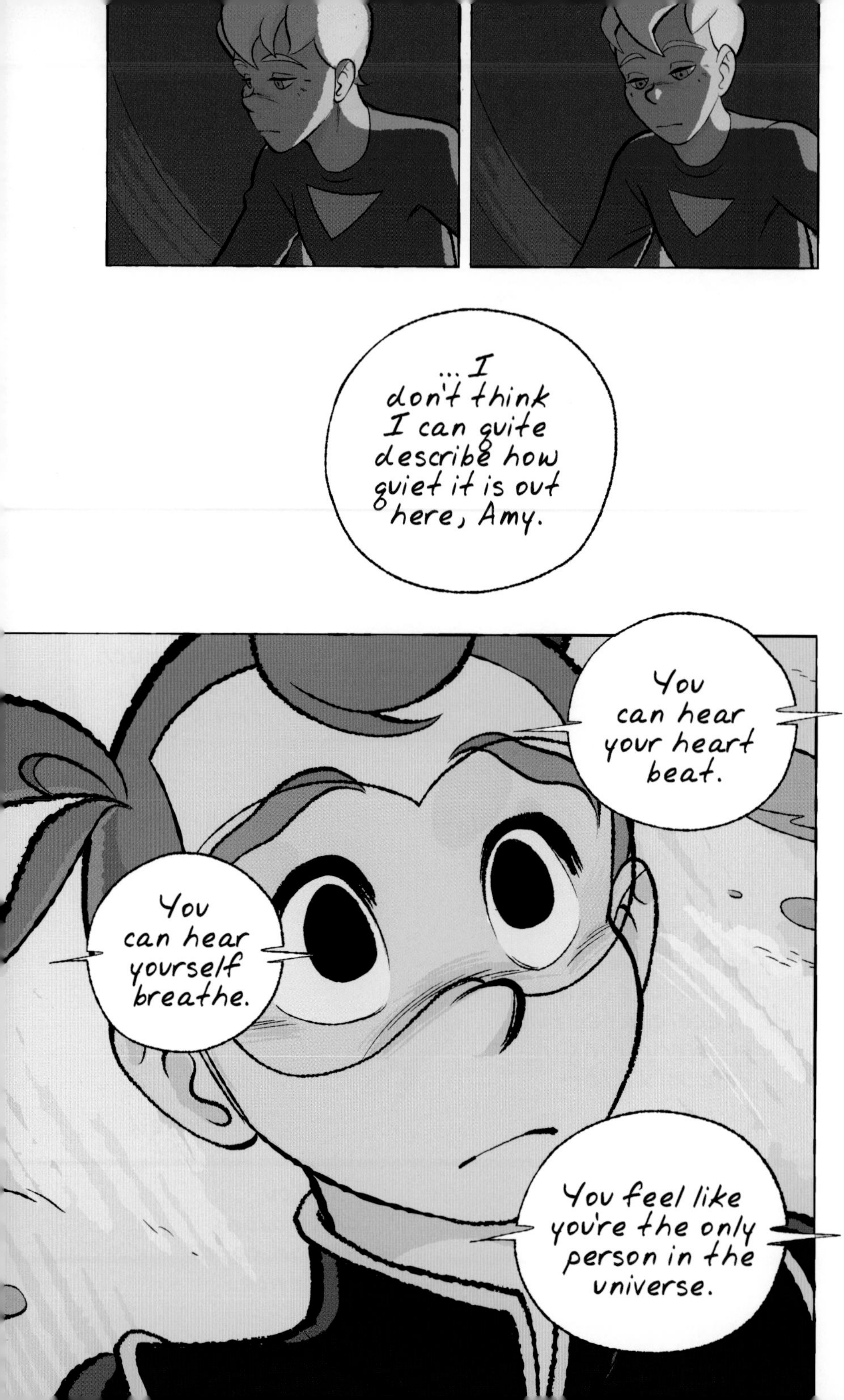
...I don't think I can quite describe how quiet it is out here, Amy.
You can hear your heart beat.
You can hear yourself breathe.
You feel like you're the only person in the universe.

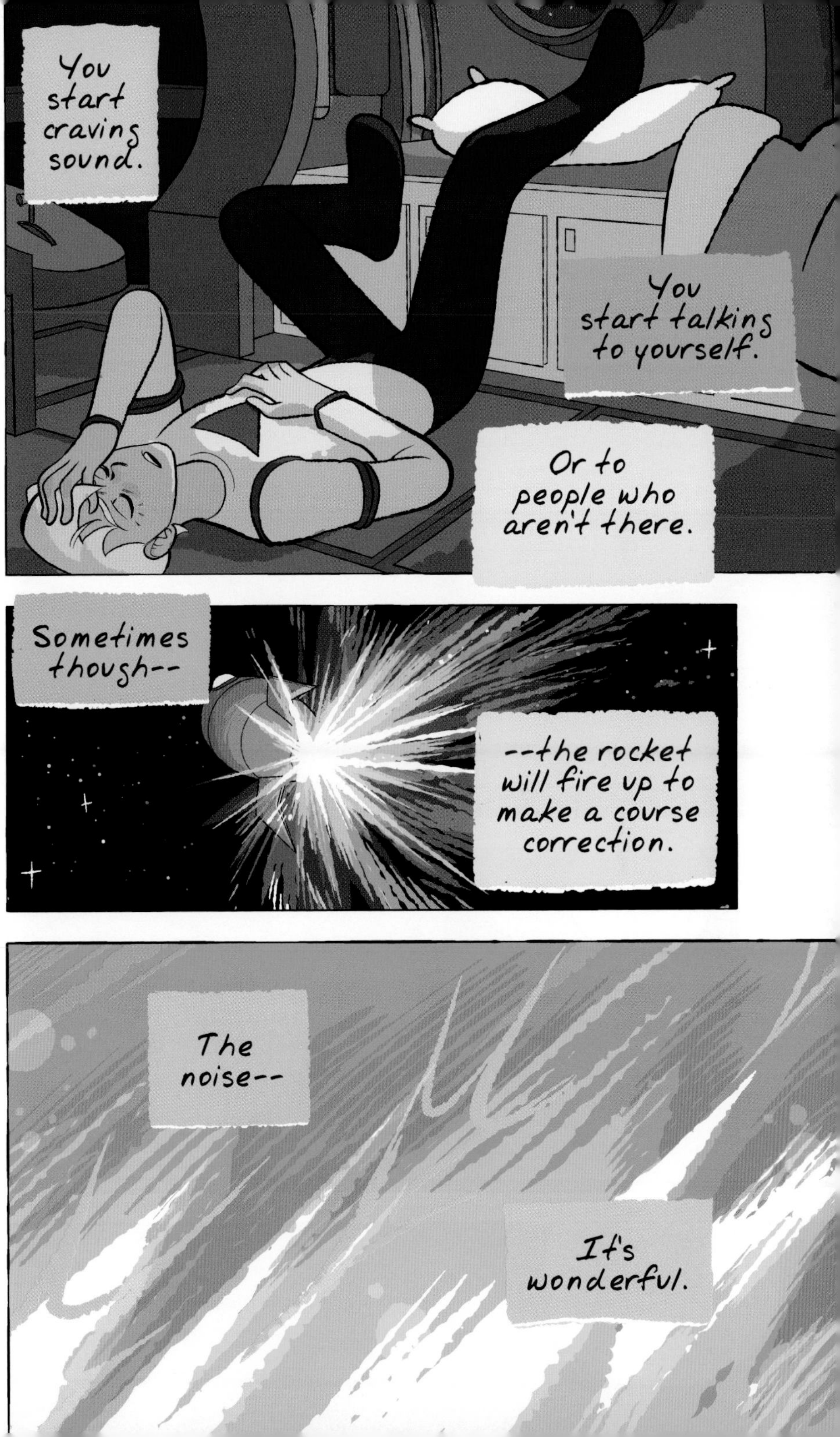
You start craving sound.
You start talking to yourself.
Or to people who aren't there.
Sometimes though--
--the rocket will fire up to make a course correction.
The noise--
It's wonderful.

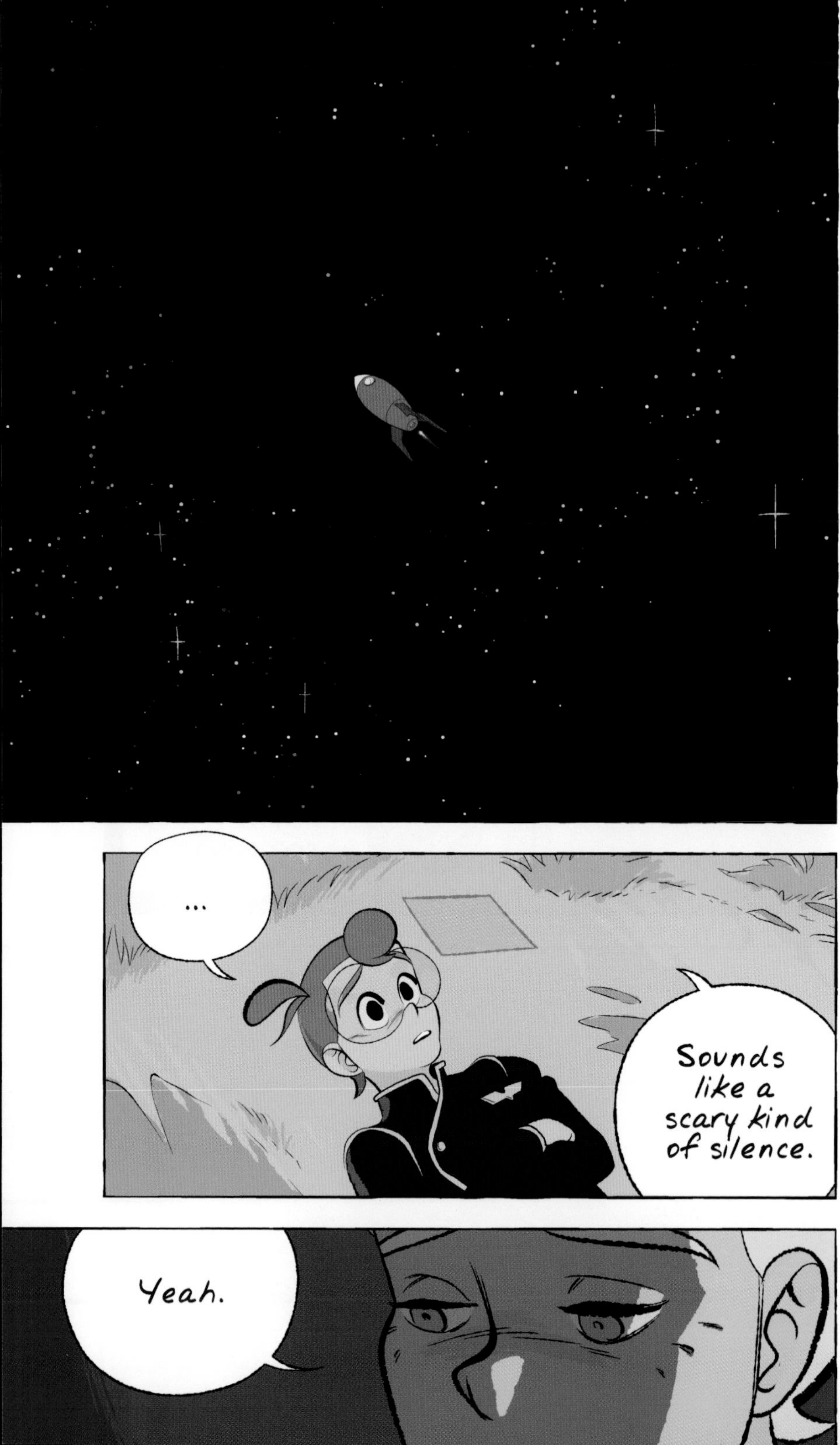
...
Sounds like a scary kind of silence.
Yeah.

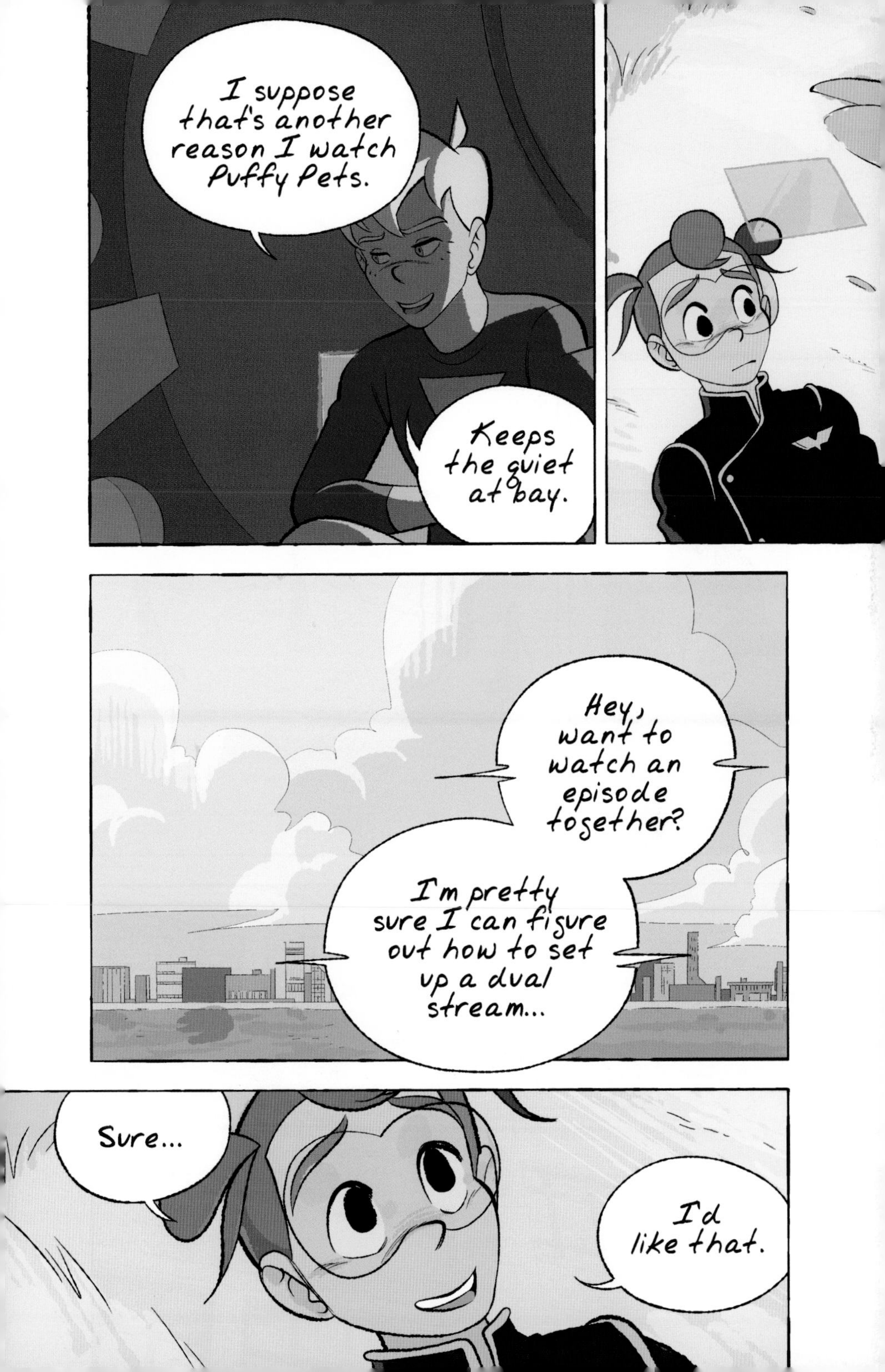
I suppose that's another reason I watch Puffy Pets.
Keeps the quiet at bay.
Hey, want to watch an episode together?
I'm pretty sure I can figure out how to set up a dual stream...
Sure...
I'd like that.

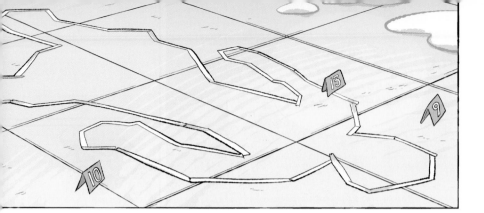

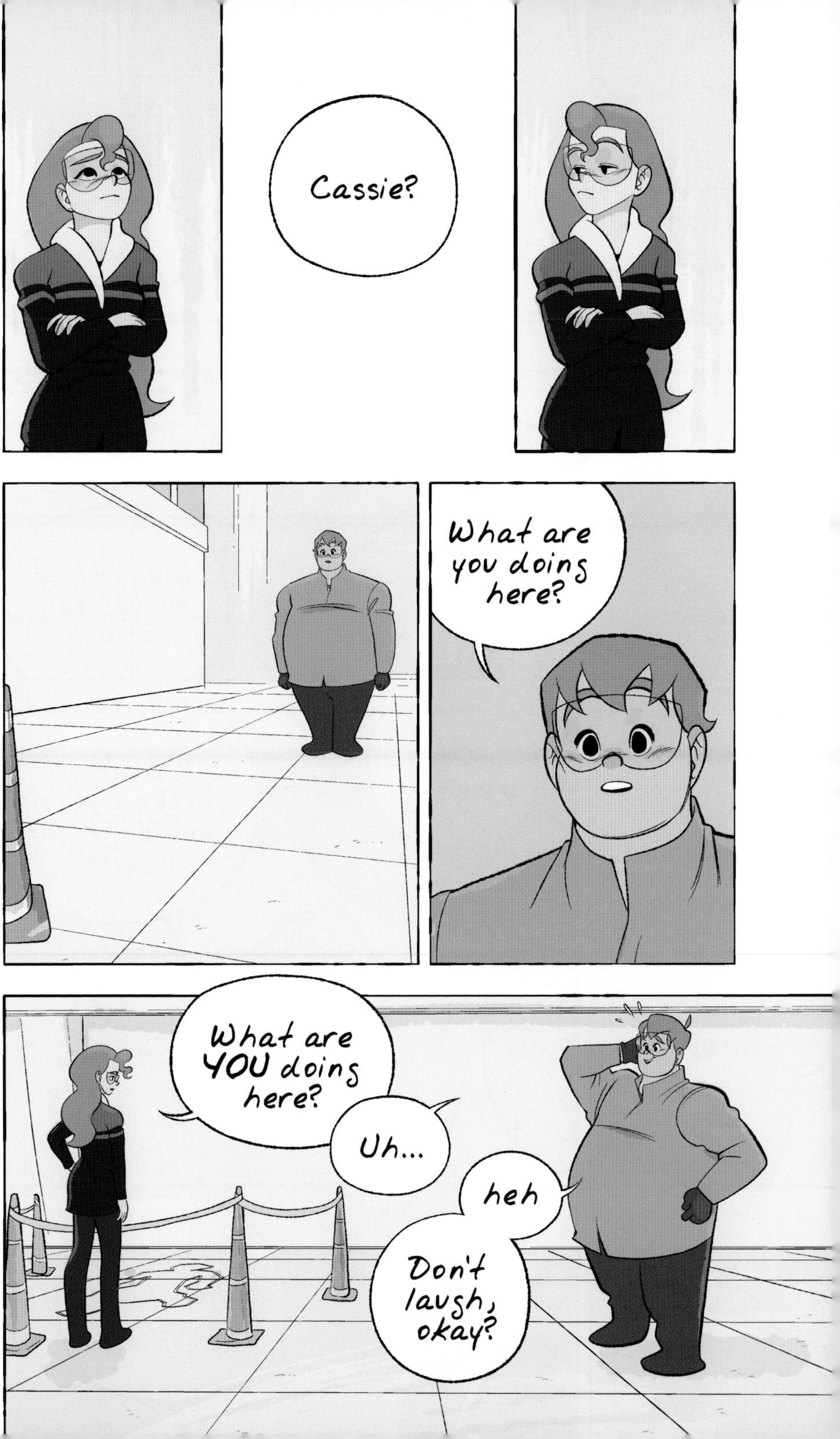
Cassie?
What are you doing here?
What are YOU doing here?
Uh...
heh
Don't laugh, okay?

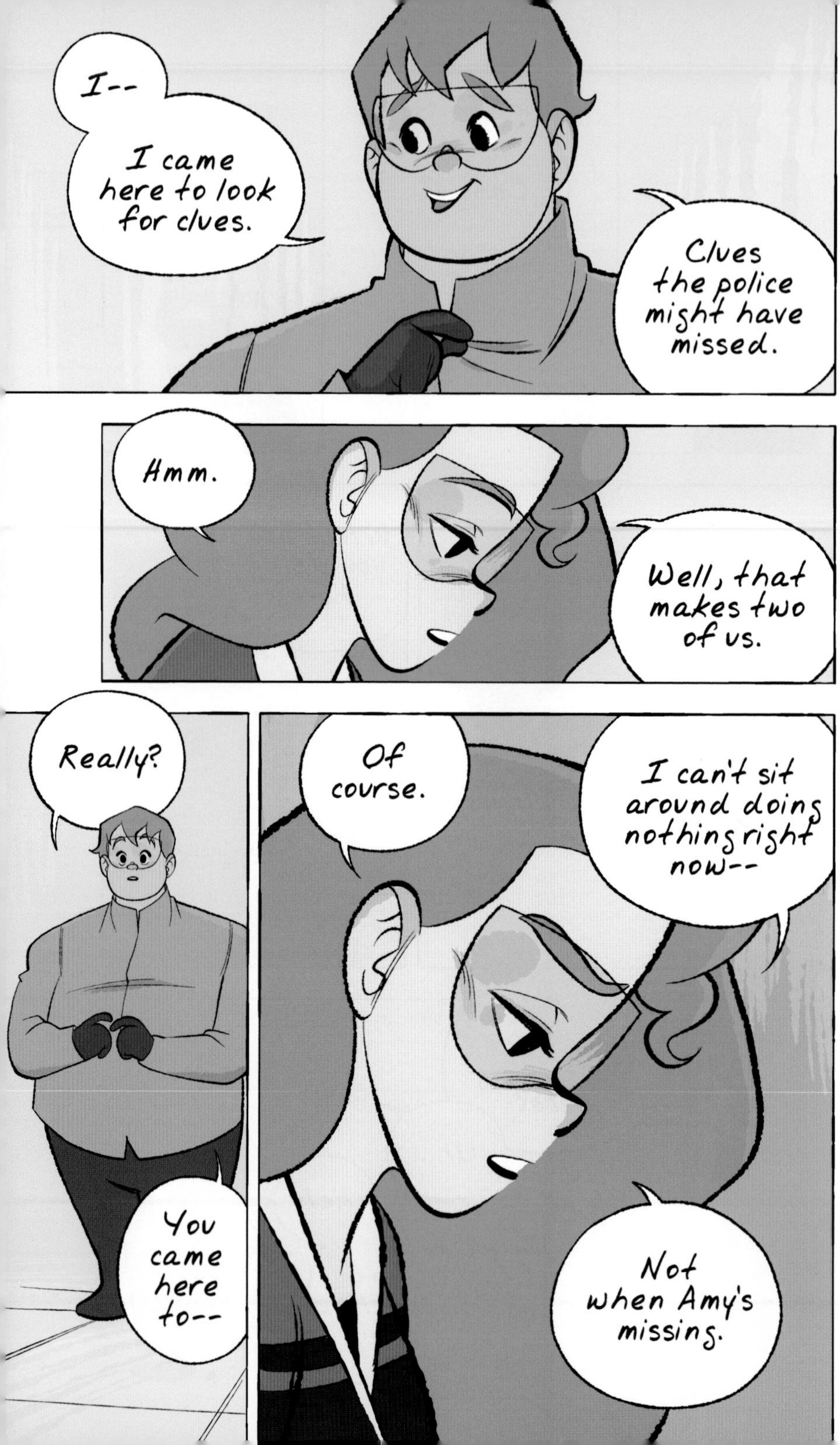
I--
I came here to look for clues.
Clues the police might have missed.
Hmm.
Well, that makes two of us.
Really?
Of course.
I can't sit around doing nothing right now--
You came here to--
Not when Amy's missing.

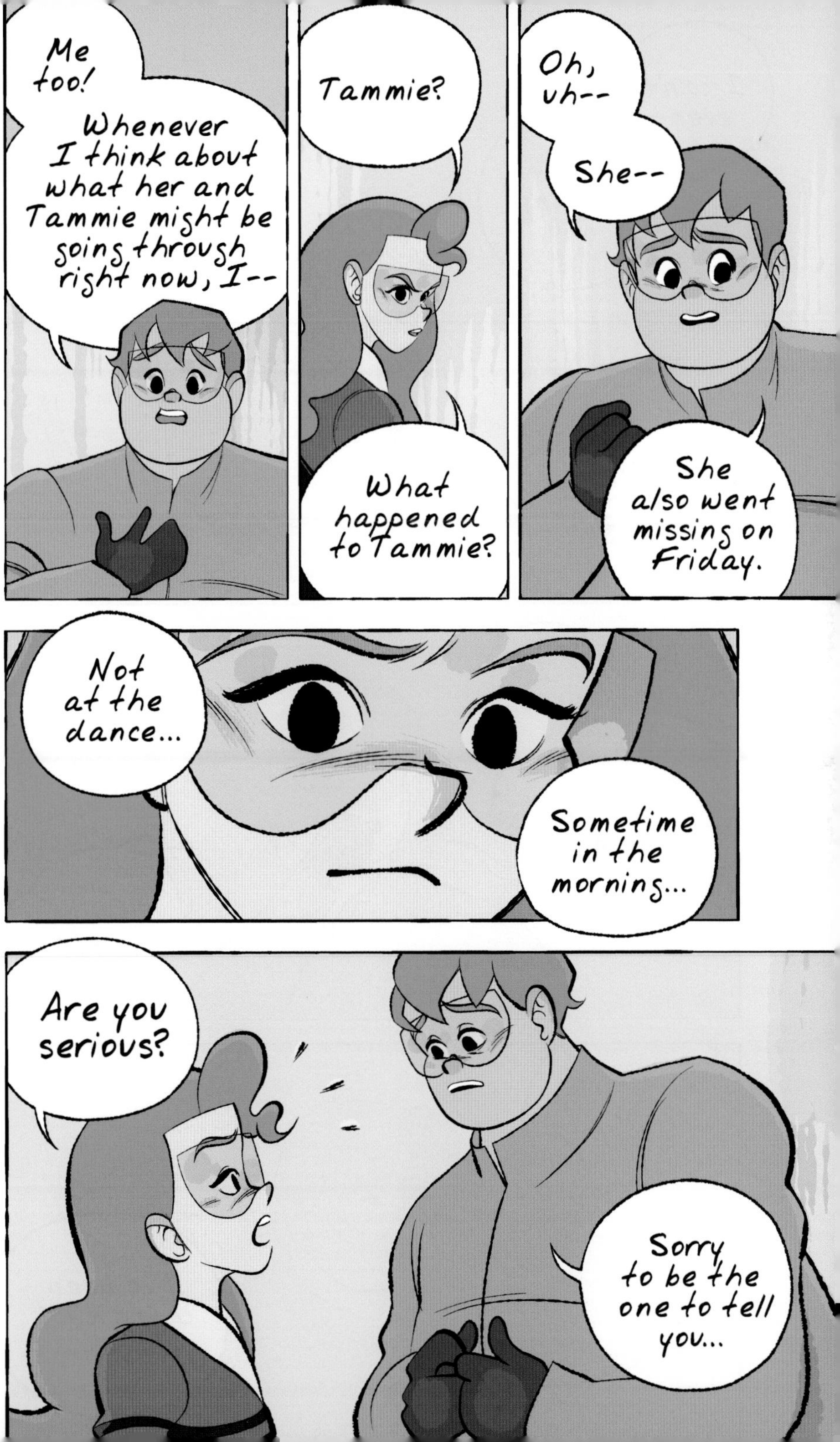
Me too!
Whenever I think about what her and Tammie might be going through right now, I--
Tammie?
What happened to Tammie?
Oh, uh--
She--
She also went missing on Friday.
Not at the dance...
Sometime in the morning...
Are you serious?
Sorry to be the one to tell you...

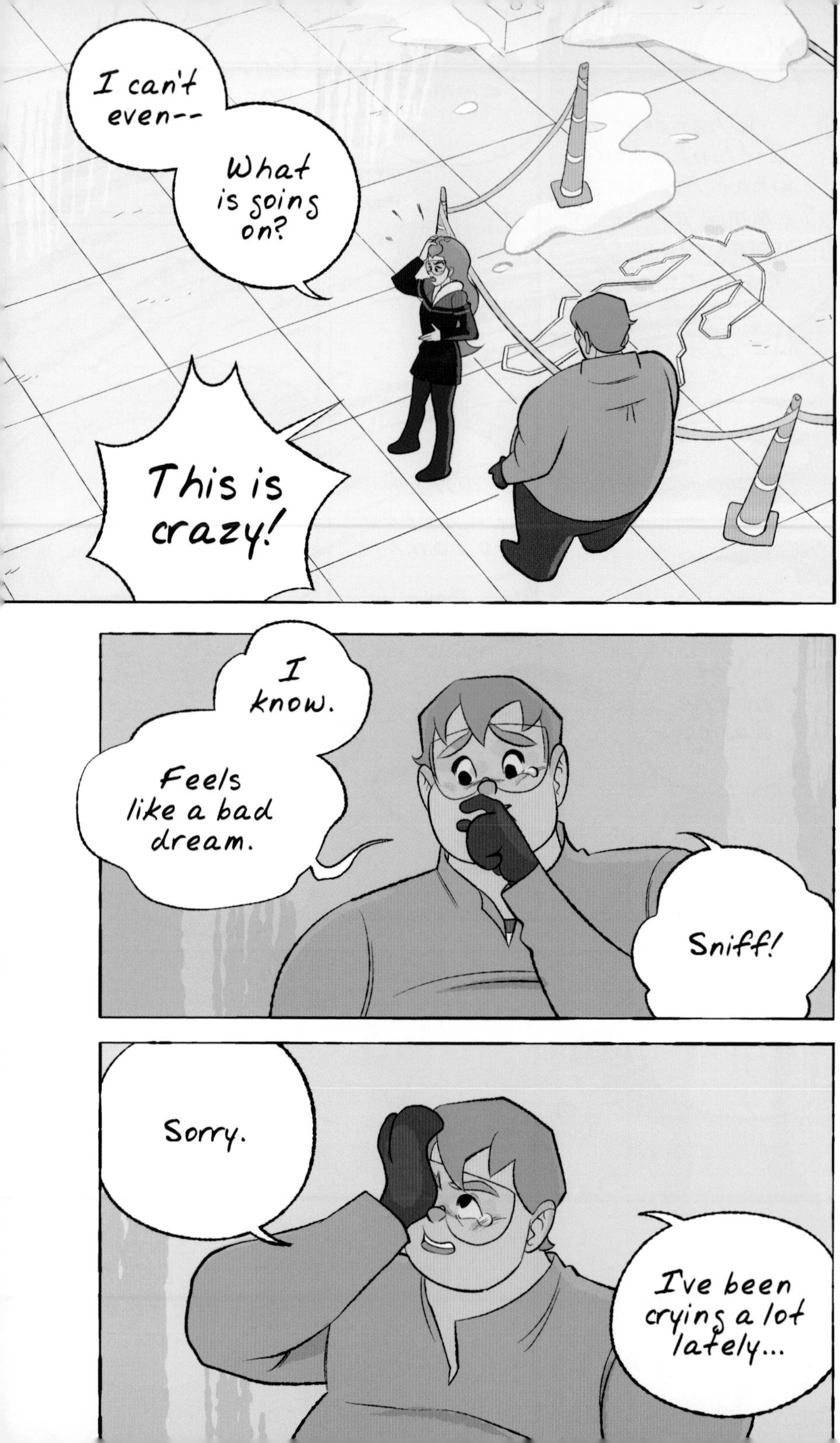
I can't even--
What is going on?
This is crazy!
I know.
Feels like a bad dream.
Sniff!
Sorry.
I've been crying a lot lately...

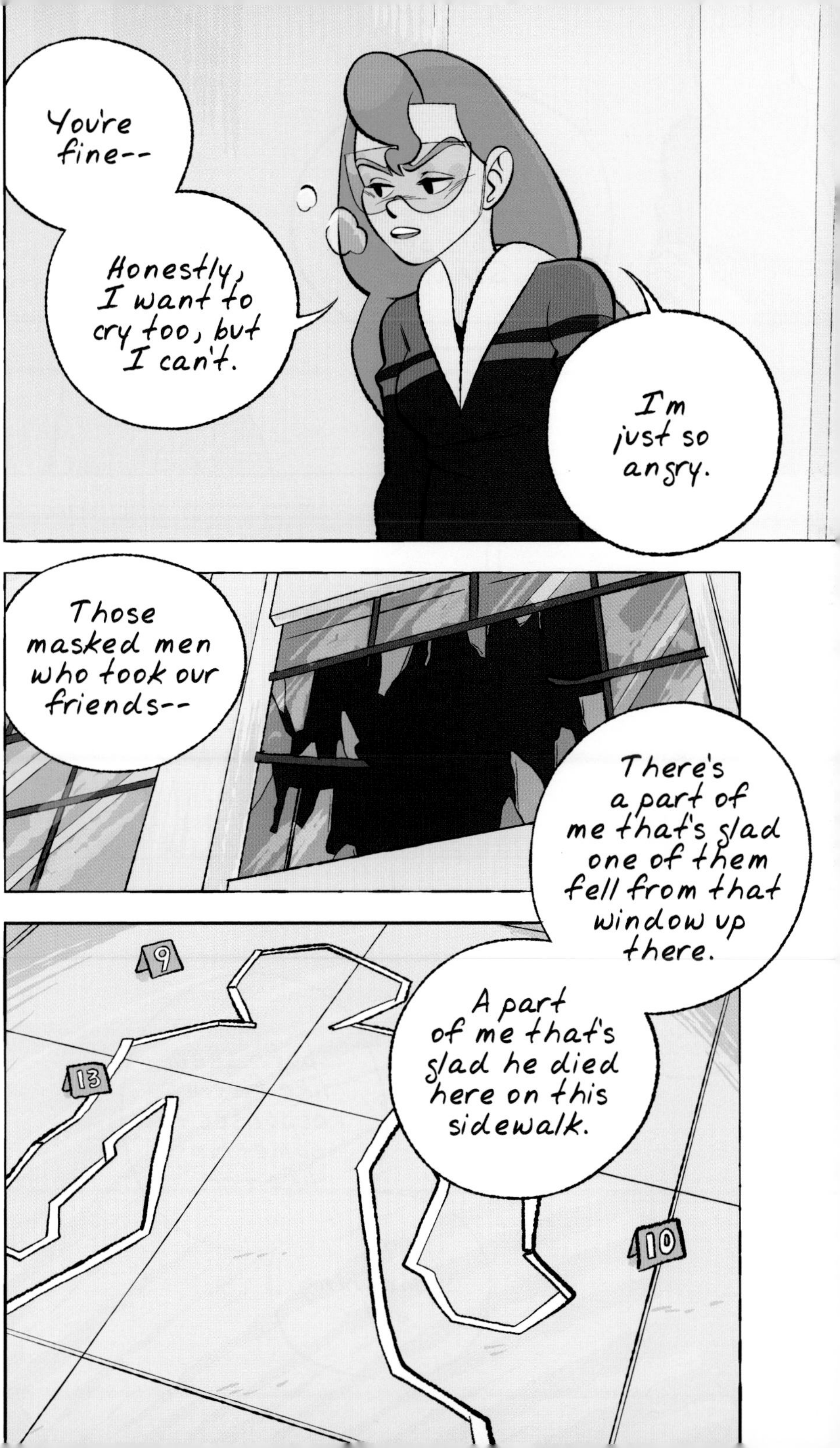

You're fine--
Honestly, I want to cry too, but I can't.
I'm just so angry.
Those masked men who took our friends--
There's a part of me that's glad one of them fell from that window up there.
A part of me that's glad he died here on this sidewalk.
9
13
10

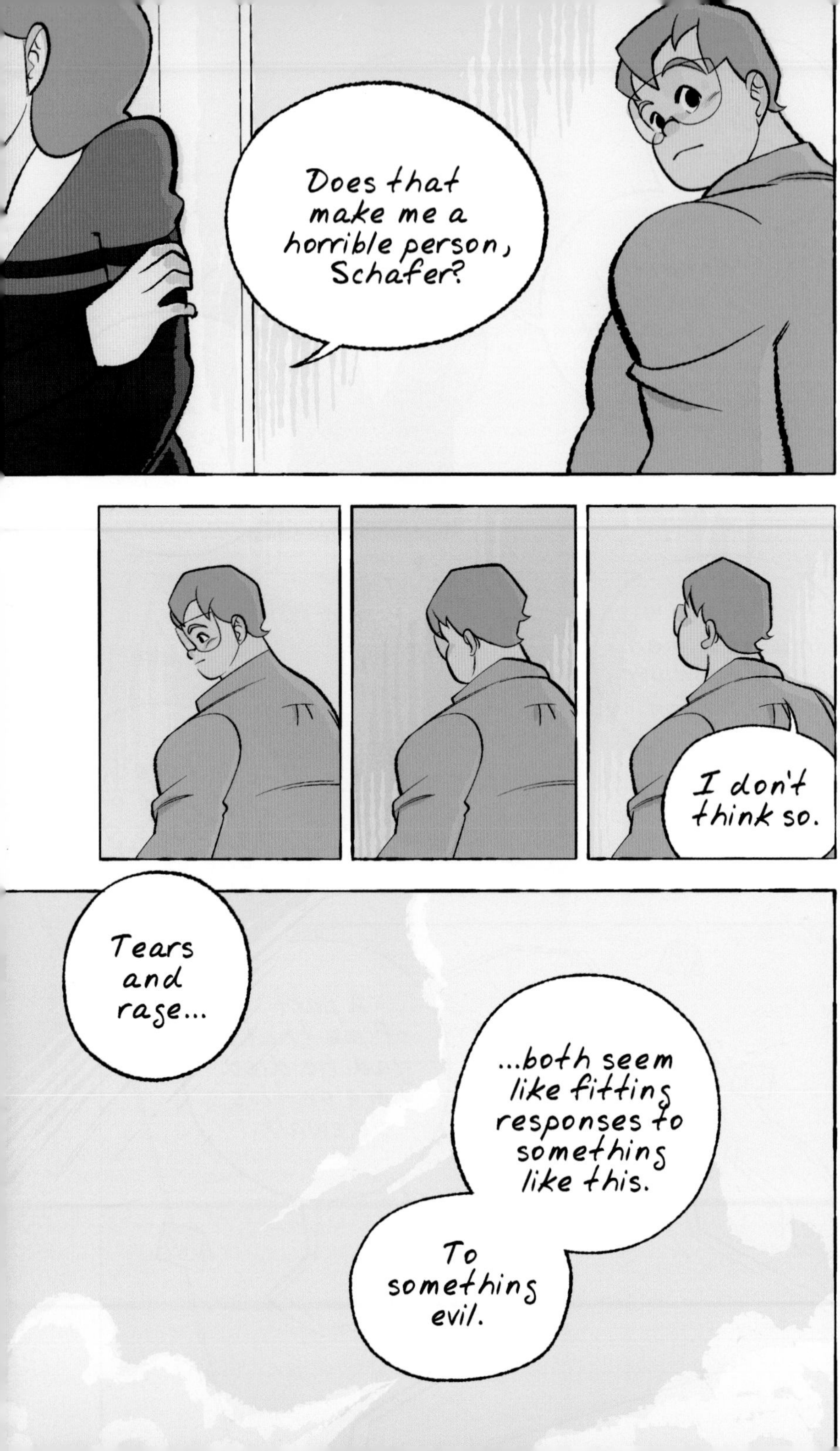
Does that make me a horrible person, Schafer?
I don't think so.
Tears and rage...
...both seem like fitting responses to something like this.
To something evil.

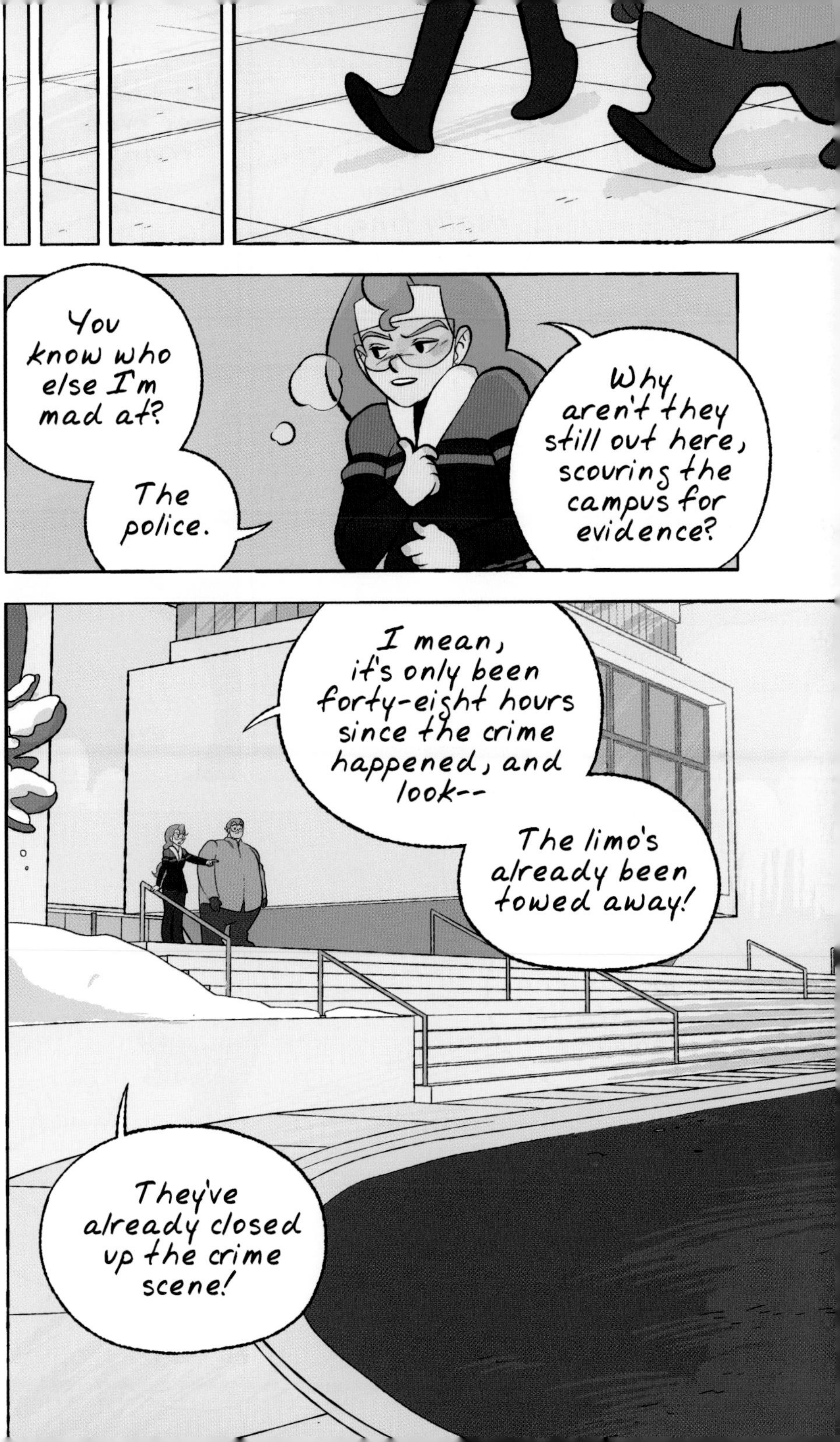
You know who else I'm mad at?
The police.
Why aren't they still out here, scouring the campus for evidence?
I mean, it's only been forty-eight hours since the crime happened, and look--
The limo's already been towed away!
They've already closed up the crime scene!

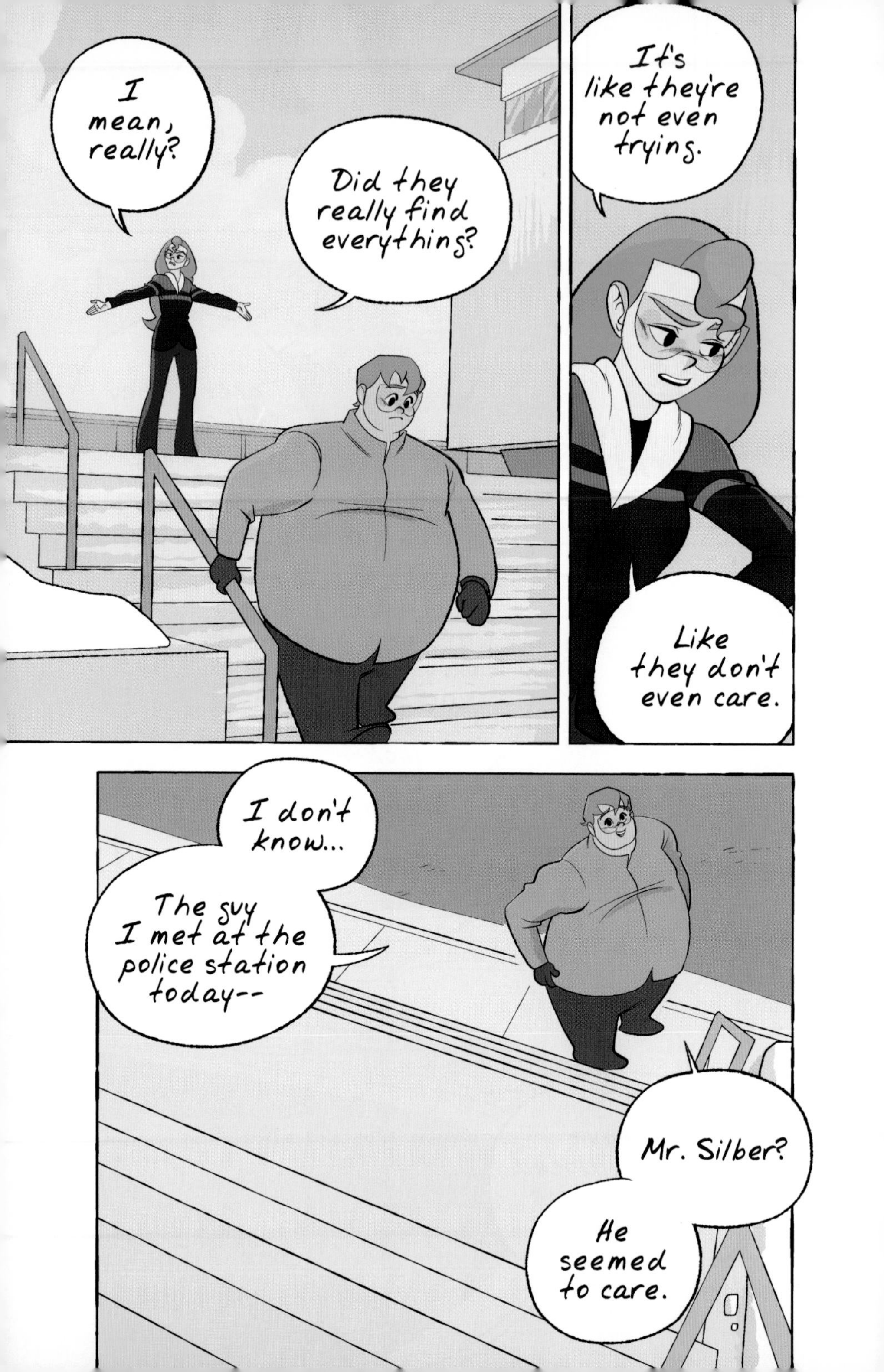
I mean, really?
Did they really find everything?
It's like they're not even trying.
Like they don't even care.
I don't know...
The guy I met at the police station today--
Mr. Silber?
He seemed to care.

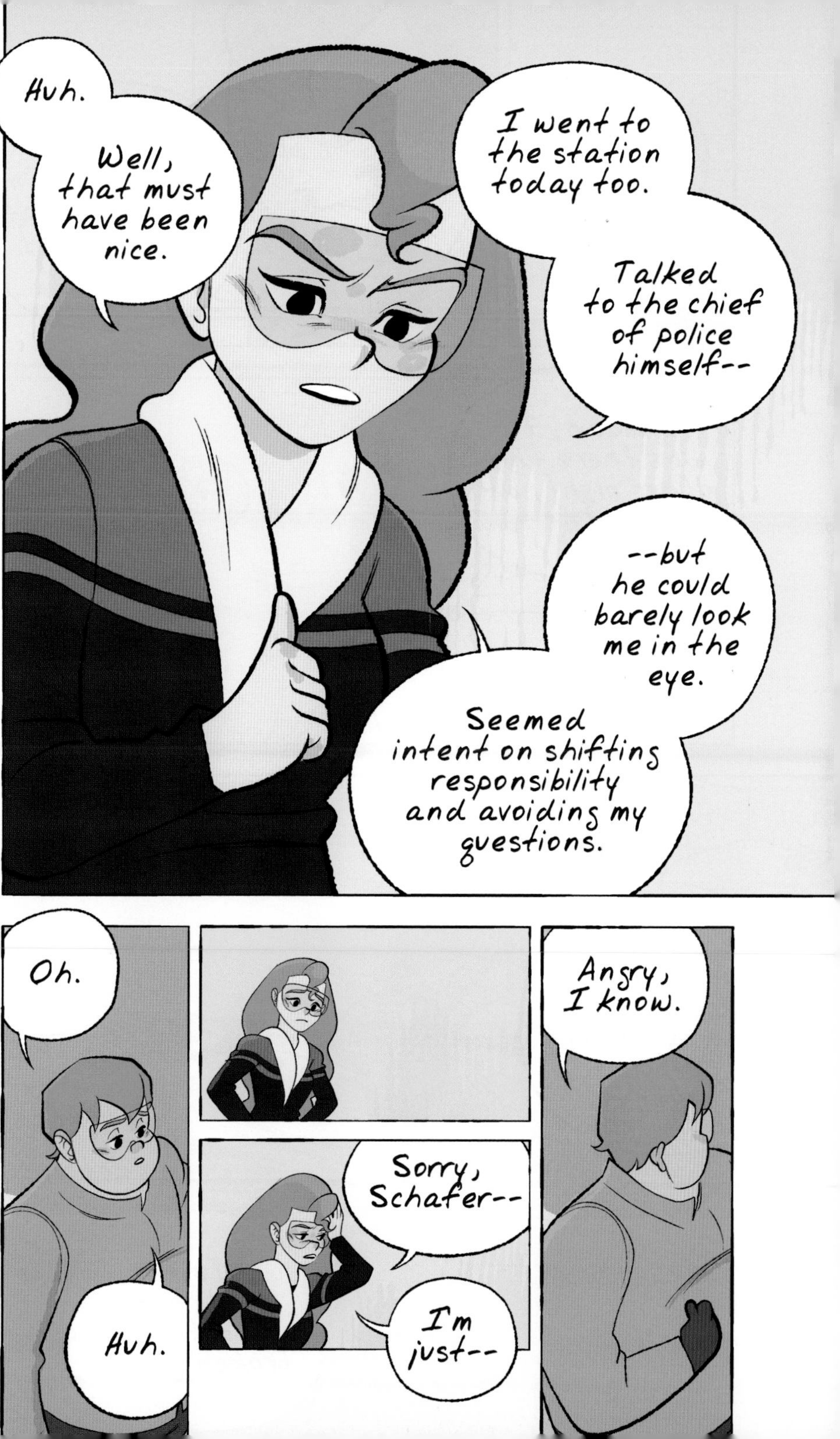
Huh.
Well, that must have been nice.
I went to the station today too.
Talked to the chief of police himself--
--but he could barely look me in the eye.
Seemed intent on shifting responsibility and avoiding my questions.
Oh.
Huh.
Sorry, Schafer--
I'm just--
Angry, I know.

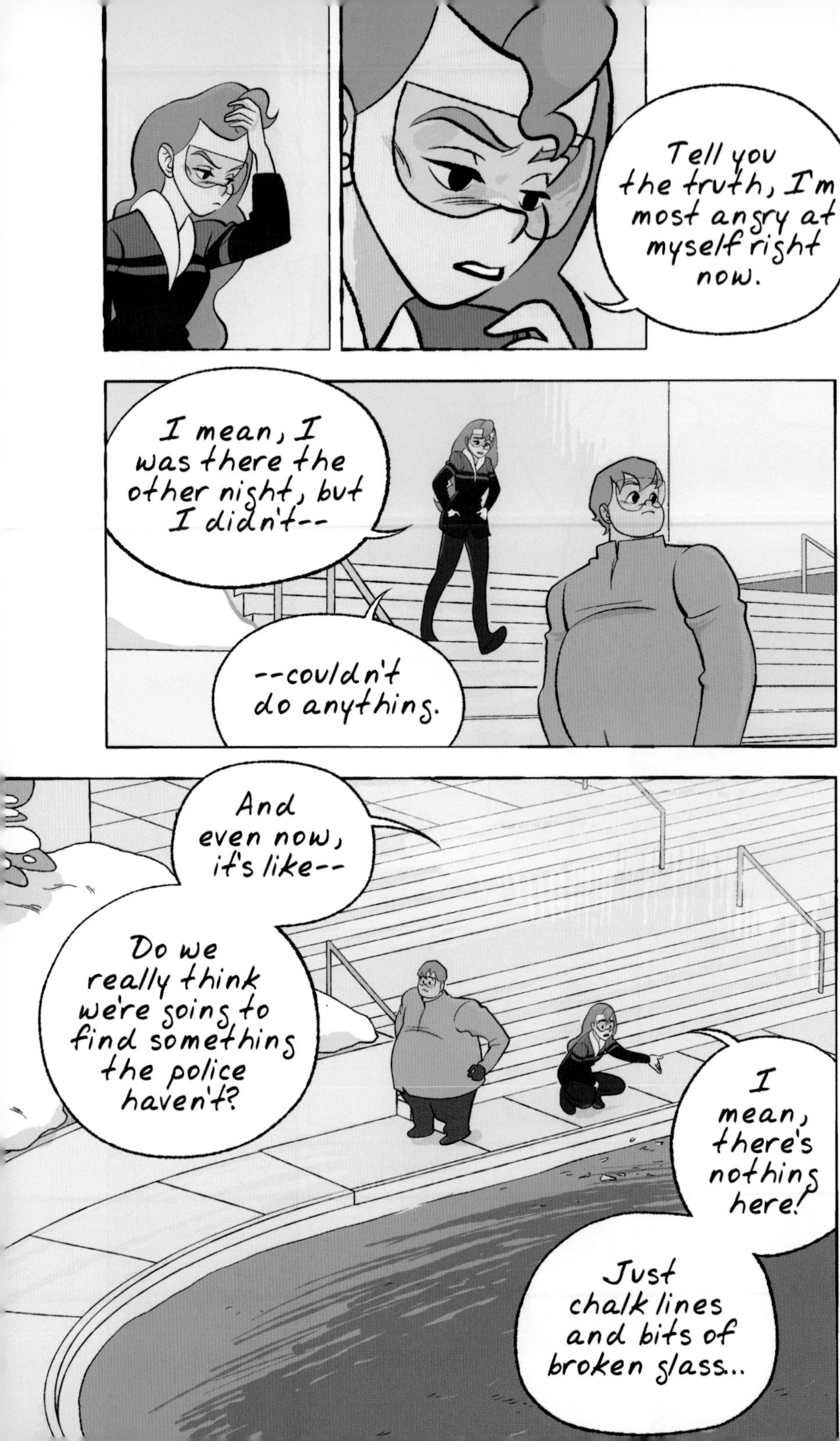
Tell you the truth, I'm most angry at myself right now.
I mean, I was there the other night, but I didn't--
--couldn't do anything.
And even now, it's like--
Do we really think we're going to find something the police haven't?
I mean, there's nothing here!
Just chalk lines and bits of broken glass..

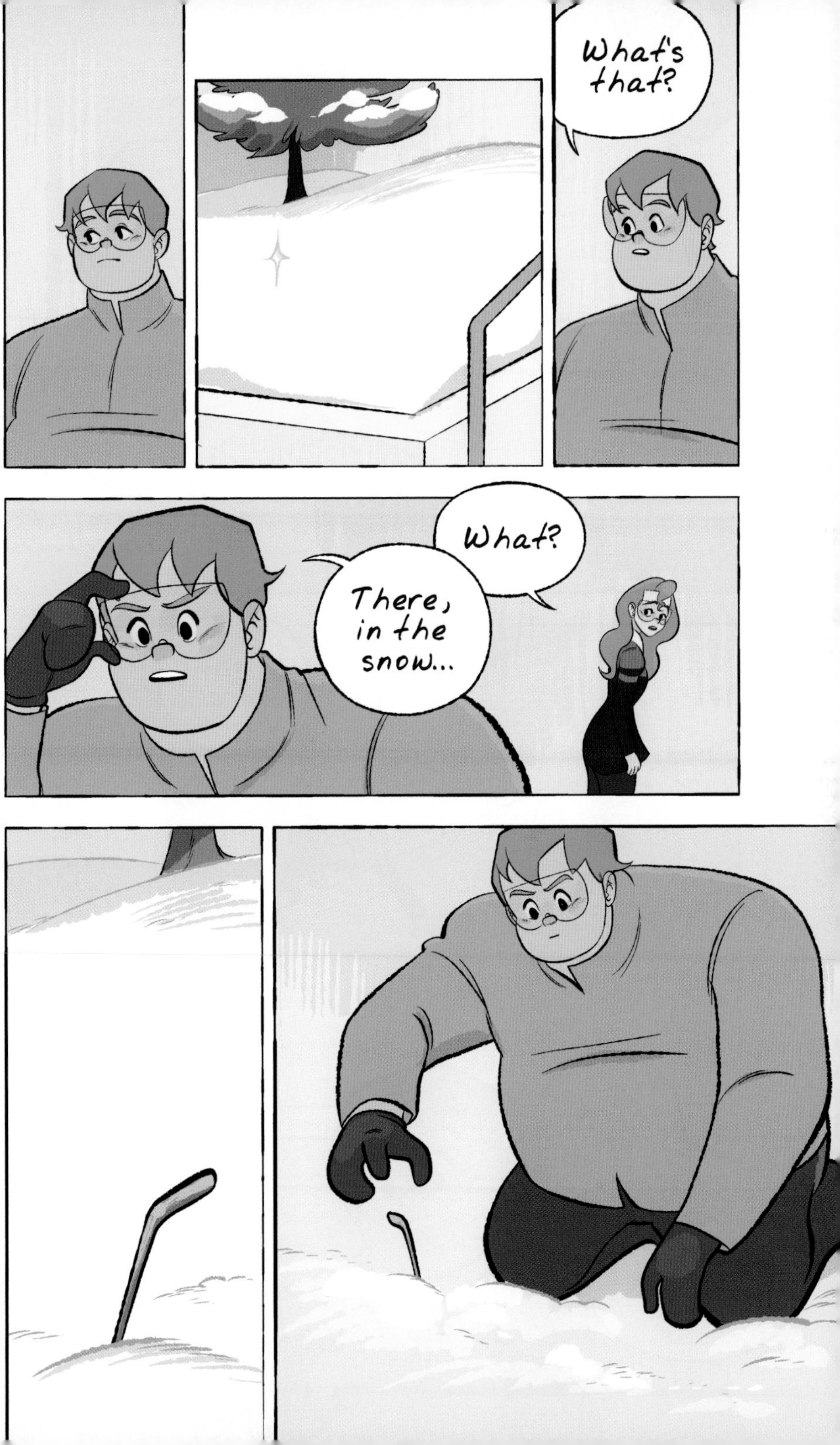
What's that?
What?
There, in the snow...

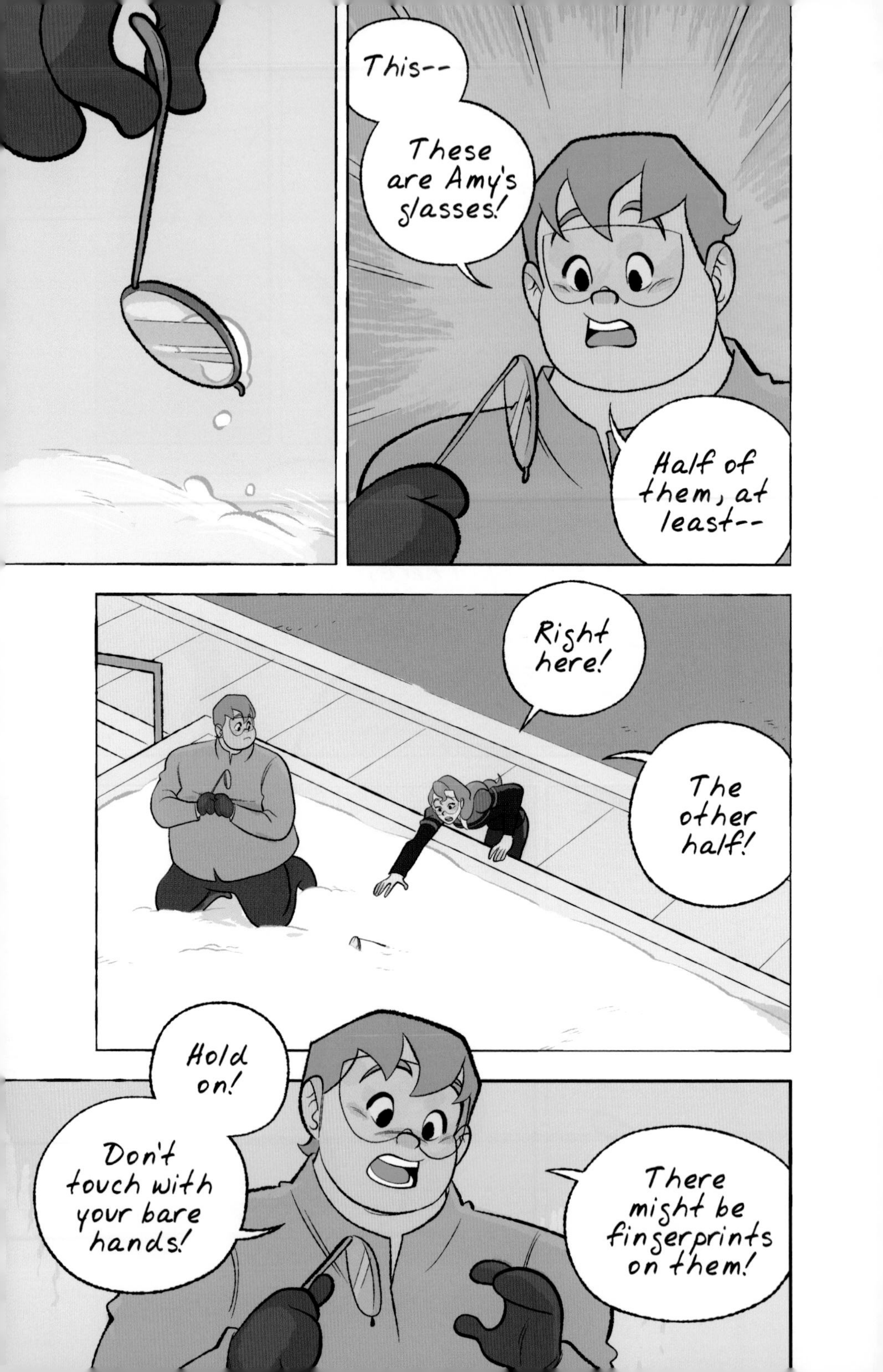
This--
These are Amy's glasses!
Half of them, at least--
Right here!
The other half!
Hold on!
Don't touch with your bare hands!
There might be fingerprints on them!

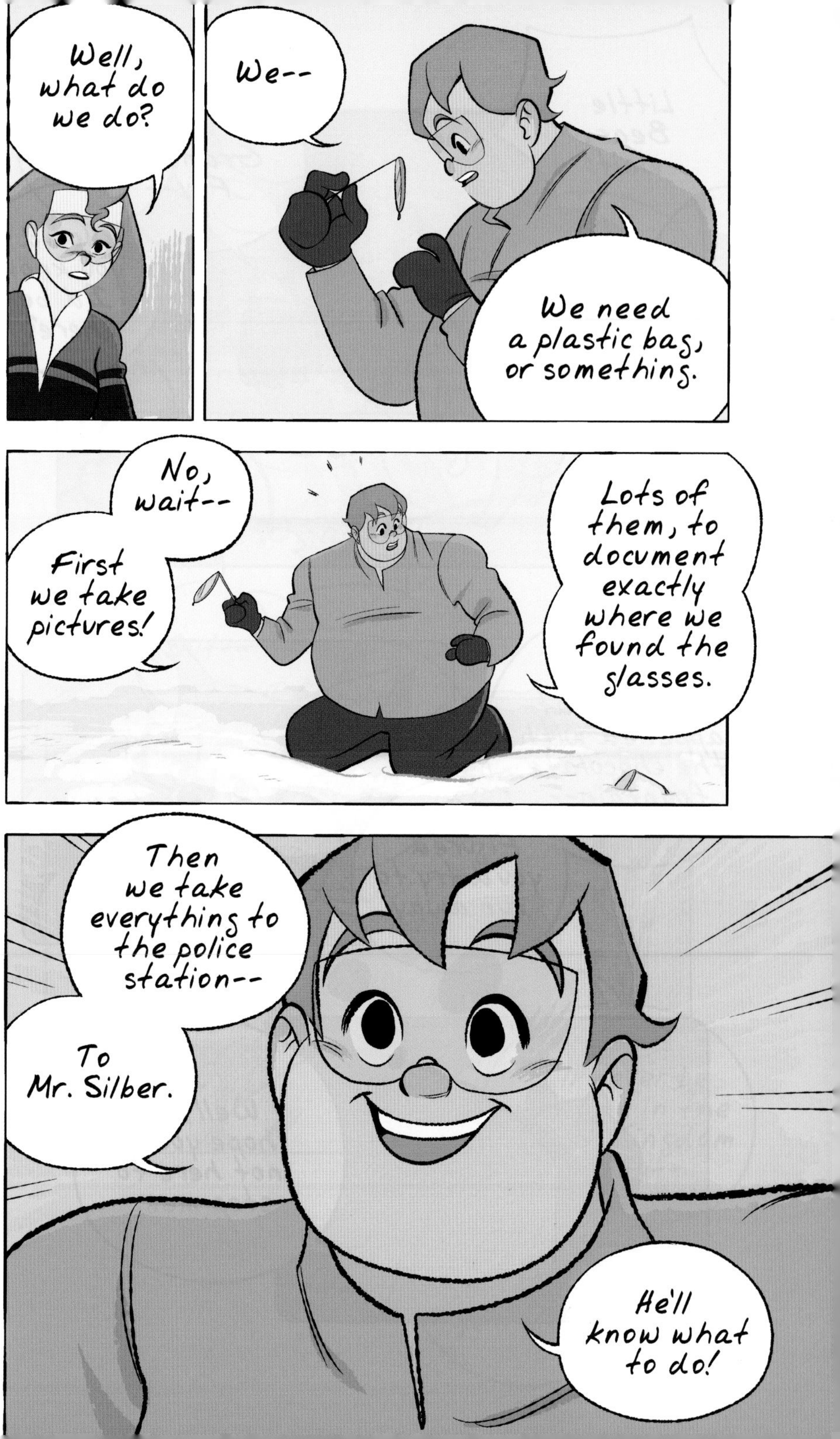
Well, what do we do?
We--
We need a plastic bag, or something.
No, wait--
First we take pictures!
Lots of them, to document exactly where we found the glasses.
Then we take everything to the police station--
To Mr. Silber.
He'll know what to do!

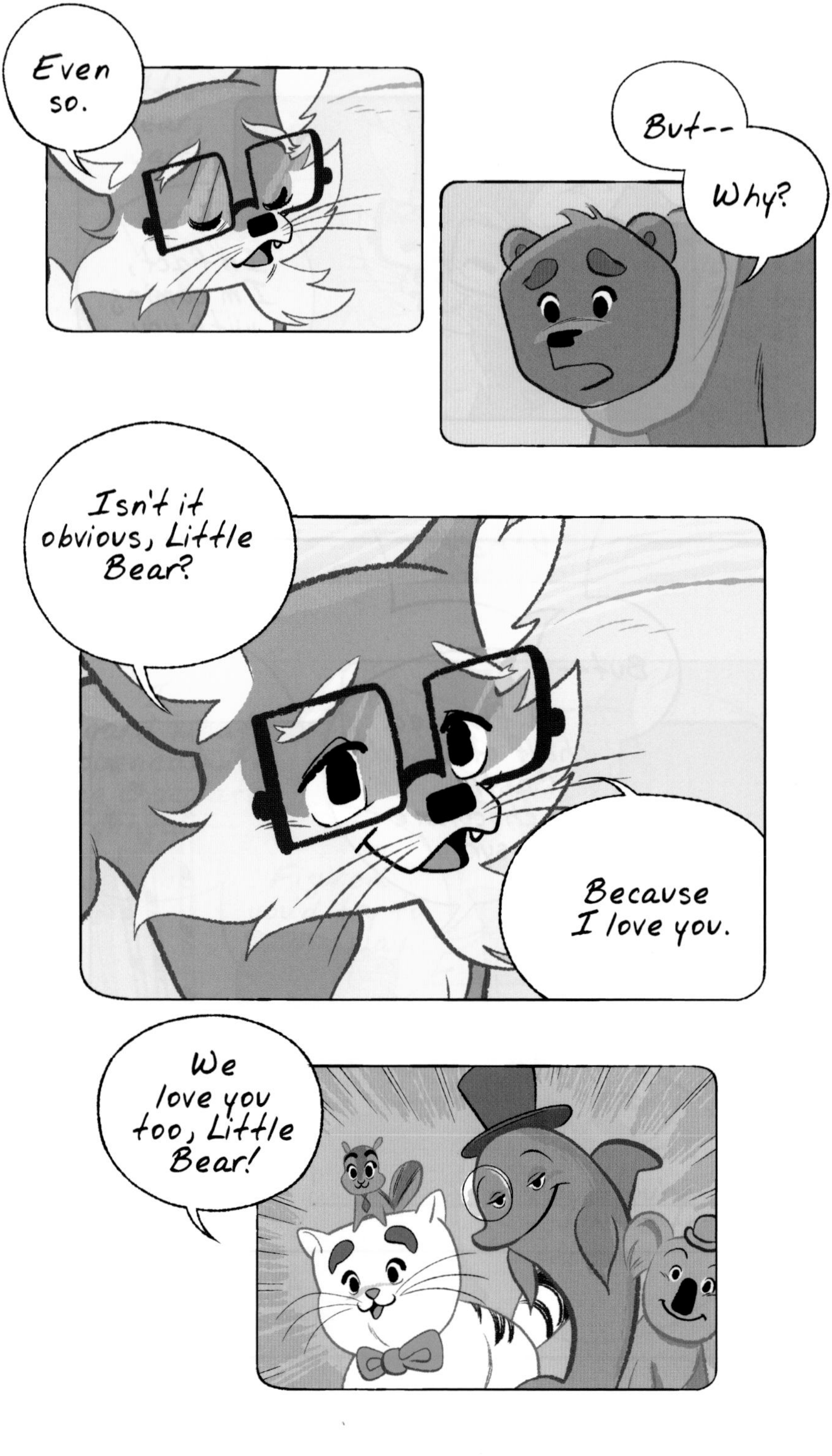
Even so.
But--
Why?
Isn't it obvious, Little Bear?
Because I love you.
We love you too, Little Bear!

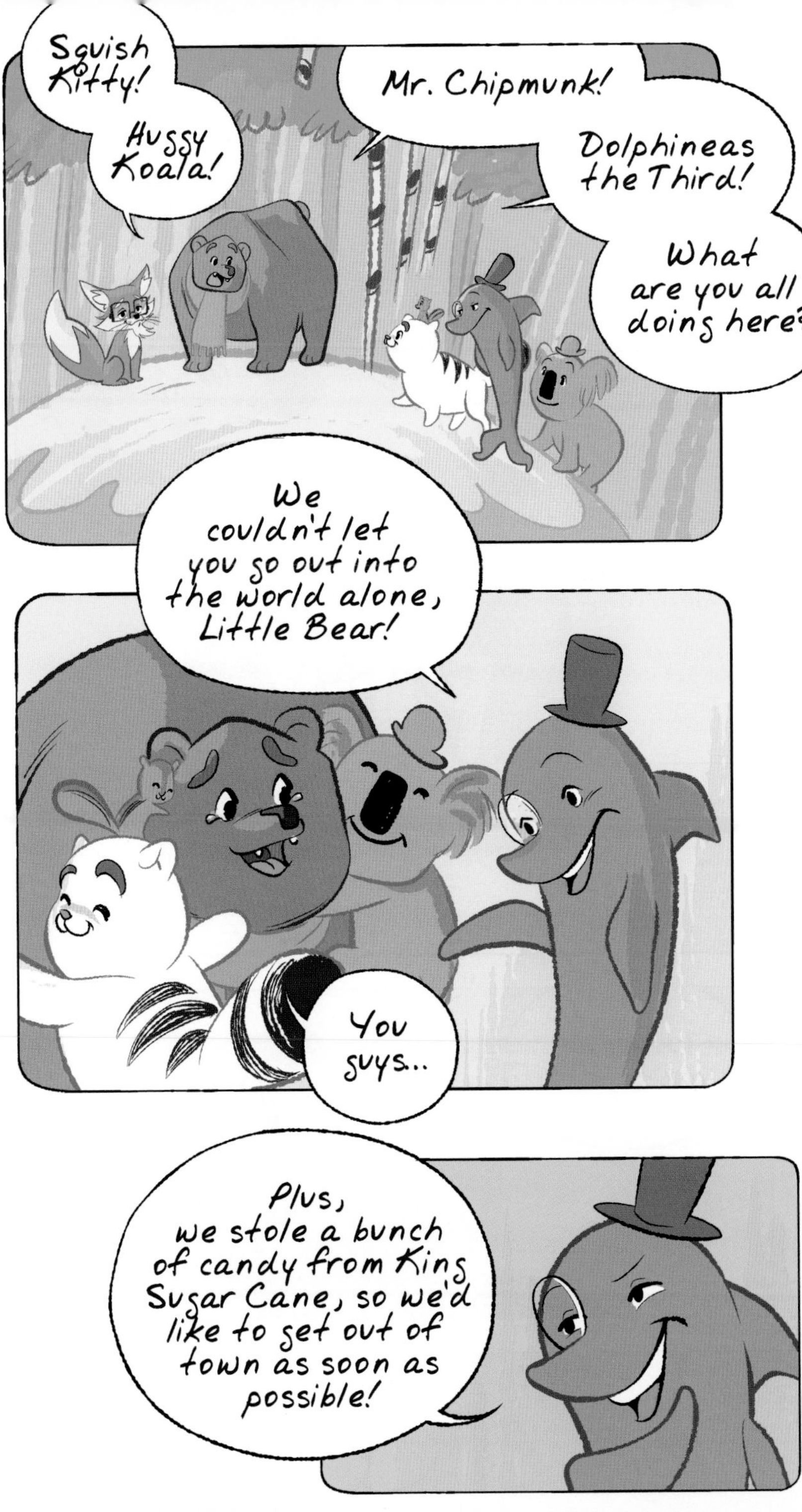

Squish Kitty!
Hussy Koala!
Mr. Chipmunk!
Dolphineas the Third!
What are you all doing here?
We couldn't let you go out into the world alone, Little Bear!
You guys...
Plus, we stole a bunch of candy from King Sugar Cane, so we'd like to get out of town as soon as possible!

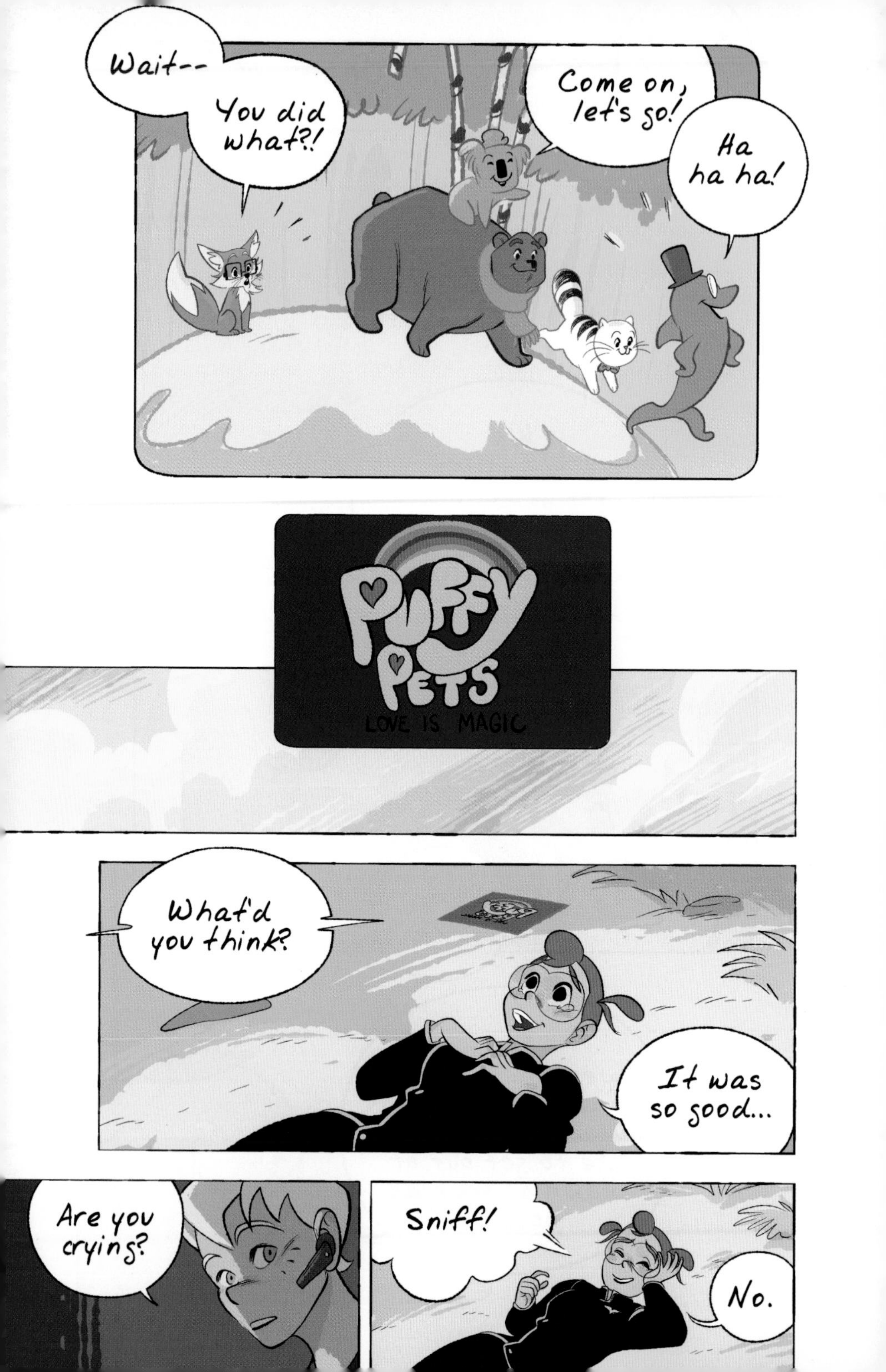
Wait--
You did what?!
Come on, let's go!
Ha ha ha!
PUFFY PETS
LOVE IS MAGIC
What'd you think?
It was so good...
Are you crying?
Sniff!
No.

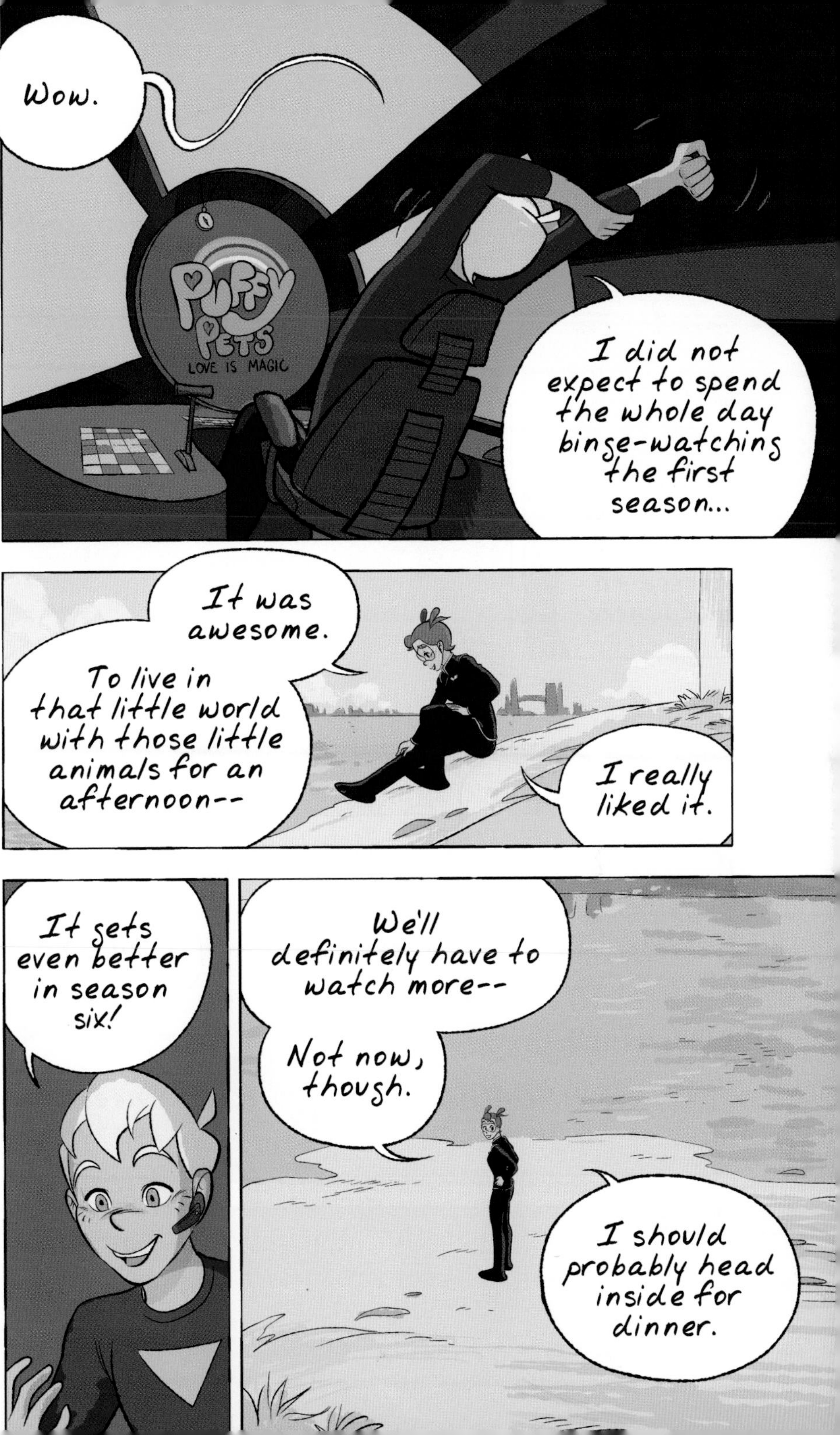
Wow.
PUFFY PETS
LOVE IS MAGIC
I did not expect to spend the whole day binge-watching the first season...
It was awesome.
To live in that little world with those little animals for an afternoon--
I really liked it.
It gets even better in season six!
We'll definitely have to watch more--
Not now, though.
I should probably head inside for dinner.

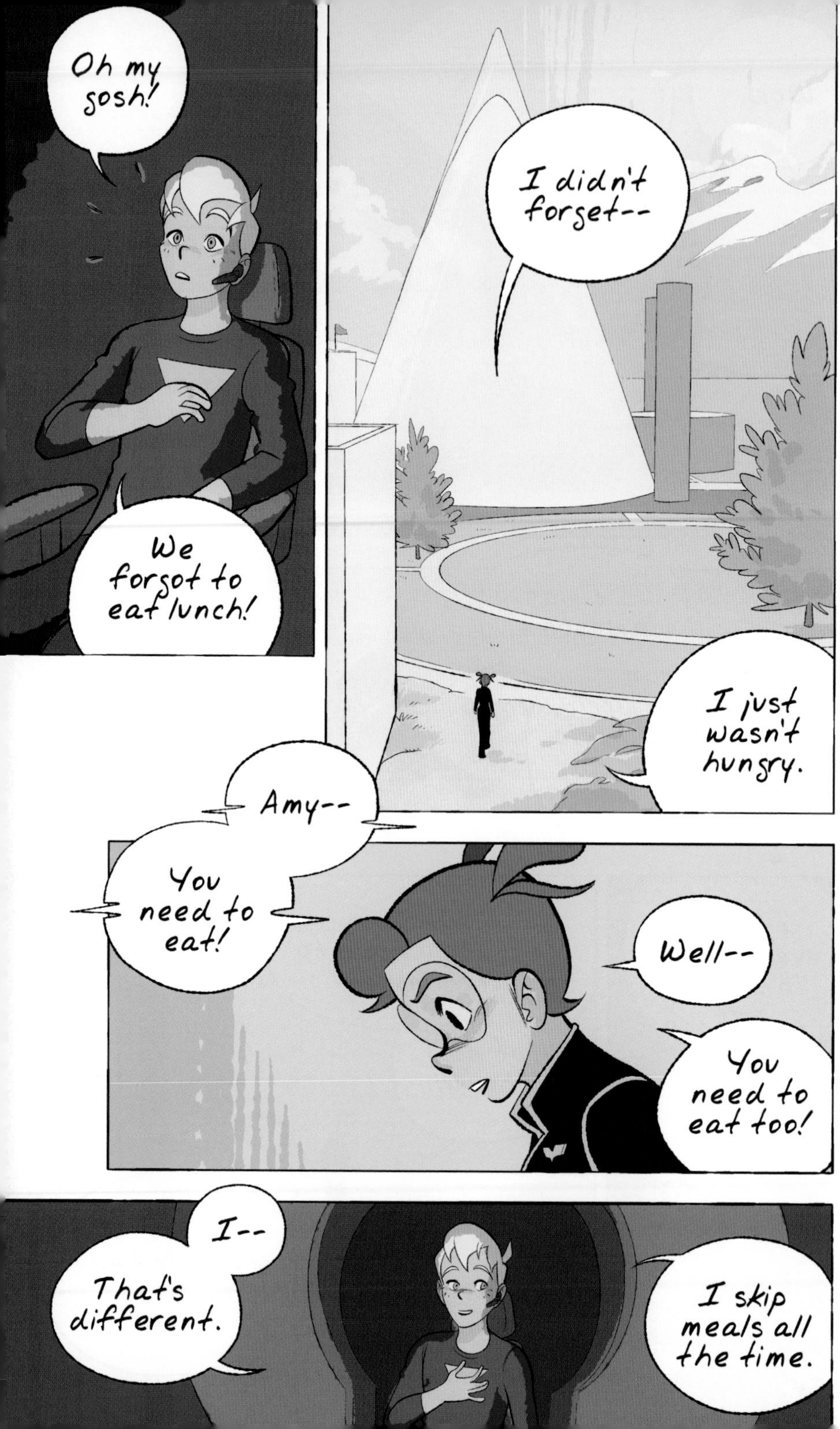
Oh my gosh!
We forgot to eat lunch!
I didn't forget--
I just wasn't hungry.
Amy--
You need to eat!
Well--
You need to eat too!
I--
That's different.
I skip meals all the time.

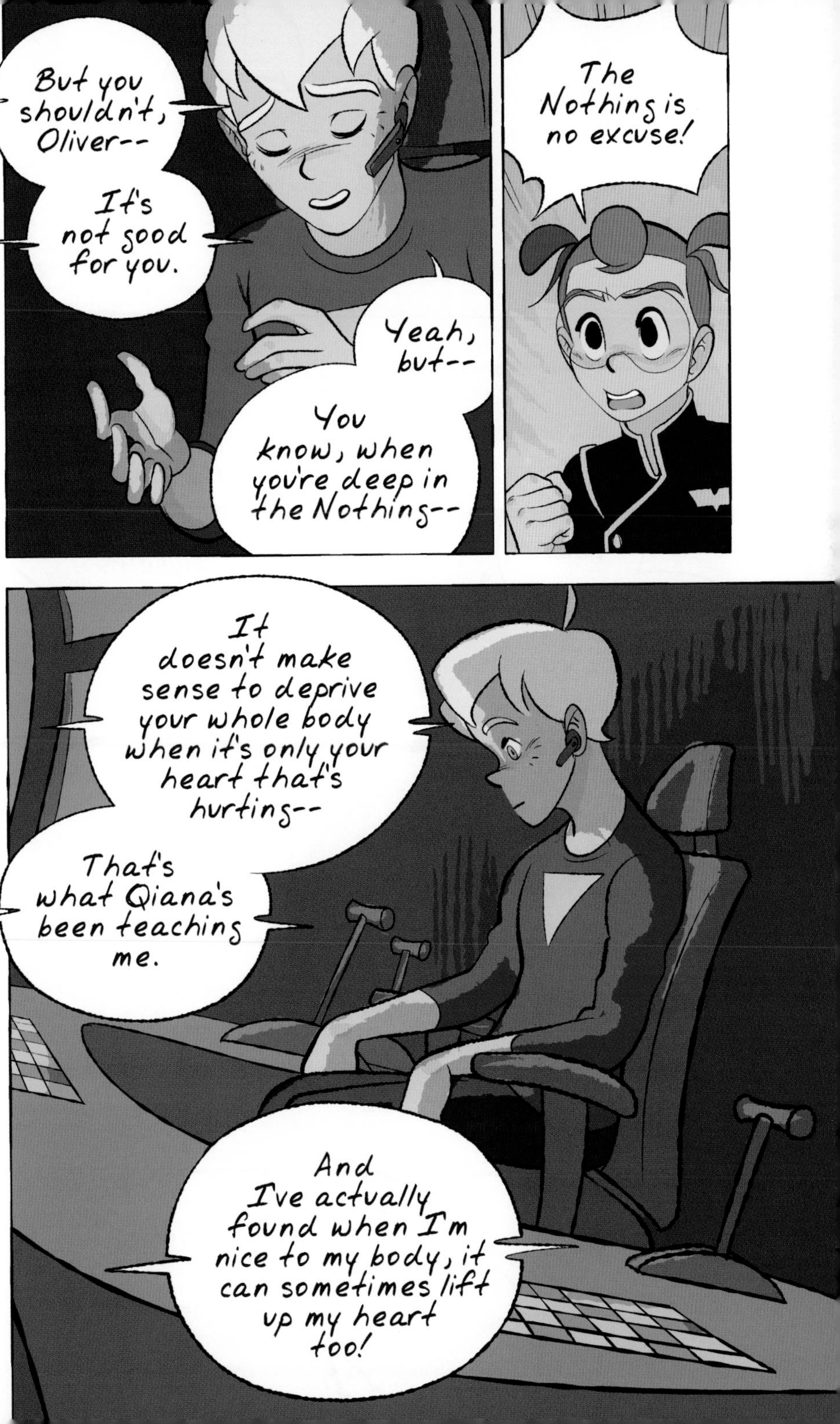
But you shouldn't, Oliver--
It's not good for you.
Yeah, but--
You know, when you're deep in the Nothing--
The Nothing is no excuse!
It doesn't make sense to deprive your whole body when it's only your heart that's hurting--
That's what Qiana's been teaching me.
And I've actually found when I'm nice to my body, it can sometimes lift up my heart too!

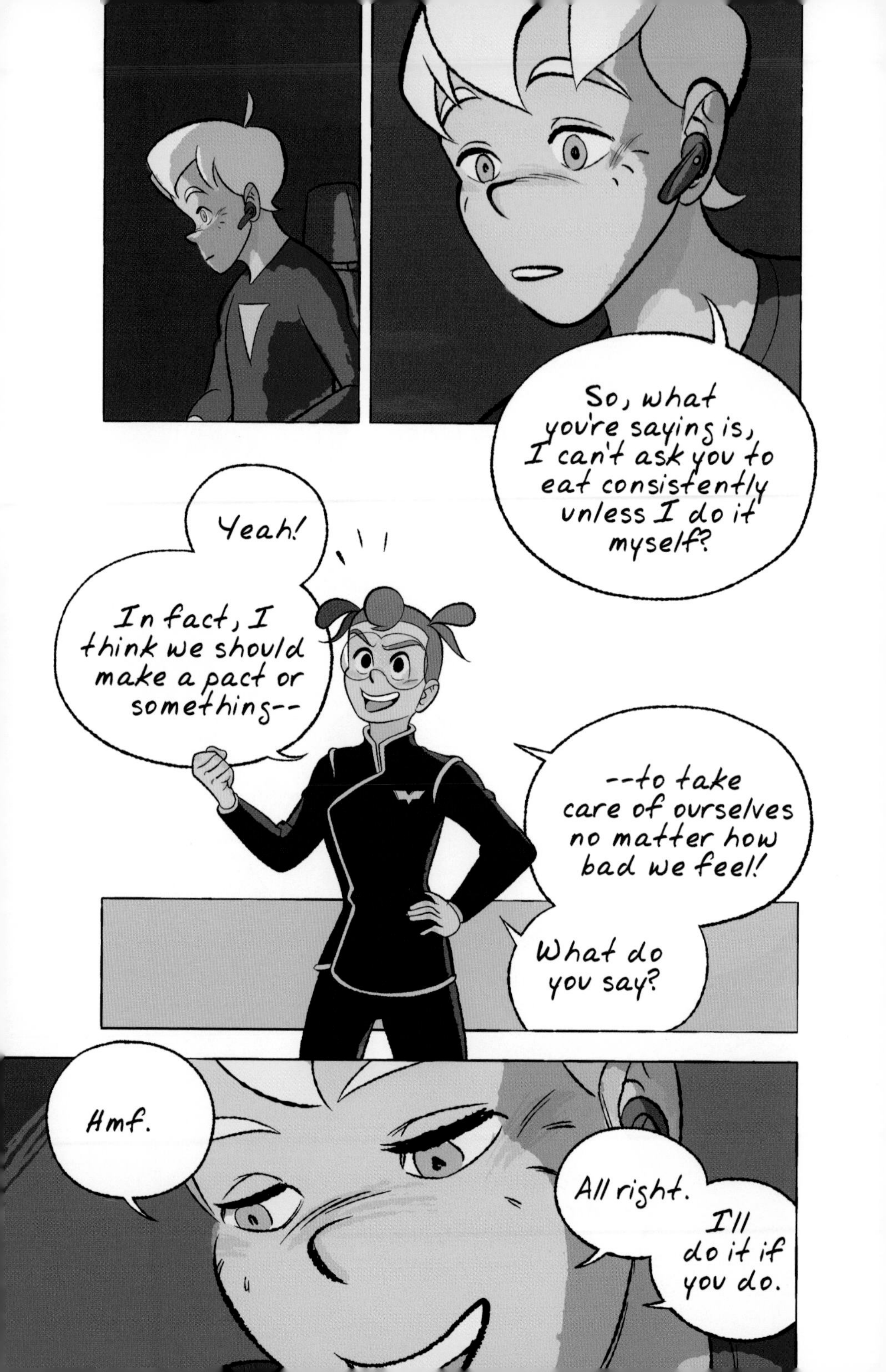
So, what you're saying is, I can't ask you to eat consistently unless I do it myself?
Yeah!
In fact, I think we should make a pact or something--
--to take care of ourselves no matter how bad we feel!
What do you say?
Hmf.
All right.
I'll do it if you do.

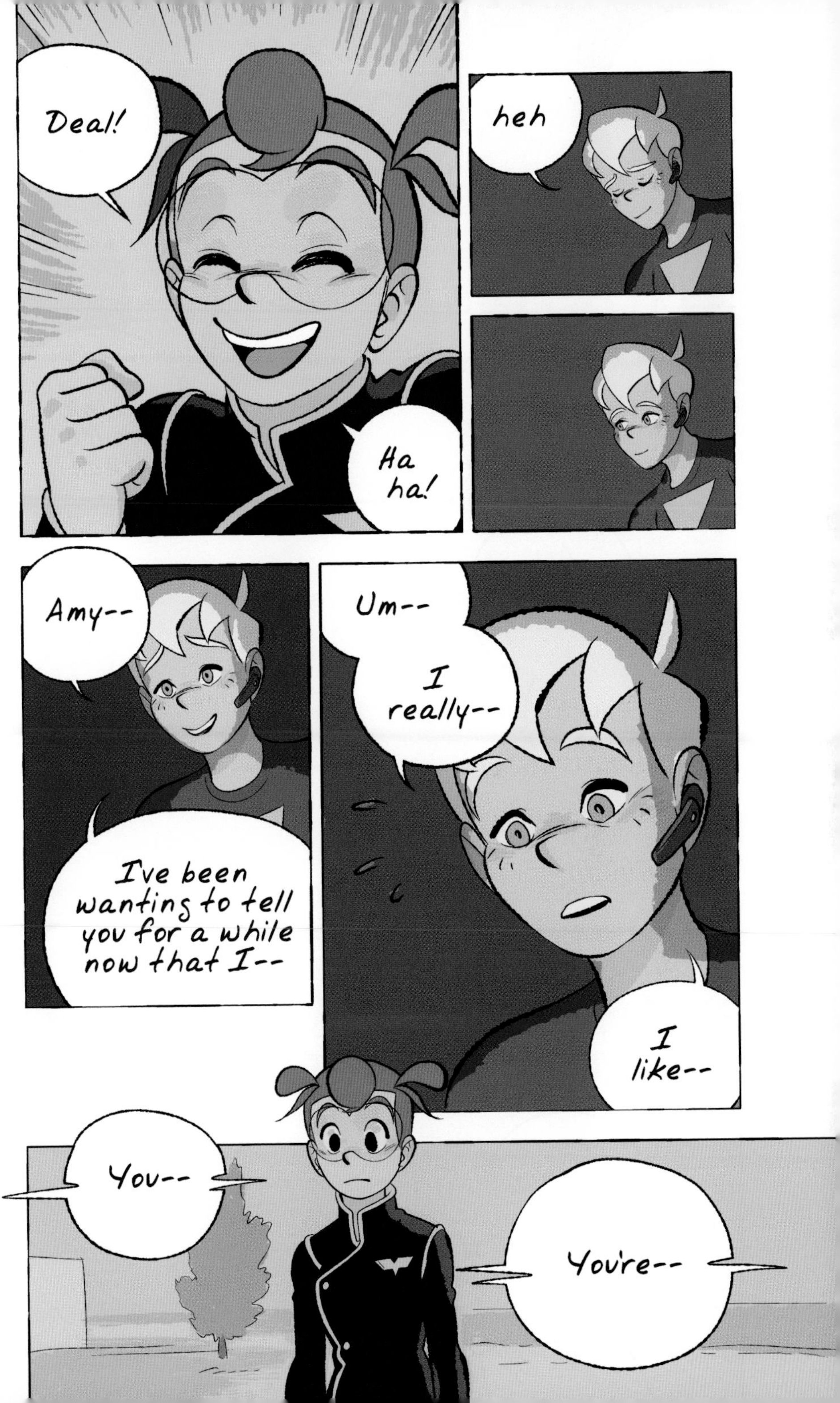
Deal!
heh
Ha ha!
Amy--
I've been wanting to tell you for a while now that I--
Um--
I really--
I like--
You--
You're--

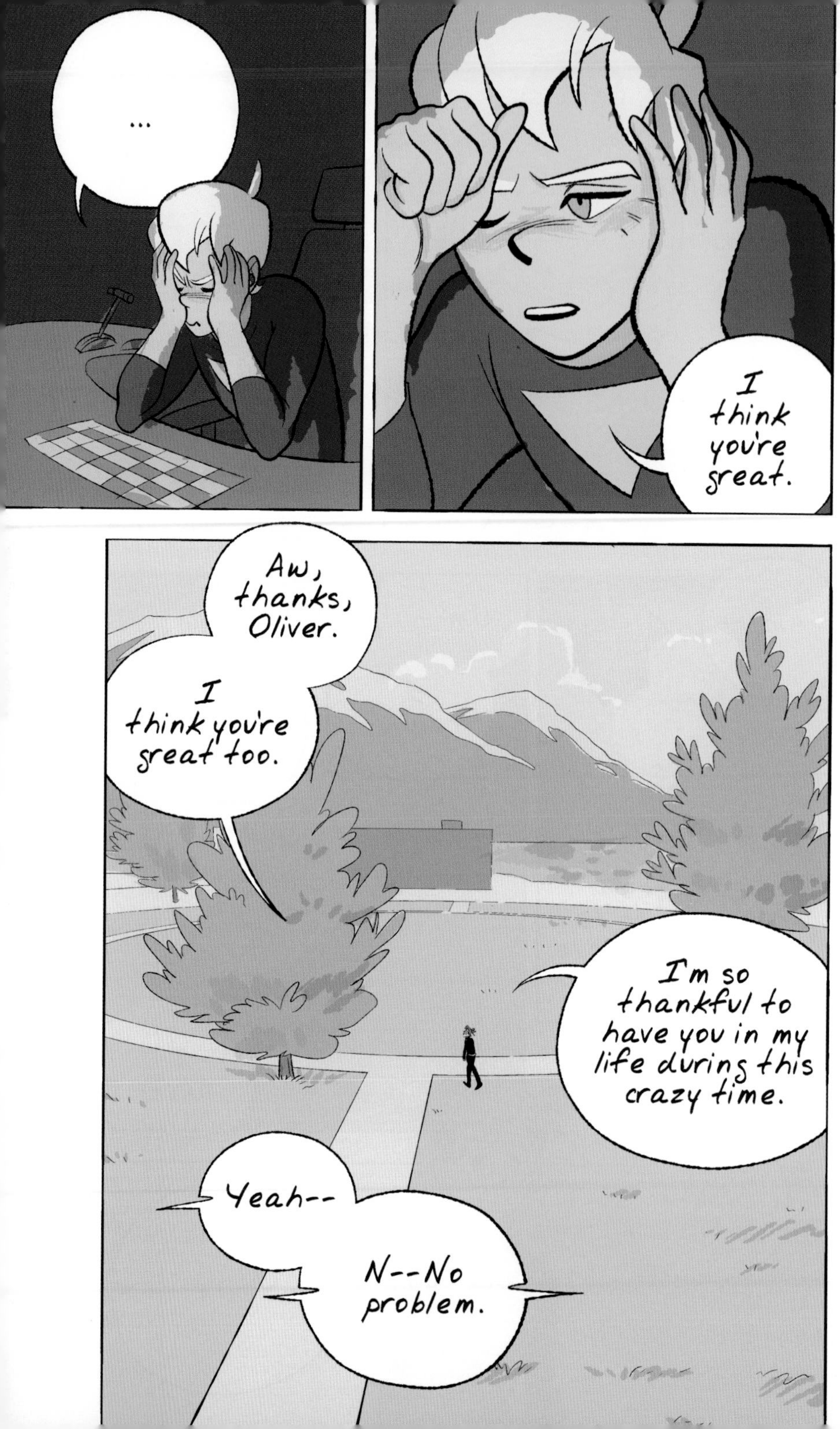
...
I think you're great.
Aw, thanks, Oliver.
I think you're great too.
I'm so thankful to have you in my life during this crazy time.
Yeah--
N--No problem.

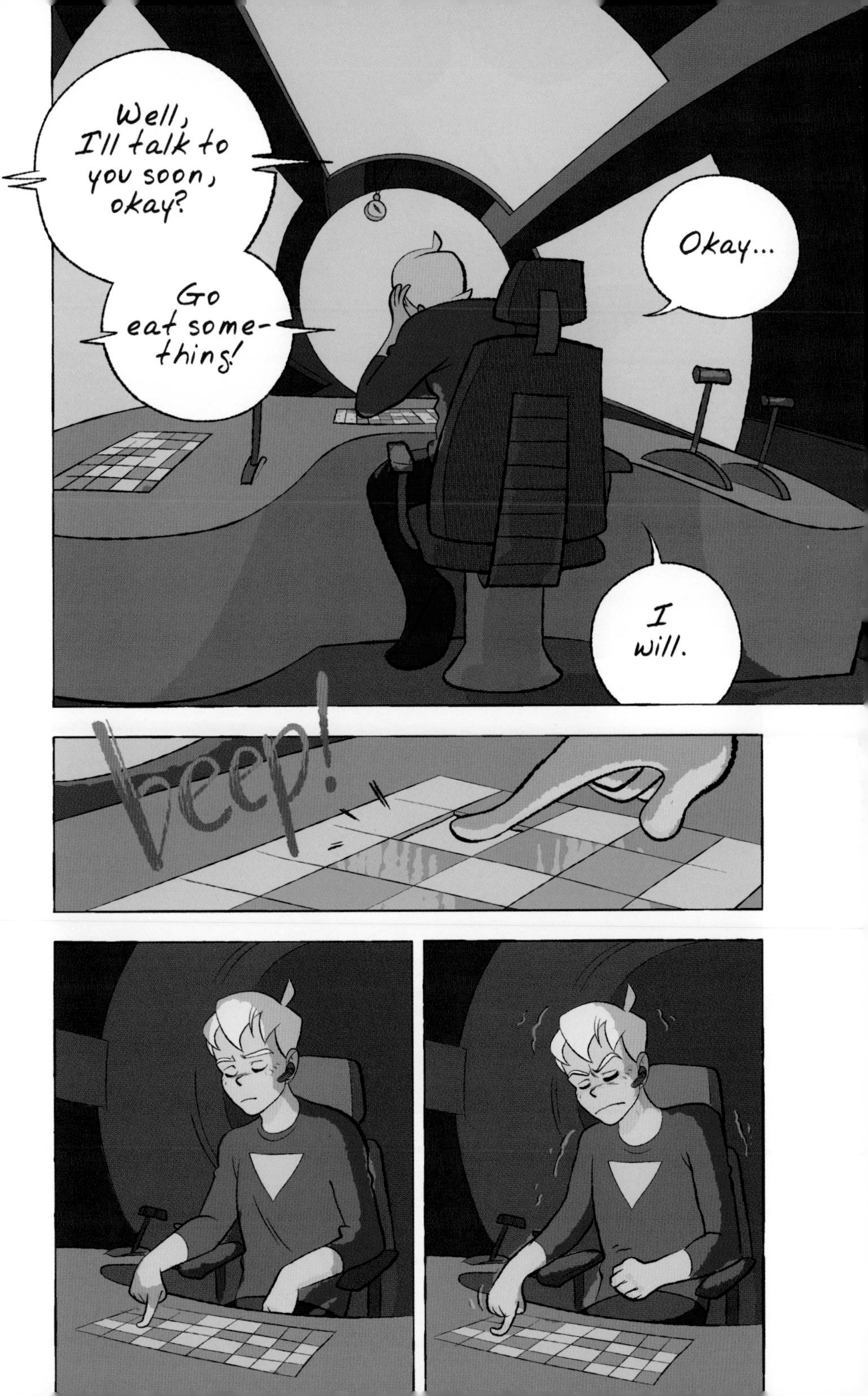
Well, I'll talk to you soon, okay?
Go eat something!
Okay...
I will.
beep!

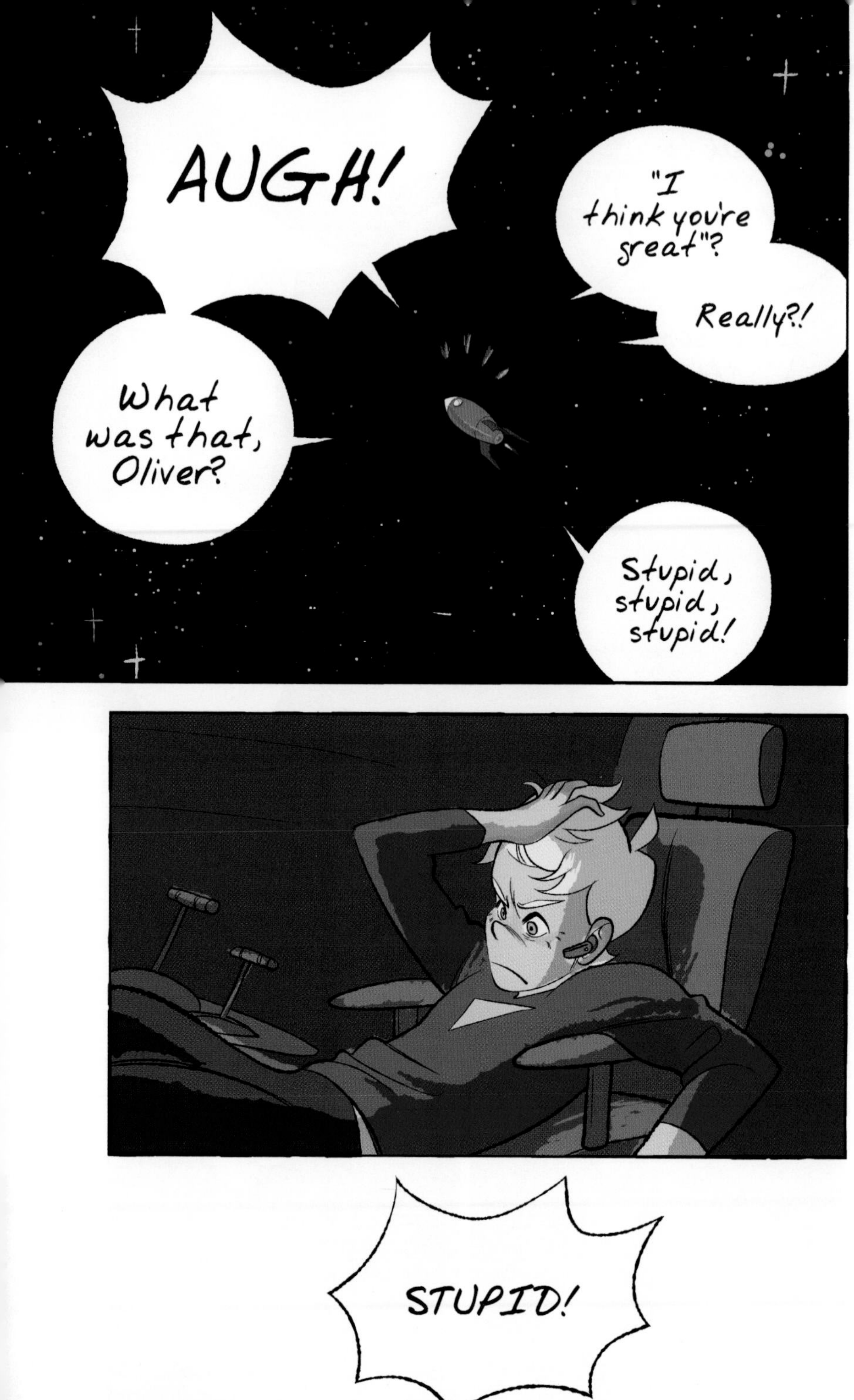
AUGH!
"I think you're great"?
Really?!
What was that, Oliver?
Stupid, stupid, stupid!
STUPID!

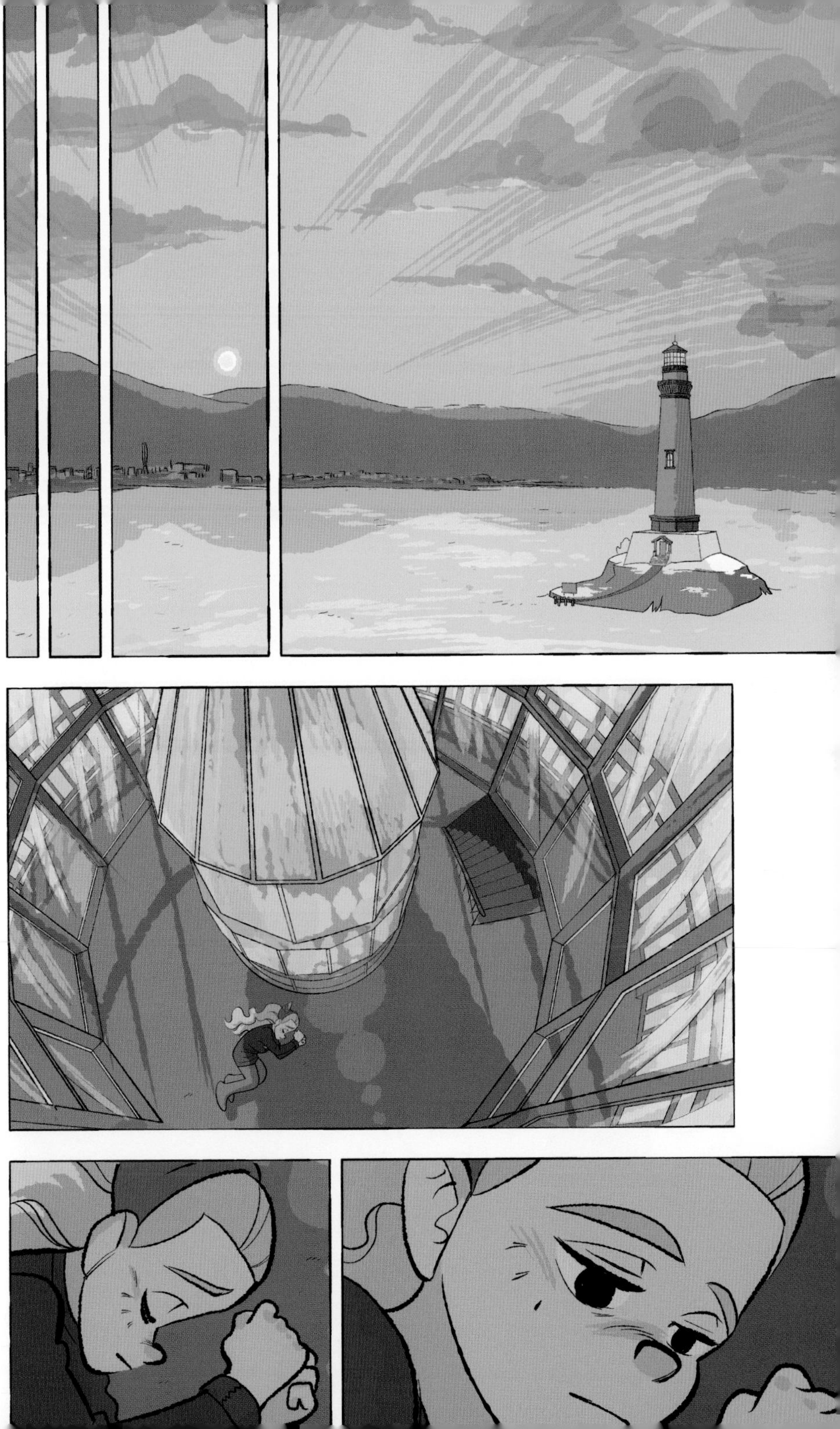

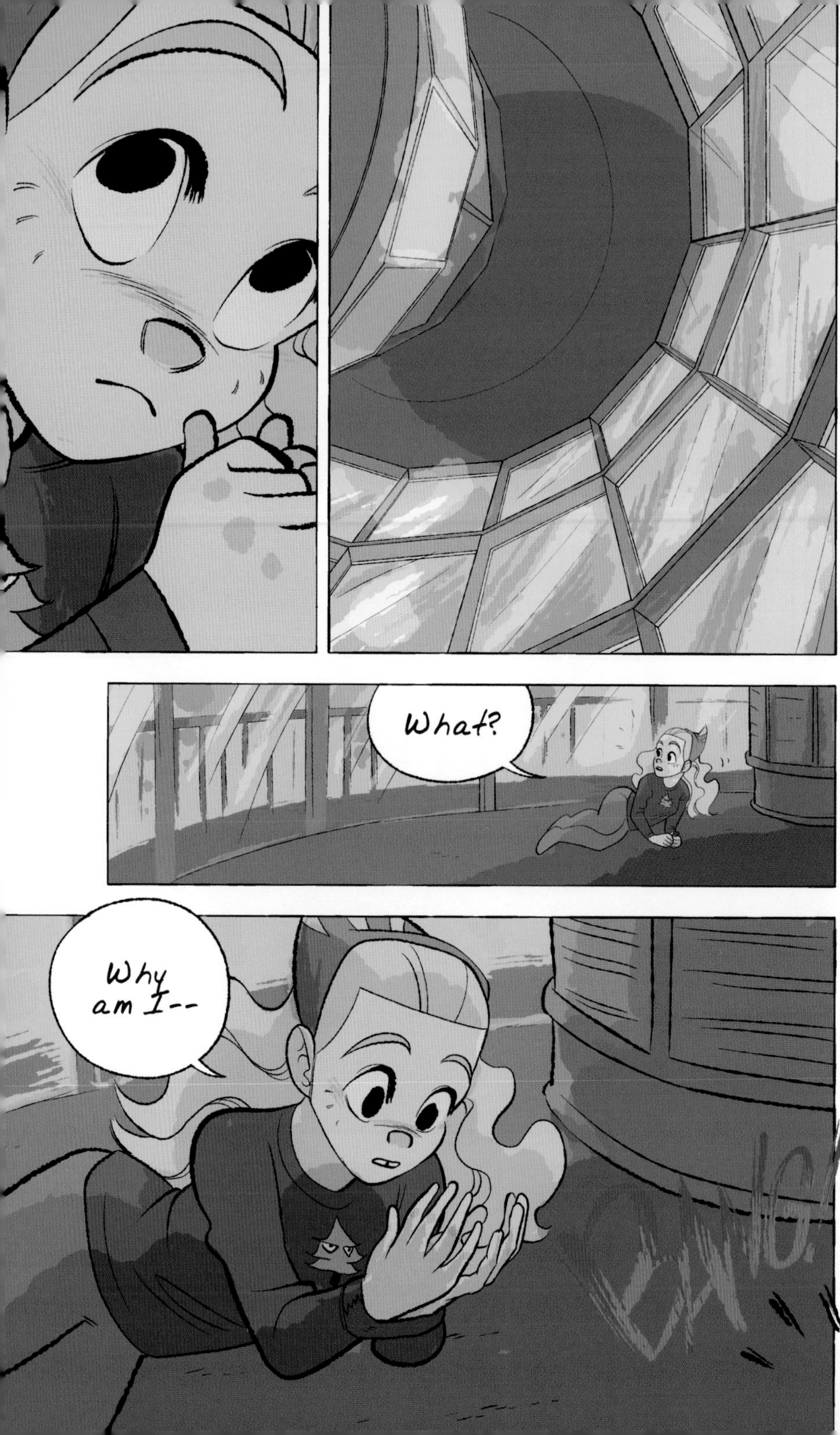
What?
Why am I--

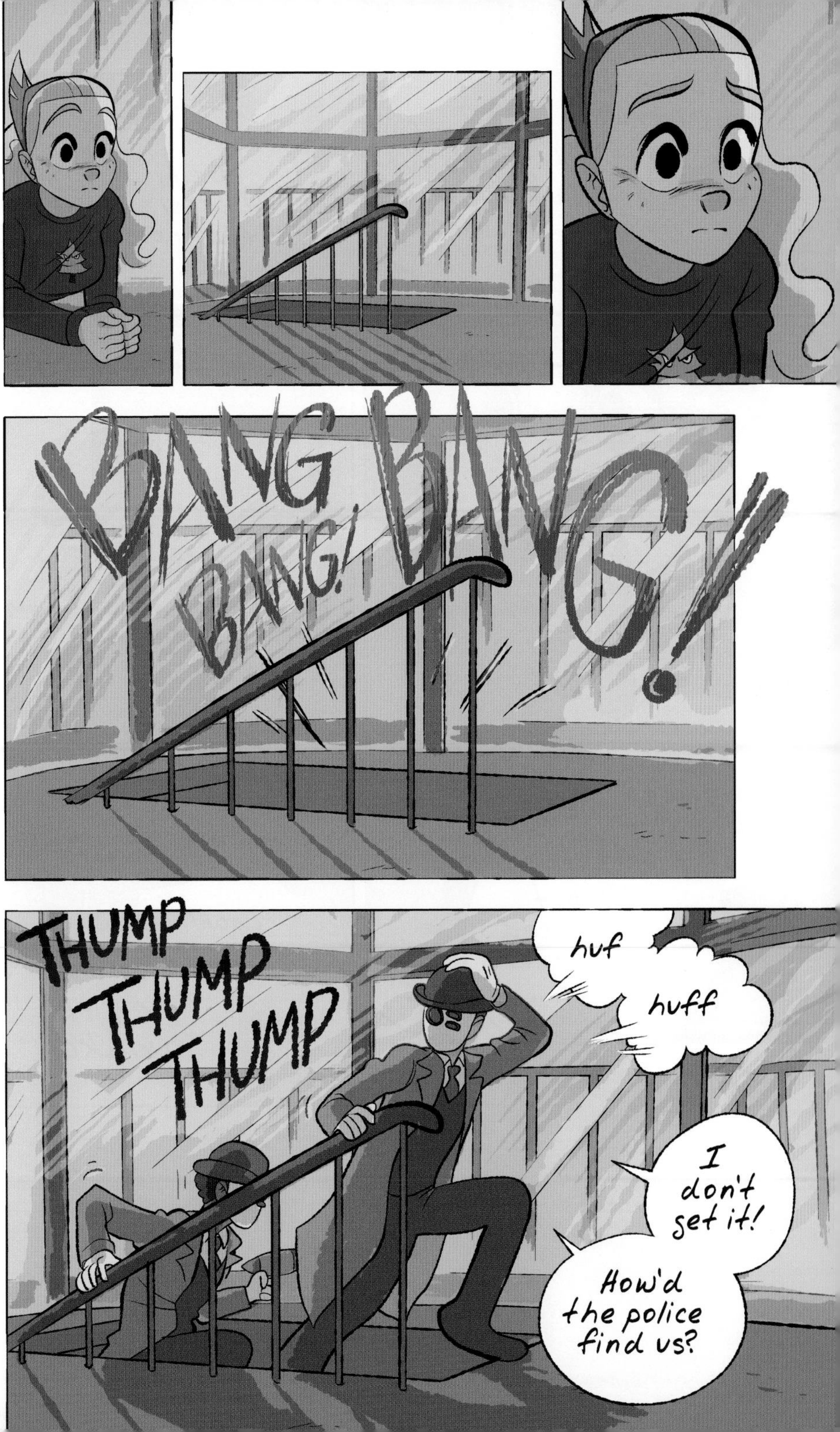
BANG
BANG!
BANG!
THUMP
THUMP
THUMP
huf
huff
I don't get it!
How'd the police find us?

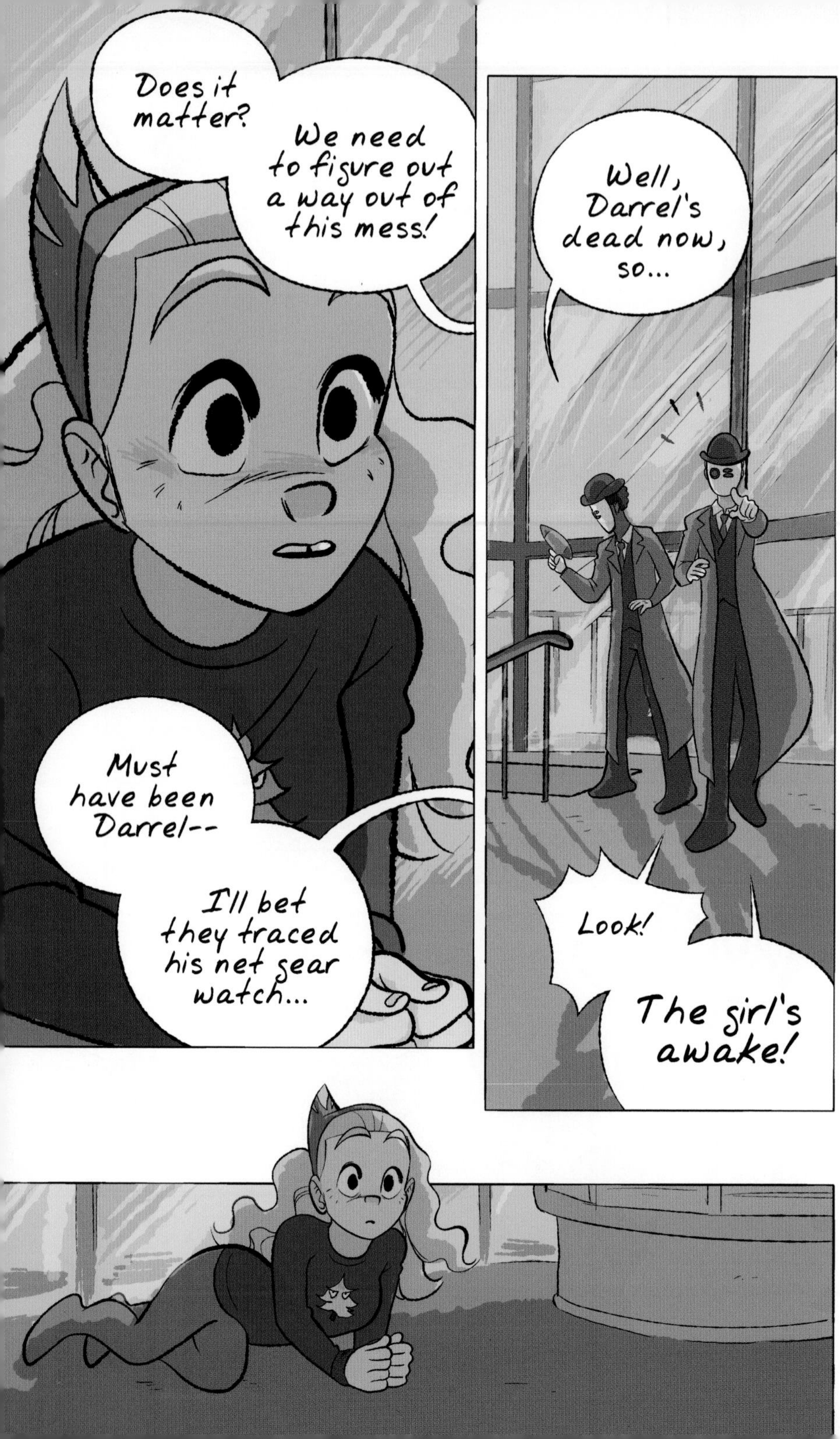

Does it matter?
We need to figure out a way out of this mess!
Well, Darrel's dead now, so...
Must have been Darrel--
I'll bet they traced his net gear watch...
Look!
The girl's awake!

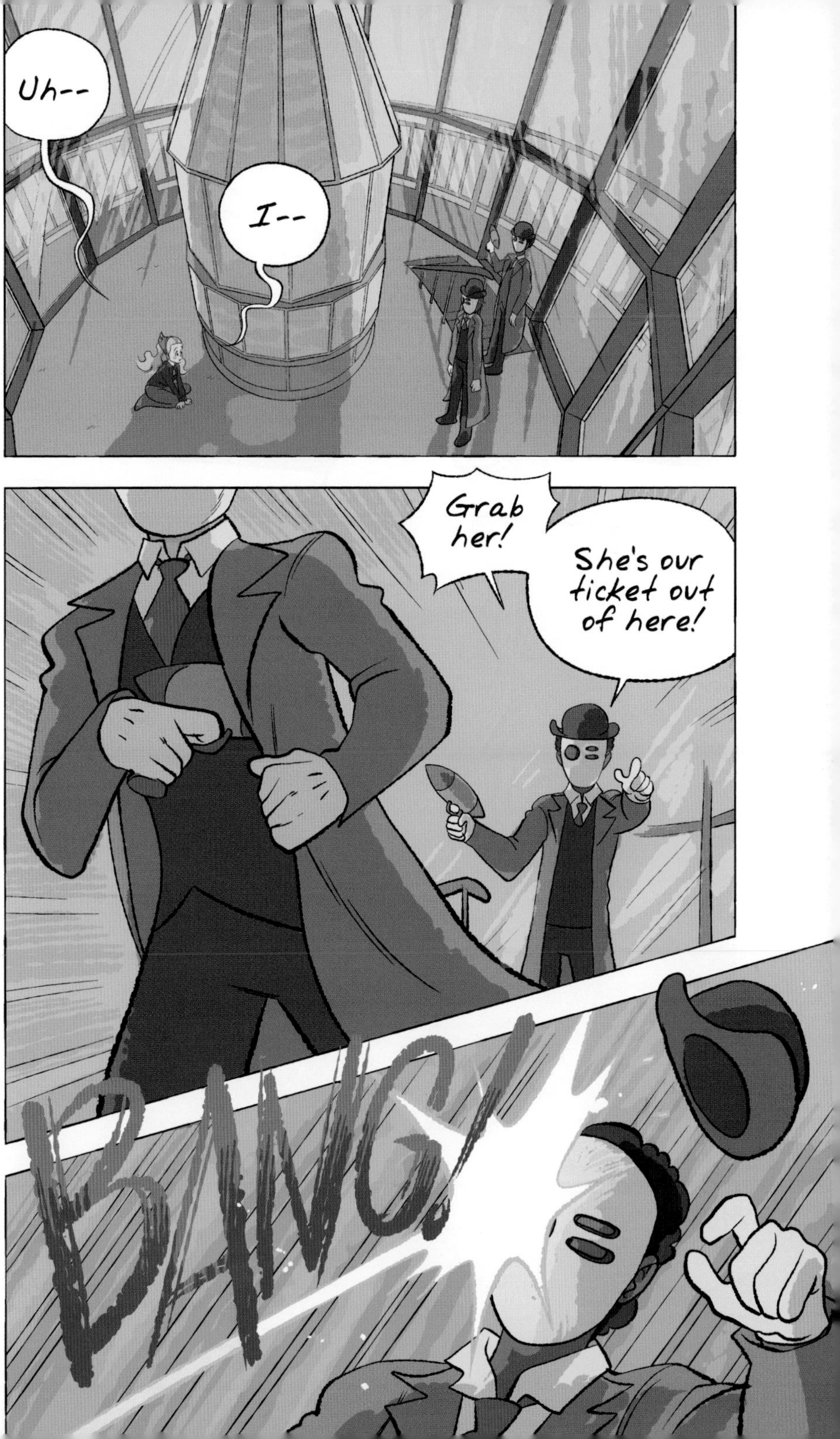
Uh--
I--
Grab her!
She's our ticket out of here!
BANG!

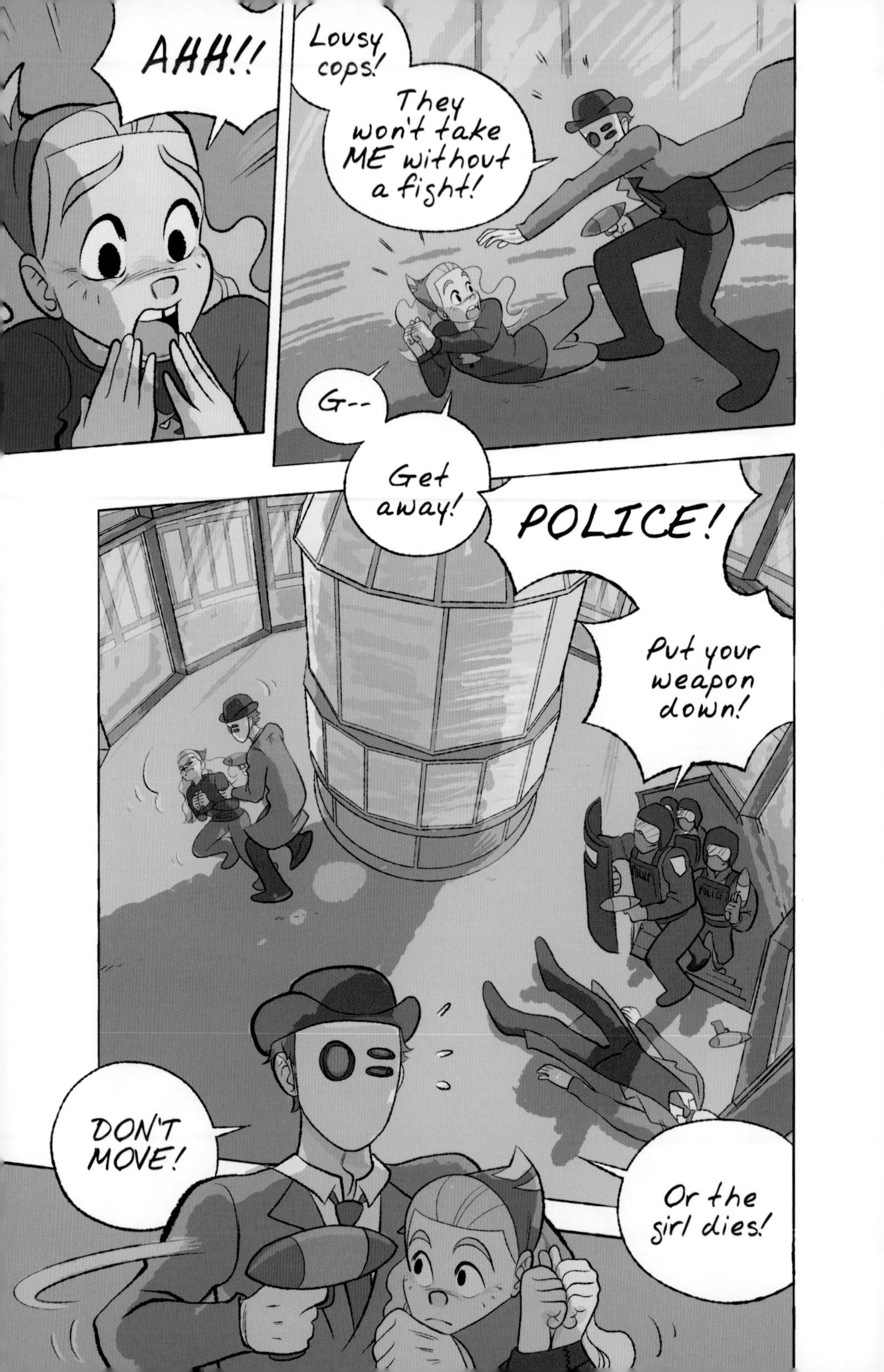
AHH!!
Lousy cops!
They won't take ME without a fight!
G--
Get away!
POLICE!
Put your weapon down!
DON'T MOVE!
Or the girl dies!

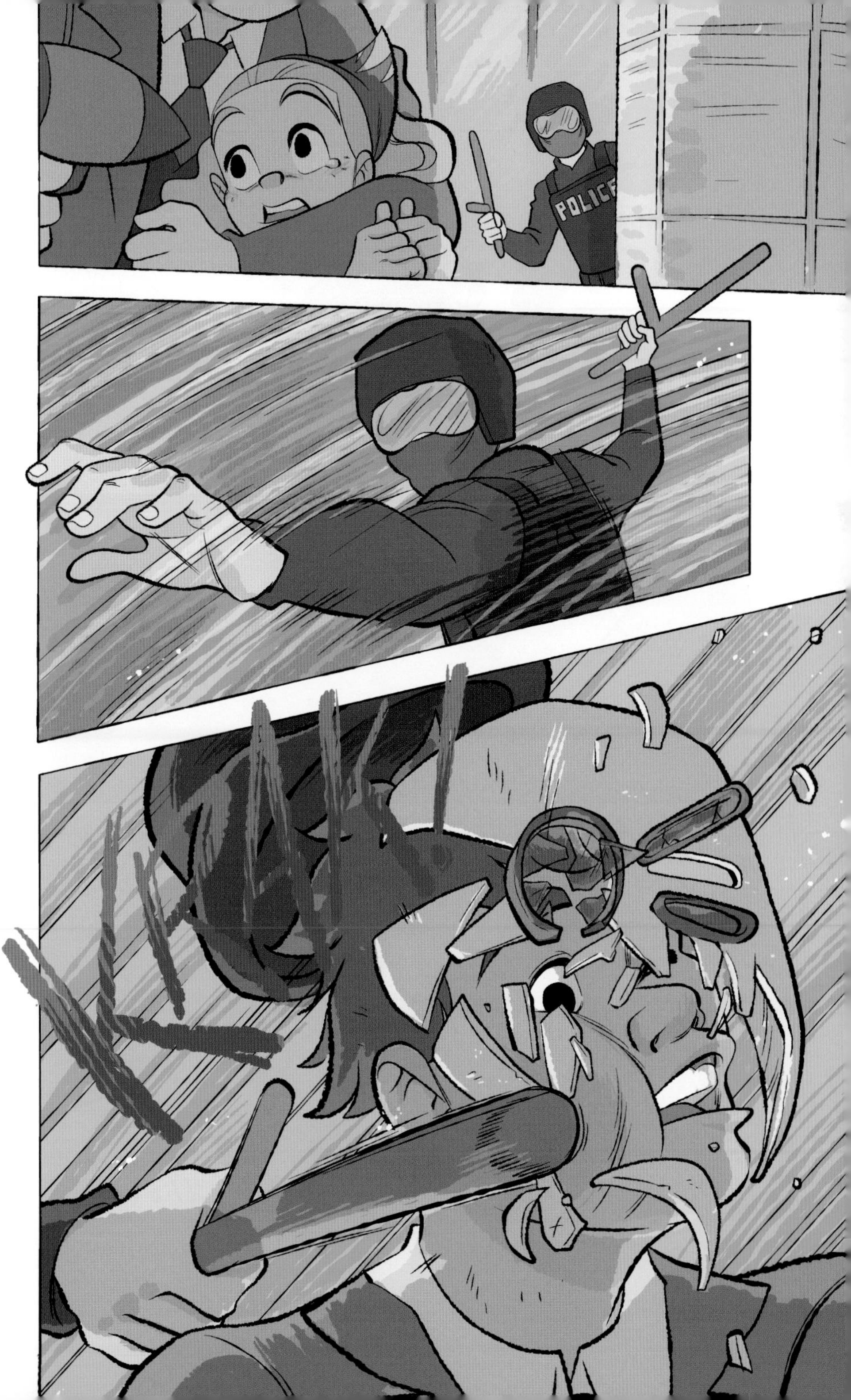
POLICE

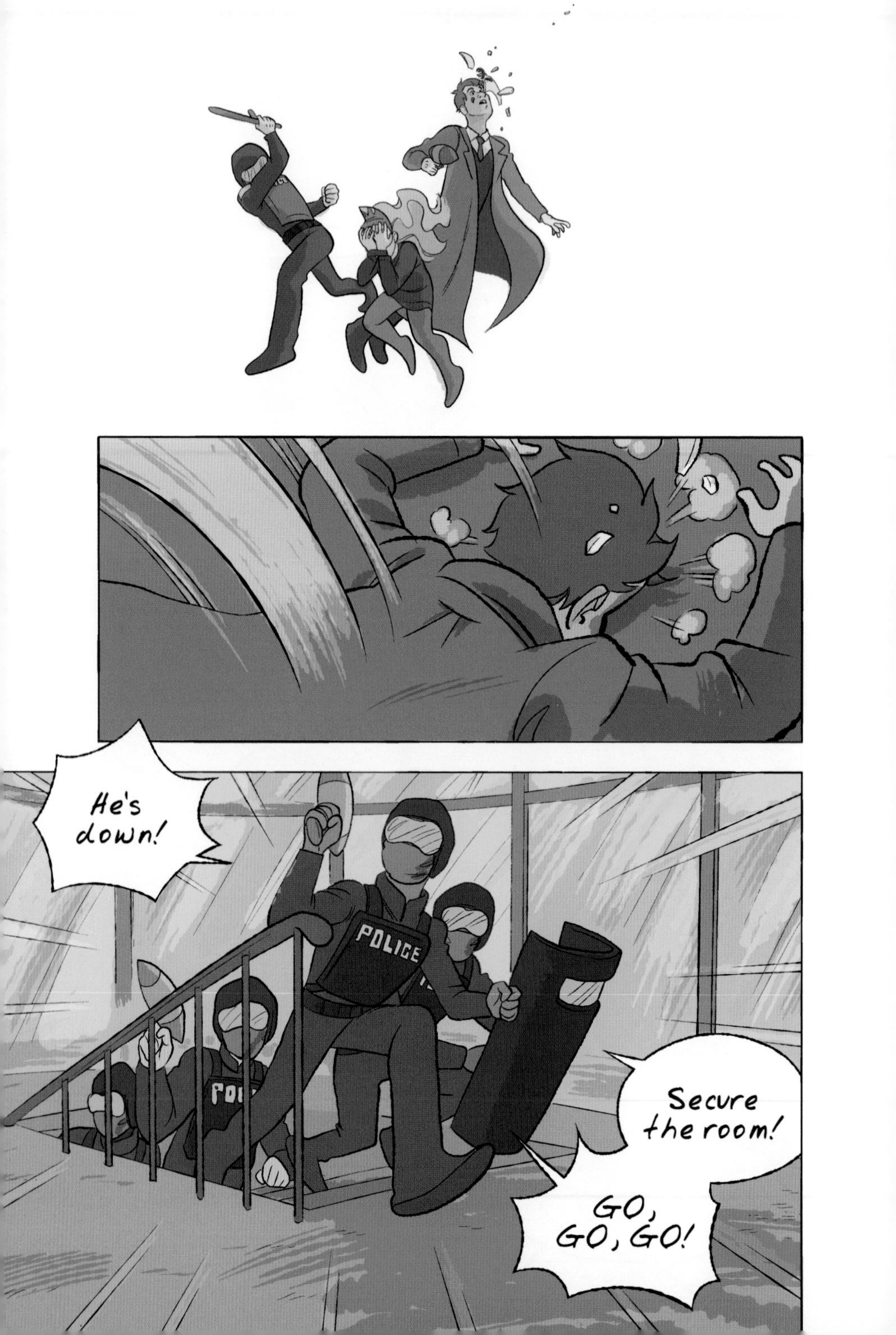
He's down!
POLICE
POLI
Secure the room!
GO, GO, GO!

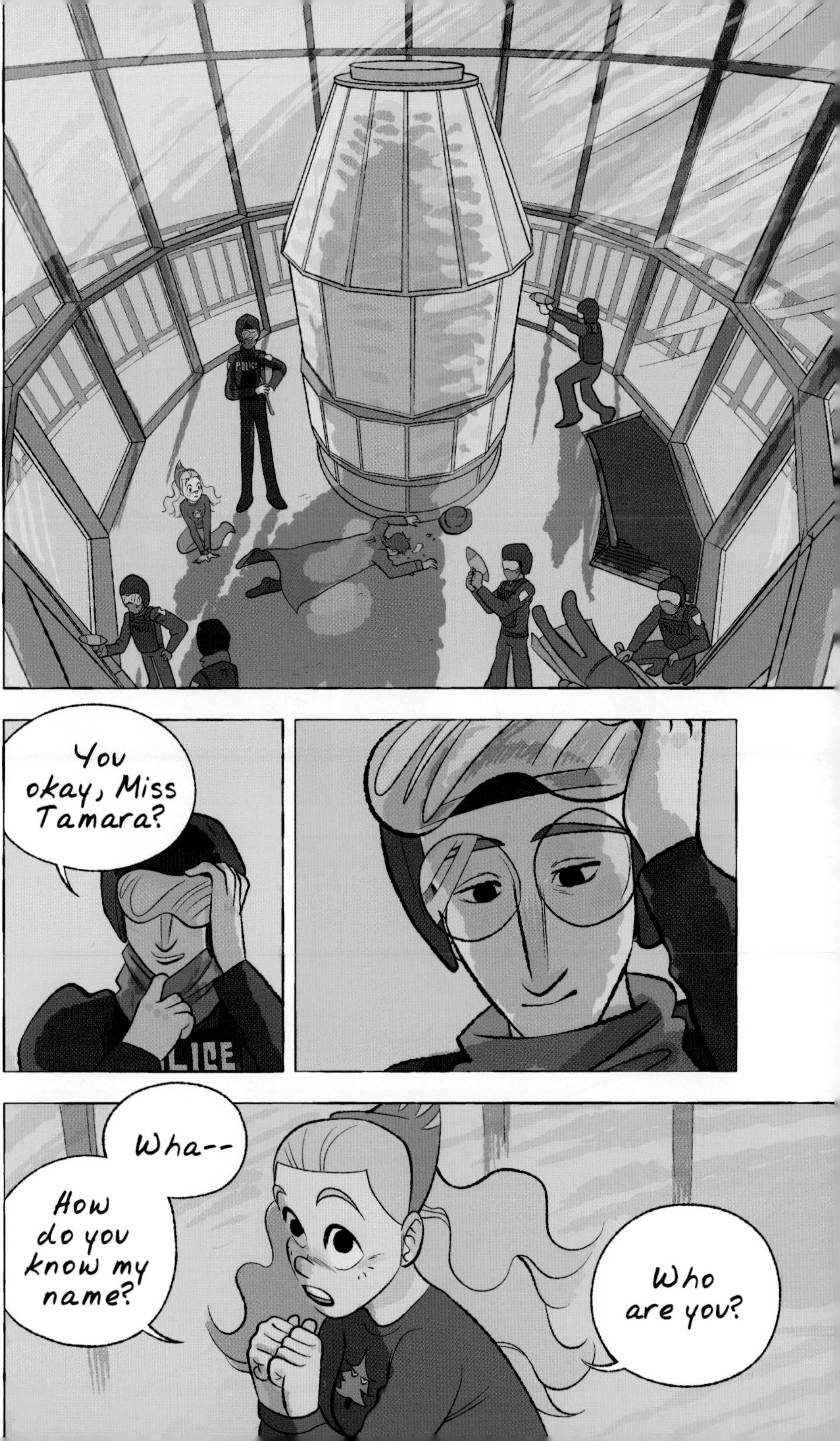
POLICE
You okay, Miss Tamara?
LICE
Wha--
How do you know my name?
Who are you?

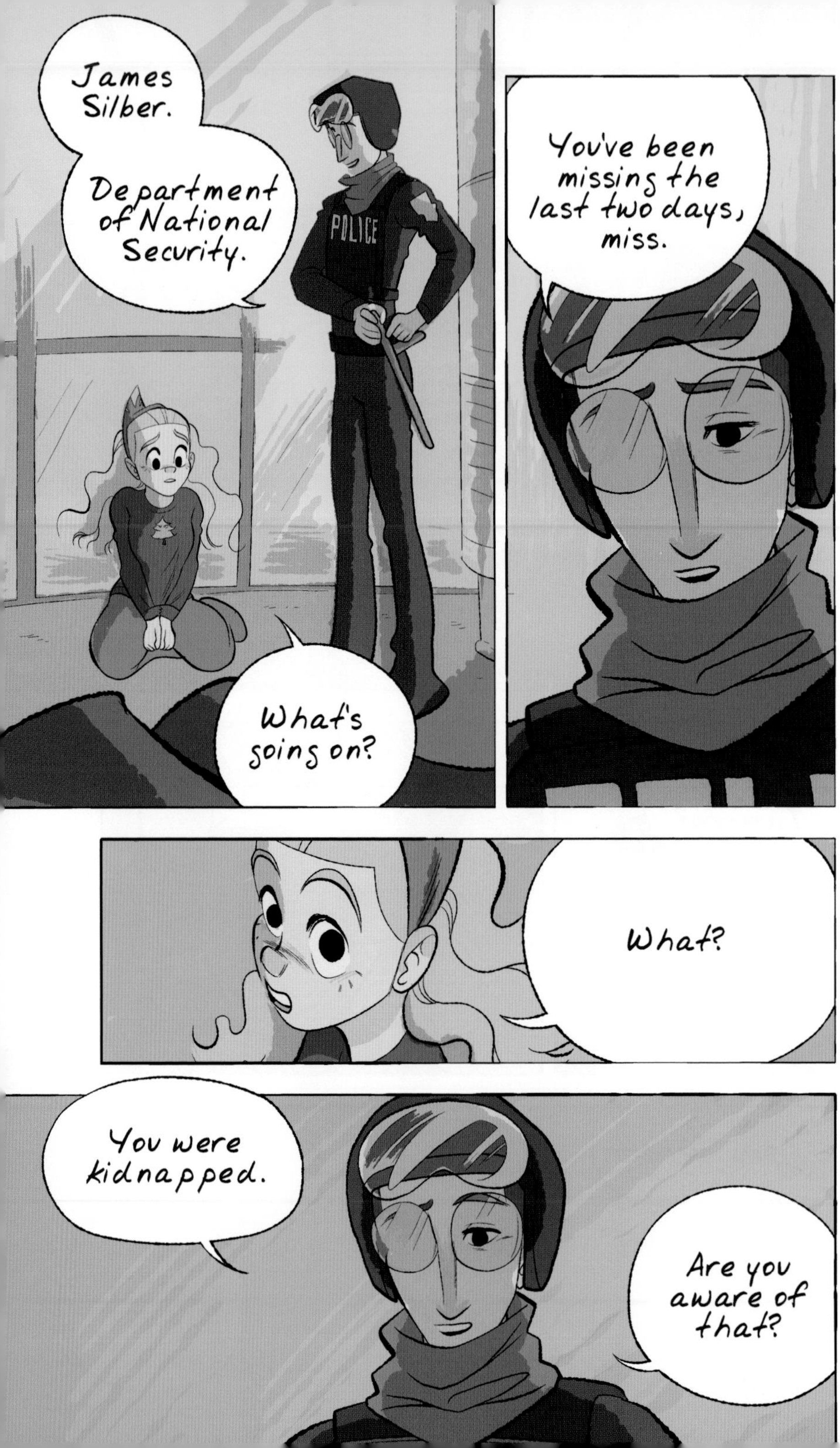
James Silber.
Department of National Security.
POLICE
What's going on?
You've been missing the last two days, miss.
What?
You were kidnapped.
Are you aware of that?

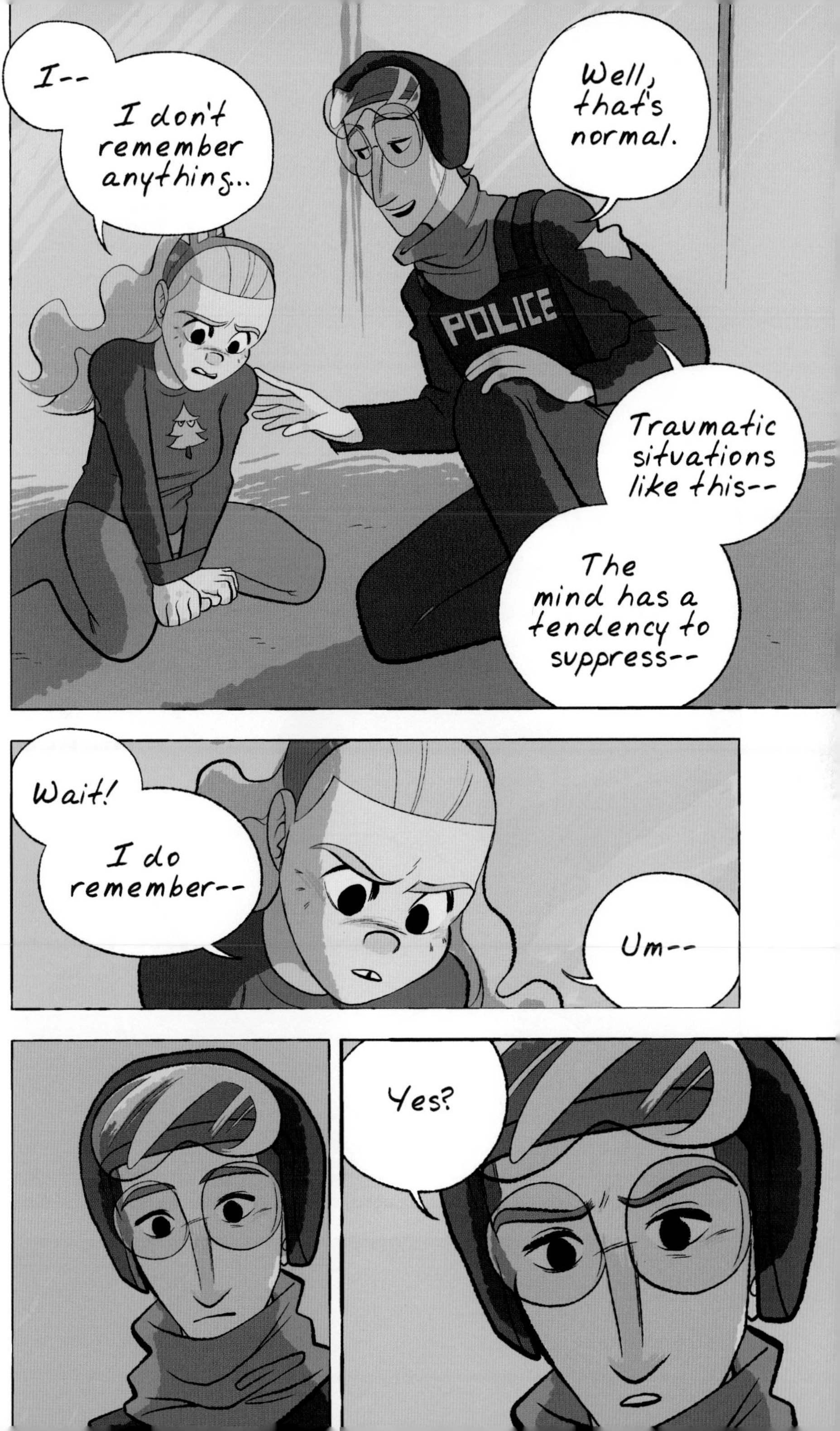
I--
I don't remember anything...
Well, that's normal.
Traumatic situations like this--
The mind has a tendency to suppress--
POLICE
Wait!
I do remember--
Um--
Yes?

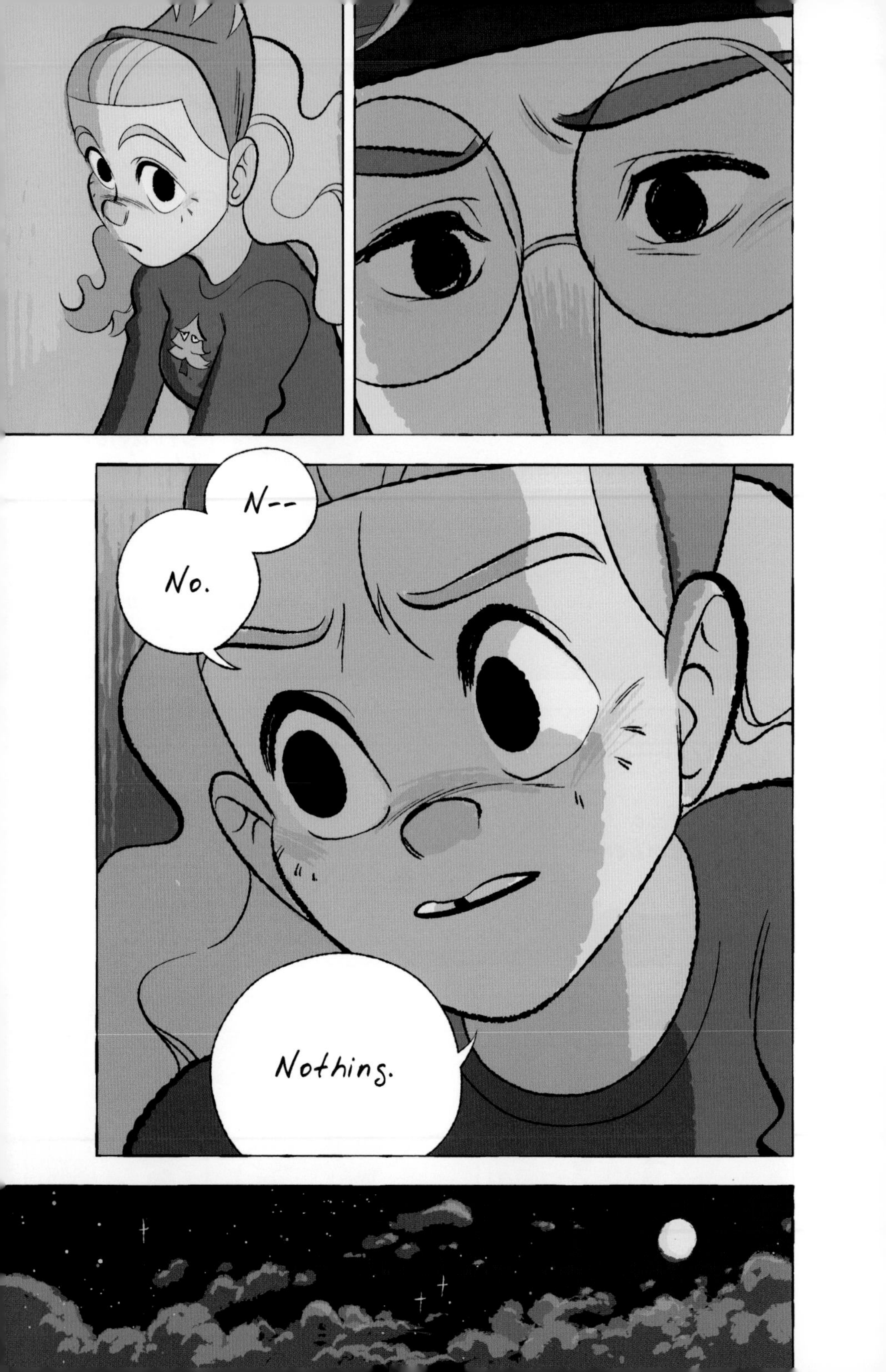
N--
No.
Nothing.

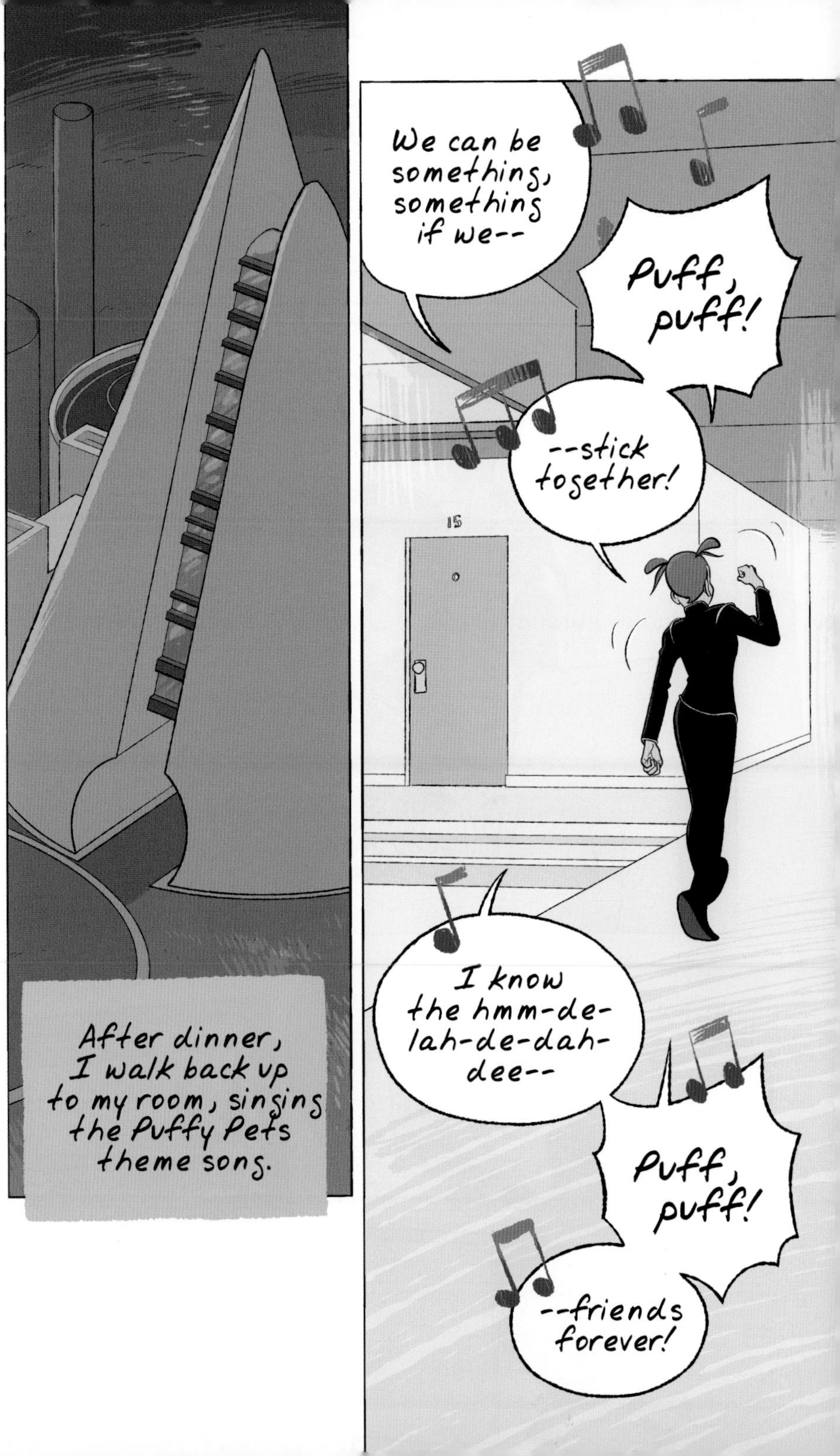
After dinner, I walk back up to my room, singing the Puffy Pets theme songs.
We can be something, something if we--
Puff, puff!
--stick together!
15
I know the hmm-de-lah-de-dah-dee--
Puff, puff!
--friends forever!

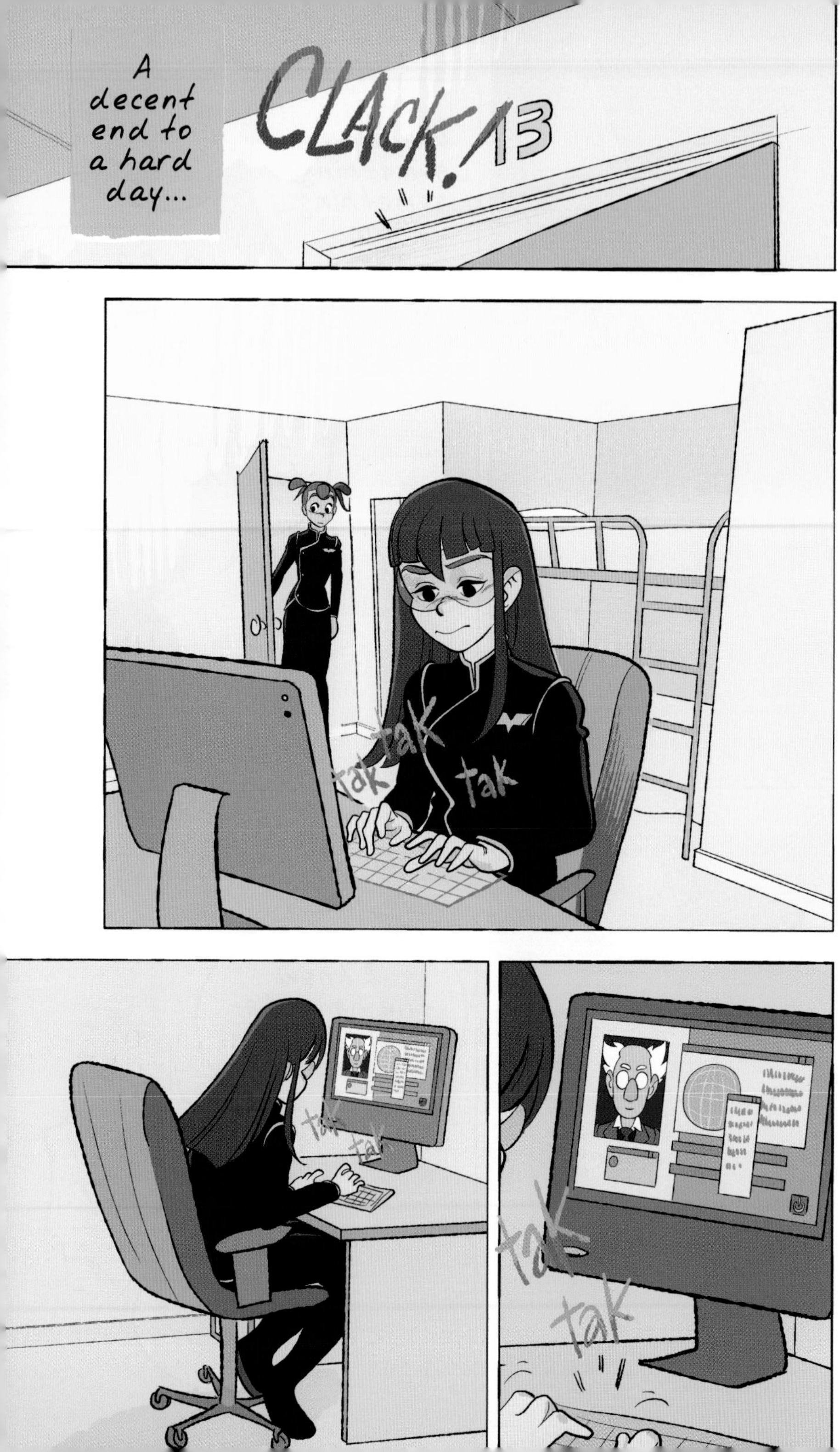

A decent end to a hard day...
CLACK!
tak tak tak tak
tak tak
tak tak

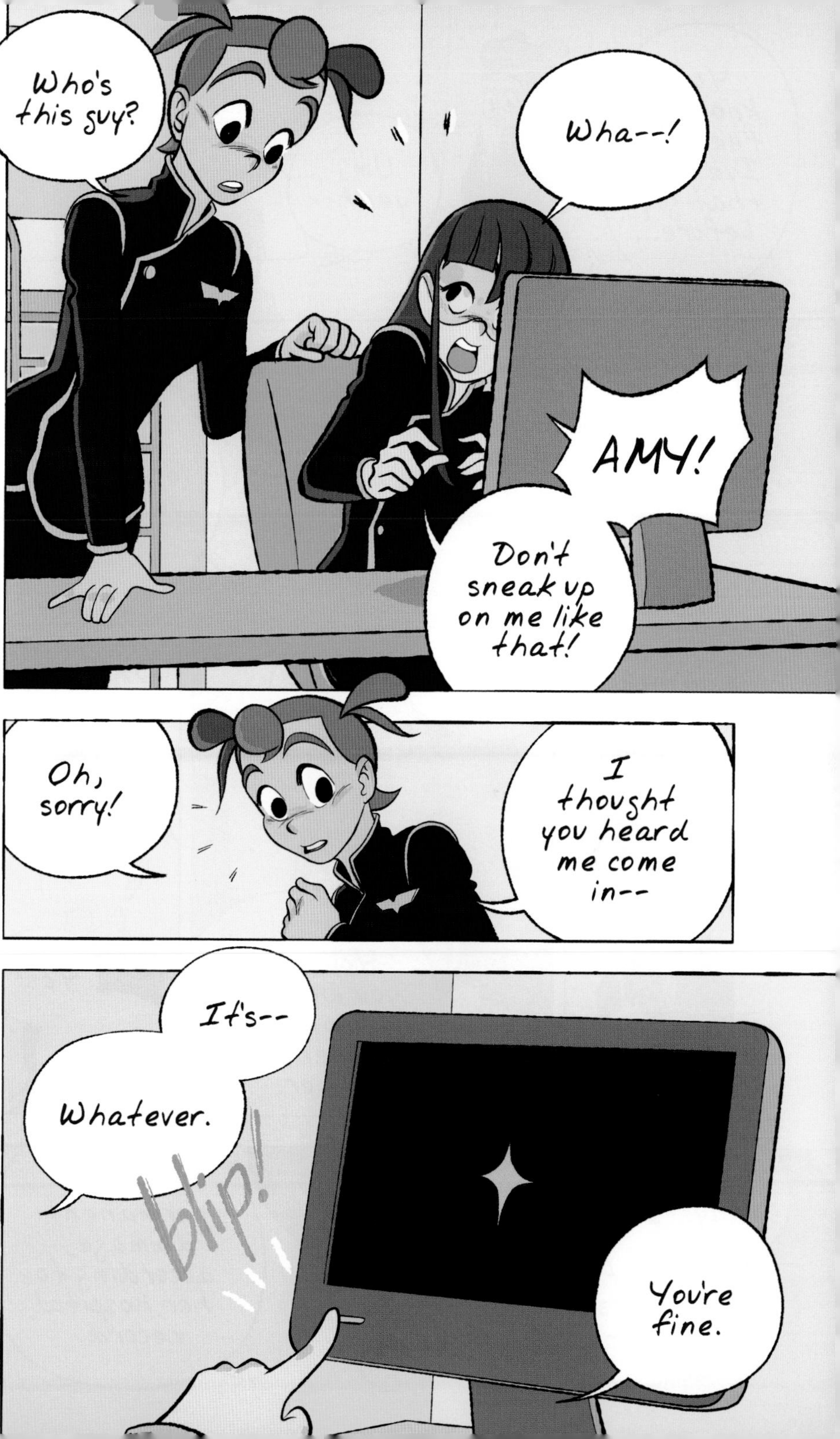
Who's this guy?
Wha--!
AMY!
Don't sneak up on me like that!
Oh, sorry!
I thought you heard me come in--
It's--
Whatever.
blip!
You're fine.

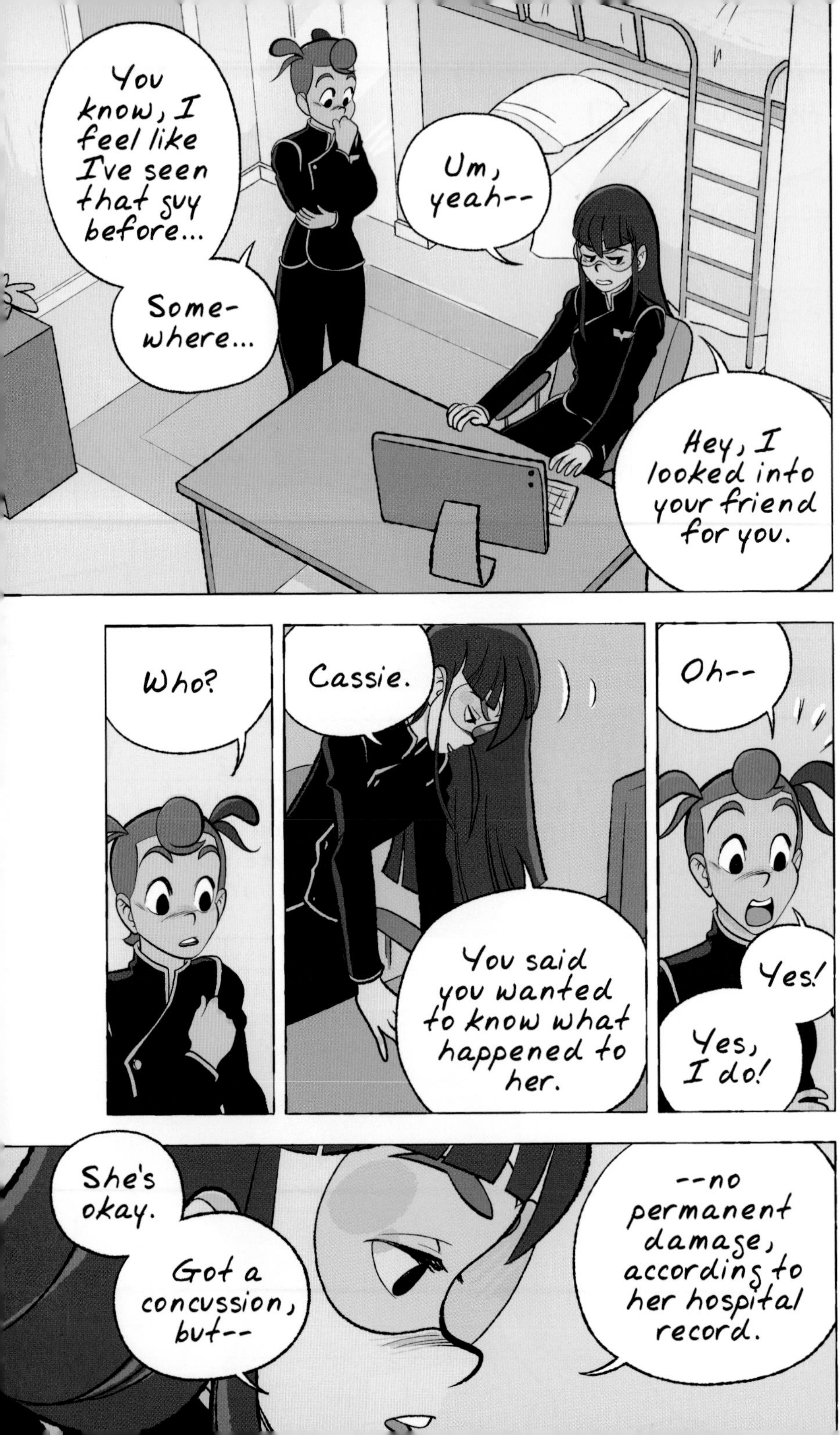
You know, I feel like I've seen that guy before...
Some-where...
Um, yeah--
Hey, I looked into your friend for you.
Who?
Cassie.
You said you wanted to know what happened to her.
Oh--
Yes!
Yes, I do!
She's okay.
Got a concussion, but--
--no permanent damage, according to her hospital record.

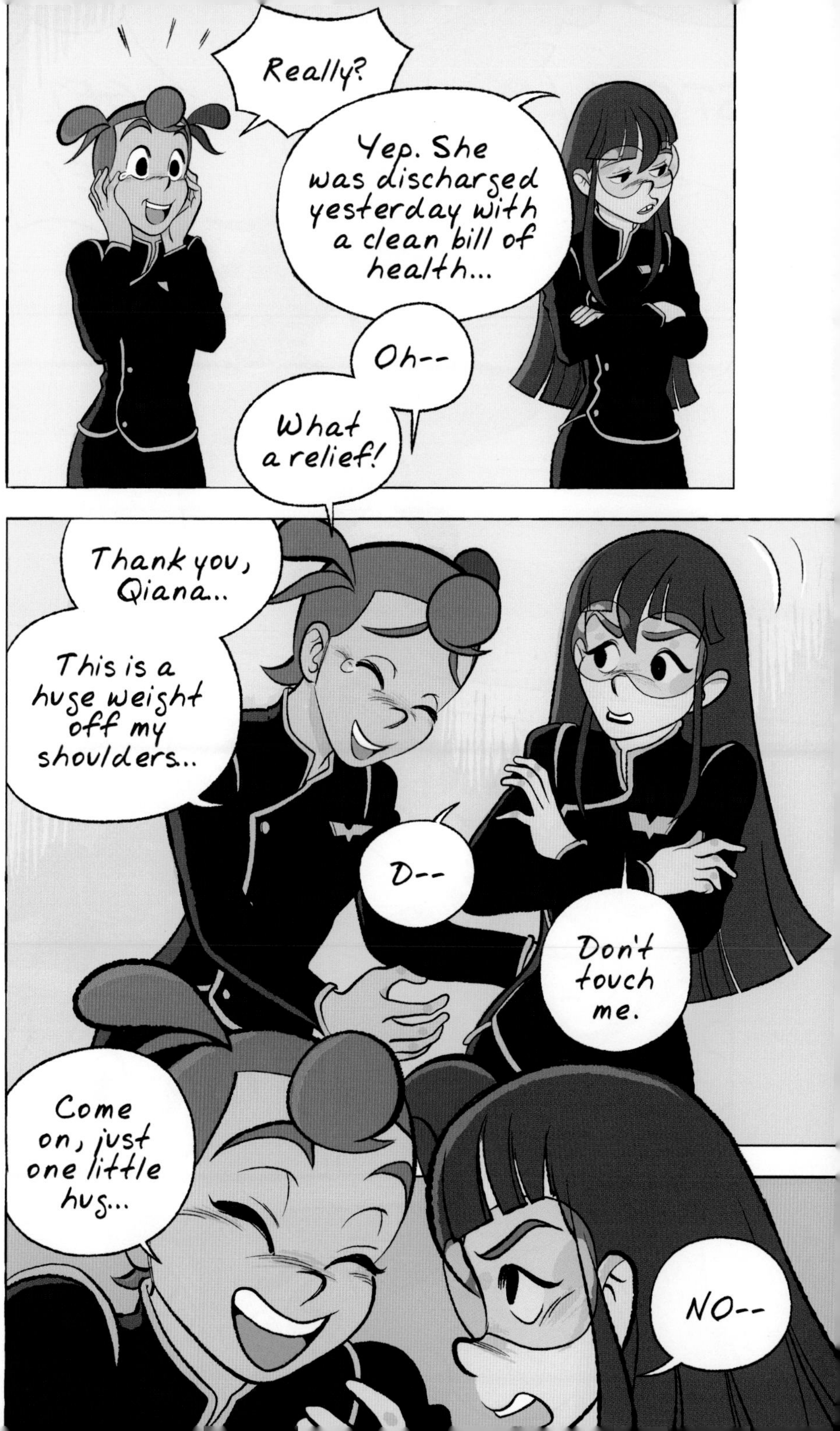
Really?
Yep. She was discharged yesterday with a clean bill of health...
Oh--
What a relief!
Thank you, Qiana..
This is a huge weight off my shoulders..
D--
Don't touch me.
Come on, just one little hug...
NO--

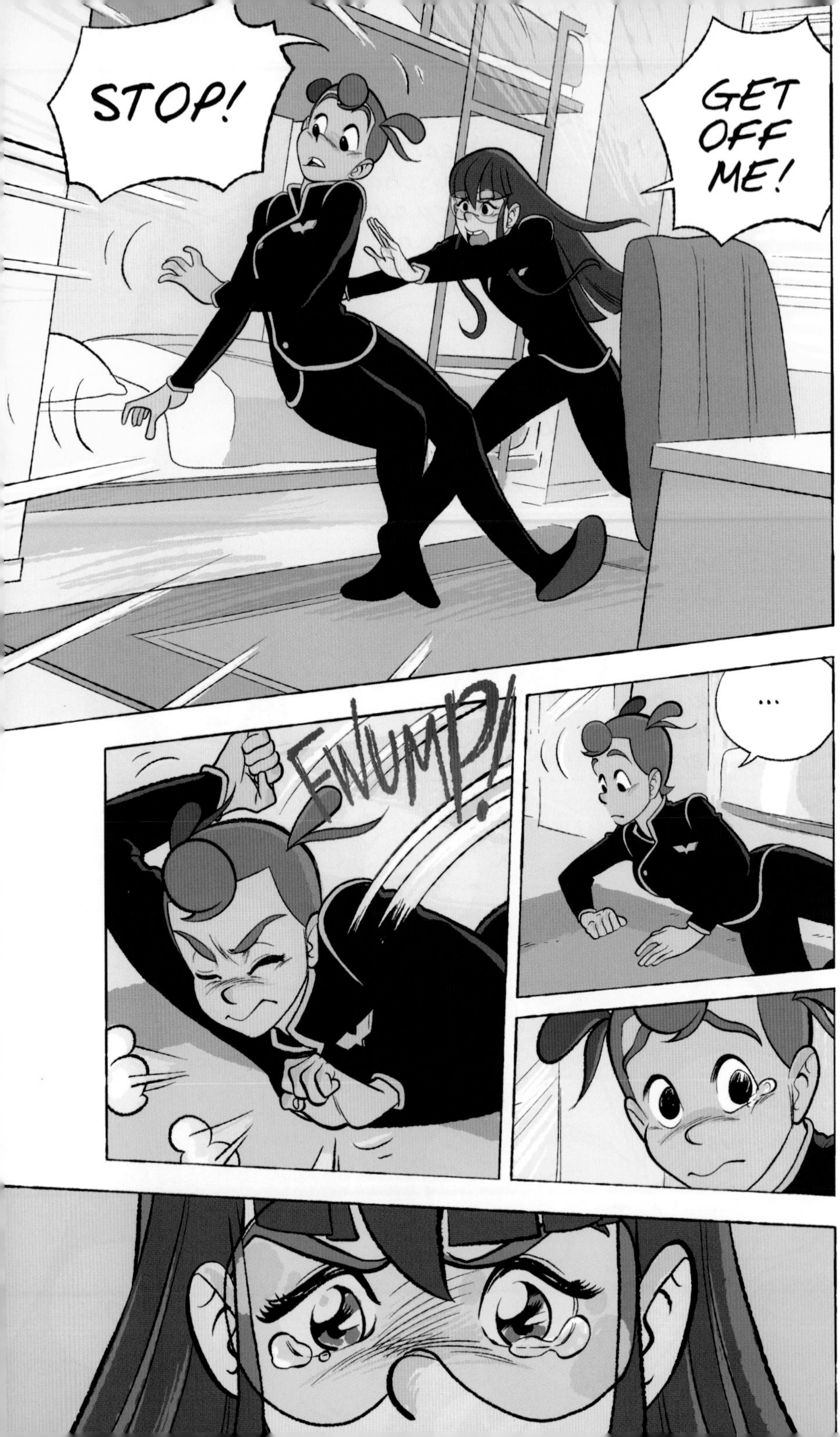
STOP!
GET OFF ME!
FWUMP!
...

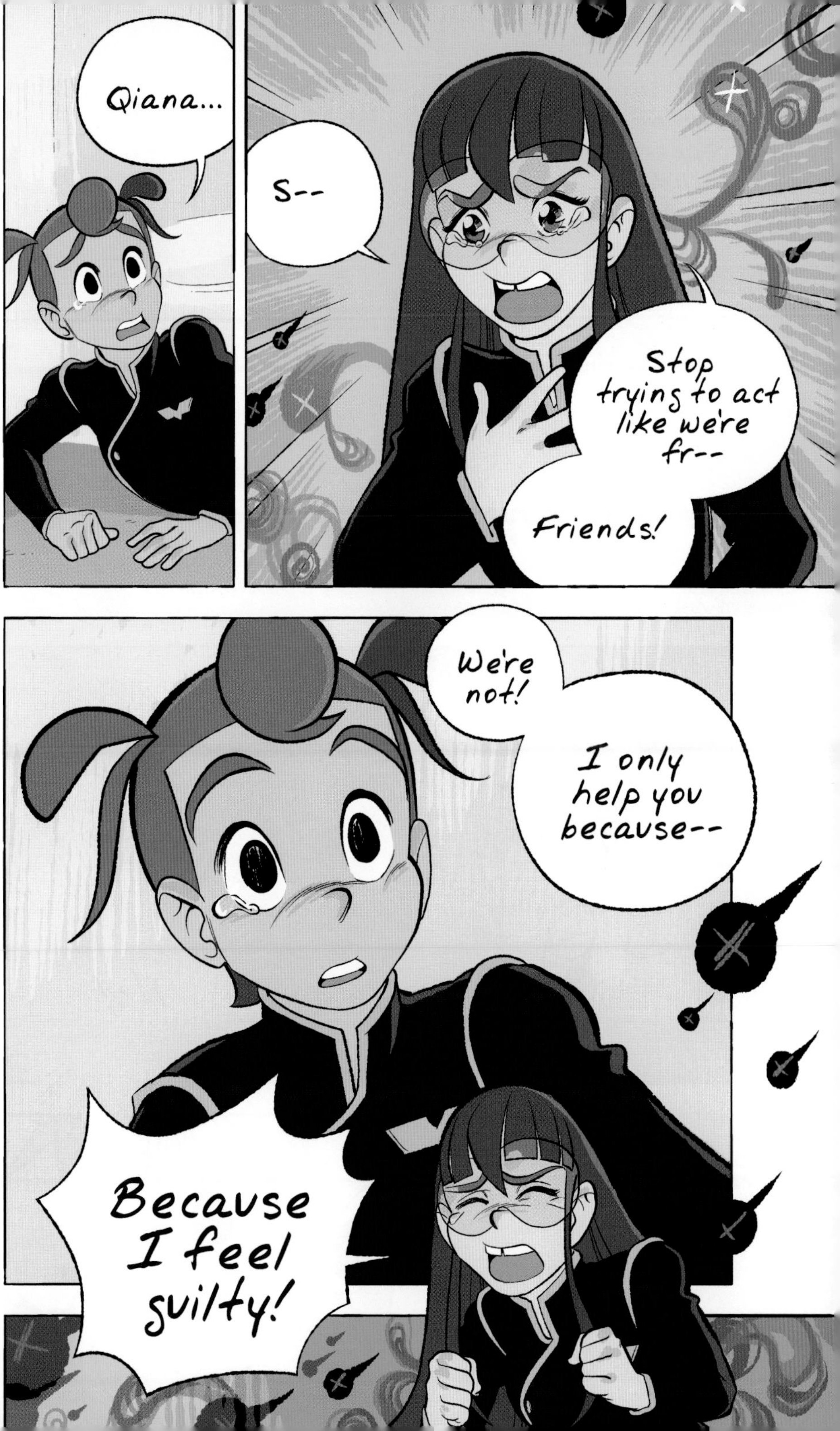
Qiana...
S--
Stop tryins to act like we're fr--
Friends!
We're not!
I only help you because--
Because I feel guilty!

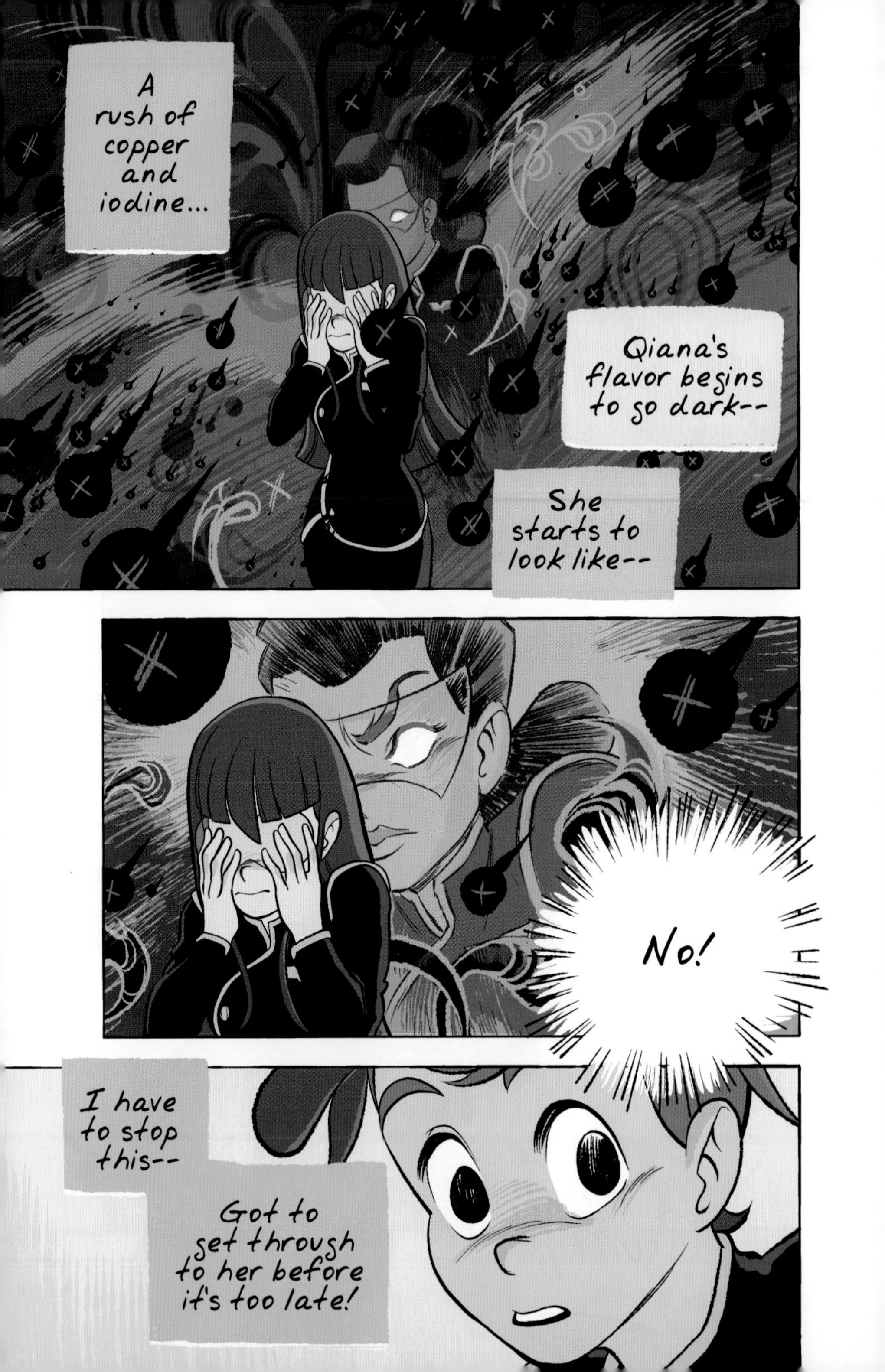

A rush of copper and iodine...
Qiana's flavor begins to go dark--
She starts to look like--
No!
I have to stop this--
Got to get through to her before it's too late!

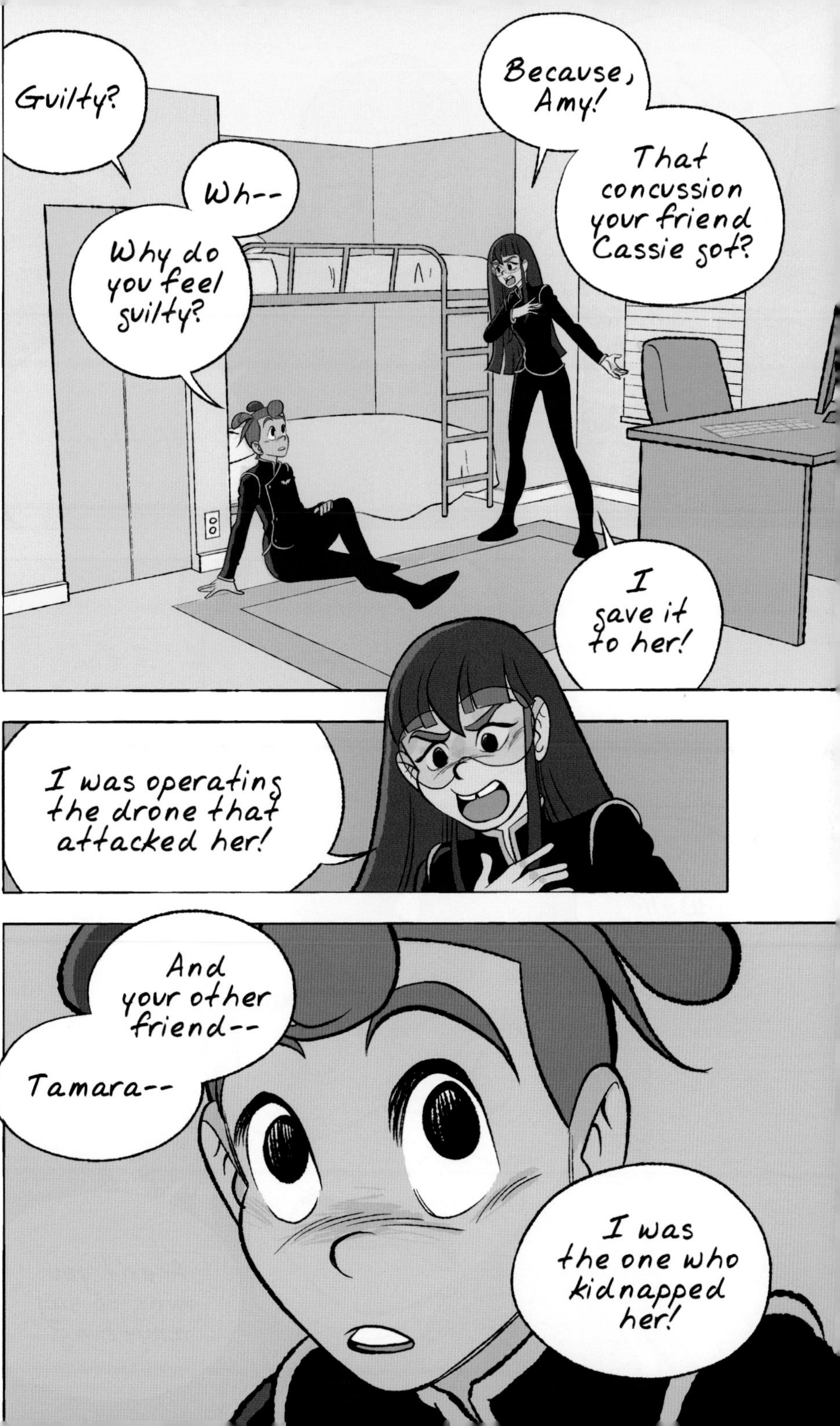
Because, Amy!
That concussion your friend Cassie got?
Guilty?
Wh--
Why do you feel guilty?
I gave it to her!
I was operating the drone that attacked her!
And your other friend--
Tamara--
I was the one who kidnapped her!

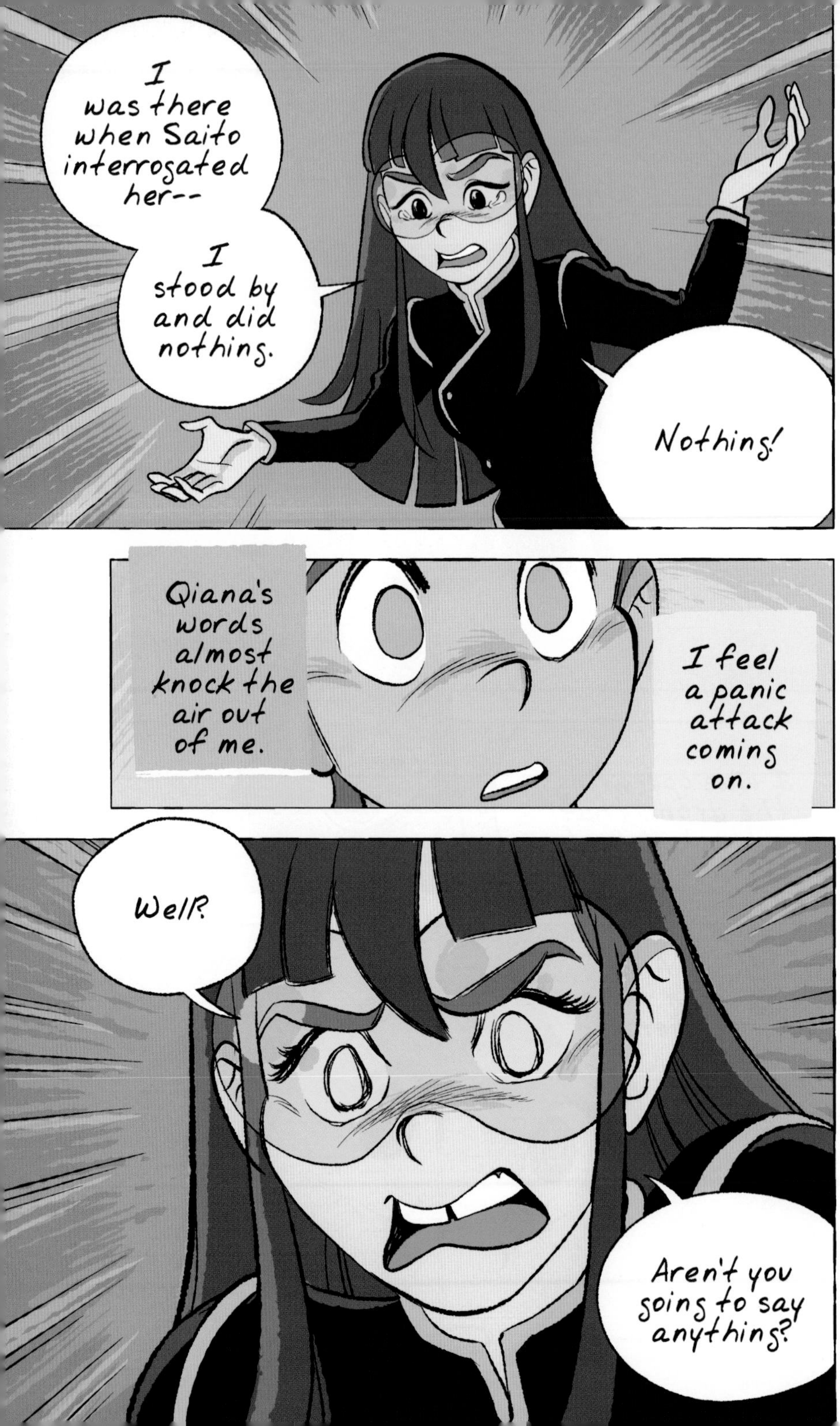
I was there when Saito interrogated her--
I stood by and did nothing.
Nothing!
Qiana's words almost knock the air out of me.
I feel a panic attack coming on.
Well?
Aren't you going to say anything?

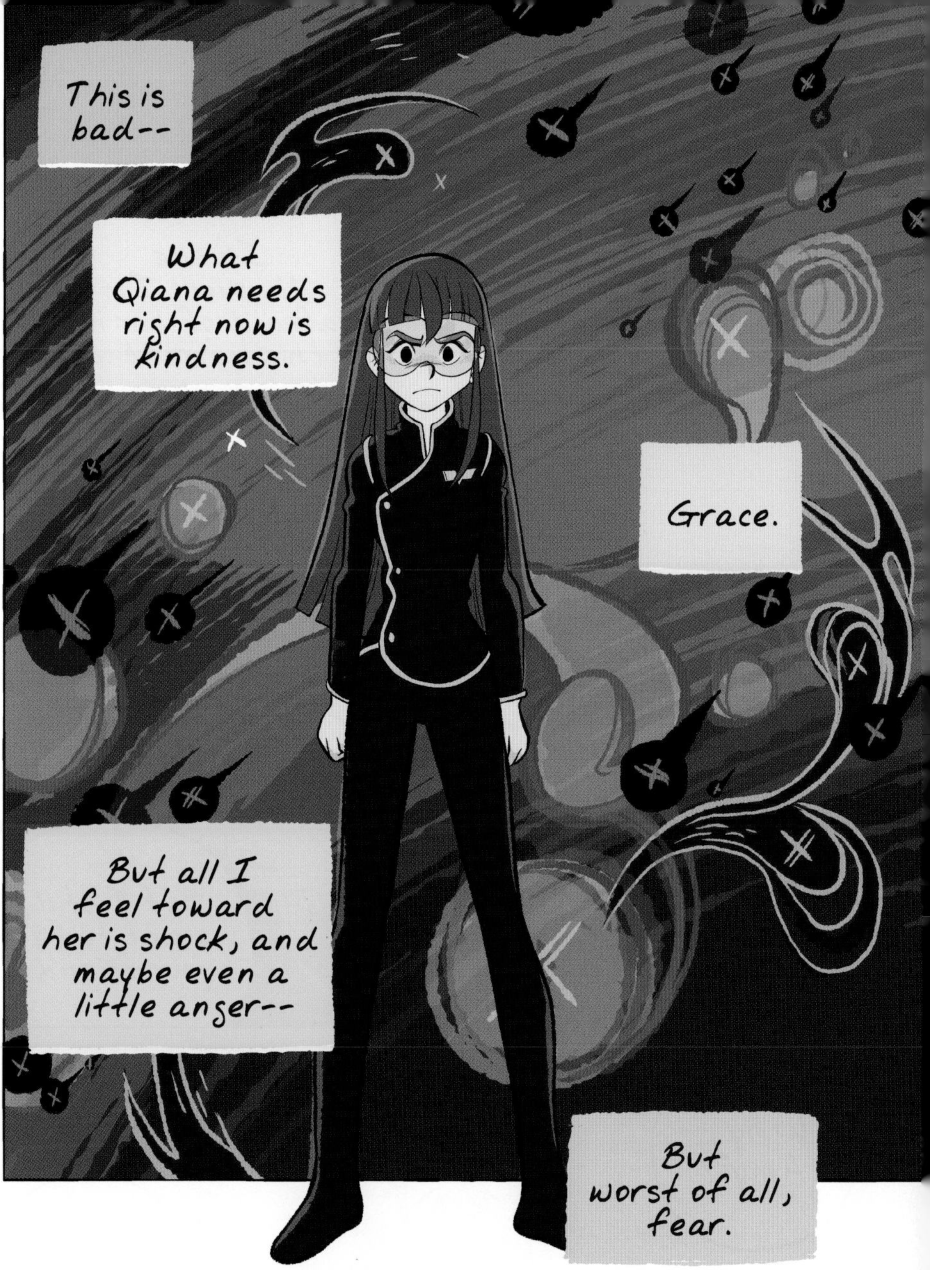
This is bad--
What Qiana needs right now is kindness.
Grace.
But all I feel toward her is shock, and maybe even a little anger--
But worst of all, fear.

Qiana thinks she's a monster right now, and that belief is threatening to actually turn her into one.

And if she sees the fear in my eyes--

If she discovers I'm afraid of her in this moment--

It will confirm her worst suspicions about herself.

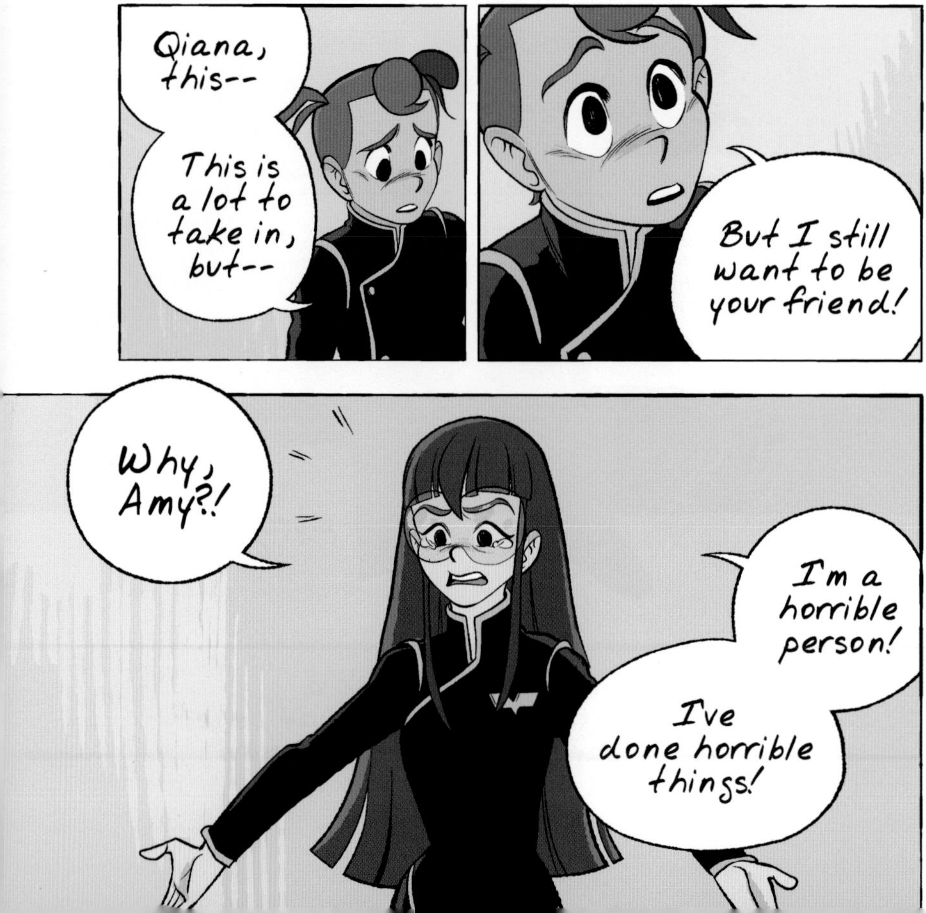
Qiana, this--
This is a lot to take in, but--
But I still want to be your friend!
Why, Amy?!
I'm a horrible person!
I've done horrible things!

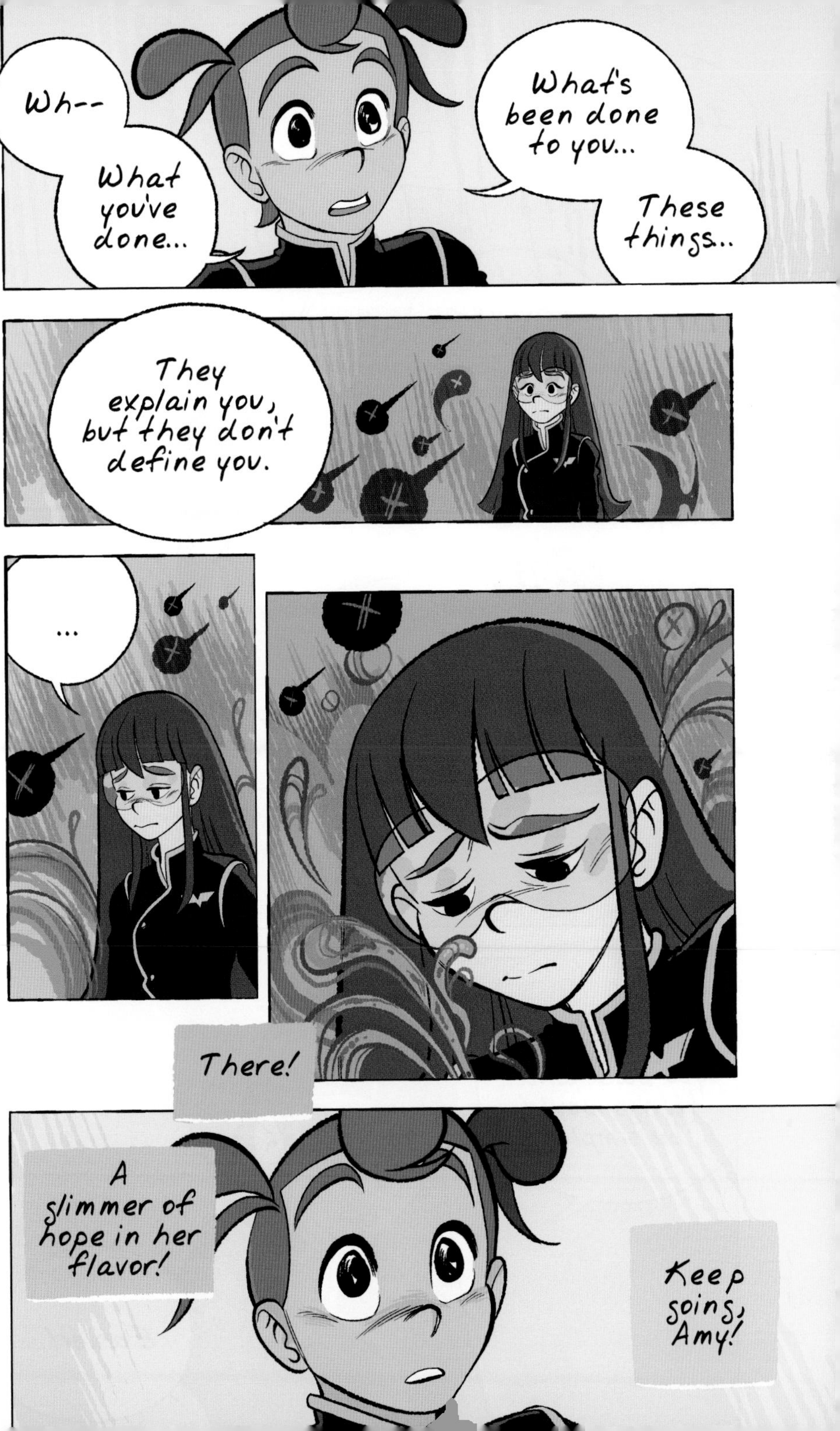
Wh--
What you've done...
What's been done to you...
These things..
They explain you, but they don't define you.
...
There!
A glimmer of hope in her flavor!
Keep going, Amy!

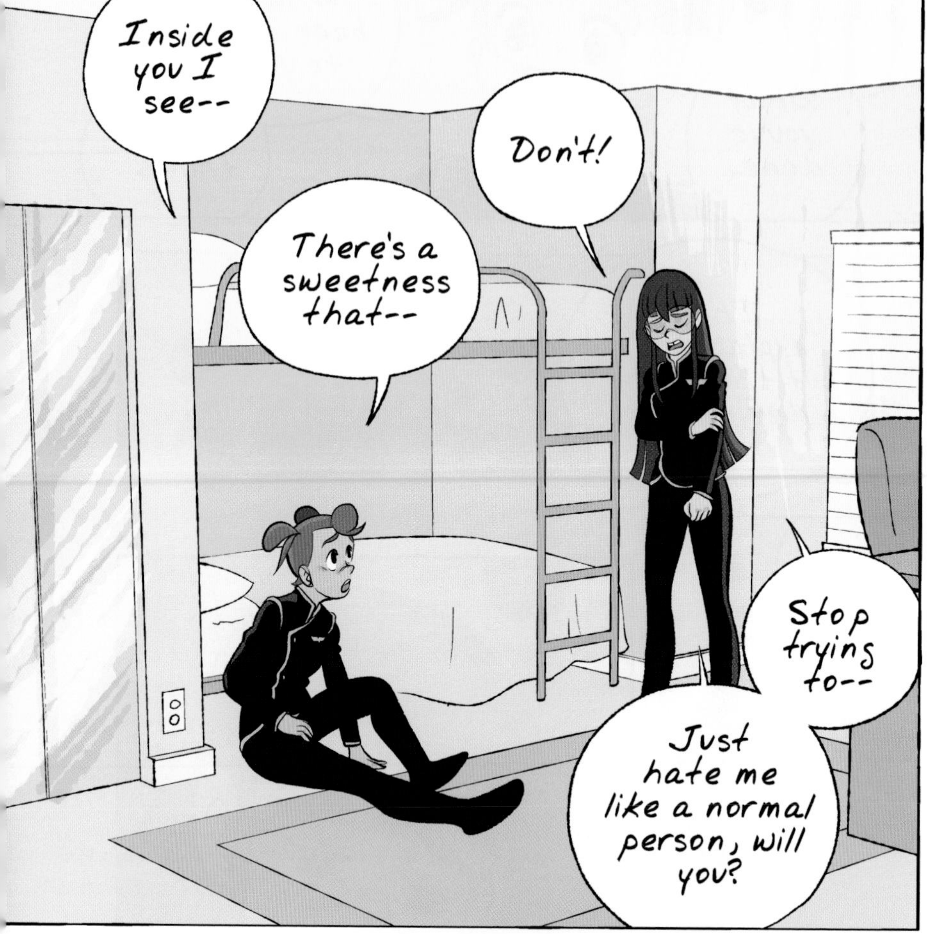
Inside you I see--
Don't!
There's a sweetness that--
Stop trying to--
Just hate me like a normal person, will you?

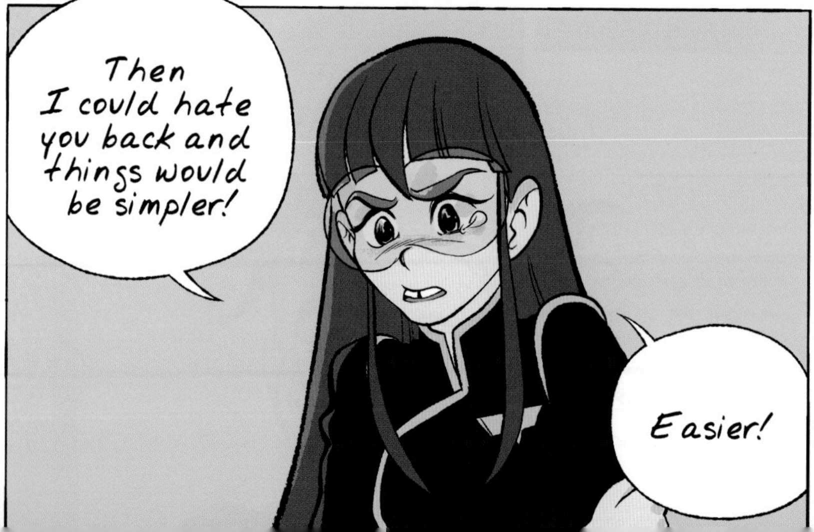
Then I could hate you back and things would be simpler!
Easier!

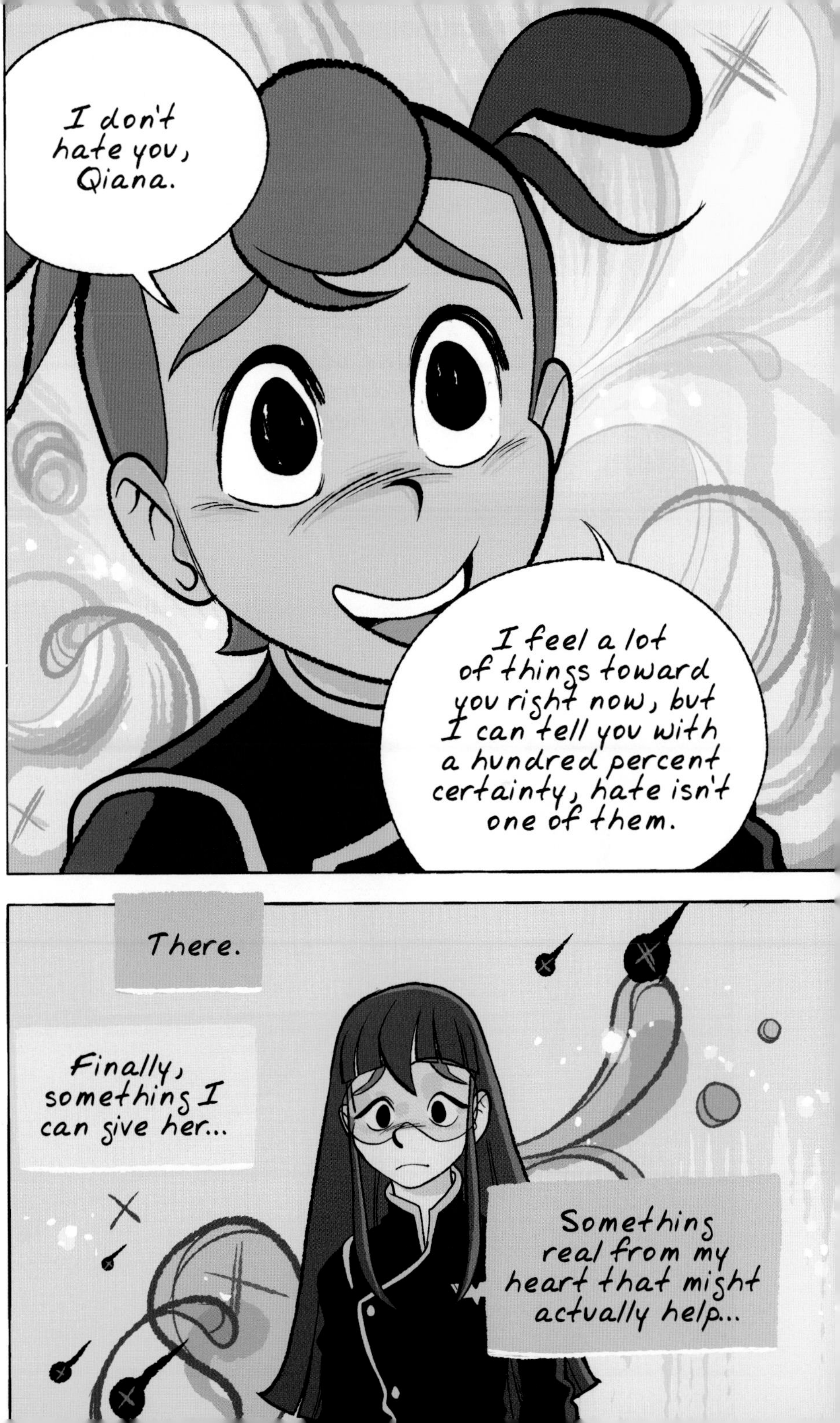
I don't hate you, Qiana.
I feel a lot of things toward you right now, but I can tell you with a hundred percent certainty, hate isn't one of them.
There.
Finally, something I can give her...
Something real from my heart that might actually help...

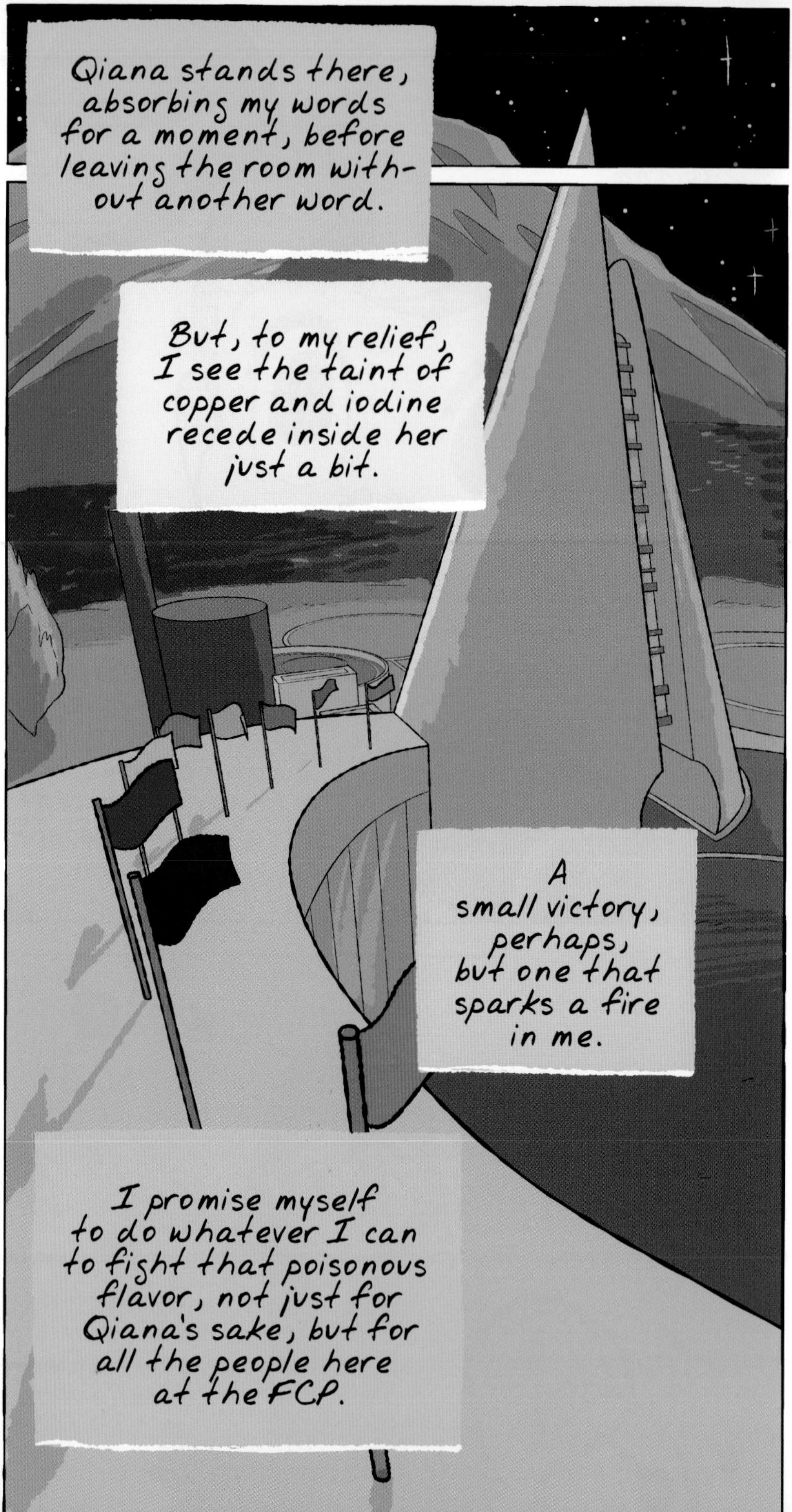
Qiana stands there, absorbing my words for a moment, before leaving the room without another word.
But, to my relief, I see the taint of copper and iodine recede inside her just a bit.
A small victory, perhaps, but one that sparks a fire in me.
I promise myself to do whatever I can to fight that poisonous flavor, not just for Qiana's sake, but for all the people here at the FCP.

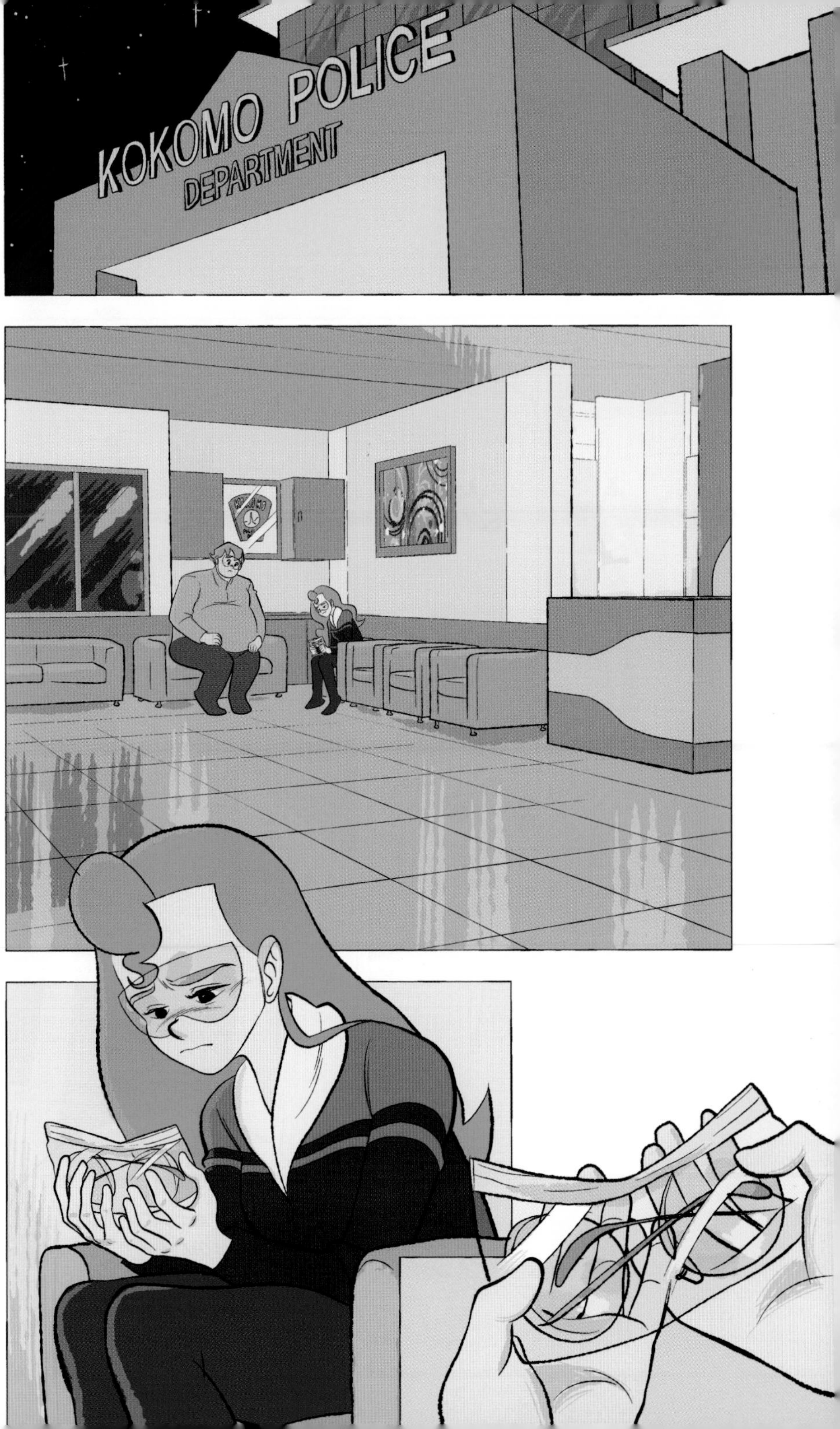

KOKOMO POLICE
DEPARTMENT

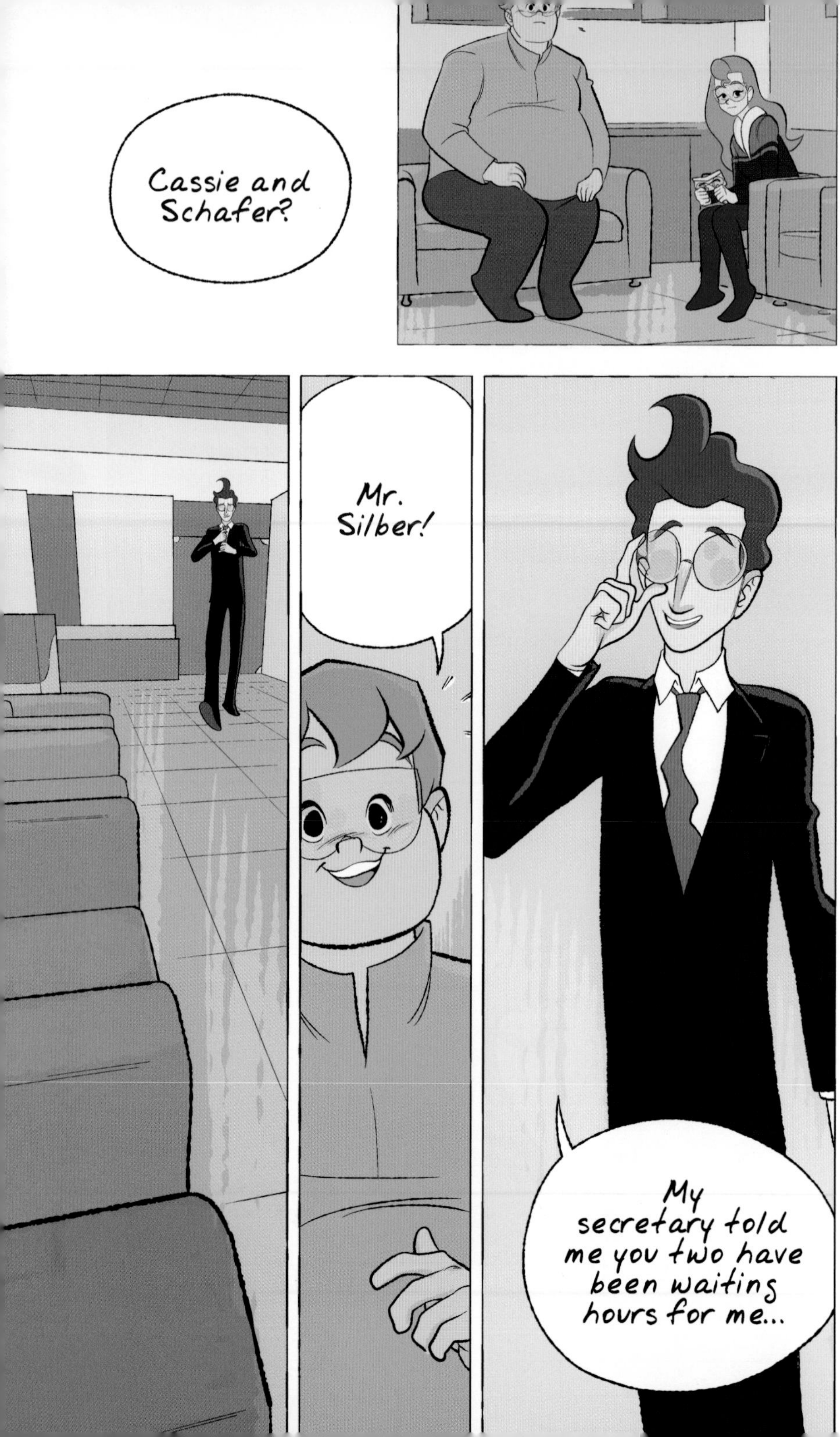
Cassie and Schafer?
Mr. Silber!
My secretary told me you two have been waiting hours for me...

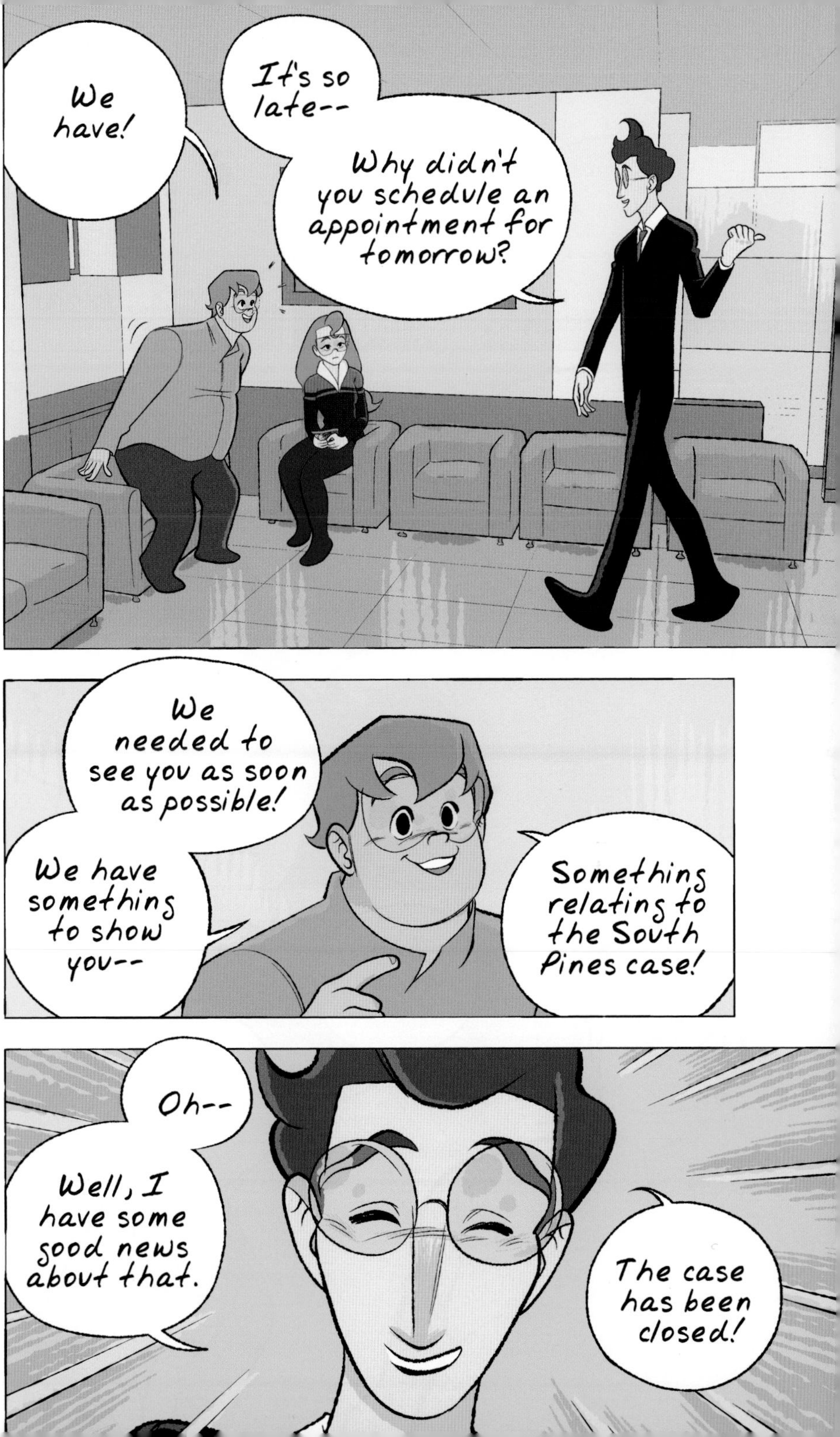
We have!
It's so late--
Why didn't you schedule an appointment for tomorrow?
We needed to see you as soon as possible!
We have somethins to show you--
Somethins relatins to the South Pines case!
Oh--
Well, I have some sood news about that.
The case has been closed!

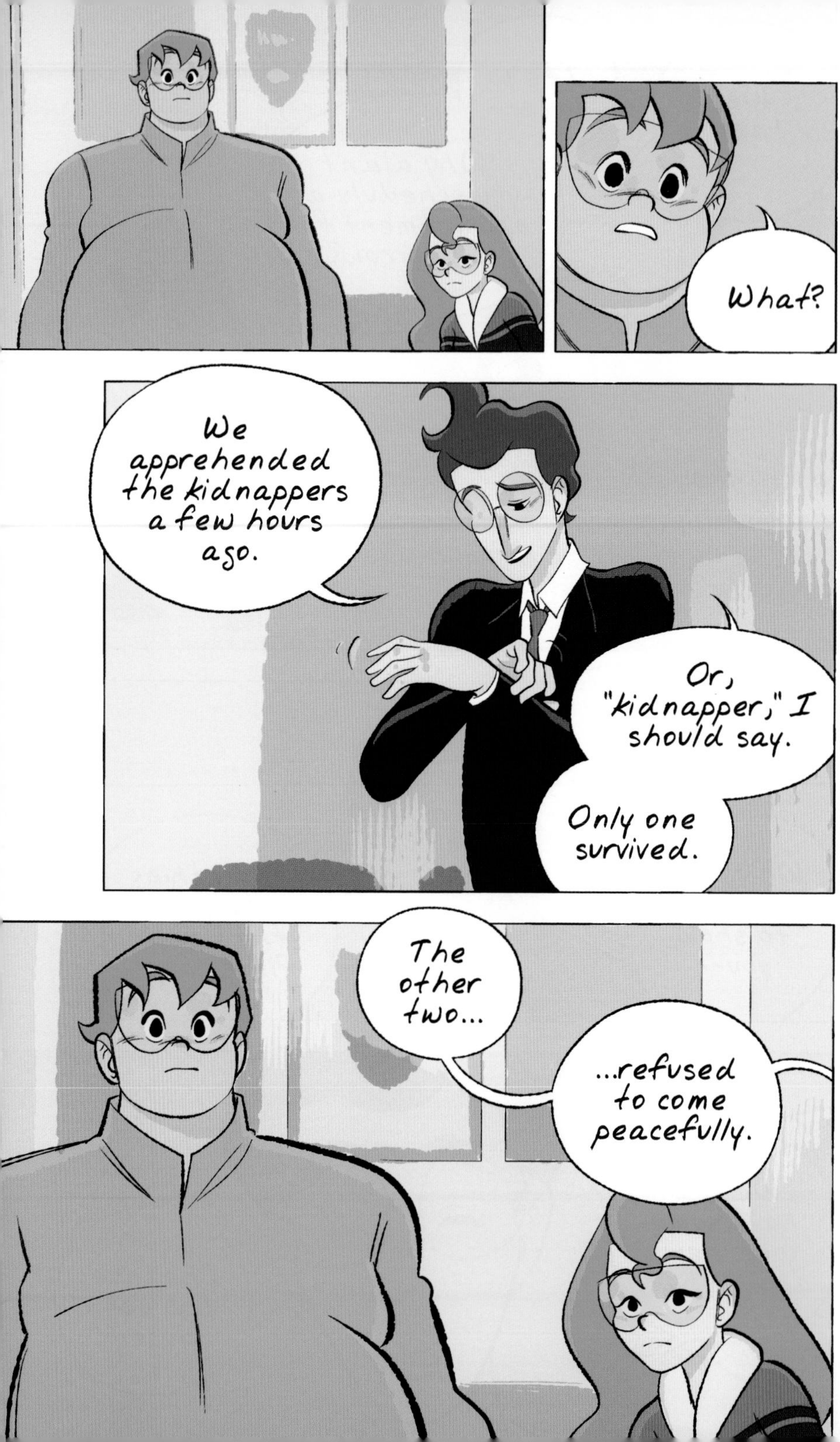
What?
We apprehended the kidnappers a few hours ago.
Or, "kidnapper," I should say.
Only one survived.
The other two...
...refused to come peacefully.

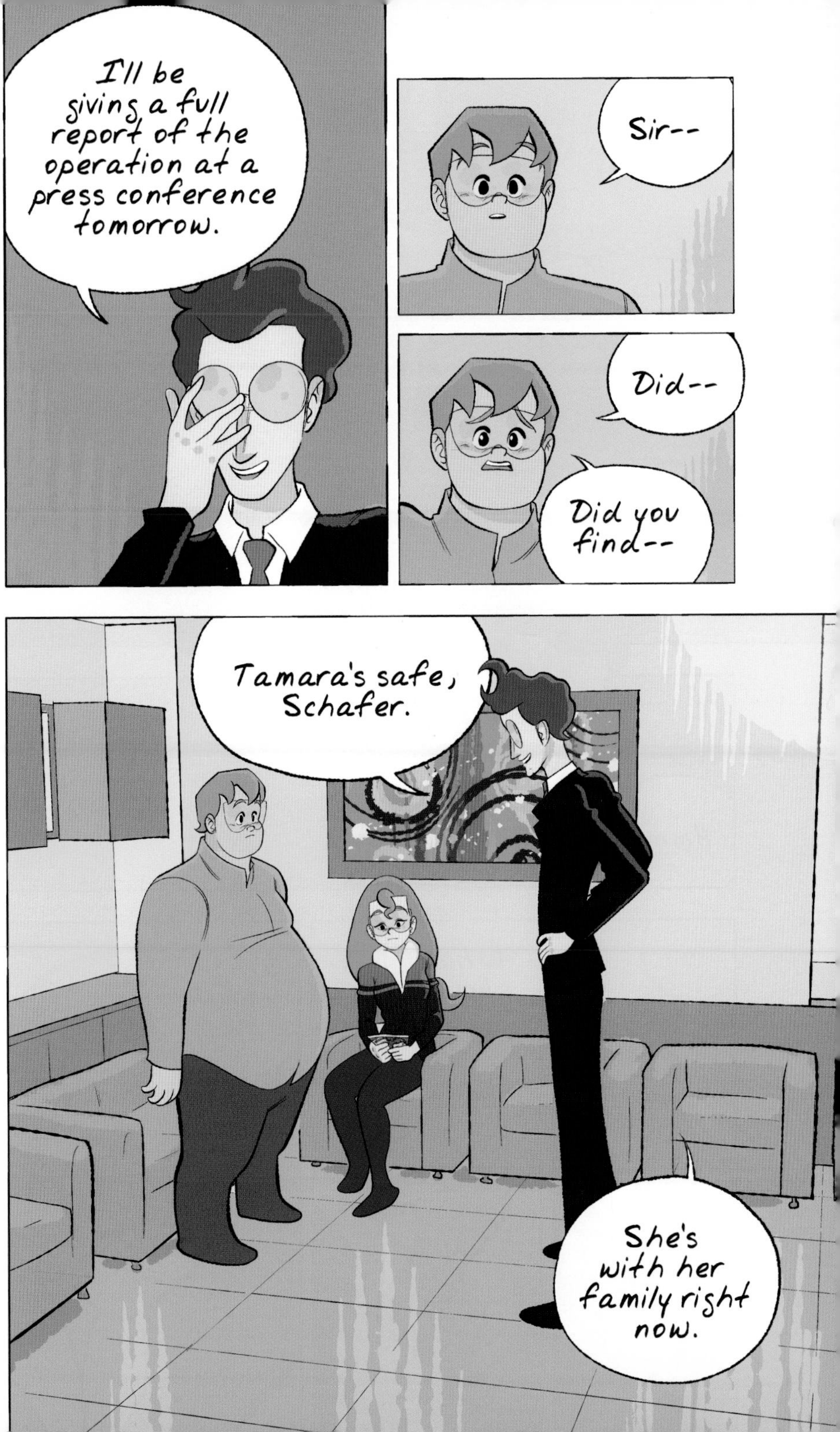
I'll be giving a full report of the operation at a press conference tomorrow.
Sir--
Did--
Did you find--
Tamara's safe, Schafer.
She's with her family right now.

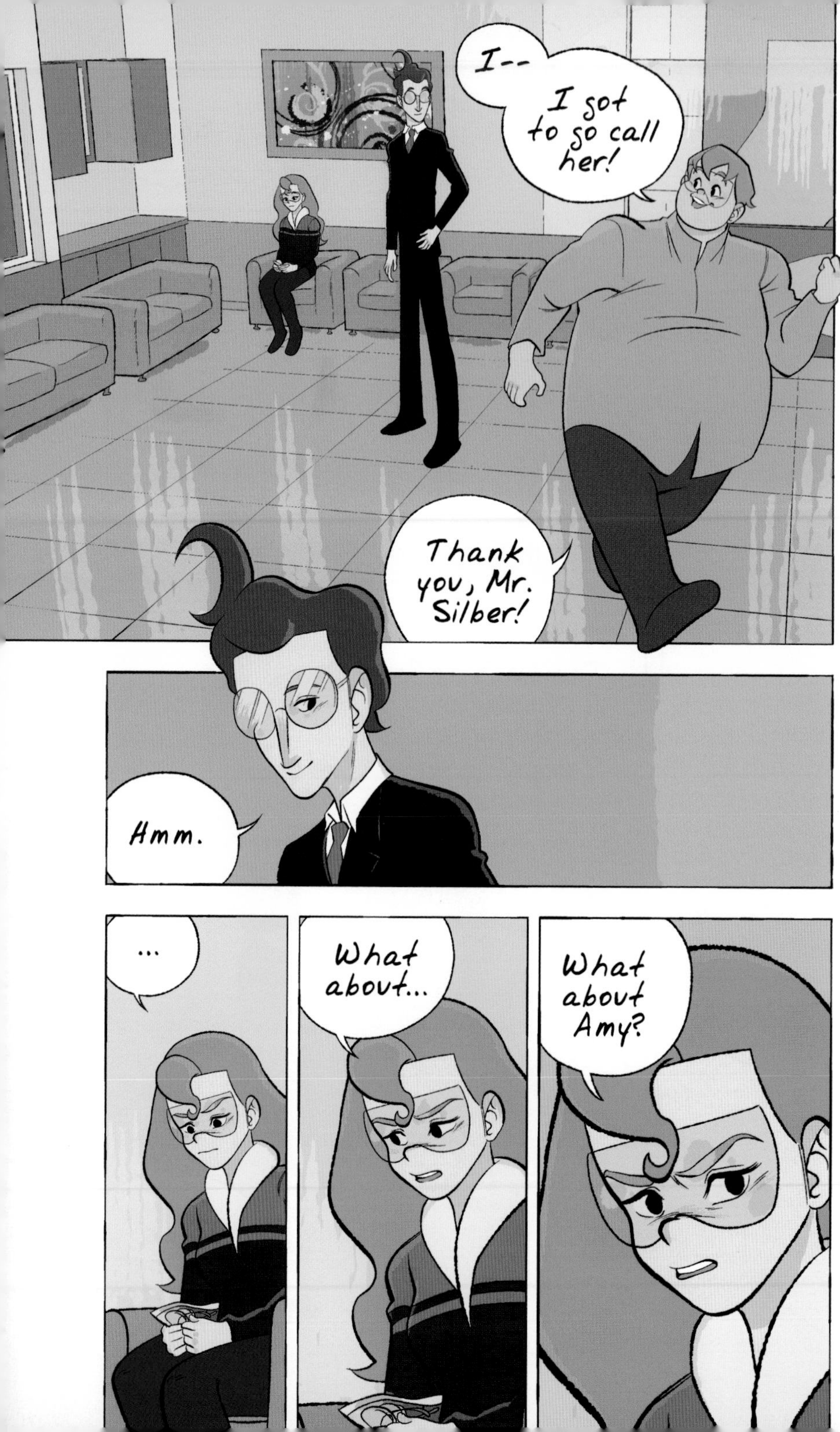
I--
I got to go call her!
Thank you, Mr. Silber!
Hmm.
...
What about...
What about Amy?

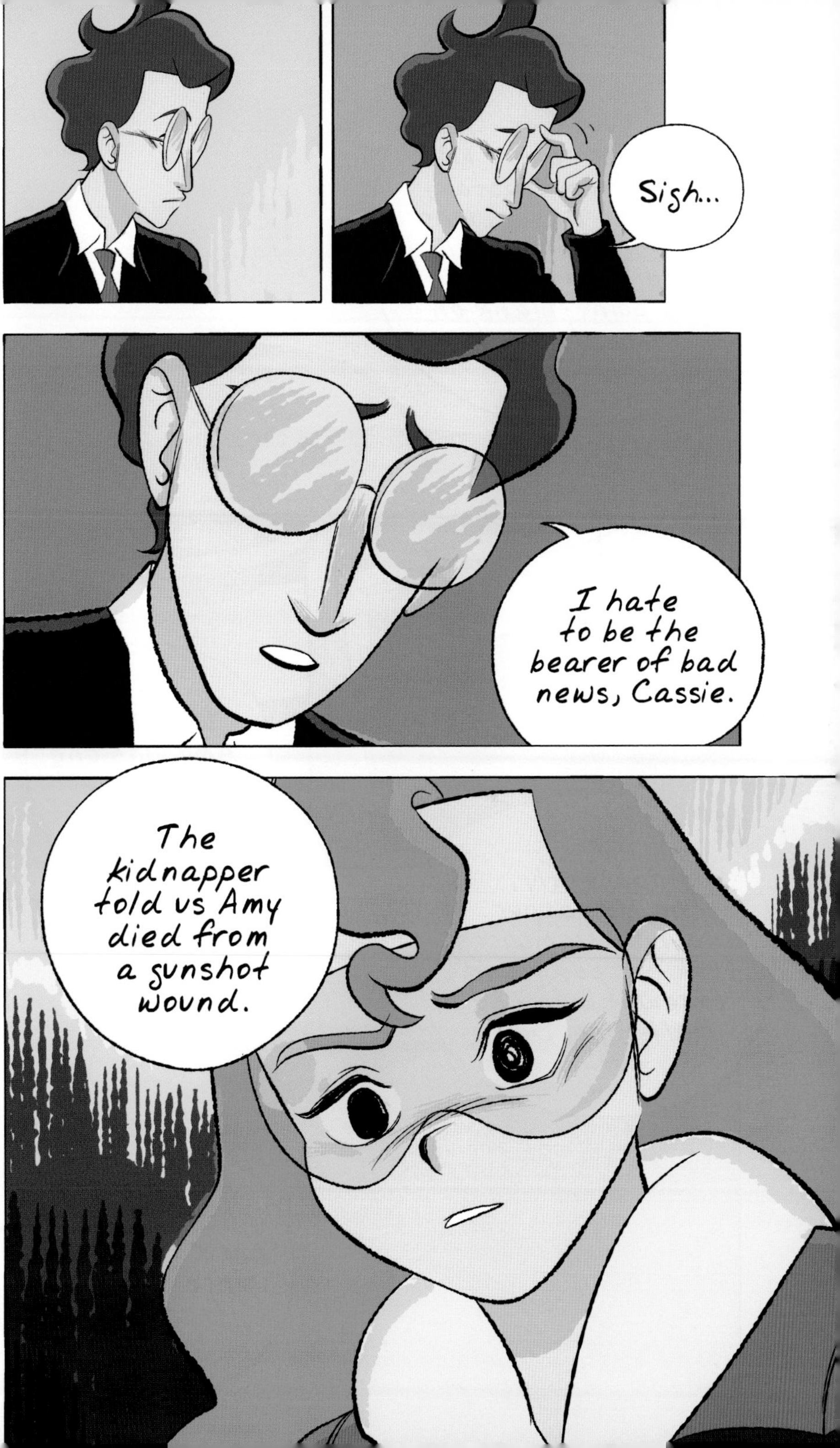
Sigh...
I hate to be the bearer of bad news, Cassie.
The kidnapper told us Amy died from a gunshot wound.

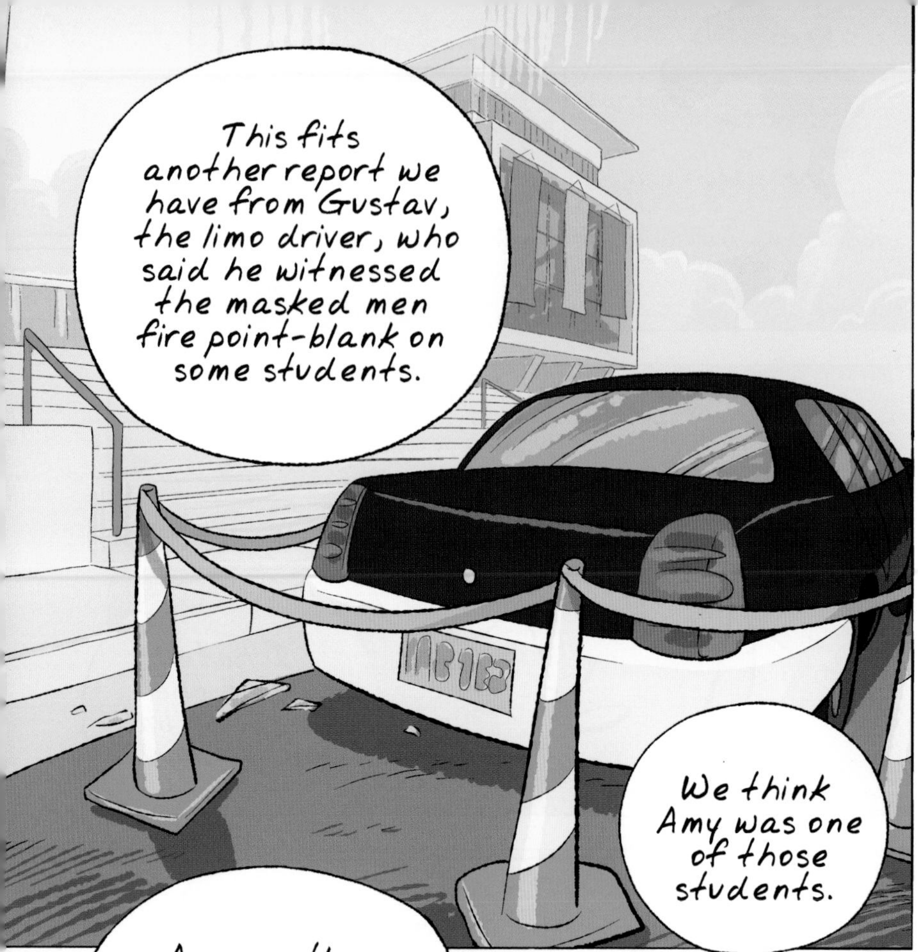
This fits another report we have from Gustav, the limo driver, who said he witnessed the masked men fire point-blank on some students.
We think Amy was one of those students.

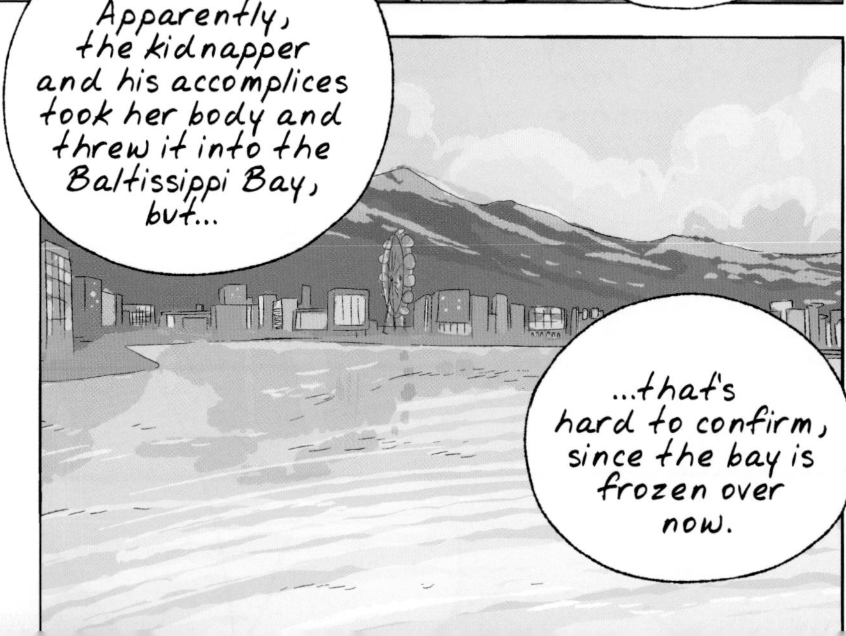
Apparently, the kidnapper and his accomplices took her body and threw it into the Baltissippi Bay, but...
...that's hard to confirm, since the bay is frozen over now.

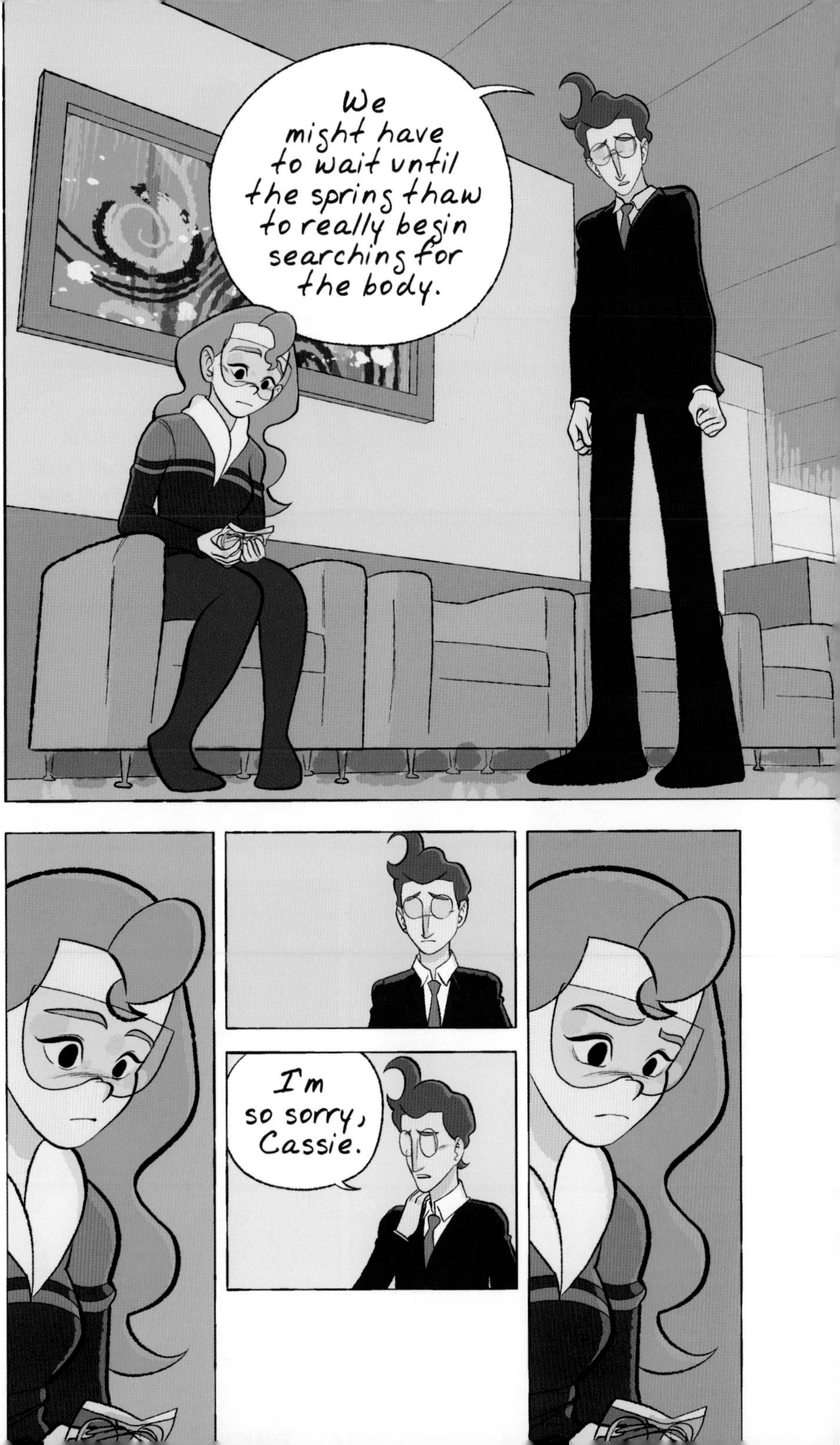
We might have to wait until the spring thaw to really begin searching for the body.
I'm so sorry, Cassie.

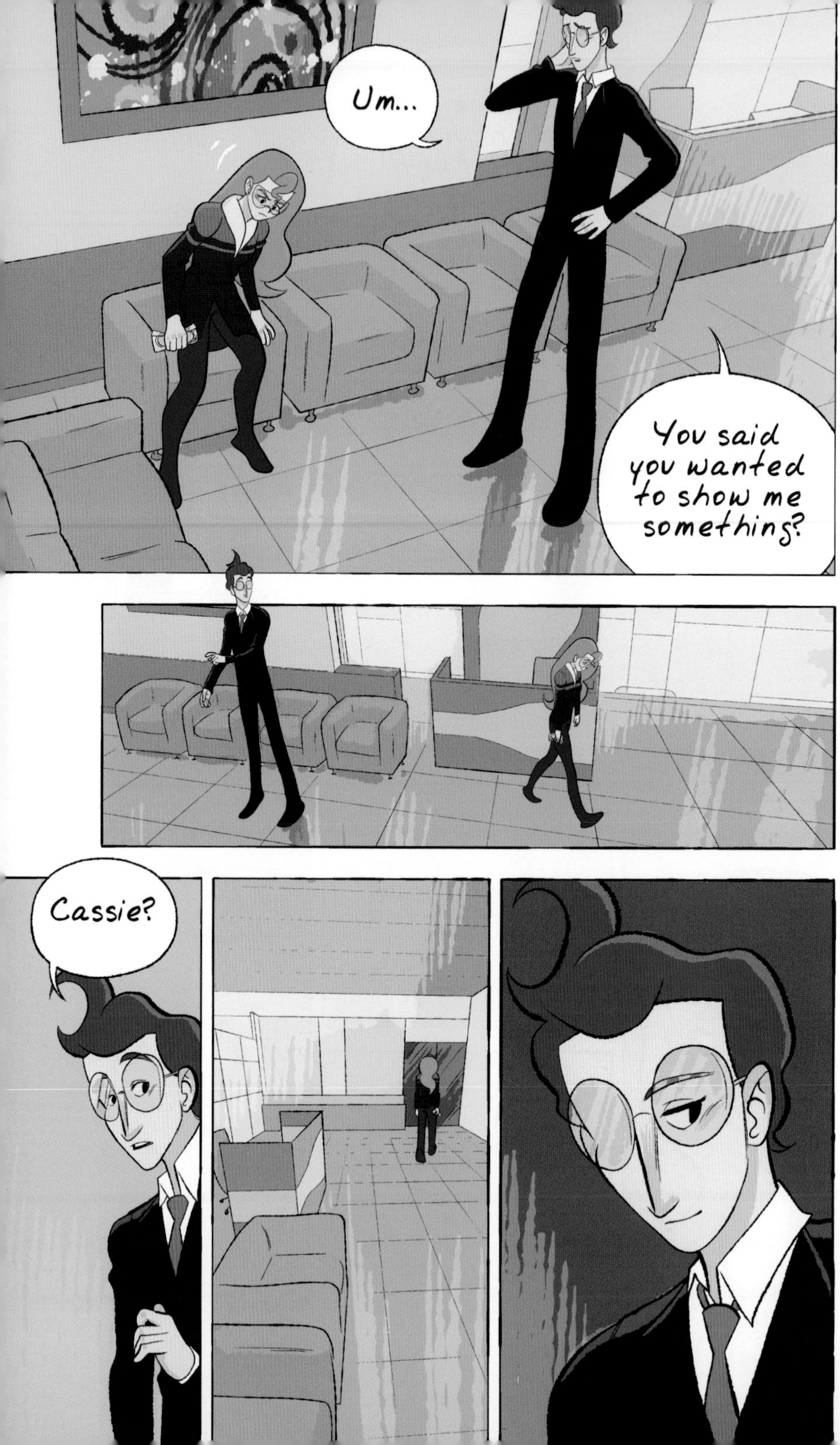
Um...
You said you wanted to show me something?
Cassie?

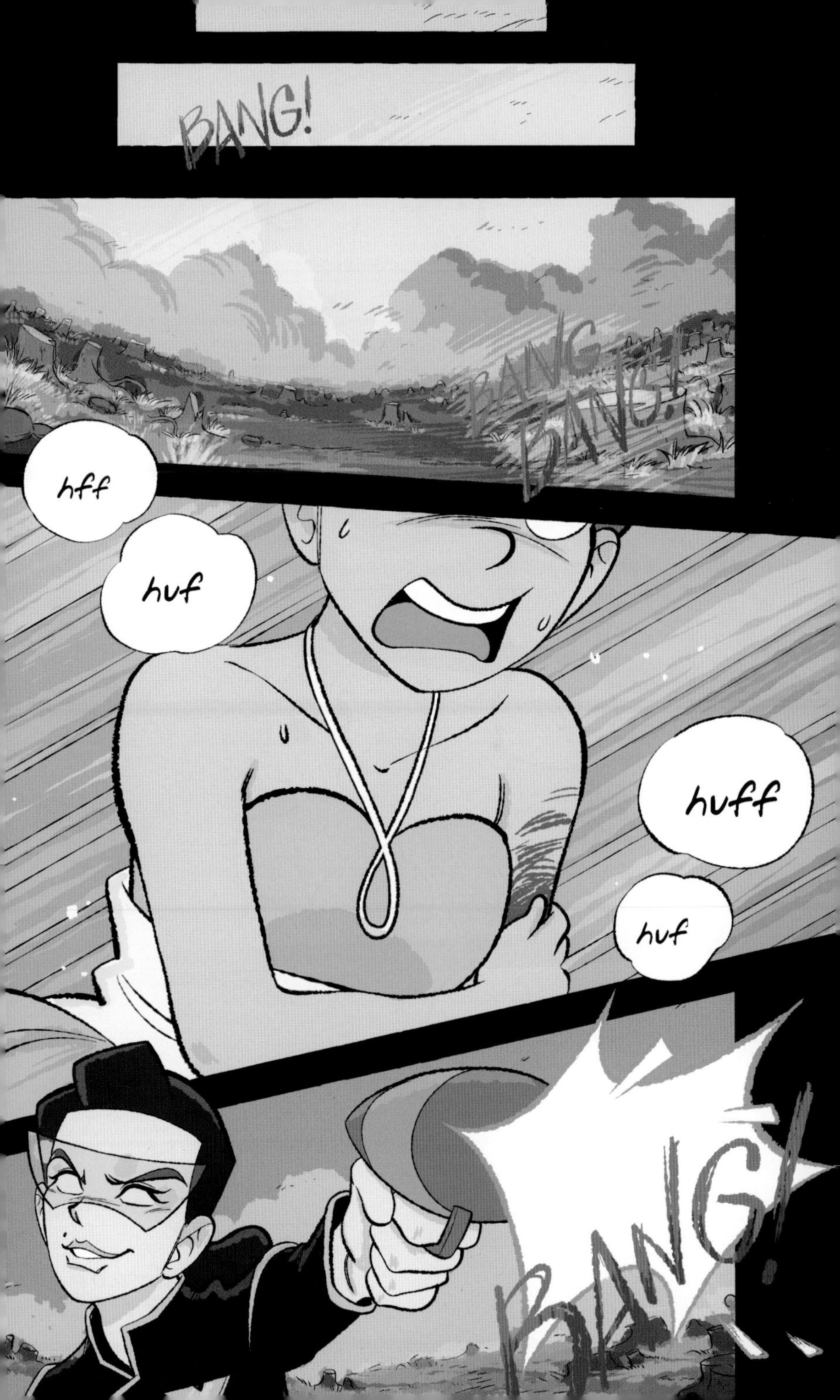
BANG!
BANG
BANG!
hff
huf
huff
huf
BANG!

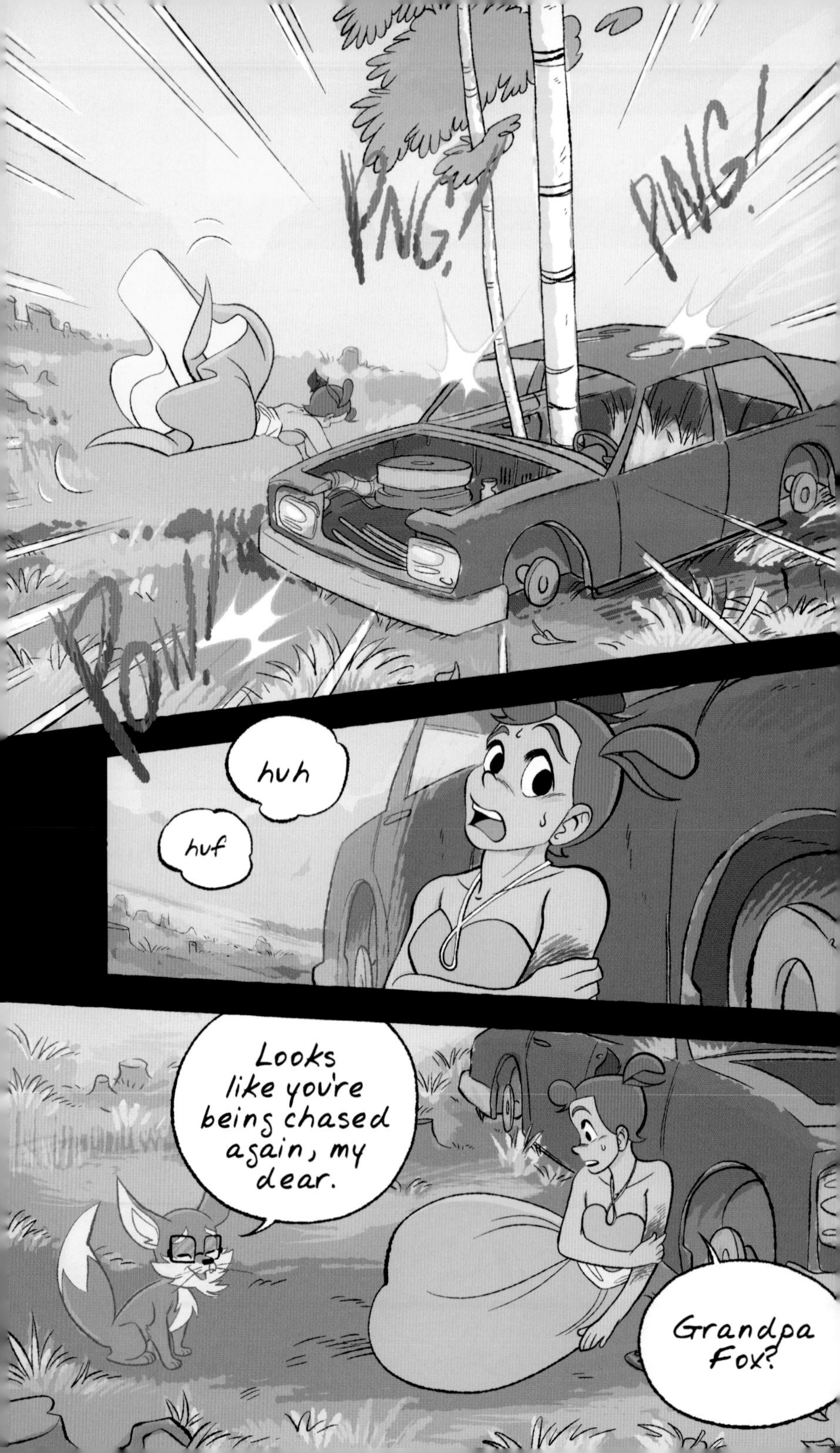
PING!
PING!
POW!
huh
huf
Looks like you're being chased again, my dear.
Grandpa Fox?

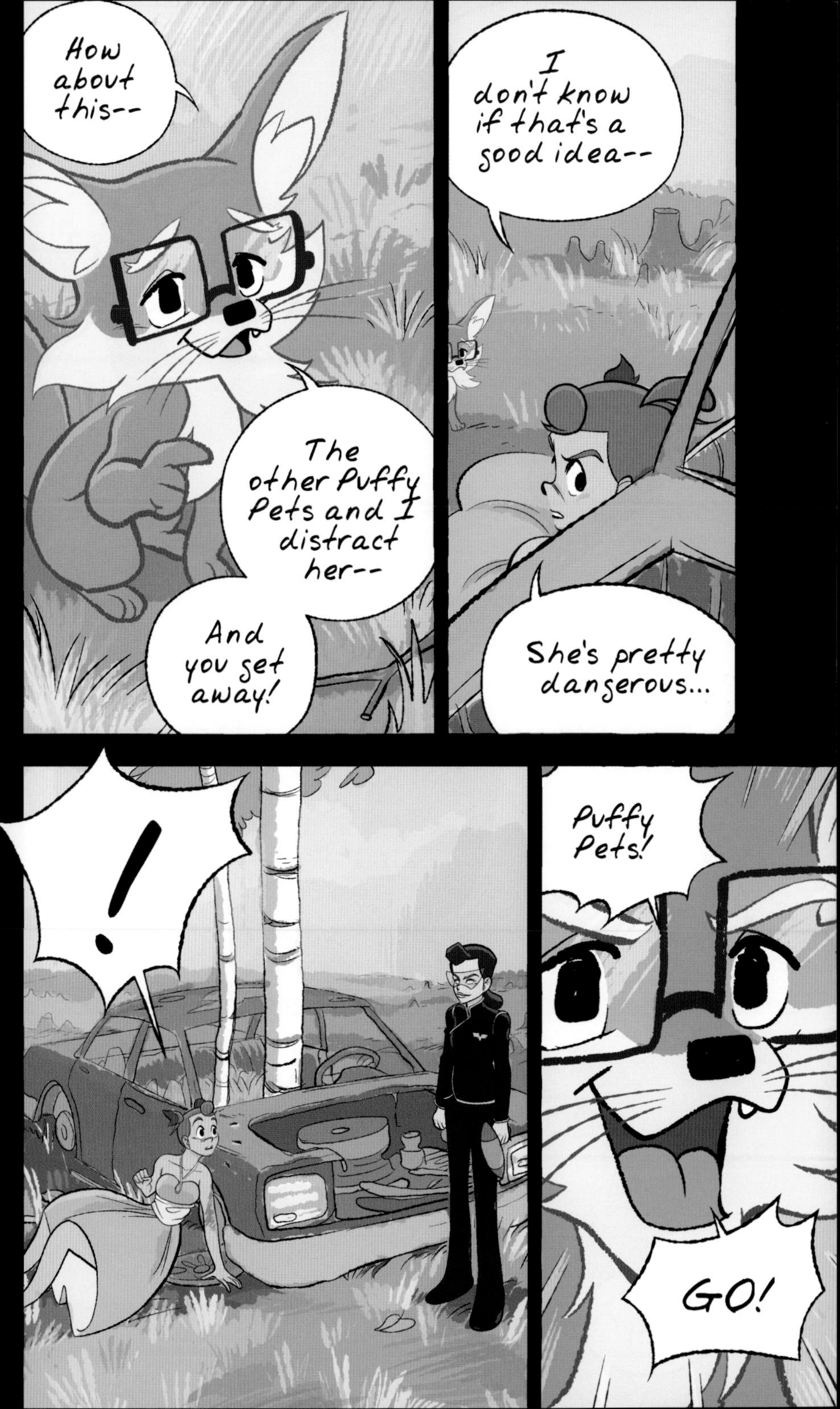
How about this--
The other Puffy Pets and I distract her--
And you get away!
I don't know if that's a good idea--
She's pretty dangerous...
!
Puffy Pets!
GO!

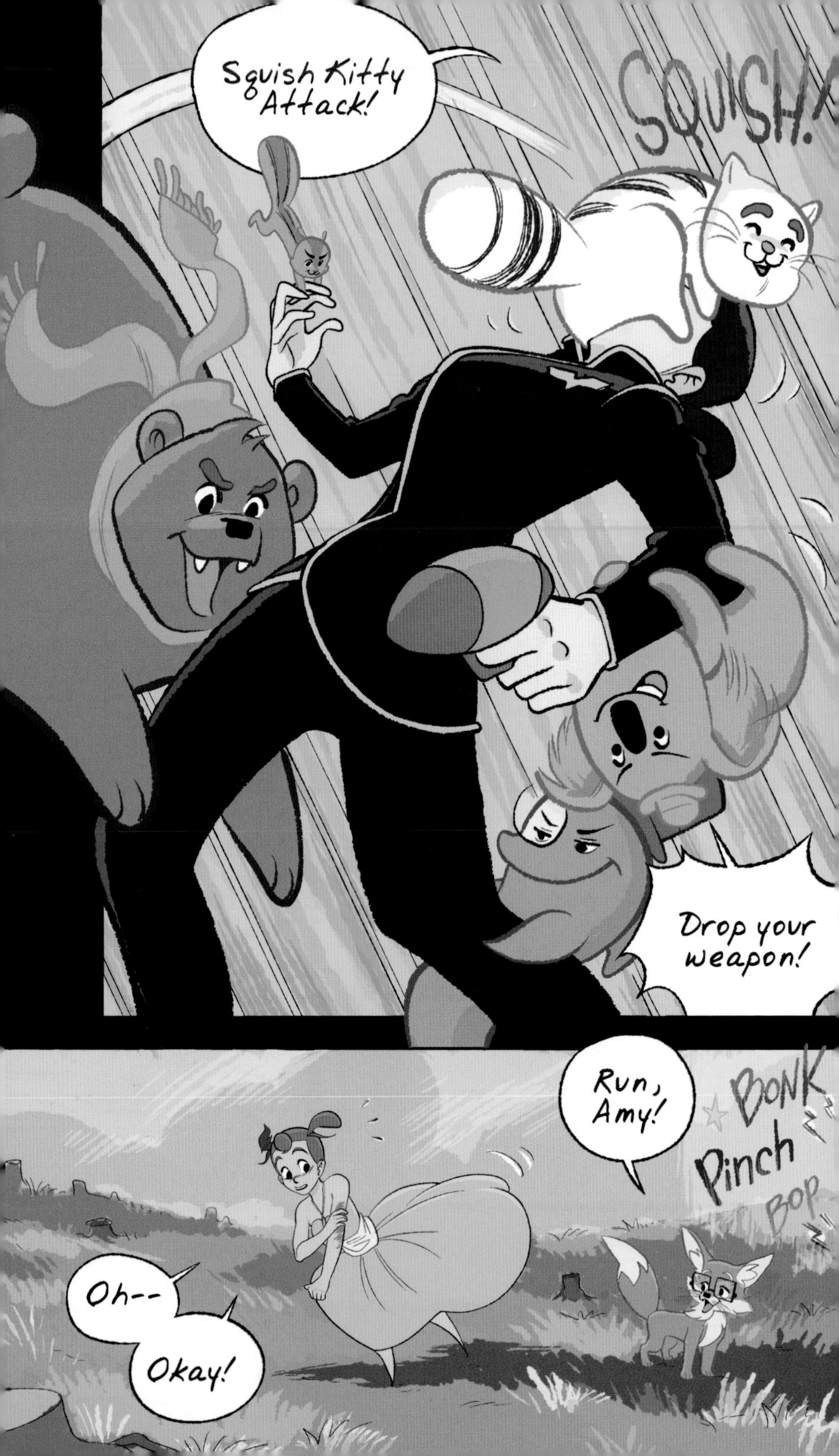
Squish Kitty Attack!
SQUISH!
Drop your weapon!
Run, Amy!
BONK
Pinch
BOP
Oh--
Okay!

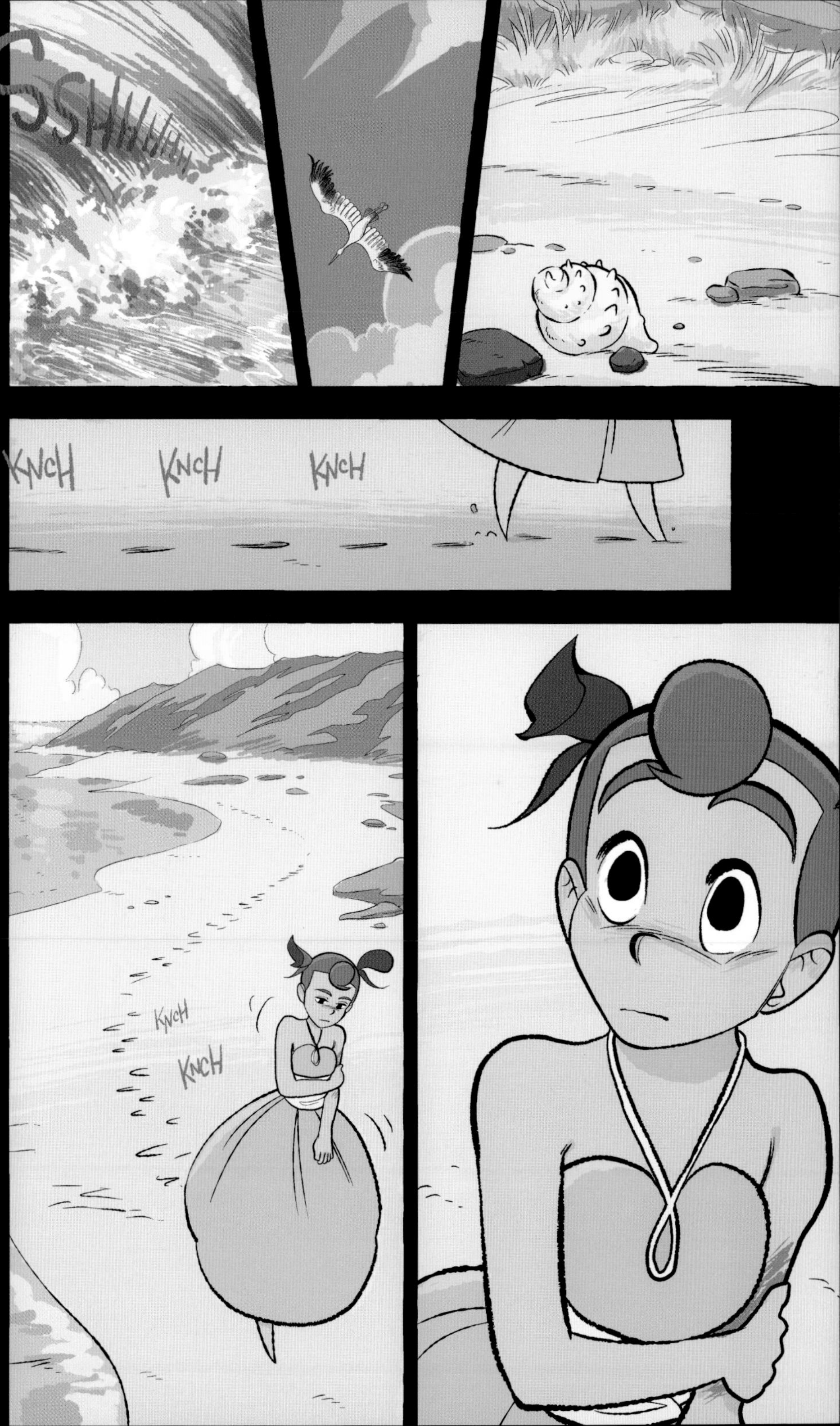
SSHHHHHH
KNCH
KNCH
KNCH
KNCH
KNCH

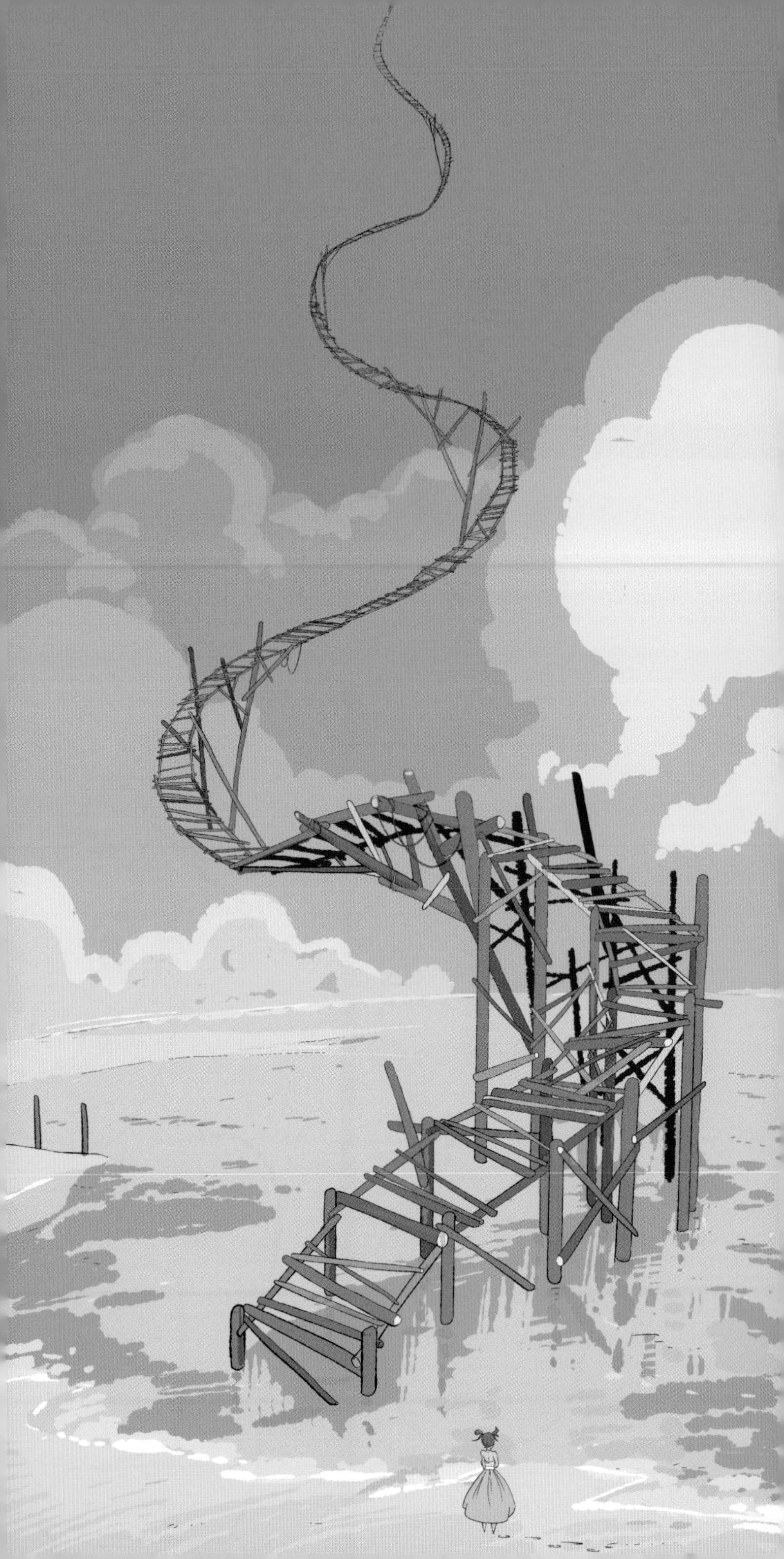

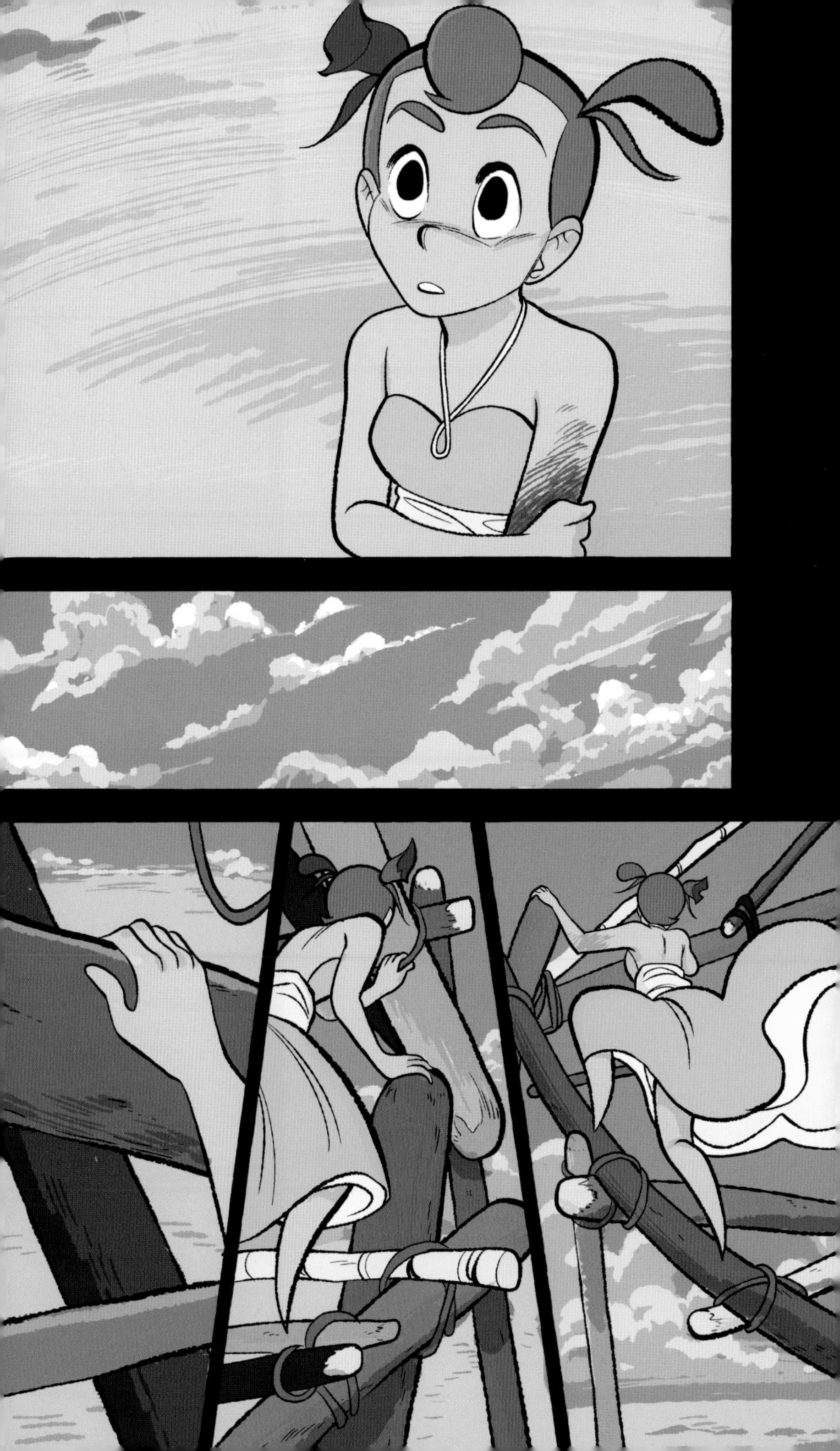

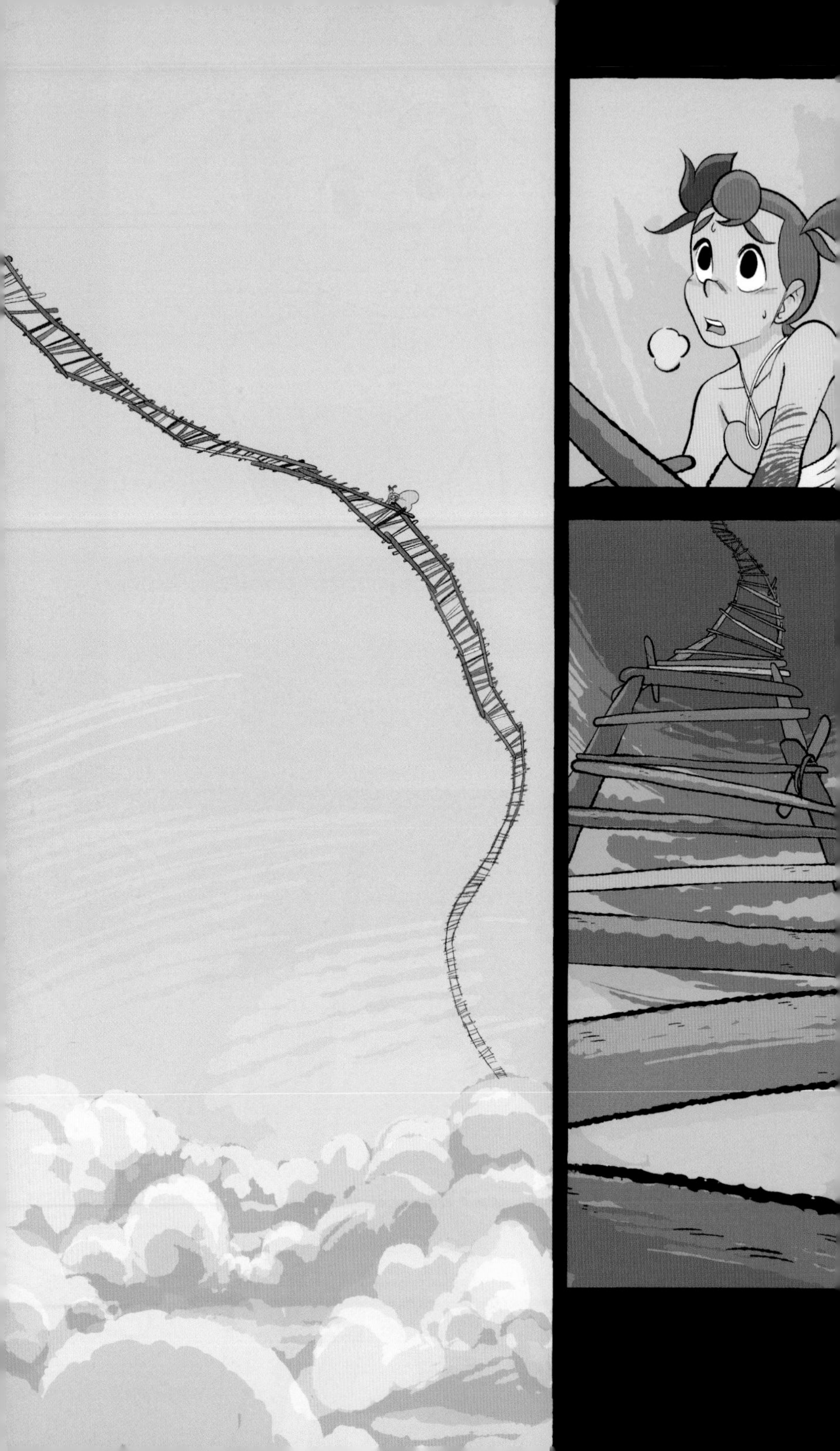

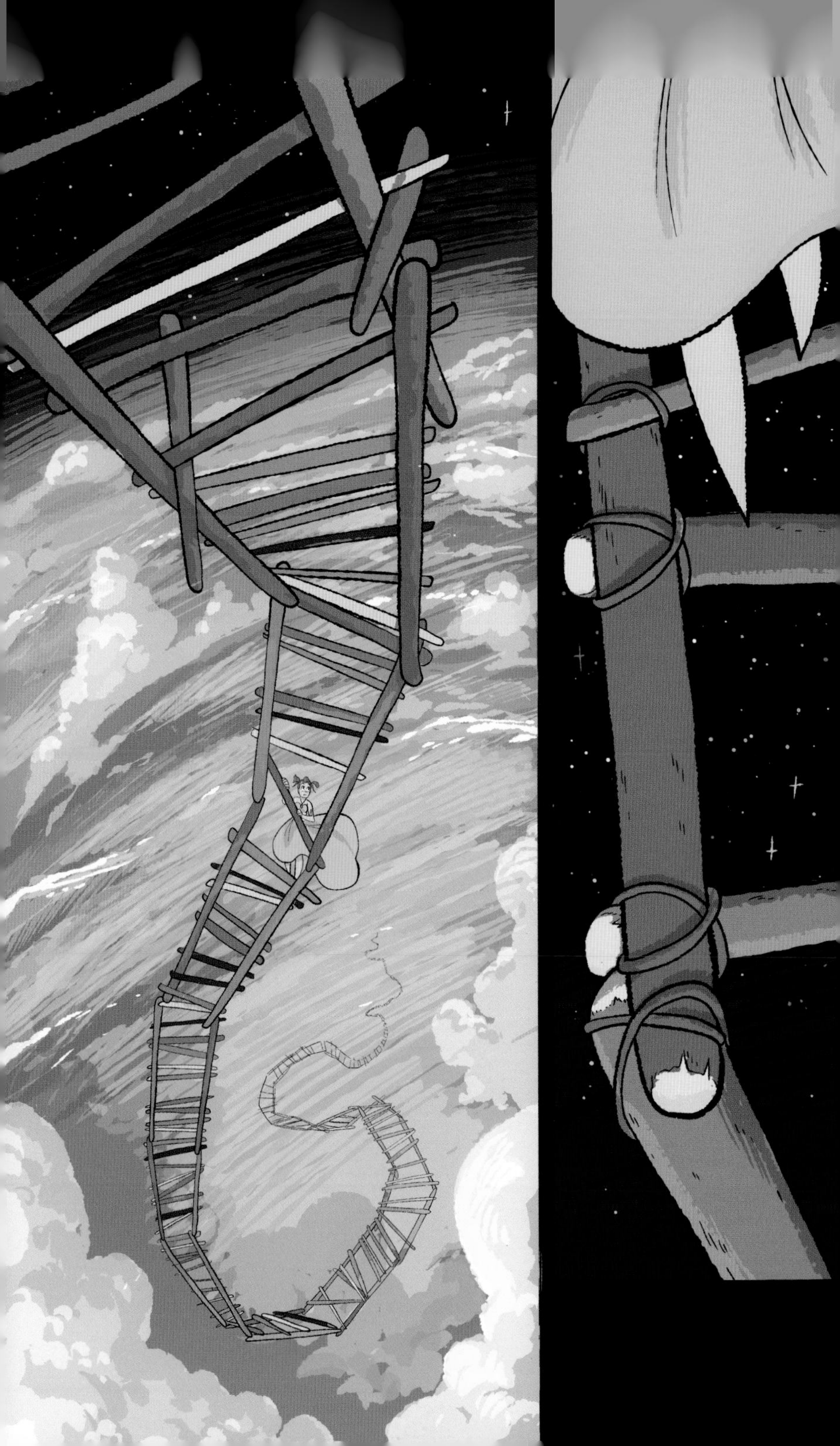

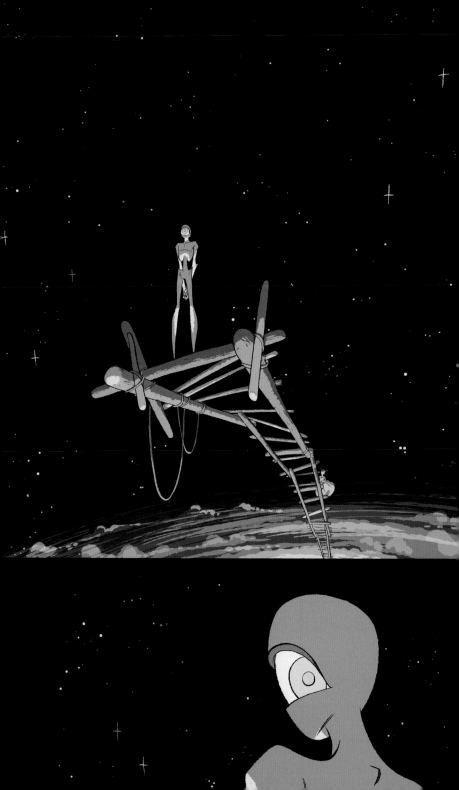

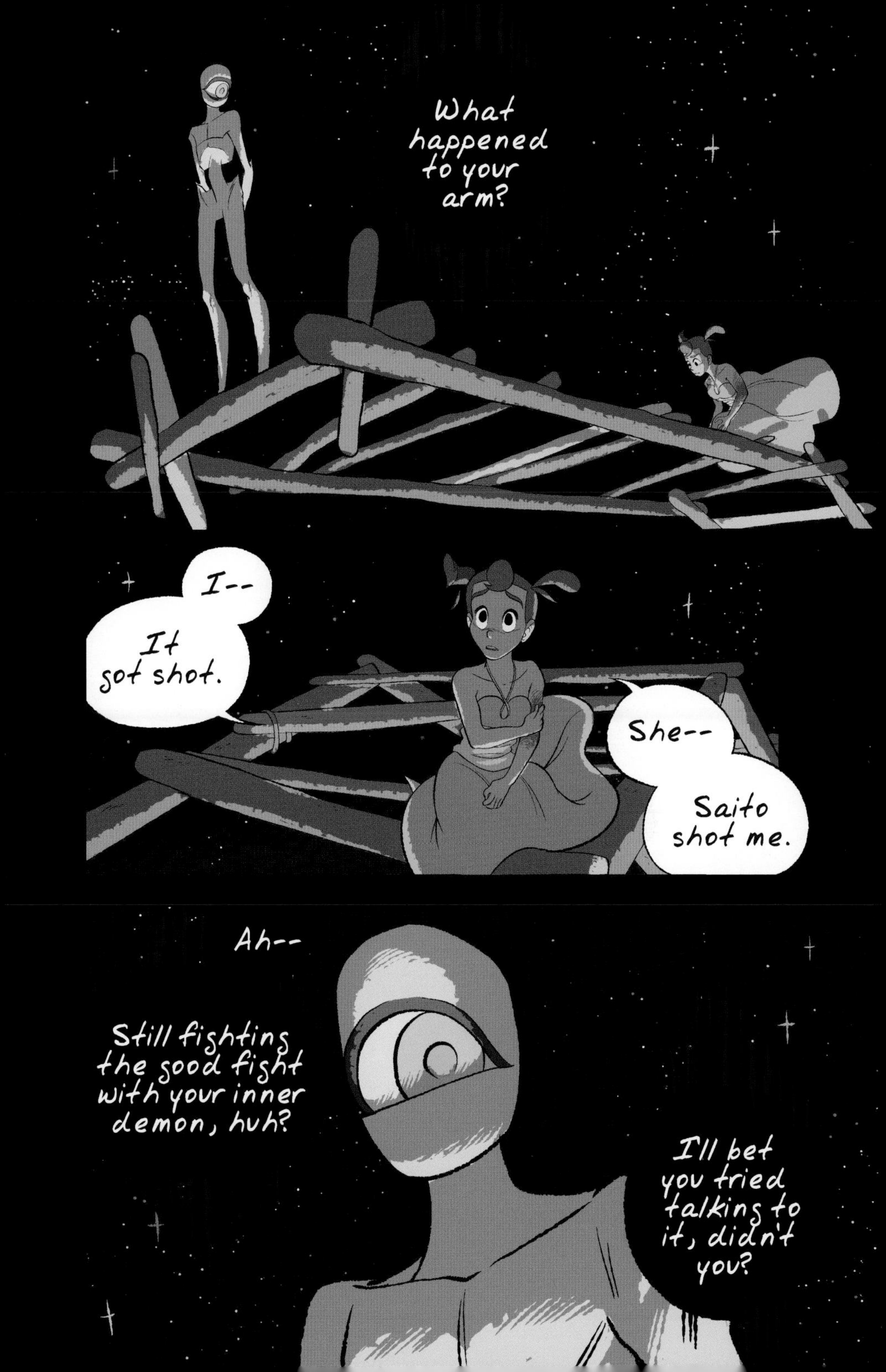
What happened to your arm?
I--
It got shot.
She--
Saito shot me.
Ah--
Still fighting the good fight with your inner demon, huh?
I'll bet you tried talking to it, didn't you?

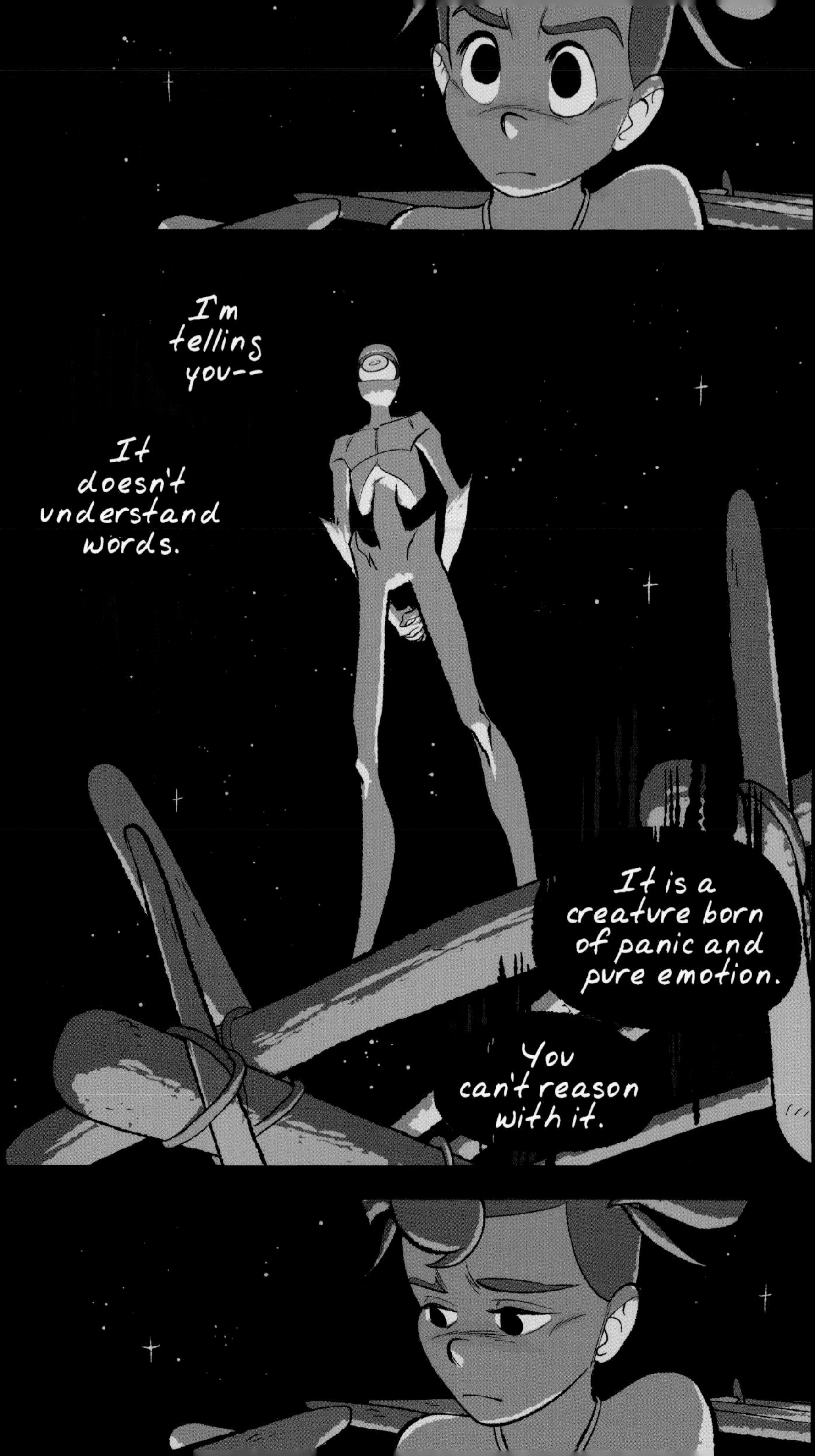
I'm telling you--
It doesn't understand words.
It is a creature born of panic and pure emotion.
You can't reason with it.

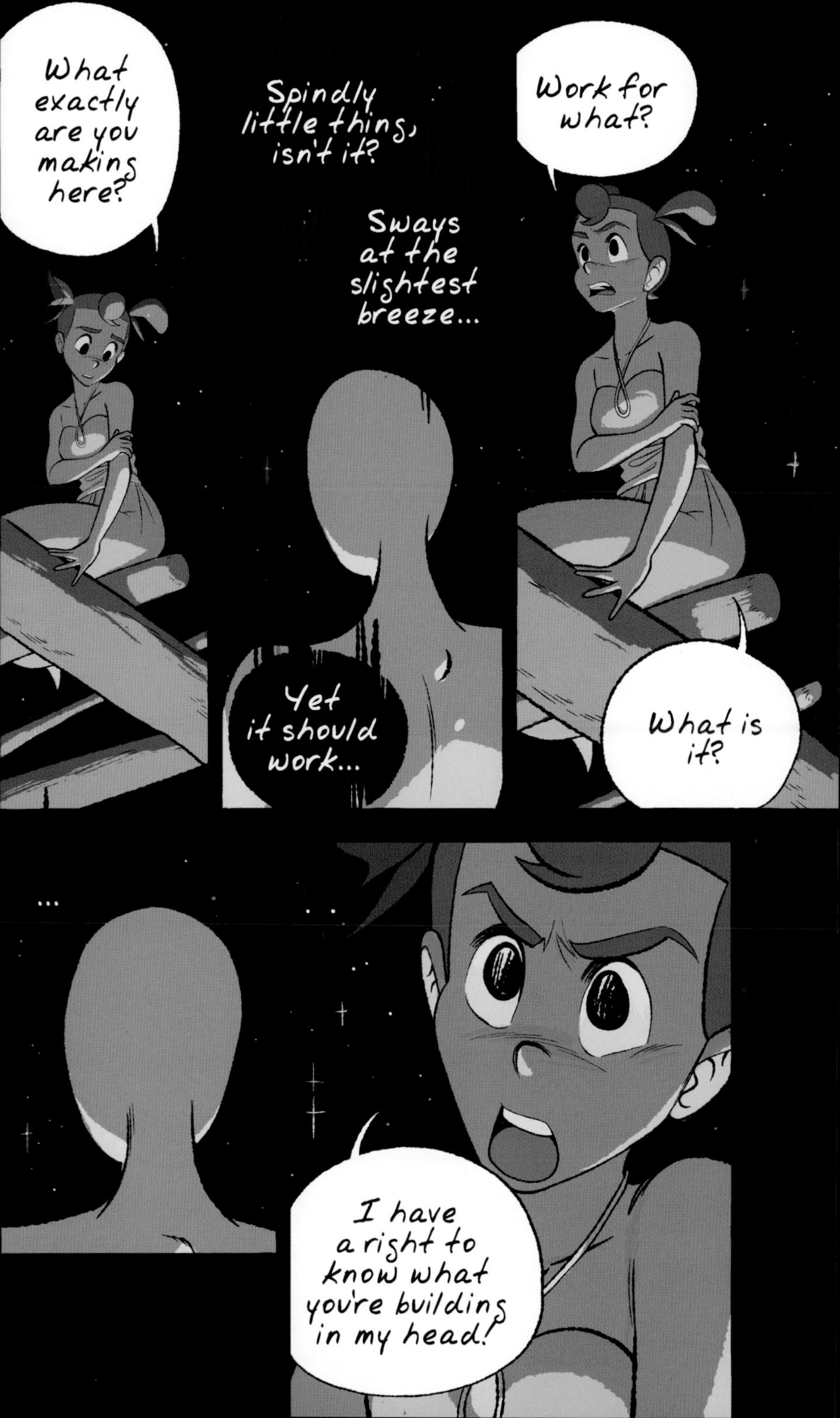
What exactly are you making here?
Spindly little thing, isn't it?
Sways at the slightest breeze...
Yet it should work...
Work for what?
What is it?
...
I have a right to know what you're building in my head!

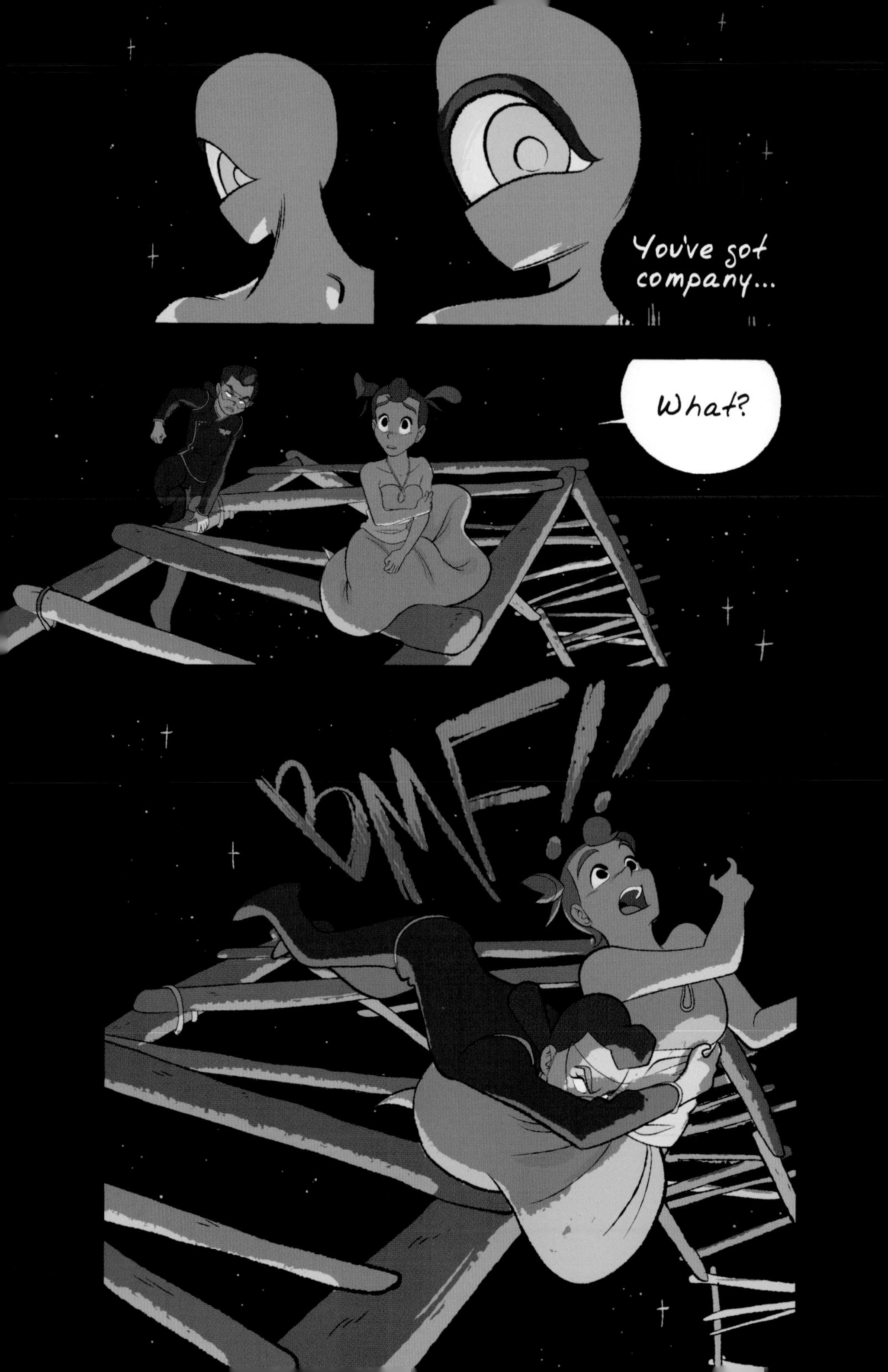

You've got company...
What?
BMF!!

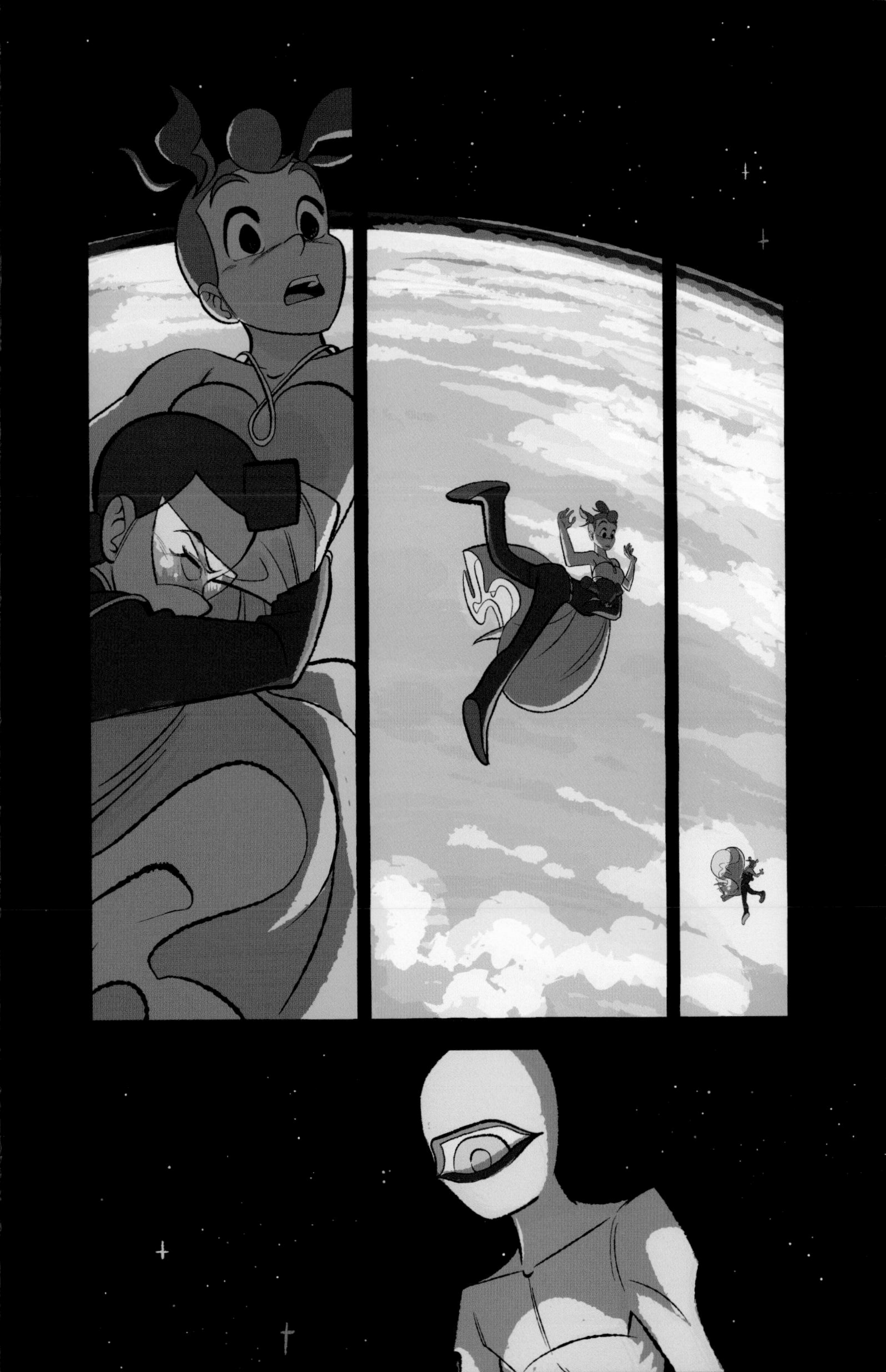

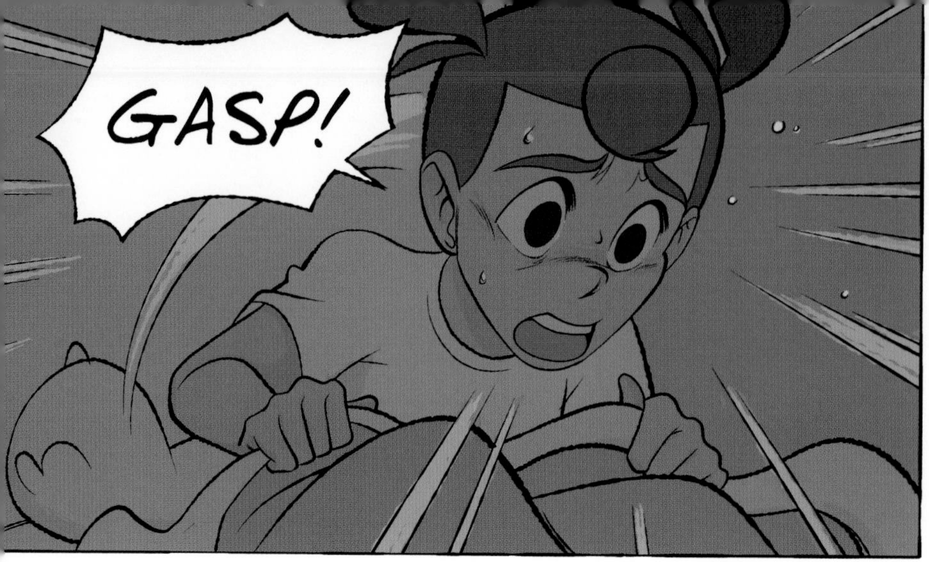
GASP!

I awake with a start.

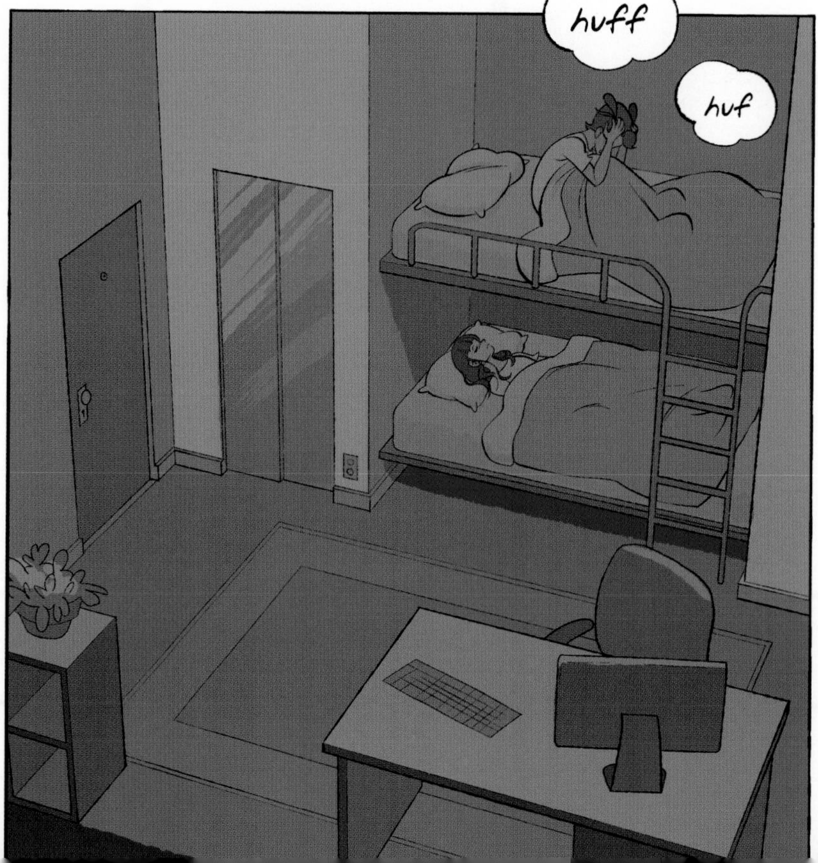
huff
huf

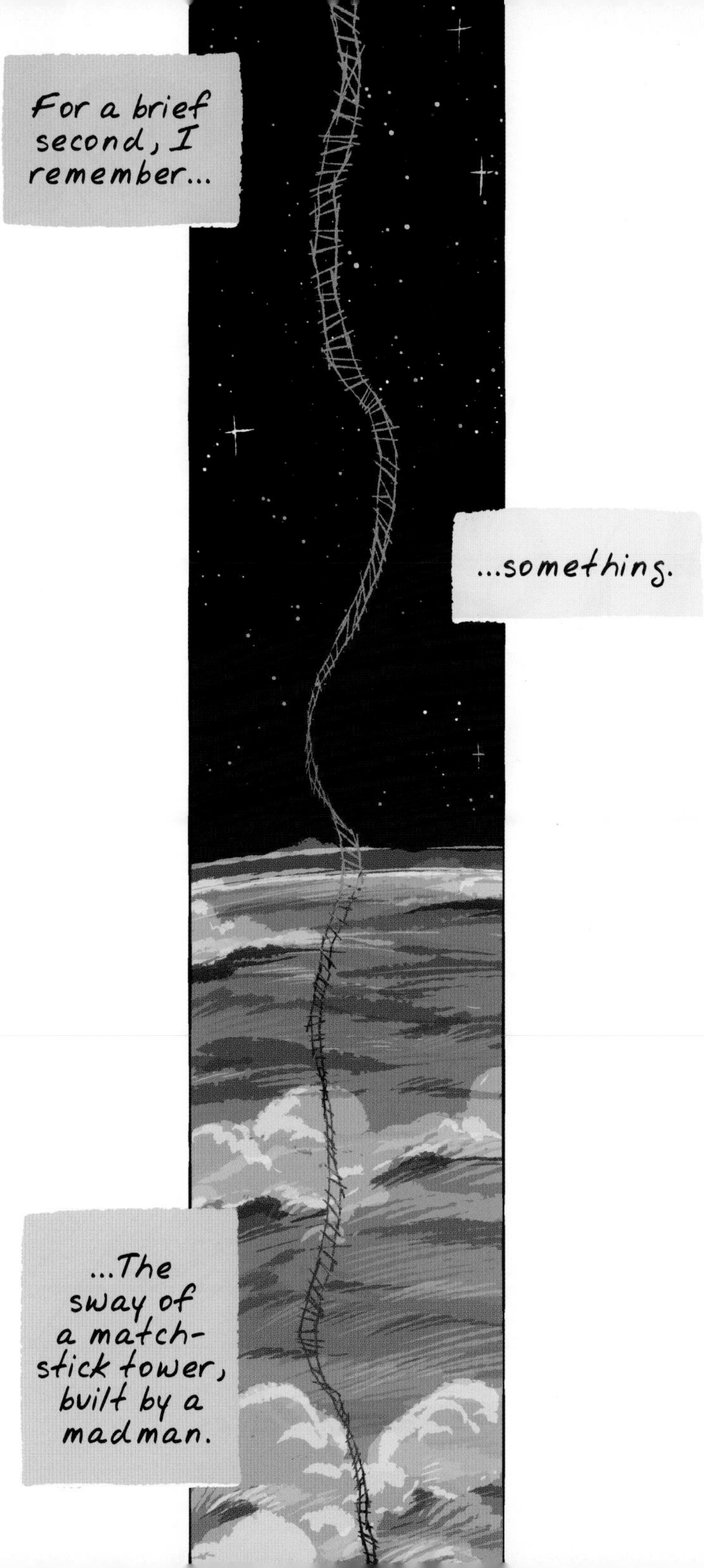
For a brief second, I remember...
...something.
...The sway of a match-stick tower, built by a madman.

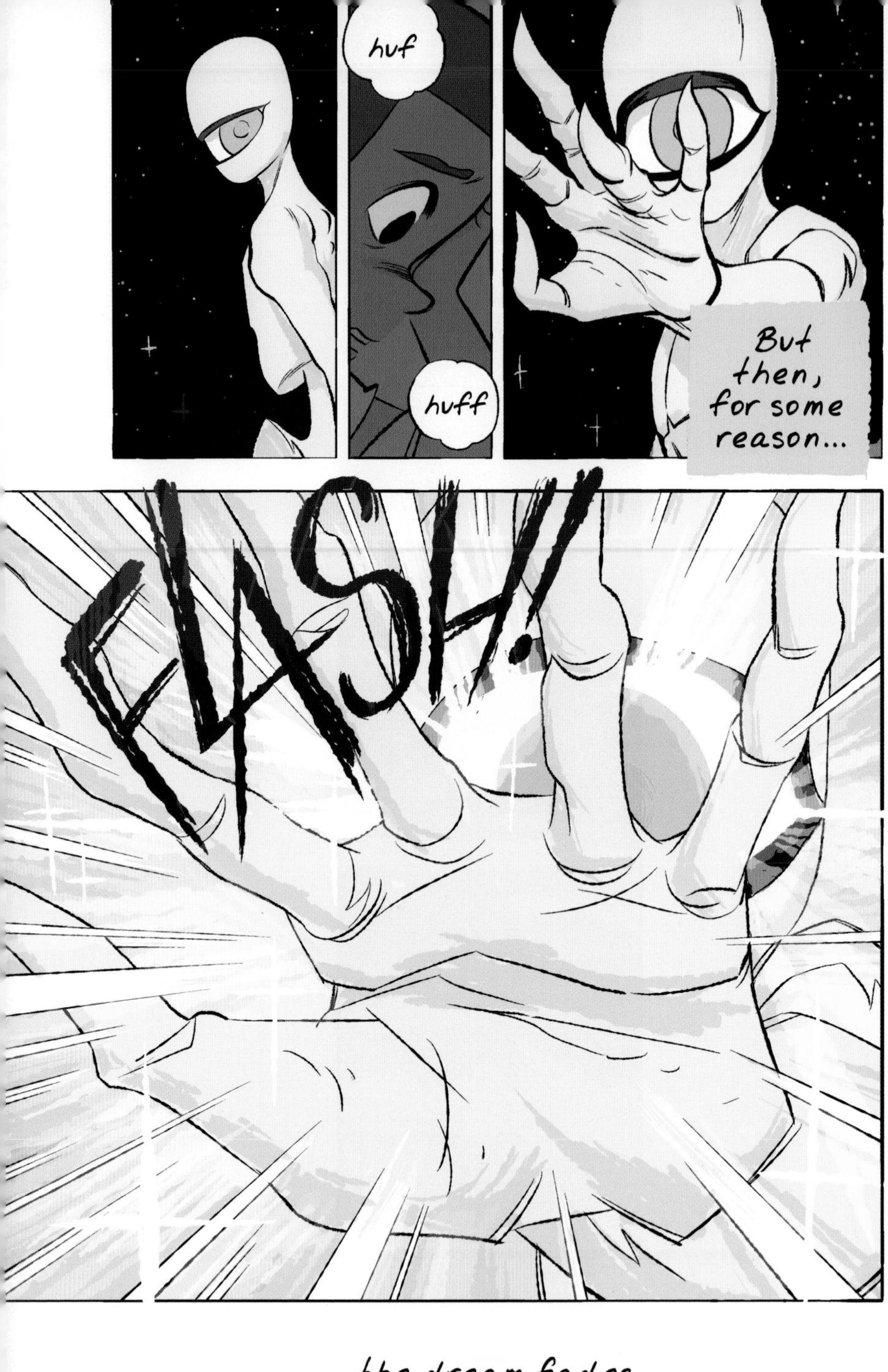
huf
huff
But then, for some reason...
FLASH!!

...the dream fades.

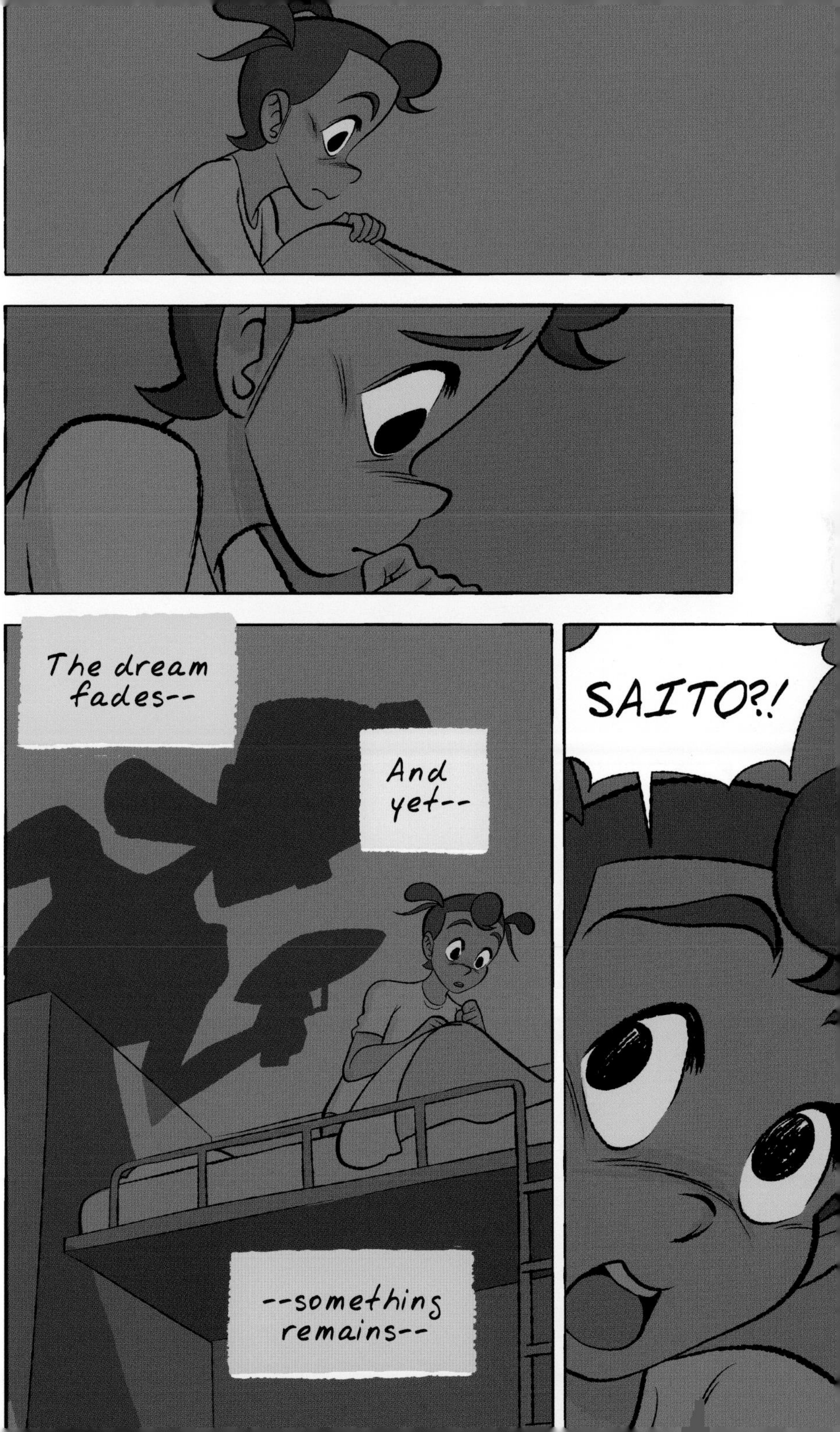
The dream fades--
And yet--
--something remains--
SAITO?!

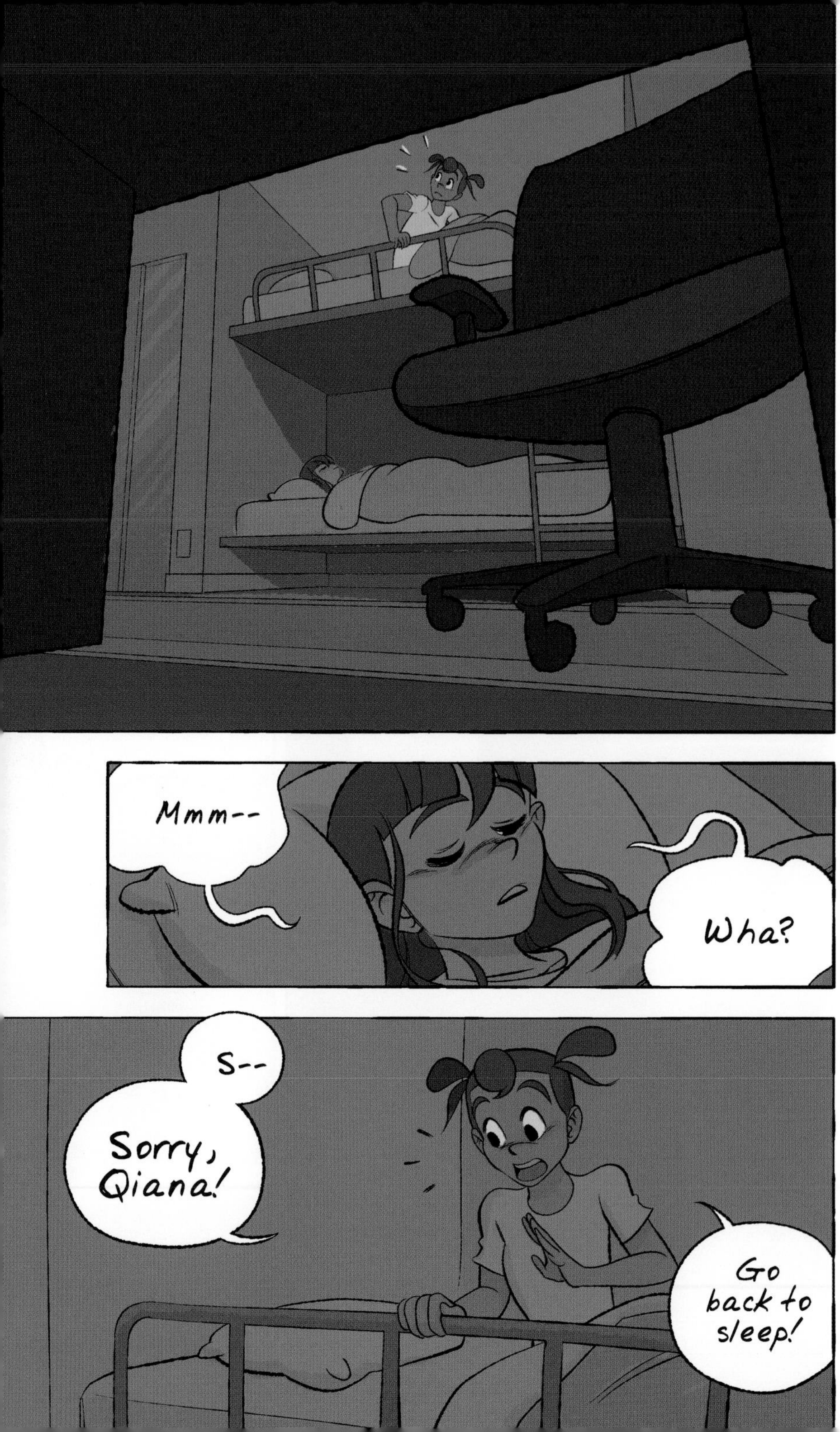
Mmm--
Wha?
S--
Sorry, Qiana!
Go back to sleep!

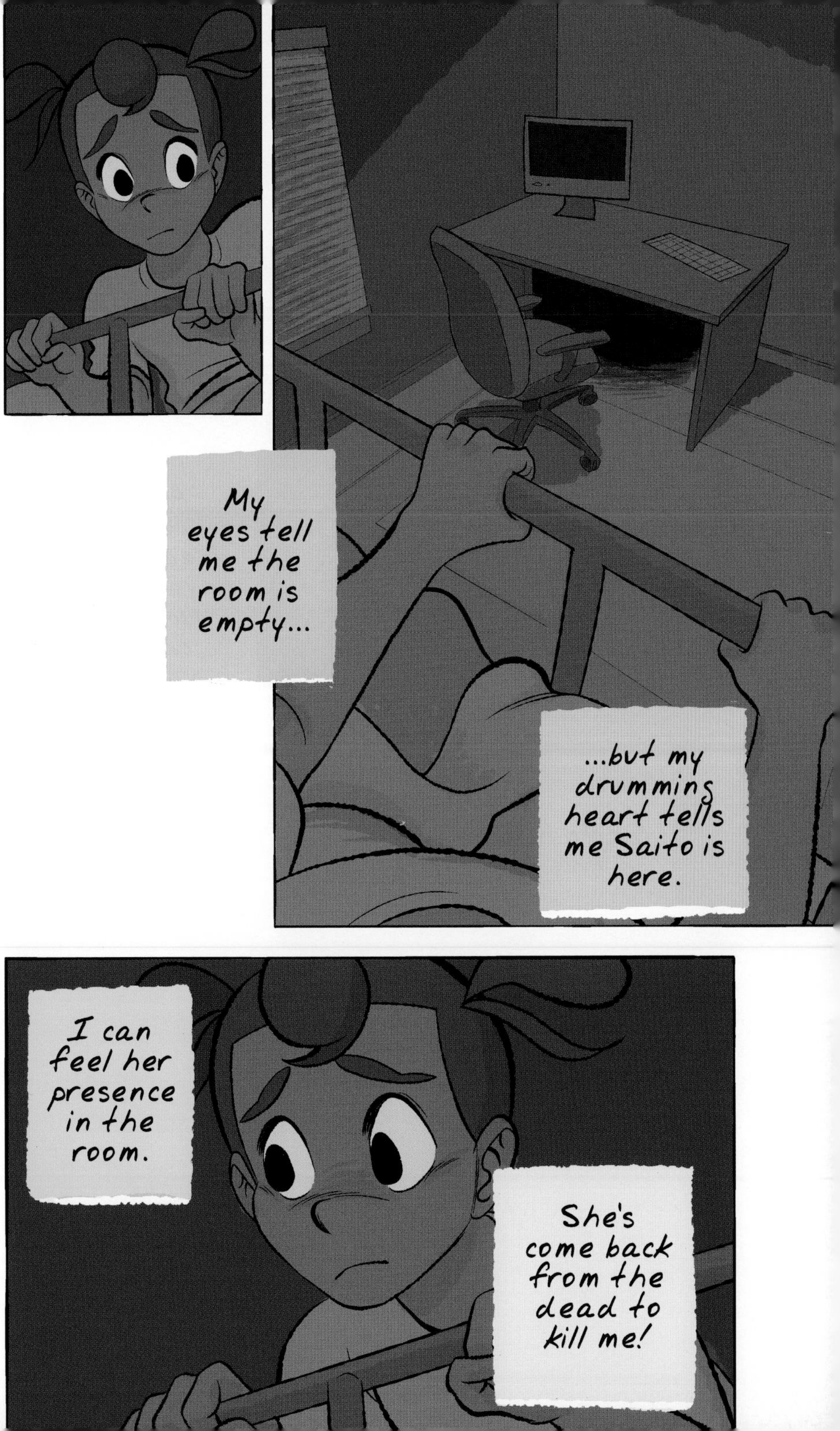
My eyes tell me the room is empty...
...but my drumming heart tells me Saito is here.
I can feel her presence in the room.
She's come back from the dead to kill me!

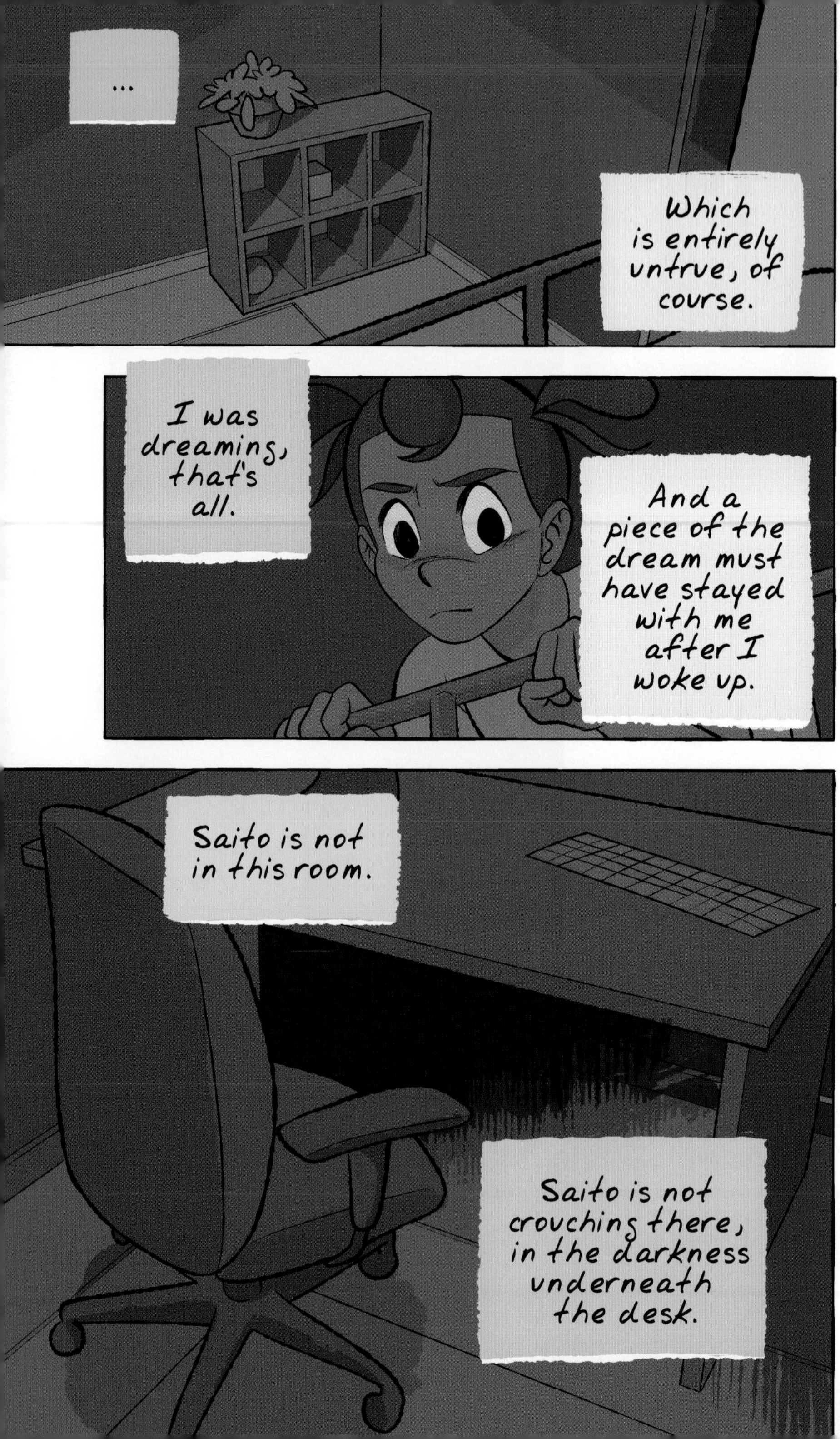
...
Which is entirely untrue, of course.
I was dreaming, that's all.
And a piece of the dream must have stayed with me after I woke up.
Saito is not in this room.
Saito is not crouching there, in the darkness underneath the desk.

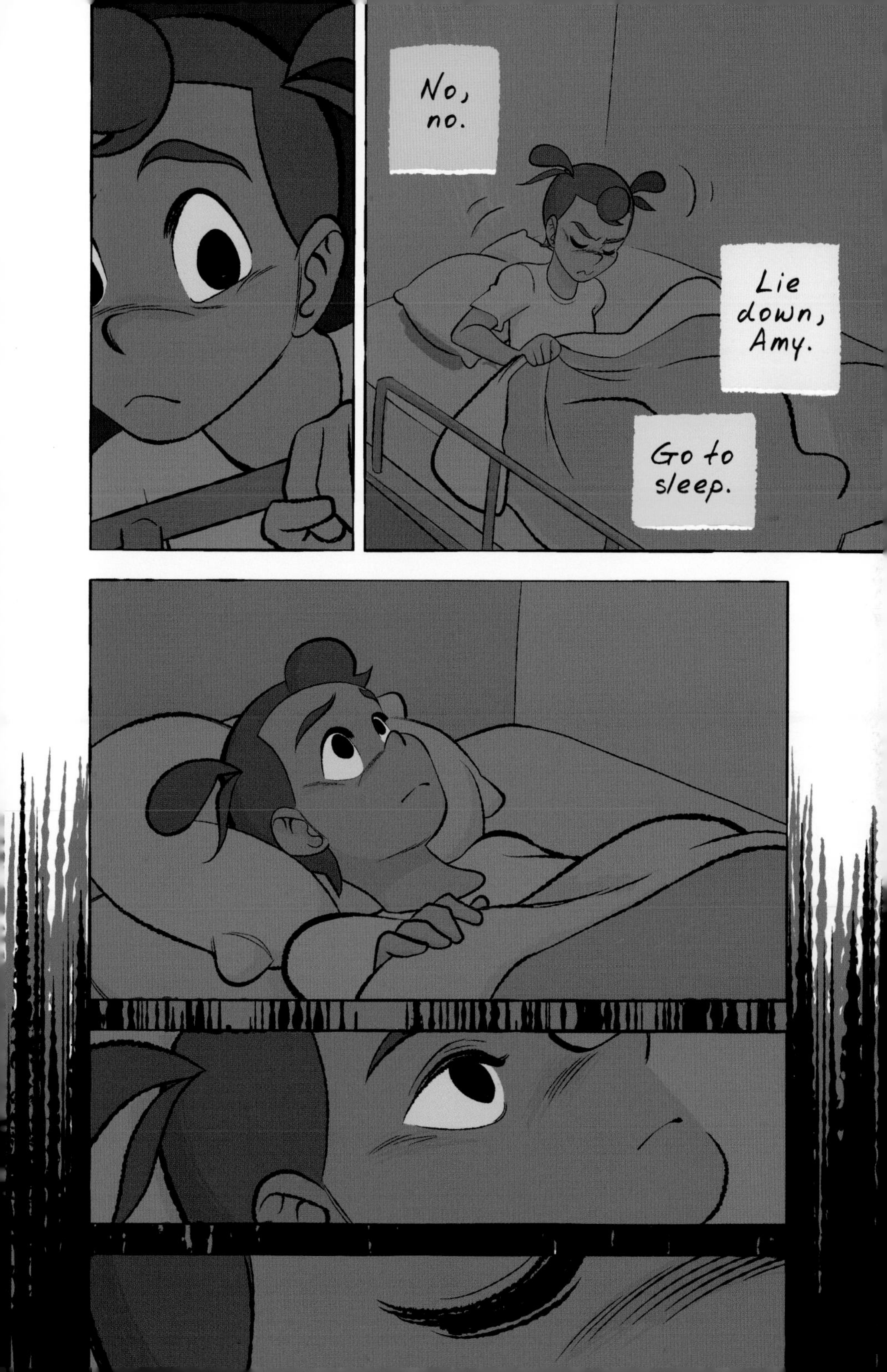
No, no.
Lie down, Amy.
Go to sleep.

"You're going to die," a voice whispers from under the desk.

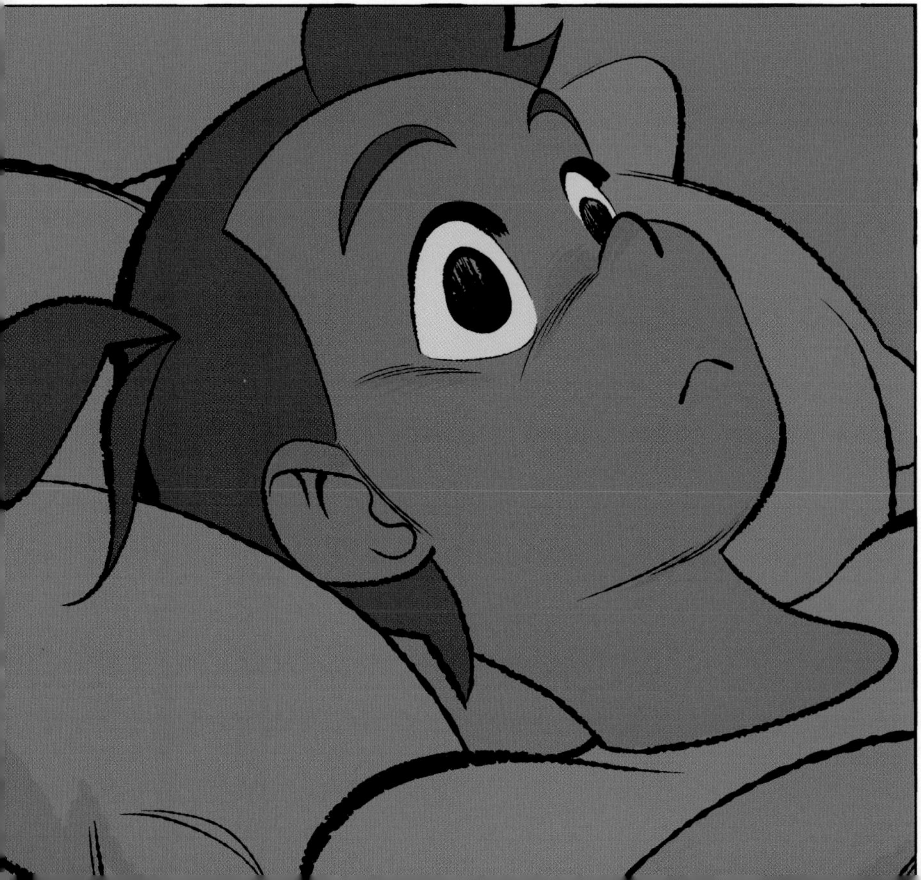

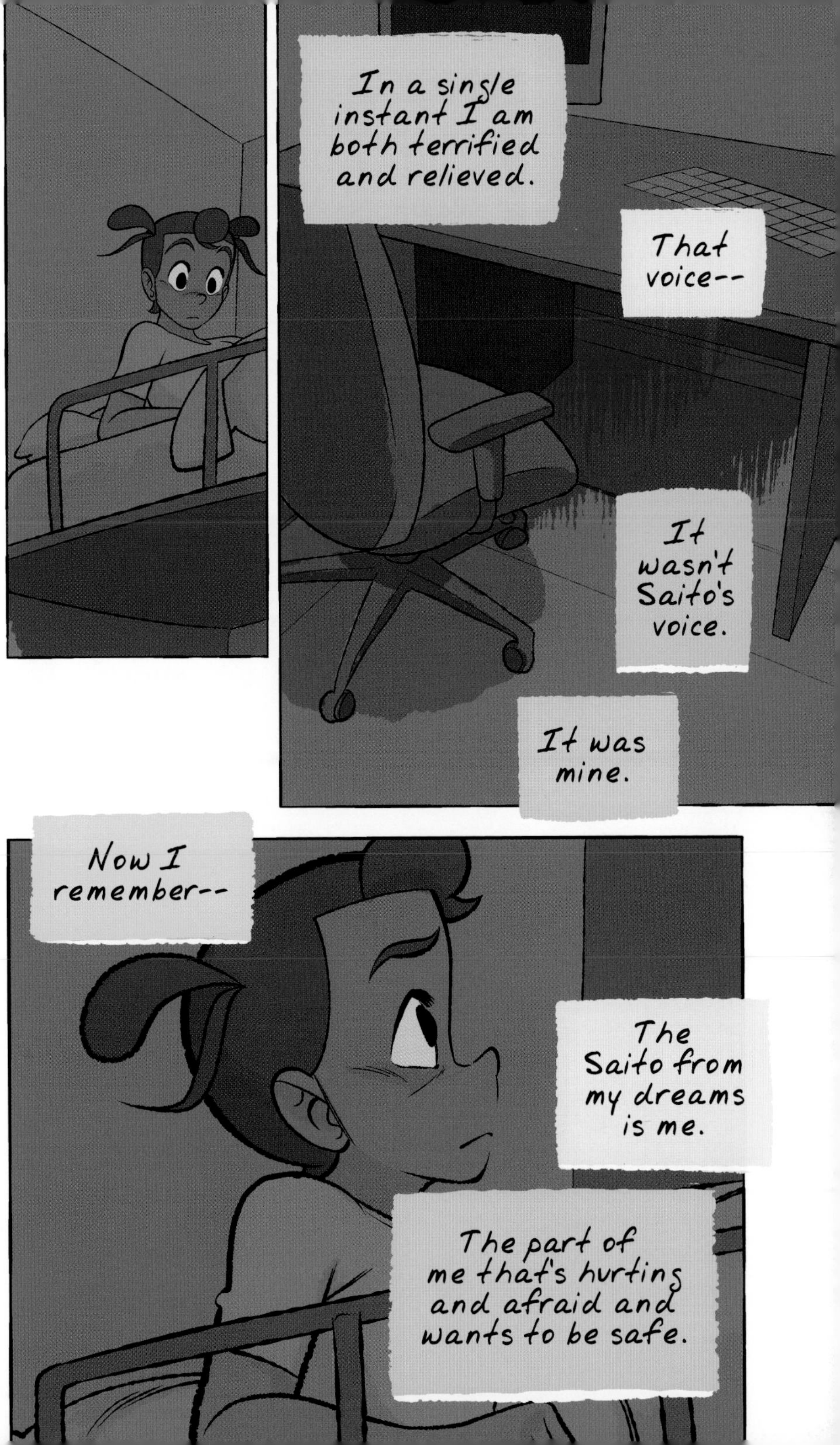
In a single instant I am both terrified and relieved.
That voice--
It wasn't Saito's voice.
It was mine.
Now I remember--
The Saito from my dreams is me.
The part of me that's hurting and afraid and wants to be safe.

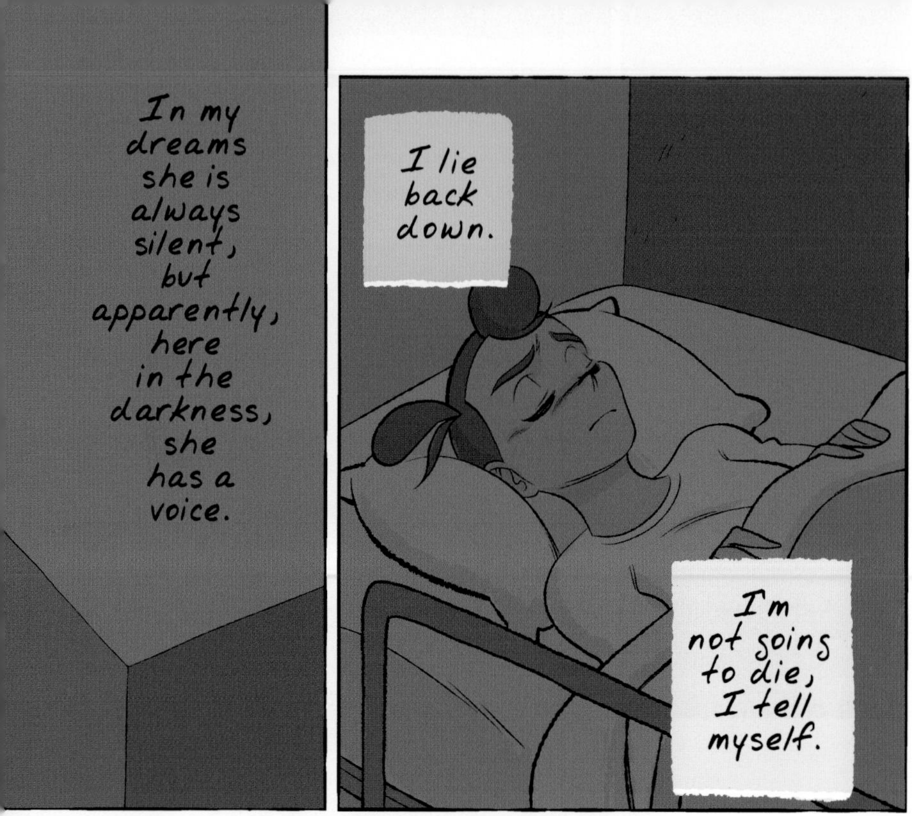
In my dreams she is always silent, but apparently, here in the darkness, she has a voice.
I lie back down.
I'm not going to die, I tell myself.

"Yes, you are," she says.

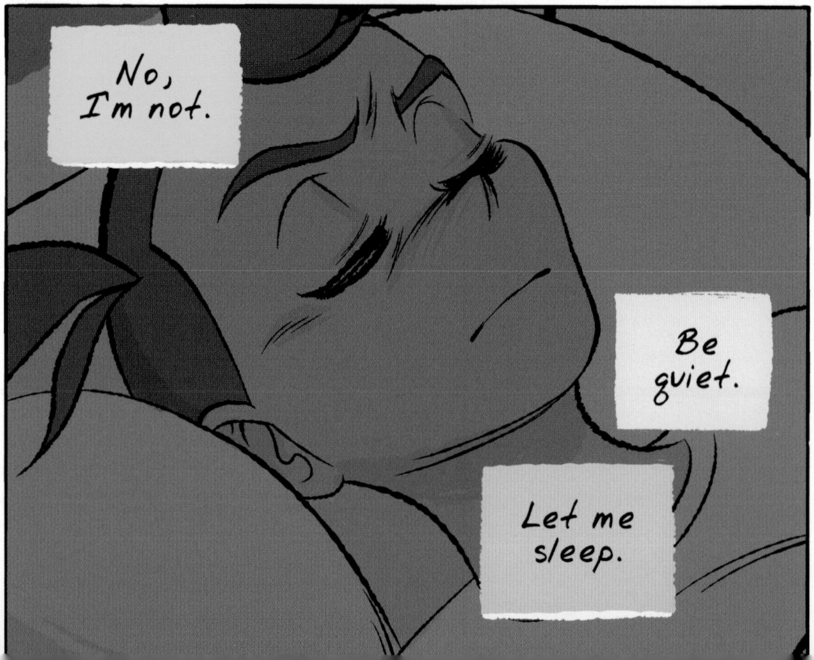
No, I'm not.
Be quiet.
Let me sleep.

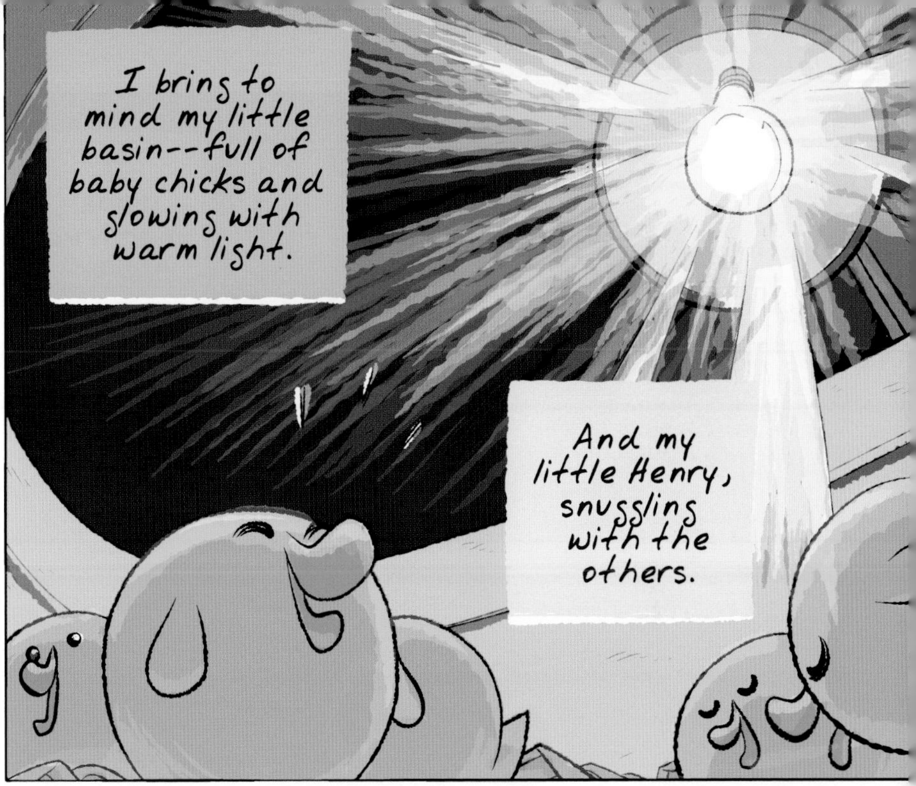
I bring to mind my little basin--full of baby chicks and glowing with warm light.
And my little Henry, snuggling with the others.

"Qiana put Cassie in the hospital," says the voice.

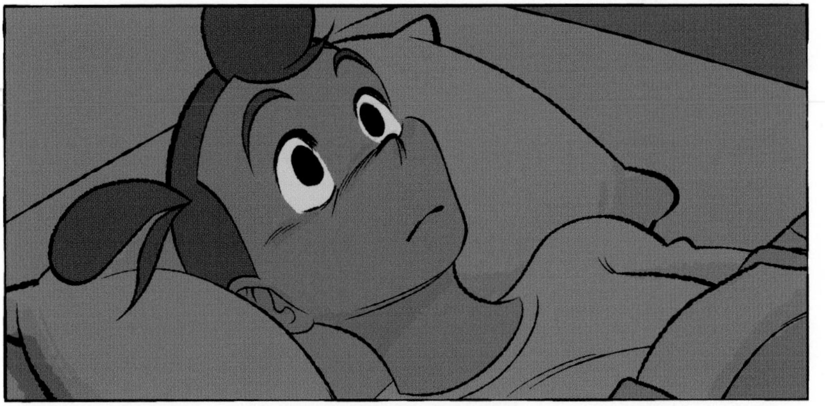

"Qiana is dangerous. You can't trust her."

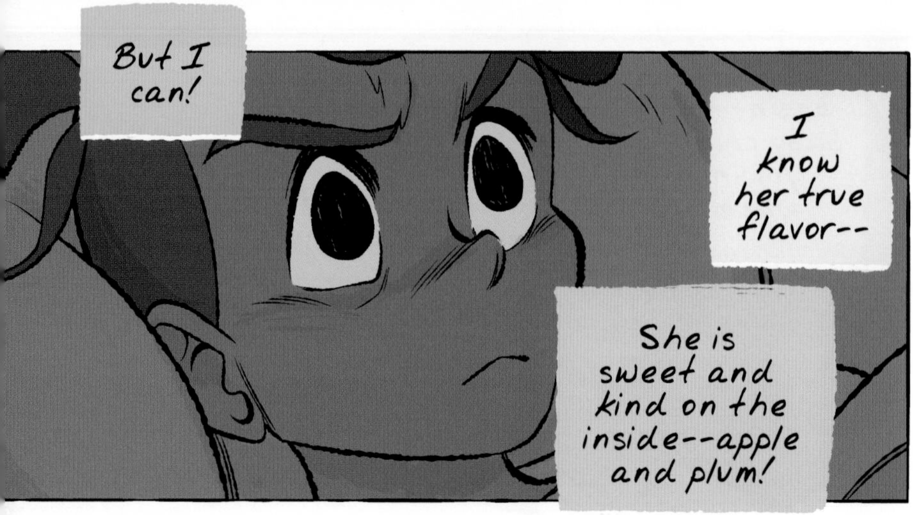
But I can!
I know her true flavor--
She is sweet and kind on the inside--apple and plum!

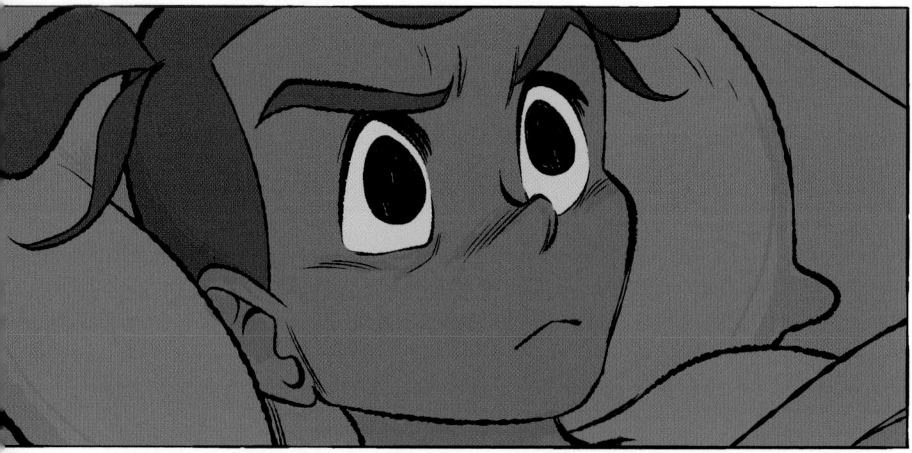

"I miss Mom," says the voice.

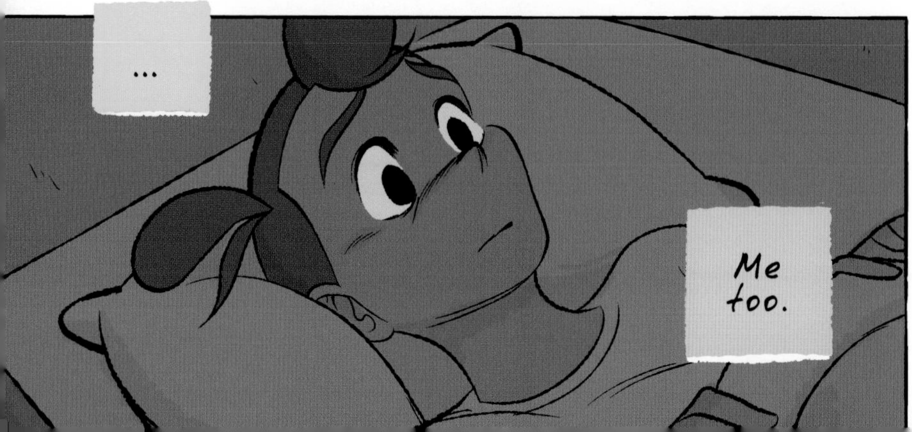
...
Me too.

"You're never going to see her again, you know. You're never going to escape this place," she says.

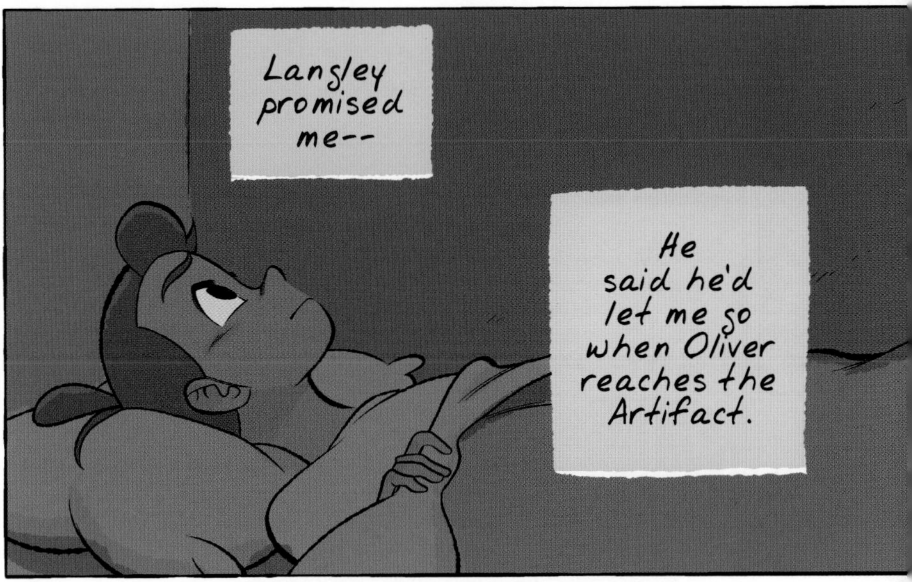
Langley promised me--
He said he'd let me go when Oliver reaches the Artifact.

"You really think you can trust a man with a crooked flavor like that? How do you know he wasn't lying to you?"

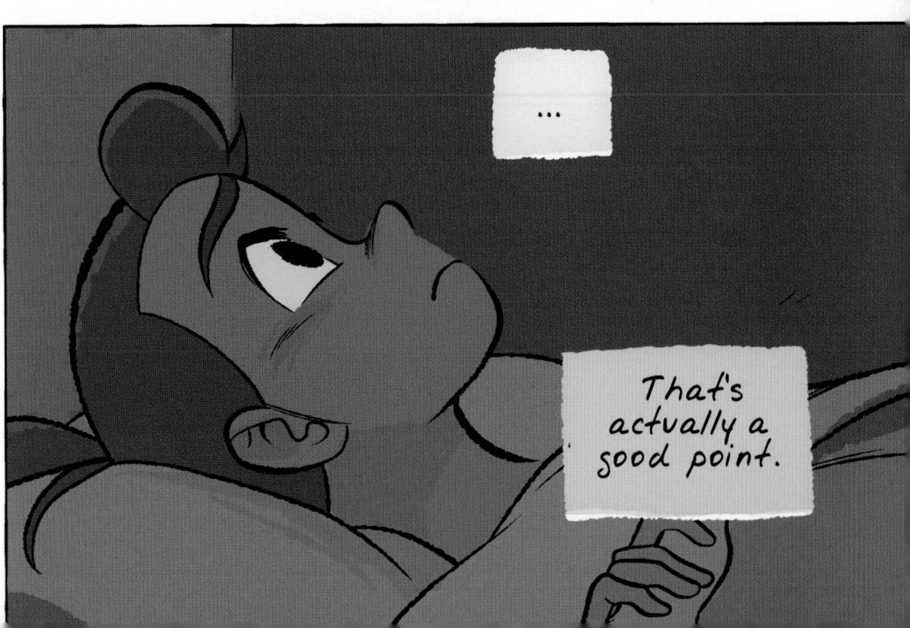
...
That's actually a good point.

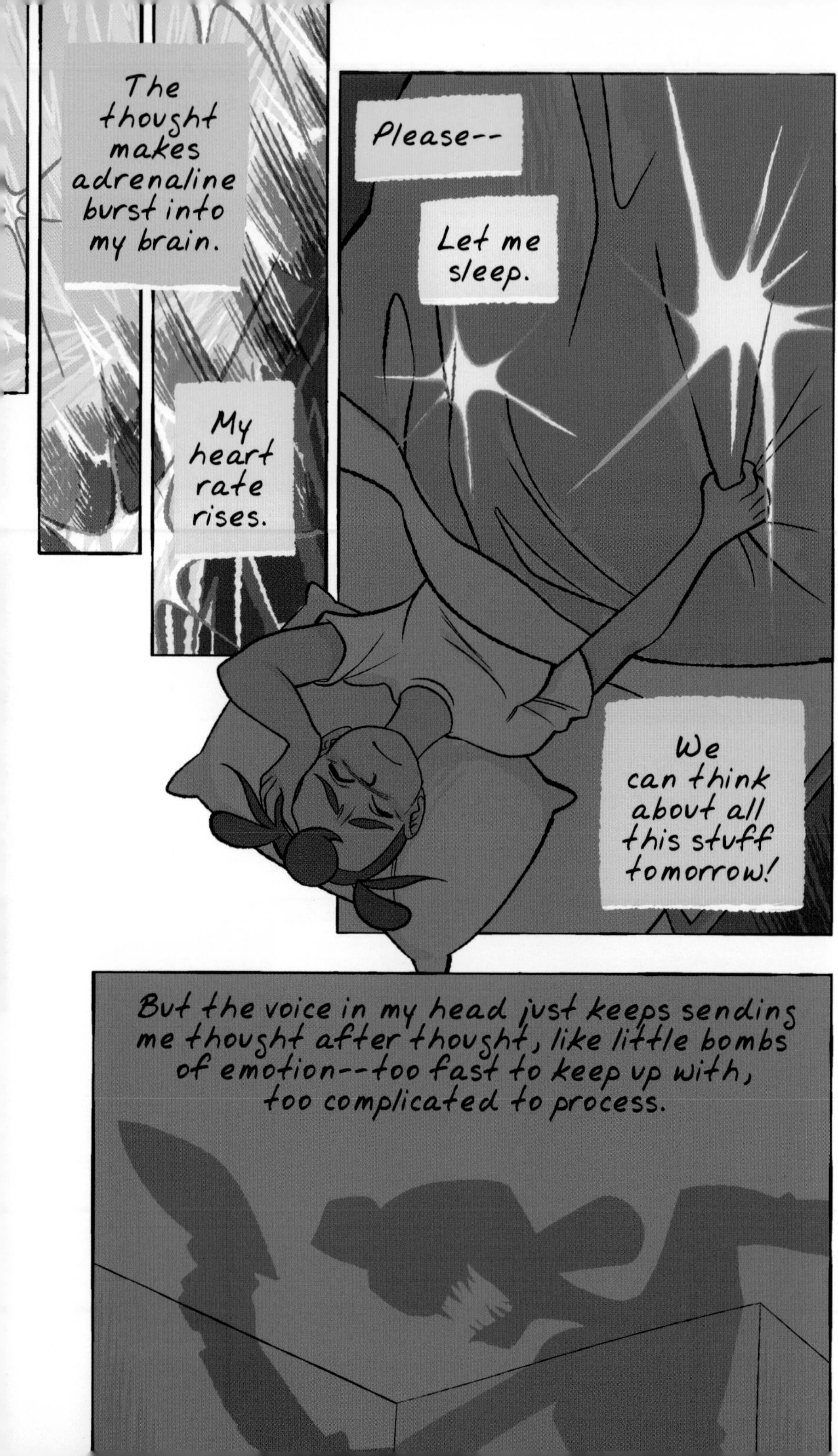
The thought makes adrenaline burst into my brain.
My heart rate rises.
Please--
Let me sleep.
We can think about all this stuff tomorrow!
But the voice in my head just keeps sending me thought after thought, like little bombs of emotion--too fast to keep up with, too complicated to process.

I spend the rest of the night in an endless half sleep, trying to untangle my troubled thoughts.

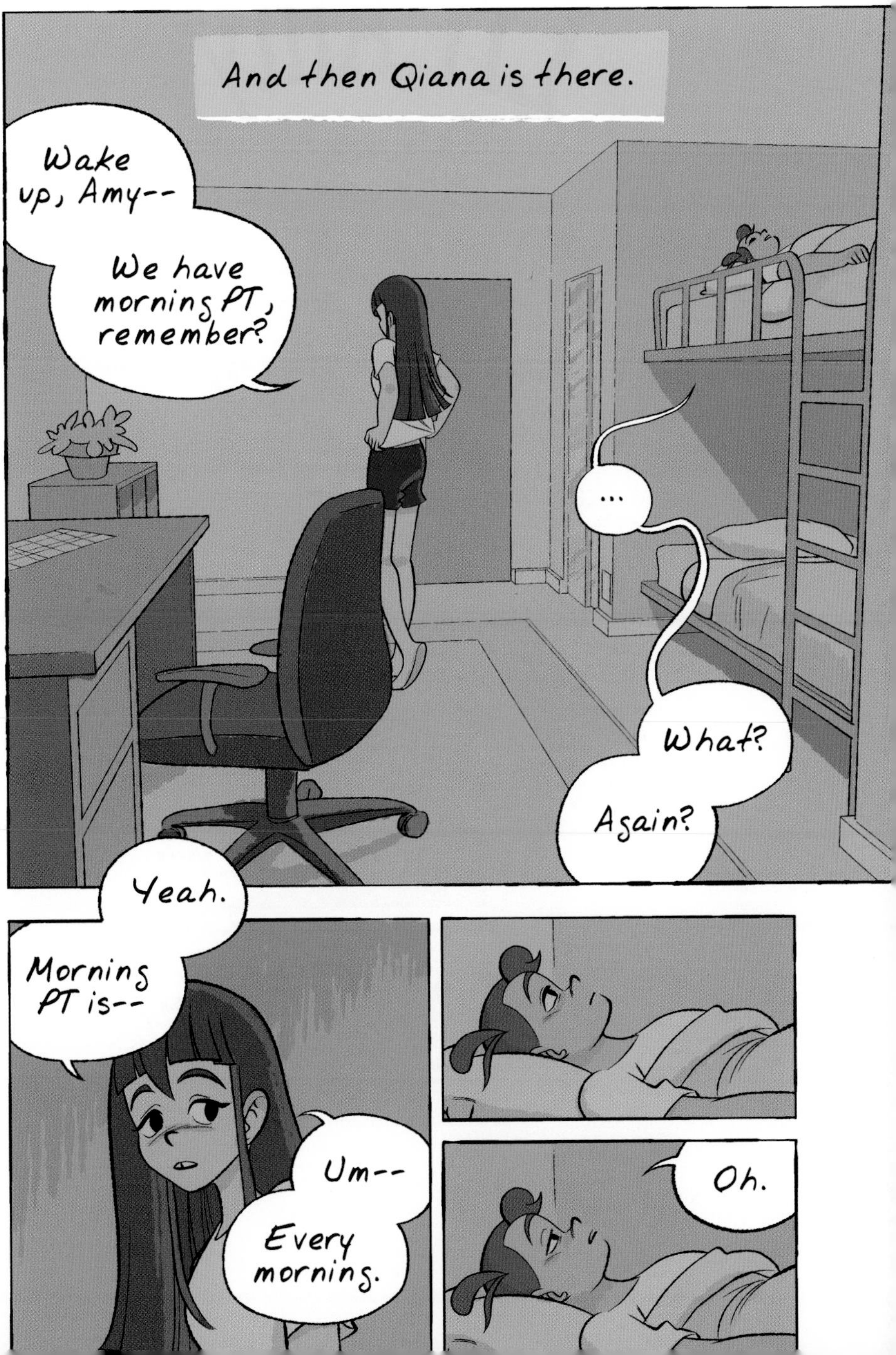
And then Qiana is there.
Wake up, Amy--
We have morning PT, remember?
...
What?
Again?
Yeah.
Morning PT is--
Um--
Every morning.
Oh.

Li'l Amy

by
Stephen McCranie

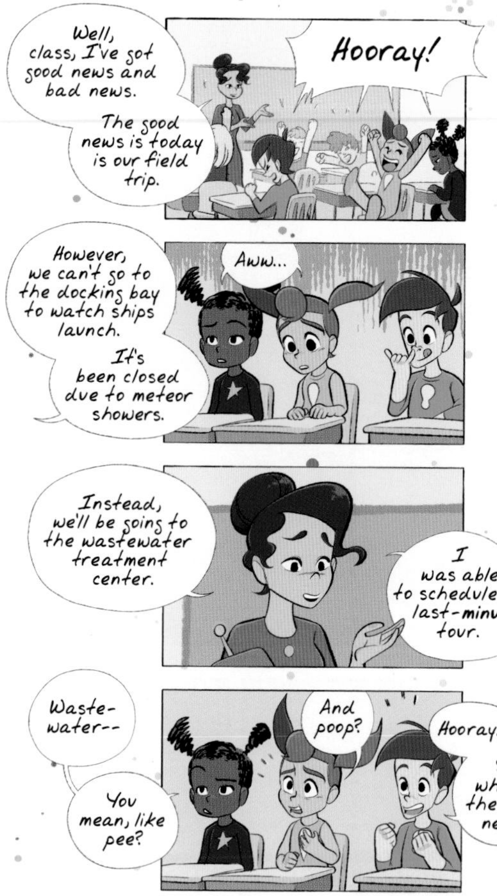
Well, class, I've got good news and bad news.
The good news is today is our field trip.
Hooray!
However, we can't go to the docking bay to watch ships launch.
It's been closed due to meteor showers.
Aww...
Instead, we'll be going to the wastewater treatment center.
I was able to schedule a last-minute tour.
Waste-water--
You mean, like pee?
And poop?
Hooray!
So what's the bad news?

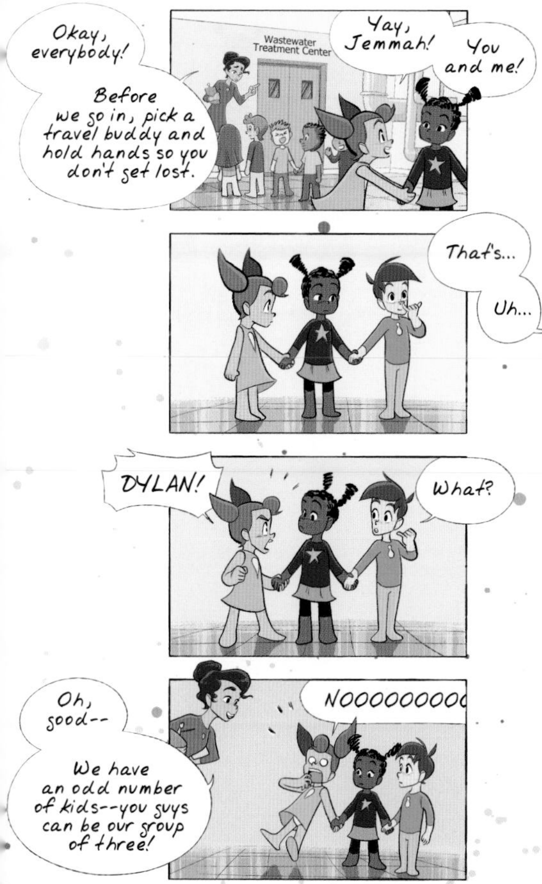
Okay, everybody!
Before we go in, pick a travel buddy and hold hands so you don't get lost.
Wastewater Treatment Center
Yay, Jemmah!
You and me!
That's...
Uh...
DYLAN!
What?
Oh, good--
We have an odd number of kids--you guys can be our group of three!
NOOOOOOOOO

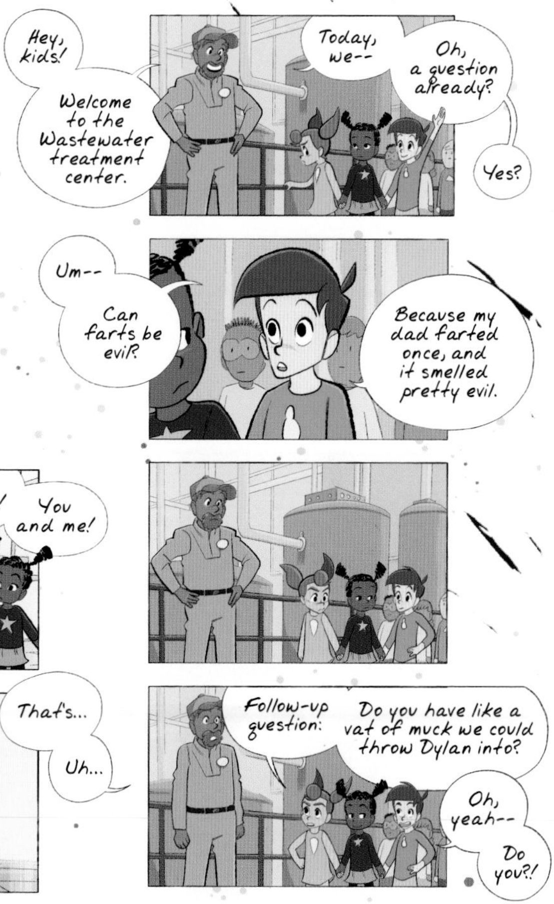
Hey, kids!
Welcome to the Wastewater treatment center.
Today, we--
Oh, a question already?
Yes?
Um--
Can farts be evil?
Because my dad farted once, and it smelled pretty evil.
Follow-up question:
Do you have like a vat of muck we could throw Dylan into?
Oh, yeah--
Do you?!

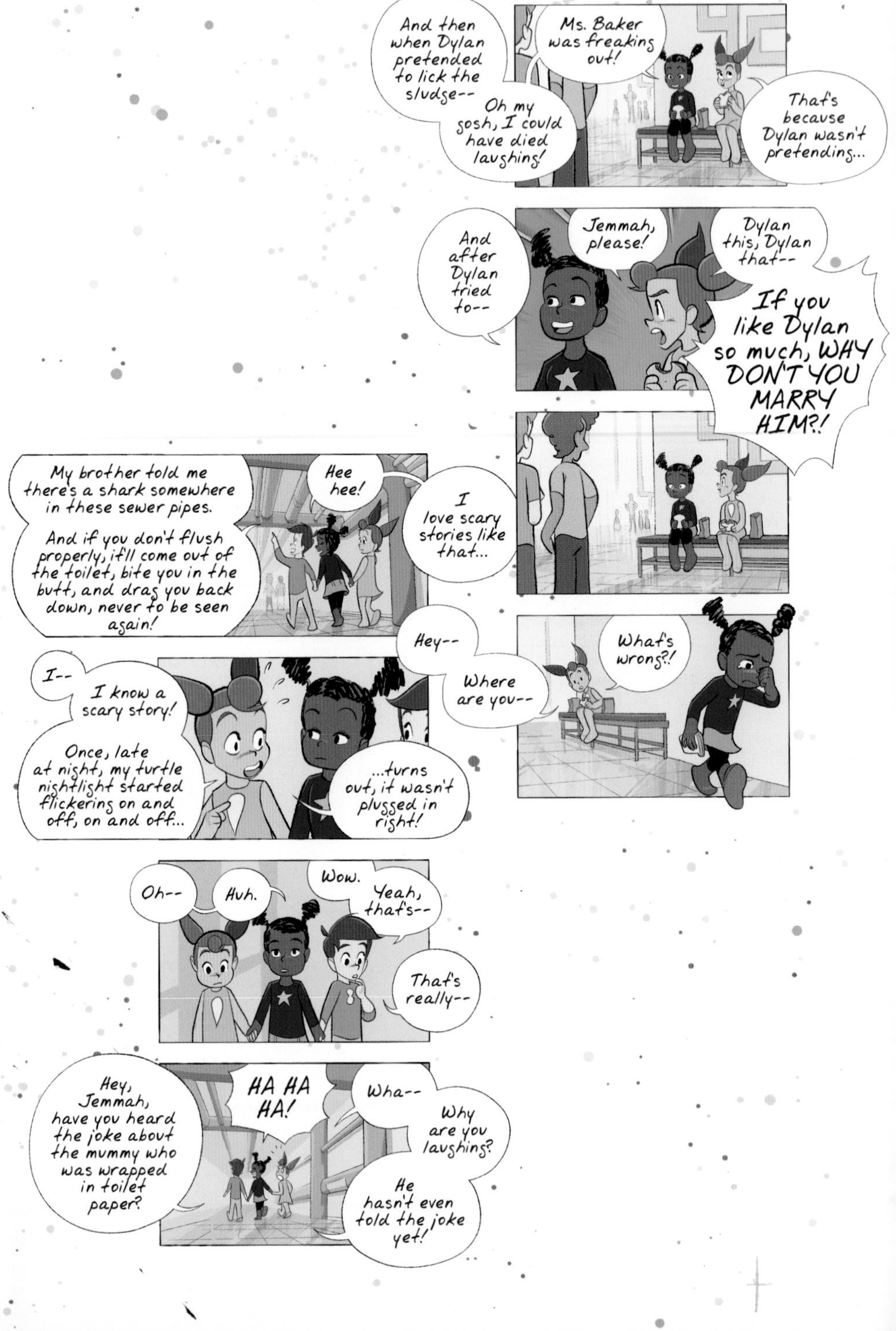
And then when Dylan pretended to lick the sludge--
Ms. Baker was freaking out!
Oh my gosh, I could have died laughing!
That's because Dylan wasn't pretending...
And after Dylan tried to--
Jemmah, please!
Dylan this, Dylan that--
If you like Dylan so much, WHY DON'T YOU MARRY HIM?!
My brother told me there's a shark somewhere in these sewer pipes.
And if you don't flush properly, it'll come out of the toilet, bite you in the butt, and drag you back down, never to be seen again!
Hee hee!
I love scary stories like that...
Hey--
Where are you--
What's wrong?!
I--
I know a scary story!
Once, late at night, my turtle nightlight started flickering on and off, on and off...
...turns out, it wasn't plugged in right!
Oh--
Huh.
Wow.
Yeah, that's--
That's really--
Hey, Jemmah, have you heard the joke about the mummy who was wrapped in toilet paper?
HA HA HA!
Wha--
Why are you laughing?
He hasn't even told the joke yet!

What happened?
Is Jemmah okay?
Oh, this is all your fault, Dylan!
Why did you have to grab Jemmah's hand this morning when Ms. Baker had us choose travel buddies?
Hey, I didn't grab her hand.
She grabbed mine.
Listen--
As your friend, I want you to be happy.
Oh, Amy--
You really mean it?
Hi, Jemmah.
Hi, Amy.
And if Dylan makes you happy, then--
He can hang out with us.
Sometimes.
I guess.
Yeah...
But we'll still be best friends forever, right?
I promise.
The tour's starting up again, you two.
Oh, hey--
My gum!
I've been looking all over for that!

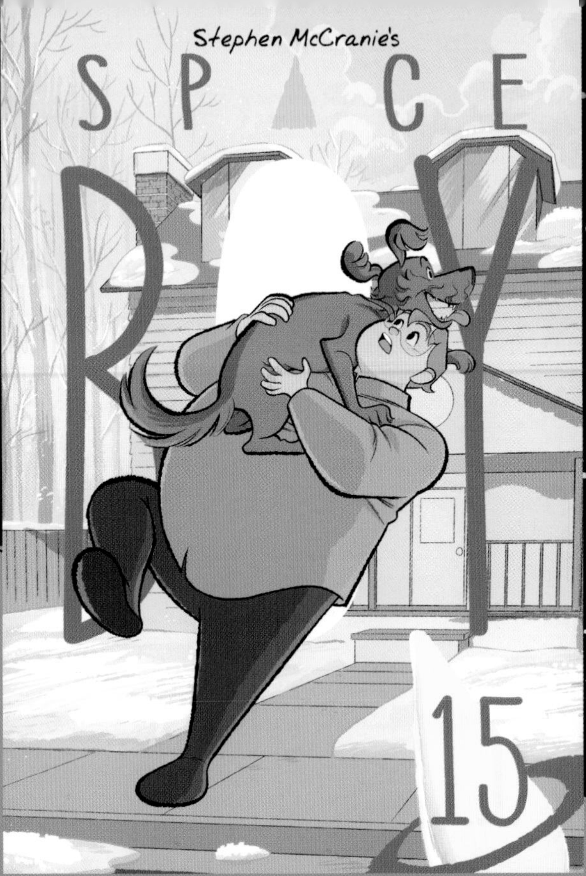
Stephen McCranie's
SPACE
BOY
15

The investigation of the Homecoming Incident is closing, but things don't add up. At least Tammie is back home safe. Along with Schafer and Cassie, she is focusing on finding out what really happened to Amy at the homecoming dance. They know they can't trust the authorities, and to everyone else Amy is officially dead. But she isn't. A prisoner at FCP headquarters, Amy is beginning a friendship with the special ops agent Qiana, and her relationship with Oliver is flourishing. The more time she is on base, the more Amy realizes the world at large has no idea that the First Contact Project is not what it seems. While Amy and Qiana investigate the dark events the FCP has been covering up, Oliver flies ever closer to the Artifact and the end of his mission.

Available March 2023!

YOU CAN ALSO READ MORE *SPACE BOY* COMICS ON WEBTOONS.COM!

HAVE YOU READ THEM ALL?

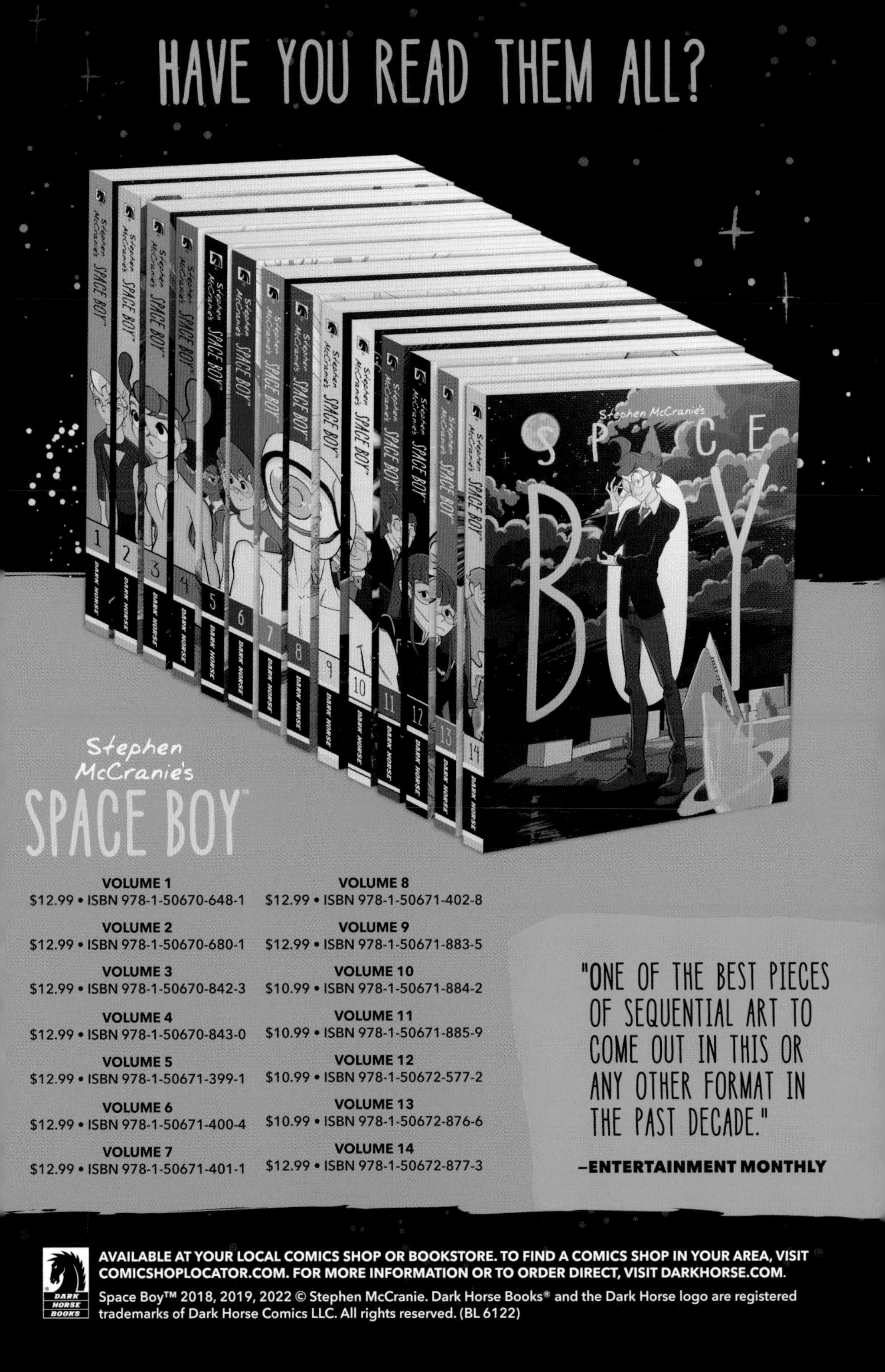
Stephen McCranie's
SPACE BOY

Stephen McCranie's
SPACE BOY™

VOLUME 1
$12.99 • ISBN 978-1-50670-648-1

VOLUME 2
$12.99 • ISBN 978-1-50670-680-1

VOLUME 3
$12.99 • ISBN 978-1-50670-842-3

VOLUME 4
$12.99 • ISBN 978-1-50670-843-0

VOLUME 5
$12.99 • ISBN 978-1-50671-399-1

VOLUME 6
$12.99 • ISBN 978-1-50671-400-4

VOLUME 7
$12.99 • ISBN 978-1-50671-401-1

VOLUME 8
$12.99 • ISBN 978-1-50671-402-8

VOLUME 9
$12.99 • ISBN 978-1-50671-883-5

VOLUME 10
$10.99 • ISBN 978-1-50671-884-2

VOLUME 11
$10.99 • ISBN 978-1-50671-885-9

VOLUME 12
$10.99 • ISBN 978-1-50672-577-2

VOLUME 13
$10.99 • ISBN 978-1-50672-876-6

VOLUME 14
$12.99 • ISBN 978-1-50672-877-3

"ONE OF THE BEST PIECES OF SEQUENTIAL ART TO COME OUT IN THIS OR ANY OTHER FORMAT IN THE PAST DECADE."

—ENTERTAINMENT MONTHLY

DARK HORSE BOOKS

AVAILABLE AT YOUR LOCAL COMICS SHOP OR BOOKSTORE. TO FIND A COMICS SHOP IN YOUR AREA, VISIT COMICSHOPLOCATOR.COM. FOR MORE INFORMATION OR TO ORDER DIRECT, VISIT DARKHORSE.COM.

DARK HORSE BRINGS YOU THE BEST IN WEBCOMICS!

These wildly popular cartoon gems were once only available online, but now can be found through Dark Horse Books with loads of awesome extras!

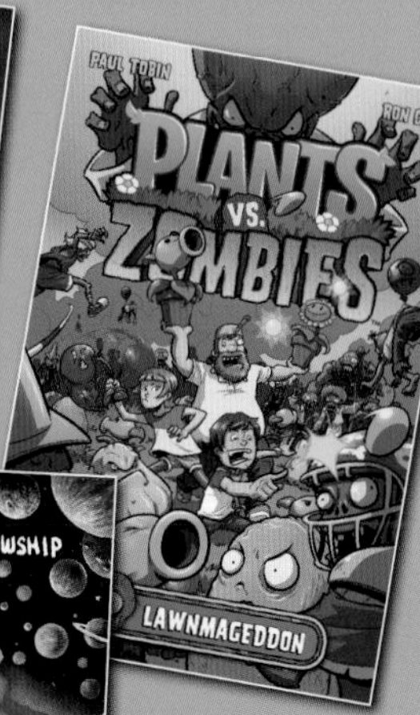

BANDETTE
By Paul Tobin, Colleen Coover, Steve Lieber, Alberto J. Albuquerque, and others

- **Volume 1: Presto!**
  ISBN 978-1-50671-923-8 | $14.99
- **Volume 2: Stealers, Keepers!**
  ISBN 978-1-50671-924-5 | $14.99
- **Volume 3: The House of the Green Mask**
  ISBN 978-1-50671-925-2 | $14.99
- **Volume 4: The Six-Finger Secret**
  ISBN 978-1-50671-925-2 | $14.99

MIKE NORTON'S BATTLEPUG
By Mike Norton

- **The Devil's Biscuit**
  ISBN 978-1-61655-864-2 | $14.99
- **The Paws of War**
  ISBN 978-1-50670-114-1 | $14.99

THE ADVENTURES OF SUPERHERO GIRL - EXPANDED EDITION HC
By Faith Erin Hicks
ISBN 978-1-50670-336-7 | $16.99

PLANTS VS. ZOMBIES
By Paul Tobin, Ron Chan, Andie Tong, and others

- **LAWNMAGEDDON**
  ISBN 978-1-61655-192-6 | $10.99
- **BULLY FOR YOU**
  ISBN 978-1-61655-889-5 | $10.99
- **GROWN SWEET HOME**
  ISBN 978-1-61655-971-7 | $10.99
- **RUMBLE AT LAKE GUMBO**
  ISBN 978-1-50670-497-5 | $10.99

THE PERRY BIBLE FELLOWSHIP 10TH ANNIVERSARY EDITION
By Nicholas Gurewitch
ISBN 978-1-50671-588-9 | $24.99

AVAILABLE AT YOUR LOCAL COMICS SHOP OR BOOKSTORE | To find a comics shop in your area, visit comicshoplocator.com. For more information or to order direct, visit DarkHorse.com

MINECRAFT™

AVAILABLE NOW...

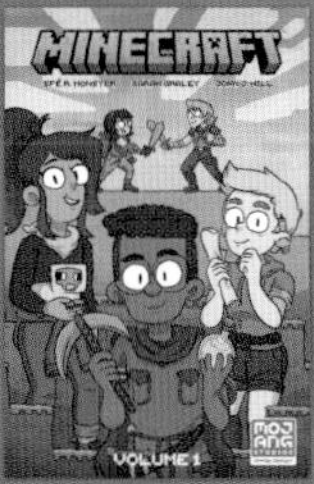
MINECRAFT
VOLUME 1
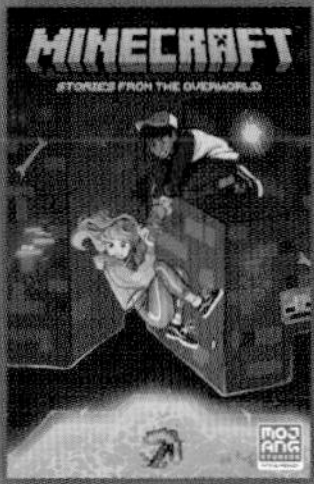
MINECRAFT
STORIES FROM THE OVERWORLD
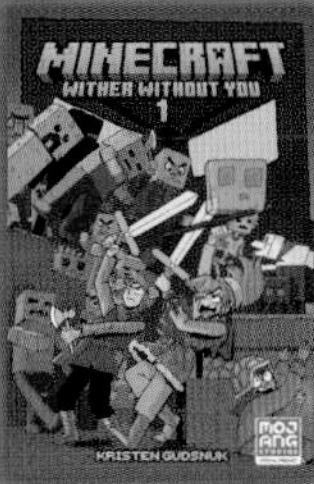
MINECRAFT
WITHER WITHOUT YOU
1
KRISTEN GUDSNUK
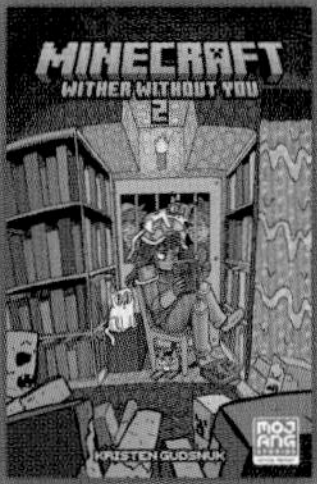
MINECRAFT
WITHER WITHOUT YOU
2
KRISTEN GUDSNUK
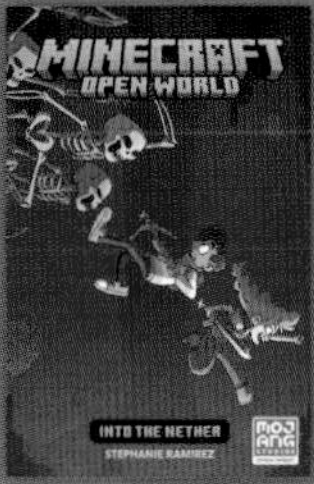
MINECRAFT
OPEN WORLD
INTO THE NETHER
STEPHANIE RAMIREZ

MINECRAFT

SFÉ R. MONSTER, SARAH GRALEY, JOHN J. HILL

Tyler is your everyday kid whose life is changed when his family has to move from the town he's always known. Thankfully, Tyler has a strong group of friends forever linked in the world of Minecraft! Tyler, along with his friends Evan, Candace, Tobi, and Grace have been going on countless adventures together across the expanses of the Overworld and are in need of a new challenge. They decide to go on the Ultimate Quest–to travel to the End and face off against the ender dragon!

Volume 1 · ISBN 978-1-50670-834-8	$10.99
Volume 2 · ISBN 978-1-50670-836-2	$10.99
Volume 3 · ISBN 978-1-50672-580-2	$10.99

MINECRAFT: STORIES FROM THE OVERWORLD

From blocks to panels, Minecraft explorations are crafted into comics in this anthology collection!

With tales of witch and pillager rivals finding common ground, a heartless griefer who bit off more than they could chew, and valiant heroes new (or not!) to the Overworld, this anthology tells tales that span the world of Minecraft. Featuring stories from star writers and exciting artists, this collection brings together stories from all realms, leaving no block unturned!

ISBN 978-1-50670-833-1 $14.99

MINECRAFT: WITHER WITHOUT YOU

KRISTEN GUDSNUK

Jump into the Overworld with the first adventure of a three-part series from the world's best-selling video-game Minecraft!

Cahira and Orion are twin monster hunters under the tutelage of Senan the Thorough. After an intense battle with an enchanted wither, their mentor is eaten and the twins are now alone! The two hunters go on a mission to get their mentor back, and meet an unlikely ally along the way!

Volume 1 · ISBN 978-1-50670-835-5	$10.99
Volume 2 · ISBN 978-1-50671-886-6	$10.99
Volume 3 · ISBN 978-1-50671-887-3	$10.99

MINECRAFT: OPEN WORLD–INTO THE NETHER

STEPHANIE RAMIREZ

Sarah is new to the world of Minecraft, and without much knowledge on the world or how to play, she finds herself looking to veteran player Hector for help. Hector's got a very different way of doing things...! Can they overcome their differences and team up?

ISBN 978-1-50671-888-0 $10.99

AVAILABLE AT YOUR LOCAL COMICS SHOP OR BOOKSTORE!

To find a comics shop in your area, visit comicshoplocator.com. For more information or to order direct visit DarkHorse.com

Do FELINES give you the FEELS?

CATS OF ALL KINDS
are featured in these titles from Dark Horse!

CATS!
Frédéric Brrémaud, Paola Antista

Light-hearted short stories following the lives of three young women and their kitties. Join in all the fun and funny that comes with raising at cat!

PURRFECT STRANGERS
$14.99 • ISBN 978-1-50672-613-7

GIRLFRIENDS AND CATFRIENDS
$14.99 • ISBN 978-1-50672-614-4

WHAT'S MICHAEL?: FATCAT COLLECTION
Makoto Kobayashi

True-to-life daily cat scenarios and off-the-wall crazy feline fantasies combine in these epic manga collections, starring the wacky and often anthropomorphic Michael!

VOLUME 1
$19.99 • ISBN 978-1-50671-414-1

VOLUME 2
$19.99 • ISBN 978-1-50671-415-8

CAT + GAMER
Wataru Nadatani

Riko Kozakura, a young office worker with an obsession for video games, finds her quiet life upended when she takes in a stray cat—and uses lessons drawn from video games to guide her in cat care!

VOLUME 1
$11.99 • ISBN 978-1-50672-741-7

VOLUME 2 – Coming Summer 2022!
$11.99 • ISBN 978-1-50672-742-4

STRAYED
Carlos Griffoni, Juan Doe

Far in the future, the galaxy's only hope against destruction is an unlikely pair: an astral-projecting cat named Lou and his loving owner Kiara.

$19.99 • ISBN 978-1-50671-428-8

TENTACLE KITTY
John Merritt, Raena Merritt, Jean-Claudio Vinci, Amy King, Brittney Williams, Aubrey Aiese, Rootis Tabootus

Tentacle Kitty is a kitty from another dimension that happens to have tentacles. She is trapped on Earth trying to find a way home, but to pass the time she explores the world with new friends.

TALES AROUND THE TEACUP Short stories of adventure told over tea!
$12.99 • ISBN 978-1-50672-396-9

TENTACLE KITTY COLORING BOOK Forty-five original illustrations to color!
$14.99 • ISBN 978-1-50670-699-3

AVAILABLE AT YOUR LOCAL COMICS SHOP OR BOOKSTORE!
To find a comics shop in your area, visit comicshoplocator.com For more information or to order direct, visit DarkHorse.com

DARK HORSE BOOKS